THE YELLO

Out of the darkness—for extinguished—staggered a woman; a woman whose pale face exhibited, despite the ravages of sorrow or illness, signs of quite unusual beauty. Her eyes were wide opened, and terror-stricken, the pupils contracted almost to vanishing point. She wore a magnificent cloak of civet fur wrapped tightly about her, and, as Leroux opened the door, she tottered past him into the lobby, glancing back over her shoulder.

With his upraised hands plunged pathetically into the mop of his hair, Leroux turned and stared at the intruder. She groped as if a darkness had descended, clutched at the sides of the study doorway, and then, unsteadily, entered—and sank down upon the big chesterfield in utter exhaustion.

Leroux, rubbing his chin, perplexedly, walked in after her. He scarcely had his foot upon the study carpet, ere the woman started up, tremulously, and shot out from the enveloping furs a bare arm and a pointing, quivering finger.

"Close the door!" she cried hoarsely. "Close the door! He has followed me!"

THE YELLOW CLAW

SAX ROHMER

WILDSIDE PRESS

THE YELLOW CLAW

Published by:

Wildside Press
P.O. Box 301
Holicong, PA 18928-0301
www.wildsidepress.com

I

THE LADY OF THE CIVET FURS

Henry Leroux wrote busily on. The light of the table-lamp, softened and enriched by its mosaic shade, gave an appearance of added opulence to the already handsome appointments of the room. The little table-clock ticked merrily from half-past eleven to a quarter to twelve.

Into the cozy, bookish atmosphere of the novelist's study penetrated the muffled chime of Big Ben; it chimed the three-quarters. But, with his mind centered upon his work, Leroux wrote on ceaselessly.

An odd figure of a man was this popular novelist, with patchy and untidy hair which lessened the otherwise striking contour of his brow. A neglected and unpicturesque figure, in a baggy, neutral-colored dressing-gown; a figure more fitted to a garret than to this spacious, luxurious workroom, with the soft light playing upon rank after rank of rare and costly editions, deepening the tones in the Persian carpet, making red morocco more red, purifying the vellum and regilding the gold of the choice bindings, caressing lovingly the busts and statuettes surmounting the book-shelves, and twinkling upon the scantily-covered crown of Henry Leroux. The door bell rang.

Leroux, heedless of external matters, pursued his work. But the door bell rang again and continued to ring.

"Soames! Soames!" Leroux raised his voice irascibly, continuing to write the while. "Where the devil are you! Can't you hear the door bell?"

Soames did not reveal himself; and to the ringing of the bell was added the unmistakable rattling of a letter-box.

"Soames!" Leroux put down his pen and stood up. "Damn it! he's out! I have no memory!"

He retied the girdle of his dressing-gown, which had become unfastened, and opened the study door. Opposite, across the entrance lobby, was the outer door; and in the light from the lobby lamp he perceived two laughing eyes peering in under the upraised flap of the letter-box. The ringing ceased.

"Are you *very* angry with me for interrupting you?" cried a girl's voice.

"My dear Miss Cumberly!" said Leroux without irritation; "on the contrary—er—I am delighted to see you—or rather to hear you. There is nobody at home, you know."

"I *do* know," replied the girl firmly, "and I know something else, also. Father assures me that you simply *starve* yourself when Mrs. Leroux is away! So I have brought down an omelette!"

"Omelette!" muttered Leroux, advancing toward the door; "you have—er—brought an omelette! I understand—yes; you have brought an omelette? Er—that is very good of you."

He hesitated when about to open the outer door, raising his hands to his dishevelled hair and unshaven chin. The flap of the letter-box dropped; and the girl outside could be heard stifling her laughter.

"You must think me—er—very rude," began Leroux; "I mean—not to open the door. But . . ."

"I quite understand," concluded the voice of the unseen one. "You are a most untidy object! And I shall tell Mira *directly* she returns that she has no right to leave you alone like this! Now I am going to hurry back upstairs; so you may appear safely. Don't let the omelette get cold. Good night!"

"No, certainly I shall not!" cried Leroux. "So good of you—I—er— do like omelette . . . . Good night!"

Calmly he returned to his writing-table, where, in the pursuit of the elusive character whose exploits he was chronicling and who had brought him fame and wealth, he forgot in the same moment Helen Cumberly and the omelette.

The table-clock ticked merrily on; *scratch—scratch—splutter— scratch*—went Henry Leroux's pen; for this up-to-date litterateur, essayist by inclination, creator of "Martin Zeda, Criminal Scientist" by popular clamor, was yet old-fashioned enough, and sufficient of an enthusiast, to pen his work, while lesser men dictated.

So, amidst that classic company, smiling or frowning upon him from the oaken shelves, where Petronius Arbiter, exquisite, rubbed shoulders with Balzac, plebeian; where Omar Khayyam leaned confidentially toward Philostratus; where Mark Twain, standing squarely beside Thomas Carlyle, glared across the room at George Meredith, Henry Leroux pursued the amazing career of "Martin Zeda."

It wanted but five minutes to the hour of midnight, when again the door bell clamored in the silence.

Leroux wrote steadily on. The bell continued to ring, and, furthermore, the ringer could be heard beating upon the outer door.

"Soames!" cried Leroux irritably, "Soames! Why the hell don't you go to the door!"

Leroux stood up, dashing his pen upon the table.

"I shall have to sack that damned man!" he cried; "he takes too many liberties—stopping out until this hour of the night!"

He pulled open the study door, crossed the hallway, and opened the door beyond.

In, out of the darkness—for the stair lights had been extinguished—staggered a woman; a woman whose pale face exhibited, despite the ravages of sorrow or illness, signs of quite unusual beauty. Her eyes were wide opened, and terror-stricken, the pupils contracted almost to vanishing point. She wore a magnificent cloak of civet fur wrapped tightly about her, and, as Leroux opened the door, she tottered past him into the lobby, glancing back over her shoulder.

With his upraised hands plunged pathetically into the mop of his hair, Leroux turned and stared at the intruder. She groped as if a darkness had descended, clutched at the sides of the study doorway, and then, unsteadily, entered—and sank down upon the big chesterfield in utter exhaustion.

Leroux, rubbing his chin, perplexedly, walked in after her. He scarcely had his foot upon the study carpet, ere the woman started up, tremulously, and shot out from the enveloping furs a bare arm and a pointing, quivering finger.

"Close the door!" she cried hoarsely. "Close the door! He has followed me!"

The disturbed novelist, as a man in a dream, turned, retraced his steps, and closed the outer door of the flat. Then, rubbing his chin more vigorously than ever and only desisting from this exercise to fumble in his dishevelled hair, he walked back into the study, whose Athenean calm had thus mysteriously been violated.

Two minutes to midnight; the most respectable flat in respectable Westminster; a lonely and very abstracted novelist—and a pale-faced, beautiful woman, enveloped in costly furs, sitting staring with fearful eyes straight before her. This was such a scene as his sense of the proprieties and of the probabilities could never have permitted Henry Leroux to create.

His visitor kept moistening her dry lips and swallowing, emotionally.

Standing at a discreet distance from her—

"Madam," began Leroux, nervously.

She waved her hand, enjoining him to silence, and at the same time intimating that she would explain herself directly speech became possible. Whilst she sought to recover her composure, Leroux, gradually forcing himself out of the dreamlike state, studied her with a sort of anxious curiosity.

It now became apparent to him that his visitor was no more than twenty-five or twenty-six years of age, but illness or trouble, or both together, had seared and marred her beauty. Amid the auburn masses of her hair, gleamed streaks, not of gray, but of purest white. The low brow was faintly wrinkled, and the big—unnaturally big—eyes were purple shaded; whilst two heavy lines traced their way from the corner of the nostrils to the corner of the mouth—of the drooping mouth with the bloodless lips.

Her pallor became more strange and interesting the longer he studied it; for, underlying the skin was a yellow tinge which he found inexplicable, but which he linked in his mind with the contracted pupils of her eyes, seeking vainly for a common cause.

He had a hazy impression that his visitor, beneath her furs, was most inadequately clothed; and seeking confirmation of this, his gaze strayed downward to where one little slippered foot peeped out from the civet furs.

Leroux suppressed a gasp. He had caught a glimpse of a bare ankle!

He crossed to his writing-table, and seated himself, glancing sideways at this living mystery. Suddenly she began, in a voice tremulous and scarcely audible—

"Mr. Leroux, at a great—at a very great personal risk, I have come to-night. What I have to ask of you—to entreat of you, will . . . will . . ."

Two bare arms emerged from the fur, and she began clutching at her throat and bosom as though choking—dying.

Leroux leapt up and would have run to her; but forcing a ghastly smile, she waved him away again.

"It is all right," she muttered, swallowing noisily. But frightful spasms of pain convulsed her, contorting her pale face.

"Some brandy—!" cried Leroux, anxiously.

"If you please," whispered the visitor.

She dropped her arms and fell back upon the chesterfield, insensible.

II

MIDNIGHT AND MR. KING

Leroux clutched at the corner of the writing-table to steady himself and stood there looking at the deathly face. Under the most favorable circumstances, he was no man of action, although in common with the rest of his kind he prided himself upon the possession of that presence of mind which he lacked. It was a situation which could not have alarmed "Martin Zeda," but it alarmed, immeasurably, nay, struck inert with horror, Martin Zeda's creator.

Then, in upon Leroux's mental turmoil, a sensible idea intruded itself.

"Dr. Cumberly!" he muttered. "I hope to God he is in!"

Without touching the recumbent form upon the chesterfield, without seeking to learn, without daring to learn, if she lived or had died, Leroux, the tempo of his life changed to a breathless gallop, rushed out of the study, across the entrance hail, and, throwing wide the flat door, leapt up the stair to the flat above—that of his old friend, Dr. Cumberly.

The patter of the slippered feet grew faint upon the stair; then, as Leroux reached the landing above, became inaudible altogether.

In Leroux's study, the table-clock ticked merrily on, seeming to hasten its ticking as the hand crept around closer and closer to midnight. The mosaic shade of the lamp mingled reds and blues and greens upon the white ceiling above and poured golden light upon the pages of manuscript strewn about beneath it. This was a typical work-room of a literary man having the ear of the public—typical in every respect, save for the fur-clad figure outstretched upon the settee.

And now the peeping light indiscreetly penetrated to the hem of a silken garment revealed by some disarrangement of the civet fur. To the eye of an experienced observer, had such an observer been present in Henry Leroux's study, this billow of silk and lace behind the sheltering fur must have proclaimed itself the edge of a night-robe, just as the ankle beneath had proclaimed itself to Henry Leroux's shocked susceptibilities to be innocent of stocking.

Thirty seconds were wanted to complete the cycle of the day, when one of the listless hands thrown across the back of the chesterfield opened and closed spasmodically. The fur at the bosom of the midnight visitor began rapidly to rise and fall.

Then, with a choking cry, the woman struggled upright; her hair, hastily dressed, burst free of its bindings and poured in gleaming cascade down about her shoulders.

Clutching with one hand at her cloak in order to keep it wrapped about her, and holding the other blindly before her, she rose, and with that same odd, groping movement, began to approach the writing-table. The pupils of her eyes were mere pin-points flow; she shuddered convulsively, and her skin was dewed with perspiration. Her breath came in agonized gasps.

"God!—I . . . am dying . . . and I cannot—tell him!" she breathed.

Feverishly, weakly, she took up a pen, and upon a quarto page, already half filled with Leroux's small, neat, illegible writing, began to scrawl a message, bending down, one hand upon the table, and with her whole body shaking.

Some three or four wavering lines she had written, when intimately, for the flat of Henry Leroux in Palace Mansions lay within sight of the clock-face—Big Ben began to chime midnight.

The writer started back and dropped a great blot of ink upon the paper; then, realizing the cause of the disturbance, forced herself to continue her task.

The chime being completed: *One!* boomed the clock; *Two!* . . . *Three!* . . . *Four!* . . .

The light in the entrance-hall went out!

Five! boomed Big Ben;—*Six!* . . . *Seven!* . . .

A hand, of old ivory hue, a long, yellow, clawish hand, with part of a sinewy forearm, crept in from the black lobby through the study doorway and touched the electric switch!

Eight! . . .

The study was plunged in darkness!

Uttering a sob—a cry of agony and horror that came from her very soul—the woman stood upright and turned to face toward the door, clutching the sheet of paper in one rigid hand.

Through the leaded panes of the window above the writing-table swept a silver beam of moonlight. It poured, searchingly, upon the fur-clad figure swaying by the table; cutting through the darkness of the room like some huge scimitar, to end in a pallid pool about the woman's shadow on the center of the Persian carpet.

Coincident with her sobbing cry—*Nine!* boomed Big Ben; *Ten!* . . .

Two hands—with outstretched, crooked, clutching fingers—leapt from the darkness into the light of the moonbeam.

"God! Oh, God!" came a frenzied, rasping shriek—*"Mr. King!"*

Straight at the bare throat leapt the yellow hands; a gurgling cry rose—fell—and died away.

Gently, noiselessly, the lady of the civet fur sank upon the carpet by the table; as she fell, a dim black figure bent over her. The tearing of paper told of the note being snatched from her frozen grip; but never for a moment did the face or the form of her assailant encroach upon the moonbeam.

Batlike, this second and terrible visitant avoided the light.

The deed had occupied so brief a time that but one note of the great bell had accompanied it.

Twelve! rang out the final stroke from the clock-tower. A low, eerie whistle, minor, rising in three irregular notes and falling in weird, unusual cadence to silence again, came from somewhere outside the room.

Then darkness—stillness—with the moon a witness of one more ghastly crime.

Presently, confused and intermingled voices from above proclaimed the return of Leroux with the doctor. They were talking in an excited key, the voice of Leroux, especially, sounding almost hysterical. They created such a disturbance that they attracted the attention of Mr. John Exel, M. P., occupant of the flat below, who at that very moment had returned from the House and was about to insert the key in the lock of his door. He looked up the stairway, but, all being in darkness, was unable to detect anything. Therefore he called out—

"Is that you, Leroux? Is anything the matter?"

"Matter, Exel!" cried Leroux; "there's a devil of a business! For mercy's sake, come up!"

His curiosity greatly excited, Mr. Exel mounted the stairs, entering the lobby of Leroux's flat immediately behind the owner and Dr. Cumberly—who, like Leroux, was arrayed in a dressing-gown; for he had been in bed when summoned by his friend.

"You are all in the dark, here," muttered Dr. Cumberly, fumbling for the switch.

"Some one has turned the light out!" whispered Leroux, nervously; "I left it on."

Dr. Cumberly pressed the switch, turning up the lobby light as Exel entered from the landing. Then Leroux, entering the study first of the three, switched on the light there, also.

One glance he threw about the room, then started back like a man physically stricken.

"Cumberly!" he gasped, "Cumberly"—and he pointed to the furry heap by the writing-table.

"You said she lay on the chesterfield," muttered Cumberly.

"I left her there. . . ."

Dr. Cumberly crossed the room and dropped upon his knees. He turned the white face toward the light, gently parted the civet fur, and pressed his ear to the silken covering of the breast. He started slightly and looked into the glazing eyes.

Replacing the fur which he had disarranged, the physician stood up and fixed a keen gaze upon the face of Henry Leroux. The latter swallowed noisily, moistening his parched lips.

"Is she . . ." he muttered. "Is she . . ."

"God's mercy, Leroux!" whispered Mr. Exel—"what does this mean?"

"The woman is dead," said Dr. Cumberly.

In common with all medical men, Dr. Cumberly was a physiognomist; he was a great physician and a proportionately great physiognomist. Therefore, when he looked into Henry Leroux's eyes, he saw there, and recognized, horror and consternation. With no further evidence than that furnished by his own powers of perception, he knew that the mystery of this woman's death was as inexplicable to Henry Leroux as it was inexplicable to himself.

He was a masterful man, with the gray eyes of a diplomat, and he knew Leroux as did few men. He laid both hands upon the novelist's shoulders.

"Brace up, old chap!" he said; "you will want all your wits about you."

"I left her," began Leroux, hesitatingly—"I left . . ."

"We know all about where you left her, Leroux," interrupted Cumberly; "but what we want to get at is this: what occurred between the time you left her, and the time of our return?"

Exel, who had walked across to the table, and with a horror-stricken face was gingerly examining the victim, now exclaimed—

"Why! Leroux! She is—she is . . . *undressed!*"

Leroux clutched at his dishevelled hair with both hands.

"My dear Exel!" he cried—"my dear, good man! Why do you use that tone? You say 'she is undressed!' as though I were responsible for the poor soul's condition!"

"On the contrary, Leroux!" retorted Exel, standing very upright, and staring through his monocle; "on the contrary, *you* misconstrue *me!* I did not intend to imply—to insinuate—"

"My dear Exel!" broke in Dr. Cumberly—"Leroux is perfectly well aware that you intended nothing unkindly. But the poor chap, quite naturally, is distraught at the moment. You *must* understand that, man!"

"I understand; and I am sorry," said Exel, casting a sidelong glance at the body. "Of course, it is a delicate subject. No doubt Leroux can explain. . . ."

"Damn your explanation!" shrieked Leroux hysterically. "I *cannot* explain! If I could explain, I . . ."

"Leroux!" said Cumberly, placing his arm paternally about the shaking man—"you are such a nervous subject. *Do* make an effort, old fellow. Pull yourself together. Exel does not know the circumstances—"

"I am curious to learn them," said the M. P. icily.

Leroux was about to launch some angry retort, but Cumberly forced him into the chesterfield, and crossing to a bureau, poured out a stiff peg of brandy from a decanter which stood there. Leroux sank upon the chesterfield, rubbing his fingers up and down his palms with a curious nervous movement and glancing at the dead woman, and at Exel, alternately, in a mechanical, regular fashion, pathetic to behold.

Mr. Exel, tapping his boot with the head of his inverted cane, was staring fixedly at the doctor.

"Here you are, Leroux," said Cumberly; "drink this up, and let us arrange our facts in decent order before we—"

"Phone for the police?" concluded Exel, his gaze upon the last speaker.

Leroux drank the brandy at a gulp and put down the glass upon a little persian coffee table with a hand which he had somehow contrived to steady.

"You are keen on the official forms, Exel?" he said, with a wry smile. "Please accept my apology for my recent—er—outburst, but picture this thing happening in your place!"

"I cannot," declared Exel, bluntly.

"You lack imagination," said Cumberly. "Take a whisky and soda, and help me to search the flat."

"Search the flat!"

The physician raised a forefinger, forensically.

"Since you, Exel, if not actually in the building, must certainly have been within sight of the street entrance at the moment of the crime, and since Leroux and I descended the stair and met you on the landing, it is reasonable to suppose that the assassin can only be in one place: *here!*"

"*Here!*" cried Exel and Leroux, together.

"Did you see anyone leave the lower hall as you entered?"

"No one; emphatically, there was no one there!"

"Then I am right."

"Good God!" whispered Exel, glancing about him, with a new, and keen apprehensiveness.

"Take your drink," concluded Cumberly, "and join me in my search."

"Thanks," replied Exel, nervously proffering a cigar-case; "but I won't drink."

"As you wish," said the doctor, who thus, in his masterful way, acted the host; "and I won't smoke. But do you light up."

"Later," muttered Exel; "later. Let us search, first."

Leroux stood up; Cumberly forced him back.

"Stay where you are, Leroux; it is elementary strategy to operate from a fixed base. This study shall be the base. Ready, Exel?"

Exel nodded, and the search commenced. Leroux sat rigidly upon the settee, his hands resting upon his knees, watching and listening. Save for the merry ticking of the table-clock, and the movements of the searchers from room to room, nothing disturbed the silence. From the table, and that which lay near to it, he kept his gaze obstinately averted.

Five or six minutes passed in this fashion, Leroux expecting each to bring a sudden outcry. He was disappointed. The searchers returned, Exel noticeably holding himself aloof and Cumberly very stern.

Exel, a cigar between his teeth, walked to the writing-table, carefully circling around the dreadful obstacle which lay in his path, to help himself to a match. As he stooped to do so, he perceived that in the closed right hand of the dead woman was a torn scrap of paper.

"Leroux! Cumberly!" he exclaimed; "come here!"

He pointed with the match as Cumberly hurriedly crossed to his side. Leroux, inert, remained where he sat, but watched with haggard eyes. Dr. Cumberly bent down and sought to detach the paper from the grip of the poor cold fingers, without tearing it. Finally he contrived to release the fragment, and, perceiving it to bear some written words, he spread it out beneath the lamp, on the table, and eagerly scanned it, lowering his massive gray head close to the writing.

He inhaled, sibilantly.

"Do you see, Exel?" he jerked—for Exel was bending over his shoulder.

"I do—but I don't understand."

"What is it?" came hollowly from Leroux.

"It is the bottom part of an unfinished note," said Cumberly, slowly. "It is written shakily in a woman's hand, and it reads—'Your wife . . .'"

Leroux sprang to his feet and crossed the room in three strides.

"Wife!" he muttered. His voice seemed to be choked in his throat; "my wife! It says something about my wife?"

"It says," resumed the doctor, quietly, "'your wife.' Then there's a piece torn out, and the two words 'Mr. King.' No stop follows, and the line is evidently incomplete."

"My wife!" mumbled Leroux, staring unseeingly at the fragment of paper. *My wife! Mr. King!* Oh! God! I shall go mad!"

"Sit down!" snapped Dr. Cumberly, turning to him; "damn it, Leroux, you are worse than a woman!"

In a manner almost childlike, the novelist obeyed the will of the stronger man, throwing himself into an armchair, and burying his face in his hands.

"My wife!" he kept muttering—"my wife. . . !"

Exel and the doctor stood staring at one another; when suddenly, from outside the flat, came a metallic clattering, followed by a little suppressed cry. Helen Cumberly, in daintiest deshabille, appeared in the lobby, carrying, in one hand, a chafing-dish, and, in the other, the lid. As she advanced toward the study, from whence she had heard her father's voice—

"Why, Mr. Leroux!" she cried, "I shall *certainly* report you to Mira, now! You have not even touched the omelette!"

"Good God! Cumberly! stop her!" muttered Exel, uneasily. "The door was not latched. . . !"

But it was too late. Even as the physician turned to intercept his daughter, she crossed the threshold of the study. She stopped short at perceiving Exel; then, with a woman's unerring intuition, divined a tragedy, and, in the instant of divination, sought for, and found, the hub of the tragic wheel.

One swift glance she cast at the fur-clad form, prostrate.

The chafing-dish fell from her hand, and the omelette rolled, a grotesque mass, upon the carpet. She swayed, dizzily, raising one hand to her brow, but had recovered herself even as Leroux sprang forward to support her.

"All right, Leroux!" cried Cumberly; "I will take her upstairs again. Wait for me, Exel."

Exel nodded, lighted his cigar, and sat down in a chair, remote from the writing-table.

"Mira—my wife!" muttered Leroux, standing, looking after Dr. Cumberly and his daughter as they crossed the lobby. "She will report to—my wife. . . ."

In the outer doorway, Helen Cumberly looked back over her shoulder, and her glance met that of Leroux. Hers was a healing glance and a strengthening glance; it braced him up as nothing else could have done. He turned to Exel.

"For Heaven's sake, Exel!" he said, evenly, "give me your advice—give me your help; I am going to 'phone for the police."

Exel looked up with an odd expression.

"I am entirely at your service, Leroux," he said. "I can quite understand how this ghastly affair has shaken you up."

"It was so sudden," said the other, plaintively. "It is incredible that so much emotion can be crowded into so short a period of a man's life. . . ."

Big Ben chimed the quarter after midnight. Leroux, eyes averted, walked to the writing-table, and took up the telephone.

III

INSPECTOR DUNBAR TAKES CHARGE

Detective-Inspector Dunbar was admitted by Dr. Cumberly. He was a man of notable height, large-boned, and built gauntly and squarely. His clothes fitted him ill, and through them one seemed to perceive the massive scaffolding of his frame. He had gray hair retiring above a high brow, but worn long and untidily at the back; a wire-like straight-cut mustache, also streaked with gray, which served to accentuate the grimness of his mouth and slightly undershot jaw. A massive head, with tawny, leonine eyes; indeed, altogether a leonine face, and a frame indicative of tremendous nervous energy.

In the entrance lobby he stood for a moment.

"My name is Cumberly," said the doctor, glancing at the card which the Scotland Yard man had proffered. "I occupy the flat above."

"Glad to know you, Dr. Cumberly," replied the detective in a light and not unpleasant voice—and the fierce eyes momentarily grew kindly.

"This—" continued Cumberly, drawing Dunbar forward into the study, "is my friend, Leroux—Henry Leroux, whose name you will know?"

"I have not that pleasure," replied Dunbar.

"Well," added Cumberly, "he is a famous novelist, and his flat, unfortunately, has been made the scene of a crime. This is Detective-Inspector Dunbar, who has come to solve our difficulties, Leroux." He turned to where Exel stood upon the hearth-rug—toying with his monocle. "Mr. John Exel, M. P."

"Glad to know you, gentlemen," said Dunbar.

Leroux rose from the armchair in which he had been sitting and stared, drearily, at the newcomer. Exel screwed the monocle into his right eye, and likewise surveyed the detective. Cumberly, taking a tumbler from the bureau, said—

"A scotch-and-soda, Inspector?"

"It is a suggestion," said Dunbar, "that, coming from a medical man, appeals."

Whilst the doctor poured out the whisky and squirted the soda into the glass, Inspector Dunbar, standing squarely in the middle of the room, fixed his eyes upon the still form lying in the shadow of the writing-table.

"You will have been called in, doctor," he said, taking the proffered tumbler, "at the time of the crime?"

"Exactly!" replied Cumberly. "Mr. Leroux ran up to my fiat and summoned me to see the woman."

"What time would that be?"

"Big Ben had just struck the final stroke of twelve when I came out on to the landing."

"Mr. Leroux would be waiting there for you?"

"He stood in my entrance-lobby whilst I slipped on my dressing-gown, and we came down together."

"I was entering from the street," interrupted Exel, "as they were descending from above . . ."

"You can enter from the street, sir, in a moment," said Dunbar, holding up his hand. "One witness at a time, if you please."

Exel shrugged his shoulders and turned slightly, leaning his elbow upon the mantelpiece and flicking off the ash from his cigar.

"I take it you were in bed?" questioned Dunbar, turning again to the doctor.

"I had been in bed about a quarter of an hour when I was aroused by the ringing of the door-bell. This ringing struck me as so urgent that I ran out in my pajamas, and found there Mr. Leroux, in a very disturbed state—"

"What did he say? Give his own words as nearly as you remember them."

Leroux, who had been standing, sank slowly back into the armchair, with his eyes upon Dr. Cumberly as the latter replied—

"He said 'Cumberly! Cumberly! For God's sake, come down at once; there is a strange woman in my flat, apparently in a dying condition!'"

"What did you do?"

"I ran into my bedroom and slipped on my dressing-gown, leaving Mr. Leroux in the entrance-hall. Then, with the clock chiming the last stroke of midnight, we came out together and I closed my door behind me. There was no light on the stair; but our conversation—Mr. Leroux was speaking in a very high-pitched voice . . ."

"What was he saying?"

"He was explaining to me how some woman, unknown to him, had interrupted his work a few minutes before by ringing his door-bell. . . ."

Inspector Dunbar held up his hand.

"I won't ask you to repeat what he said, doctor; Mr. Leroux, presently, can give me his own words."

"We had descended to this floor, then," resumed Cumberly, "when Mr. Exel, entering below, called up to us, asking if anything was the matter. Leroux replied, 'Matter, Exel! There's a devil of a business! For mercy's sake, come up!'"

"Well?"

"Mr. Exel thereupon joined us at the door of this flat."

"Was it open?"

"Yes. Mr. Leroux had rushed up to me, leaving the door open behind him. The light was out, both in the lobby and in the study, a fact upon which I commented at the time. It was all the more curious as Mr. Leroux had left both lights on. . . !"

"Did he say so?"

"He did. The circumstances surprised him to a marked degree. We came in and I turned up the light in the lobby. Then Leroux, entering the study, turned up the light there, too. I entered next, followed by Mr. Exel—and we saw the body lying where you see it now."

"Who saw it first?"

"Mr. Leroux; he drew my attention to it, saying that he had left her lying on the chesterfield and *not* upon the floor."

"You examined her?"

"I did. She was dead, but still warm. She exhibited signs of recent illness, and of being addicted to some drug habit; probably morphine. This, beyond doubt, contributed to her death, but the direct cause was asphyxiation. She had been strangled!"

"My God!" groaned Leroux, dropping his face into his hands.

"You found marks on her throat?"

"The marks were very slight. No great pressure was required in her weak condition."

"You did not move the body?"

"Certainly not; a more complete examination must be made, of course. But I extracted a piece of torn paper from her clenched right hand."

Inspector Dunbar lowered his tufted brows.

"I'm not glad to know you did that," he said. "It should have been left."

"It was done on the spur of the moment, but without altering the position of the hand or arm. The paper lies upon the table, yonder."

Inspector Dunbar took a long drink. Thus far he had made no attempt to examine the victim. Pulling out a bulging note-case from the inside pocket of his blue serge coat, he unscrewed a fountain-pen, carefully tested the nib upon his thumb nail, and made three or four brief entries. Then, stretching out one long arm, he laid the wallet and the pen beside his glass upon the top of a bookcase, without otherwise changing his position, and glancing aside at Exel, said—

"Now, Mr. Exel, what help can you give us?"

"I have little to add to Dr. Cumberly's account," answered Exel, offhandedly. "The whole thing seemed to me . . ."

"What it seemed," interrupted Dunbar, " does not interest Scotland Yard, Mr. Exel, and won't interest the jury."

Leroux glanced up for a moment, then set his teeth hard, so that his jaw muscles stood out prominently under the pallid skin.

"What do you want to know, then?" asked Exel.

"I will be wanting to know," said Dunbar, "where you were coming from, to-night?"

"From the House of Commons."

"You came direct?"

"I left Sir Brian Malpas at the corner of Victoria Street at four minutes to twelve by Big Ben, and walked straight home, actually entering here, from the street, as the clock was chiming the last stroke of midnight."

"Then you would have walked up the street from an easterly direction?"

"Certainly."

"Did you meet any one or anything?"

"A taxi-cab, empty—for the hood was lowered—passed me as I turned the corner. There was no other vehicle in the street, and no person."

"You don't know from which door the cab came?"

"As I turned the corner," replied Exel, "I heard the man starting his engine, although when I actually saw the cab, it was in motion; but judging by the sound to which I refer, the cab had been stationary, if not at the door of Palace Mansions, certainly at that of the next block—St. Andrew's Mansions."

"Did you hear, or see anything else?"

"I saw nothing whatever. But just as I approached the street door, I heard a peculiar whistle, apparently proceeding from the gardens in the center of the square. I attached no importance to it at the time."

"What kind of whistle?"

"I have forgotten the actual notes, but the effect was very odd in some way."

"In what way?"

"An impression of this sort is not entirely reliable, Inspector; but it struck me as Oriental."

"Ah!" said Dunbar, and reached out the long arm for his notebook.

"Can I be of any further assistance?" said Exel, glancing at his watch.

"You had entered the hall-way and were about to enter your own flat when the voices of Dr. Cumberly and Mr. Leroux attracted your attention?"

"I actually had the key in my hand," replied Exel.

"Did you actually have the key in the lock?"

"Let me think," mused Exel, and he took out a bunch of keys and dangled them, reflectively, before his eyes. "No! I was fumbling for the right key when I heard the voices above me."

"But were you facing your door?"

"No," averred Exel, perceiving the drift of the inspector's inquiries; "I was facing the stairway the whole time, and although it was in darkness, there is a street lamp immediately outside on the pavement, and I can swear, positively, that no one descended; that there was no one in the hall nor on the stair, except Mr. Leroux and Dr. Cumberly."

"Ah!" said Dunbar again, and made further entries in his book. "I need not trouble you further, sir. Good night!"

Exel, despite his earlier attitude of boredom, now ignored this official dismissal, and, tossing the stump of his cigar into the grate, lighted a cigarette, and with both hands thrust deep in his pockets, stood leaning back against the mantelpiece. The detective turned to Leroux.

"Have a brandy-and-soda?" suggested Dr. Cumberly, his eyes turned upon the pathetic face of the novelist.

But Leroux shook his head, wearily.

"Go ahead, Inspector!" he said. "I am anxious to tell you all I know. God knows I am anxious to tell you."

A sound was heard of a key being inserted in the lock of a door.

Four pairs of curious eyes were turned toward the entrance lobby, when the door opened, and a sleek man of medium height, clean shaven, but with his hair cut low upon the cheek bones, so as to give the impression of short side-whiskers, entered in a manner at once furtive and servile.

He wore a black overcoat and a bowler hat. Reclosing the door, he turned, perceived the group in the study, and fell back as though someone had struck him a fierce blow.

Abject terror was written upon his features, and, for a moment, the idea of flight appeared to suggest itself urgently to him; but finally, he took a step forward toward the study.

"Who's this?" snapped Dunbar, without removing his leonine eyes from the newcomer.

"It is Soames," came the weary voice of Leroux.

"Butler?"

"Yes."

"Where's he been?"

"I don't know. He remained out without my permission."

"He did, eh?"

Inspector Dunbar thrust forth a long finger at the shrinking form in the doorway.

"Mr. Soames," he said, "you will be going to your own room and waiting there until I ring for you."

"Yes, sir," said Soames, holding his hat in both bands, and speaking huskily. "Yes, sir: certainly, sir."

He crossed the lobby and disappeared.

"There is no other way out, is there?" inquired the detective, glancing at Dr. Cumberly.

"There is no other way," was the reply; "but surely you don't suspect . . ."

"I would suspect the Archbishop of Westminster," snapped Dunbar, "if he came in like that! Now, sir,"—he turned to Leroux—"you were alone, here, to-night?"

"Quite alone, Inspector. The truth is, I fear, that my servants take liberties in the absence of my wife."

"In the absence of your wife? Where is your wife?"

"She is in Paris."

"Is she a Frenchwoman?"

"No! oh, no! But my wife is a painter, you understand, and—er—I met her in Paris—er— . . . Must you insist upon these—domestic particulars, Inspector?"

"If Mr. Exel is anxious to turn in," replied the inspector, "after his no doubt exhausting duties at the House, and if Dr. Cumberly—"

"I have no secrets from Cumberly!" interjected Leroux. "The doctor has known me almost from boyhood, but—er—" turning to the politician—"don't you know, Exel—no offense, no offense . . ."

"My dear Leroux," responded Exel hastily, "I am the offender! Permit me to wish you all good night."

He crossed the study, and, at the door, paused and turned.

"Rely upon me, Leroux," he said, "to help in any way within my power."

He crossed the lobby, opened the outer door, and departed.

"Now, Mr. Leroux," resumed Dunbar, "about this matter of your wife's absence."

IV

A WINDOW IS OPENED

Whilst Henry Leroux collected his thoughts, Dr. Cumberly glanced across at the writing-table where lay the fragment of paper which had been clutched in the dead woman's hand, then turned his head again toward the inspector, staring at him curiously. Since Dunbar had not yet attempted even to glance at the strange message, he wondered what had prompted the present line of inquiry.

"My wife," began Leroux, "shared a studio in Paris, at the time that I met her, with an American lady a very talented portrait painter—er—a Miss Denise Ryland. You may know her name?—but of course, you don't, no! Well, my wife is, herself, quite clever with her brush; in fact she has exhibited more than once at the Paris Salon. We agreed at—er—the time of our—of our—engagement, that she should be free to visit her old artistic friends in Paris at any time. You understand? There was to be no let or hindrance . . . . Is this really necessary, Inspector?"

"Pray go on, Mr. Leroux."

"Well, you understand, it was a give-and-take arrangement; because I am afraid that I, myself, demand certain—sacrifices from my wife—and—er—I did not feel entitled to—interfere . . ."

"You see, Inspector," interrupted Dr. Cumberly, "they are a Bohemian pair, and Bohemians, inevitably, bore one another at times! This little arrangement was intended as a safety-valve. Whenever ennui attacked Mrs. Leroux, she was at liberty to depart for a week to her own friends in Paris, leaving Leroux to the bachelor's existence which is really his proper state; to go unshaven and unshorn, to dine upon bread and cheese and onions, to work until all hours of the morning, and generally to enjoy himself!"

"Does she usually stay long?" inquired Dunbar.

"Not more than a week, as a rule," answered Leroux.

"You must excuse me," continued the detective, "if I seem to pry into intimate matters; but on these occasions, how does Mrs. Leroux get on for money?"

"I have opened a credit for her," explained the novelist, wearily, "at the Credit Lyonnais, in Paris."

Dunbar scribbled busily in his notebook.

"Does she take her maid with her?" he jerked, suddenly.

"She has no maid at the moment," replied Leroux; "she has been without one for twelve months or more, now."

"When did you last hear from her?"

"Three days ago."

"Did you answer the letter?"

"Yes; my answer was amongst the mail which Soames took to the post, to-night."

"You said, though, if I remember rightly, that he was out without permission?"

Leroux ran his fingers through his hair.

"I meant that he should only have been absent five minutes or so; whilst he remained out for more than an hour."

Inspector Dunbar nodded, comprehendingly, tapping his teeth with the head of the fountain-pen.

"And the other servants?"

"There are only two: a cook and a maid. I released them for the evening—glad to get rid of them—wanted to work."

"They are late?"

"They take liberties, damnable liberties, because I am easy-going."

"I see," said Dunbar. "So that you were quite alone this evening, when"—he nodded in the direction of the writing-table—"your visitor came?"

"Quite alone."

"Was her arrival the first interruption?"

"No—er—not exactly. Miss Cumberly . . ."

"My daughter," explained Dr. Cumberly, knowing that Mr. Leroux, at these times, was very neglectful in regard to meals, prepared him an omelette, and brought it down in a chafing-dish."

"How long did she remain?" asked the inspector of Leroux.

"I—er—did not exactly open the door. We chatted, through—er—through the letter-box, and she left the omelette outside on the landing."

"What time would that be?"

"It was a quarter to twelve," declared Cumberly. "I had been supping with some friends, and returned to find Helen, my daughter, engaged in preparing the omelette. I congratulated her upon the happy thought, knowing that Leroux was probably starving himself."

"I see. The omelette, though, seems to be upset here on the floor?" said the inspector.

Cumberly briefly explained how it came to be there, Leroux punctuating his friend's story with affirmative nods.

"Then the door of the flat was open all the time?" cried Dunbar.

"Yes," replied Cumberly; "but whilst Exel and I searched the other rooms—and our search was exhaustive—Mr. Leroux remained here in the study, and in full view of the lobby—as you see for yourself."

"No living thing," said Leroux, monotonously, "left this flat from the time that the three of us, Exel, Cumberly, and I, entered, up to the time that Miss Cumberly came, and, with the doctor, went out again."

"H'm!" said the inspector, making notes; "it appears so, certainly. I will ask you then, for your own account, Mr. Leroux, of the arrival of the woman in the civet furs. Pay special attention"—he pointed with his fountain-pen—"to the *time* at which the various incidents occurred."

Leroux, growing calmer as he proceeded with the strange story, complied with the inspector's request. He had practically completed his account when the door-bell rang.

"It's the servants," said Dr. Cumberly. "Soames will open the door."

But Soames did not appear.

The ringing being repeated—

"I told him to remain in his room," said Dunbar, "until I rang for him, I remember—"

"I will open the door," said Cumberly.

"And tell the servants to stay in the kitchen," snapped Dunbar.

Dr. Cumberly opened the door, admitting the cook and housemaid.

"There has been an unfortunate accident," he said—"but not to your master; you need not be afraid. But be good enough to remain in the kitchen for the present."

Peeping in furtively as they passed, the two women crossed the lobby and went to their own quarters.

"Mr. Soames next," muttered Dunbar, and, glancing at Cumberly as he returned from the lobby—"Will you ring for him?" he requested.

Dr. Cumberly nodded, and pressed a bell beside the mantelpiece. An interval followed, in which the inspector made notes and Cumberly stood looking at Leroux, who was beating his palms upon his knees, and staring unseeingly before him.

Cumberly rang again; and in response to the second ring, the housemaid appeared at the door.

"I rang for Soames," said Dr. Cumberly.

"He is not in, sir," answered the girl.

Inspector Dunbar started as though he had been bitten.

"What!" he cried; "not in?"

"No, sir," said the girl, with wide-open, frightened eyes.

Dunbar turned to Cumberly.

"You said there was no other way out!"

"There *is* no other way, to my knowledge."

"Where's his room?"

Cumberly led the way to a room at the end of a short corridor, and Inspector Dunbar, entering, and turning up the light, glanced about the little apartment. It was a very neat servants' bedroom; with comfortable, quite simple, furniture; but the chest-of-drawers had been hastily ransacked, and the contents of a trunk—or some of its contents—lay strewn about the floor.

"He has packed his grip!" came Leroux's voice from the doorway. "It's gone!"

The window was wide open. Dunbar sprang forward and leaned out over the ledge, looking to right and left, above and below.

A sort of square courtyard was beneath, and for the convenience of tradesmen, a hand-lift was constructed outside the kitchens of the three flats comprising the house; i. e.—Mr. Exel's, ground floor, Henry Leroux's second floor, and Dr. Cumberly's, top. It worked in a skeleton shaft which passed close to the left of Soames' window.

For an active man, this was a good enough ladder, and the inspector withdrew his head shrugging his square shoulders, irritably.

"My fault entirely!" he muttered, biting his wiry mustache. "I should have come and seen for myself if there was another way out."

Leroux, in a new flutter of excitement, now craned from the window.

"It might be possible to climb down the shaft," he cried, after a brief survey "but not if one were carrying a heavy grip, such as that which he has taken!"

"H'm!" said Dunbar. "You are a writing gentleman, I understand, and yet it does not occur to you that he could have lowered the bag on a cord, if he wanted to avoid the noise of dropping it!"

"Yes—er—of course!" muttered Leroux. "But really—but really— oh, good God! I am bewildered! What in Heaven's name does it all mean!"

"It means trouble," replied Dunbar, grimly; "bad trouble."

They returned to the study, and Inspector Dunbar, for the first time since his arrival, walked across and examined the fragmentary message, raising his eyebrows when he discovered that it was written upon the same paper as Leroux's MSS. He glanced, too, at the pen lying on a page of "Martin Zeda" near the lamp and at the inky splash which told how hastily the pen had been dropped.

Then—his brows drawn together—he stooped to the body of the murdered woman. Partially raising the fur cloak, he suppressed a gasp of astonishment.

"Why! she only wears a silk night-dress, and a pair of suede slippers!"

He glanced back over his shoulder.

"I had noted that," said Cumberly. "The whole business is utterly extraordinary."

"Extraordinary is no word for it!" growled the inspector, pursuing his examination . . . . "Marks of pressure at the throat—yes; and generally unhealthy appearance."

"Due to the drug habit," interjected Dr. Cumberly.

"What drug?"

"I should not like to say out of hand; possibly morphine."

"No jewelry," continued the detective, musingly; "wedding ring—not a new one. Finger nails well cared for, but recently neglected. Hair dyed to hide gray patches; dye wanted renewing. Shoes, French. Night-robe, silk; good lace; probably French, also. Faint perfume—don't know what it is—apparently proceeding from civet fur. Furs, magnificent; very costly."

He slightly moved the table-lamp in order to direct its light upon the white face. The bloodless lips were parted and the detective bent, closely peering at the teeth thus revealed.

"Her teeth were oddly discolored, doctor," he said, taking out a magnifying glass and examining them closely. "They had been recently scaled, too; so that she was not in the habit of neglecting them."

Dr. Cumberly nodded.

"The drug habit, again," he said guardedly; "a proper examination will establish the full facts."

The inspector added brief notes to those already made, ere he rose from beside the body. Then—

"You are absolutely certain," he said, deliberately, facing Leroux, "that you had never set eyes on this woman prior to her coming here, to-night?"

"I can swear it!" said Leroux.

"Good!" replied the detective, and closed his notebook with a snap. "Usual formalities will have to be gone through, but I don't think I need trouble you, gentlemen, any further, to-night."

V

DOCTORS DIFFER

Dr. Cumberly walked slowly upstairs to his own flat, a picture etched indelibly upon his mind, of Henry Leroux, with a face of despair, sitting below in his dining-room and listening to the ominous sounds proceeding from the study, where the police were now busily engaged. In the lobby he met his daughter Helen, who was waiting for him in a state of nervous suspense.

"Father!" she began, whilst rebuke died upon the doctor's lips— "tell me quickly what has happened."

Perceiving that an explanation was unavoidable, Dr. Cumberly outlined the story of the night's gruesome happenings, whilst Big Ben began to chime the hour of one.

Helen, eager-eyed, and with her charming face rather pale, hung upon every word of the narrative.

"And now," concluded her father, "you must go to bed. I insist."

"But father!" cried the girl—"there is some thing . . ."

She hesitated, uneasily.

"Well, Helen, go on," said the doctor.

"I am afraid you will refuse."

"At least give me the opportunity."

"Well—in the glimpse, the half-glimpse, which I had of her, I seemed . . ."

Dr. Cumberly rested his hands upon his daughter's shoulders characteristically, looking into the troubled gray eyes.

"You don't mean . . ." he began.

"I thought I recognized her!" whispered the girl.

"Good God! can it be possible?"

"I have been trying, ever since, to recall where we had met, but without result. It might mean so much . . ."

Dr. Cumberly regarded her, fixedly.

"It might mean so much to—Mr. Leroux. But I suppose you will say it is impossible?"

"It *is* impossible," said Dr. Cumberly firmly; "dismiss the idea, Helen."

"But father," pleaded the girl, placing her hands over his own, "consider what is at stake . . ."

"I am anxious that you should not become involved in this morbid business."

"But you surely know me better than to expect me to faint or become hysterical, or anything silly like that! I was certainly shocked when I came down to-night, because—well, it was all so frightfully unexpected . . ."

Dr. Cumberly shook his head. Helen put her arms about his neck and raised her eyes to his.

"You have no right to refuse," she said, softly: "don't you see that?"

Dr. Cumberly frowned. Then—

"You are right, Helen," he agreed. "I should know your pluck well enough. But if Inspector Dunbar is gone, the police may refuse to admit us . . ."

"Then let us hurry!" cried Helen. "I am afraid they will take away . . ."

Side by side they descended to Henry Leroux's flat, ringing the bell, which, an hour earlier, the lady of the civet furs had rung.

A sergeant in uniform opened the door.

"Is Detective-Inspector Dunbar here?" inquired the physician.

"Yes, sir."

"Say that Dr. Cumberly wishes to speak to him. And"—as the man was about to depart—"request him not to arouse Mr. Leroux."

Almost immediately the inspector appeared, a look of surprise upon his face, which increased on perceiving the girl beside her father.

"This is my daughter, Inspector," explained Cumberly; "she is a contributor to the Planet, and to various magazines, and in this journalistic capacity, meets many people in many walks of life. She thinks she may be of use to you in preparing your case."

Dunbar bowed rather awkwardly.

"Glad to meet you, Miss Cumberly," came the inevitable formula. "Entirely at your service."

"I had an idea, Inspector," said the girl, laying her hand confidentially upon Dunbar's arm, "that I recognized, when I entered Mr. Leroux's study, tonight"—Dunbar nodded—"that I recognized—the—the victim!"

"Good!" said the inspector, rubbing his palms briskly together. His tawny eyes sparkled. "And you would wish to see her again before we take her away. Very plucky of you, Miss Cumberly! But then, you are a doctor's daughter."

They entered, and the inspector closed the door behind them.

"Don't arouse poor Leroux," whispered Cumberly to the detective. "I left him on a couch in the dining-room."

"He is still there," replied Dunbar; "poor chap! It is . . ."

He met Helen's glance, and broke off shortly.

In the study two uniformed constables, and an officer in plain clothes, were apparently engaged in making an inventory—or such was the impression conveyed. The clock ticked merrily on; its ticking a desecration, where all else was hushed in deference to the grim visitor. The body of the murdered woman had been laid upon the chesterfield, and a little, dark, bearded man was conducting an elaborate examination; when, seeing the trio enter, he hastily threw the coat of civet fur over the body, and stood up, facing the intruders.

"It's all right, doctor," said the inspector; "and we shan't detain you a moment." He glanced over his shoulder. "Mr. Hilton, M. R. C. S." he said, indicating the dark man—"Dr. Cumberly and Miss Cumberly."

The divisional surgeon bowed to Helen and eagerly grasped the hand of the celebrated physician.

"I am fortunate in being able to ask your opinion," he began. . . .

Dr. Cumberly nodded shortly, and with upraised hand, cut him short.

"I shall willingly give you any assistance in my power," he said; "but my daughter has voluntarily committed herself to a rather painful ordeal, and I am anxious to get it over."

He stooped and raised the fur from the ghastly face.

Helen, her hand resting upon her father's shoulder, ventured one rapid glance and then looked away, shuddering slightly. Dr. Cumberly replaced the coat and gazed anxiously at his daughter. But Helen, with admirable courage, having closed her eyes for a moment, reopened them, and smiled at her father's anxiety. She was pale, but perfectly composed.

"Well, Miss Cumberly?" inquired the inspector, eagerly; whilst all in the room watched this slim girl in her charming deshabille, this dainty figure so utterly out of place in that scene of morbid crime.

She raised her gray eyes to the detective.

"I still believe that I have seen the face, somewhere, before. But I shall have to reflect a while—I meet so many folks, you know, in a casual way—before I can commit myself to any statement."

In the leonine eyes looking into hers gleamed the light of admiration and approval. The canny Scotsman admired this girl for her beauty, as a matter of course, for her courage, because courage was a quality standing high in his estimation, but, above all, for her admirable discretion.

"Very proper, Miss Cumberly," he said; "very proper and wise on your part. I don't wish to hurry you in any way, but"—he hesitated, glancing at the man in plain clothes, who had now resumed a careful perusal of a newspaper—"but her name doesn't happen to be Vernon—"

"Vernon!" cried the girl, her eyes lighting up at sound of the name. "Mrs. Vernon! it is! it is! She was pointed out to me at the last Arts Ball—where she appeared in a most monstrous Chinese costume—"

"Chinese?" inquired Dunbar, producing the bulky notebook.

"Yes. Oh! poor, poor soul!"

"You know nothing further about her, Miss Cumberly?"

"Nothing, Inspector. She was merely pointed out to me as one of the strangest figures in the hall. Her husband, I understand, is an art expert—"

"He *was!*" said Dunbar, closing the book sharply. "He died this afternoon; and a paragraph announcing his death appears in the newspaper which we found in the victim's fur coat!"

"But how—"

"It was the only paragraph on the half-page folded outwards which was in any sense *personal*. I am greatly indebted to you, Miss Cumberly; every hour wasted on a case like this means a fresh plait in the rope around the neck of the wrong man!"

Helen Cumberly grew slowly quite pallid.

"Good night," she said; and bowing to the detective and to the surgeon, she prepared to depart.

Mr. Hilton touched Dr. Cumberly's arm, as he, too, was about to retire.

"May I hope," he whispered, "that you will return and give me the benefit of your opinion in making out my report?"

Dr. Cumberly glanced at his daughter; and seeing her to be perfectly composed—"For the moment, I have formed no opinion, Mr. Hilton," he said, quietly, "not having had an opportunity to conduct a proper examination."

Hilton bent and whispered, confidentially, in the other's ear—

"She was drugged!"

The innuendo underlying the words struck Dr. Cumberly forcibly, and he started back with his brows drawn together in a frown.

"Do you mean that she was addicted to the use of drugs?" he asked, sharply; "or that the drugging took place to-night."

"The drugging *did* take place to-night!" whispered the other. "An injection was made in the left shoulder with a hypodermic syringe; the mark is quite fresh."

Dr. Cumberly glared at his fellow practitioner, angrily.

"Are there no other marks of injection?" he asked.

"On the left forearm, yes. Obviously self-administered. Oh, I don't deny the habit! But my point is this: the injection in the shoulder was *not* self-administered."

"Come, Helen," said Cumberly, taking his daughter's arm; for she had drawn near, during the colloquy—"you must get to bed."

His face was very stern when he turned again to Mr. Hilton.

"I shall return in a few minutes," he said, and escorted his daughter from the room.

VI

AT SCOTLAND YARD

Matters of vital importance to some people whom already we have met, and to others whom thus far we have not met, were transacted in a lofty and rather bleak looking room at Scotland Yard between the hours of nine and ten A. M.; that is, later in the morning of the fateful day whose advent we have heard acclaimed from the Tower of Westminster.

The room, which was lighted by a large French window opening upon a balcony, commanded an excellent view of the Thames Embankment. The floor was polished to a degree of brightness, almost painful. The distempered walls, save for a severe and solitary etching of a former Commissioner, were nude in all their unloveliness. A heavy deal table (upon which rested a blotting-pad, a pewter ink-pot, several newspapers and two pens) together with three deal chairs, built rather as monuments of durability than as examples of art, constituted the only furniture, if we except an electric lamp with a green glass shade, above the table.

This was the room of Detective-Inspector Dunbar; and Detective-Inspector Dunbar, at the hour of our entrance, will be found seated in the chair, placed behind the table, his elbows resting upon the blotting-pad.

At ten minutes past nine, exactly, the door opened, and a thick-set, florid man, buttoned up in a fawn colored raincoat and wearing a bowler hat of obsolete build, entered. He possessed a black mustache, a breezy, bustling manner, and humorous blue eyes; furthermore, when he took off his hat, he revealed the possession of a head of very bristly, upstanding, black hair. This was Detective-Sergeant Sowerby, and the same who was engaged in examining a newspaper in the study of Henry Leroux when Dr. Cumberly and his daughter had paid their second visit to that scene of an unhappy soul's dismissal.

"Well?" said Dunbar, glancing up at his subordinate, inquiringly.

"I have done all the cab depots," reported Sergeant Sowerby, "and a good many of the private owners; but so far the man seen by Mr. Exel has not turned up."

"The word will be passed round now, though," said Dunbar, "and we shall probably have him here during the day."

"I hope so," said the other good-humoredly, seating himself upon one of the two chairs ranged beside the wall. "If he doesn't show up. . . ."

"Well?" jerked Dunbar—"if he doesn't?"

"It will look very black against Leroux."

Dunbar drummed upon the blotting-pad with the fingers of his left hand.

"It beats anything of the kind that has ever come my way," he confessed. "You get pretty cautious at weighing people up, in this business; but I certainly don't think—mind you, I go no further—but I certainly don't think Mr. Henry Leroux would willingly kill a fly; yet there is circumstantial evidence enough to hang him."

Sergeant Sowerby nodded, gazing speculatively at the floor.

"I wonder," he said, slowly, "why the girl—Miss Cumberly—hesitated about telling us the woman's name?"

"I am not wondering about that at all," replied Dunbar, bluntly. "She must meet thousands in the same way. The wonder to me is that she remembered at all. I am open to bet half-a-crown that *you* couldn't remember the name of every woman you happened to have pointed out to you at an Arts Ball?"

"Maybe not," agreed Sowerby; "she's a smart girl, I'll allow. I see you have last night's papers there?"

"I have," replied Dunbar; "and I'm wondering . . ."

"If there's any connection?"

"Well," continued the inspector, "it looks on the face of it as though the news of her husband's death had something to do with Mrs. Vernon's presence at Leroux's flat. It's not a natural thing for a woman, on the evening of her husband's death, to rush straight away to another man's place . . ."

"It's strange we couldn't find her clothes . . ."

"It's not strange at all! You're simply obsessed with the idea that this was a love intrigue! Think, man! the most abandoned woman wouldn't run to keep an appointment with a lover at a time like that! And remember she had the news in her pocket! She came to that flat dressed—or undressed—just as we found her; I'm sure of it. And a point like that sometimes means the difference between hanging and acquittal."

Sergeant Sowerby digested these words, composing his jovial countenance in an expression of unnatural profundity. Then—

"*The* point to my mind," he said, "is the one raised by Mr. Hilton. By gum! didn't Dr. Cumberly tell him off!"

"Dr. Cumberly," replied Dunbar, "is entitled to his opinion, that the injection in the woman's shoulder was at least eight hours old; whilst Mr. Hilton is equally entitled to maintain that it was less than *one* hour old. Neither of them can hope to prove his case."

"If either of them could?"

"It might make a difference to the evidence—but I'm not sure."

"What time is your appointment?"

"Ten o'clock," replied Dunbar. "I am meeting Mr. Debnam—the late Mr. Vernon's solicitor. There is something in it. Damme! I am sure of it!"

"Something in what?"

"The fact that Mr. Vernon died yesterday evening, and that his wife was murdered at midnight."

"What have you told the press?"

"As little as possible, but you will see that the early editions will all be screaming for the arrest of Soames."

"I shouldn't wonder. He would be a useful man to have; but he's probably out of London now."

"I think not. He's more likely to wait for instructions from his principal."

"His principal?"

"Certainly. You don't think Soames did the murder, do you?"

"No; but he's obviously an accessory."

"I'm not so sure even of that."

"Then why did he bolt?"

"Because he had a guilty conscience."

"Yes," agreed Sowerby; "it does turn out that way sometimes. At any rate, Stringer is after him, but he's got next to nothing to go upon. Has any reply been received from Mrs. Leroux in Paris?"

"No," answered Dunbar, frowning thoughtfully. "Her husband's wire would reach her first thing this morning; I am expecting to hear of a reply at any moment."

"They're a funny couple, altogether," said Sowerby. "I can't imagine myself standing for Mrs. Sowerby spending her week-ends in Paris. Asking for trouble, I call it!"

"It does seem a daft arrangement," agreed Dunbar; "but then, as you say, they're a funny couple."

"I never saw such a bundle of nerves in all my life!"

"Leroux?"

Sowerby nodded.

"I suppose," he said, "it's the artistic temperament! If Mrs. Leroux has got it, too, I don't wonder that they get fed up with one another's company."

"That's about the secret of it. And now, I shall be glad, Sowerby, if you will be after that taxi-man again. Report at one o'clock. I shall be here."

With his hand on the door-knob: "By the way," said Sowerby, "who the blazes is Mr. King?"

Inspector Dunbar looked up.

"Mr. King," he replied slowly, "is the solution of the mystery."

VII

THE MAN IN THE LIMOUSINE

The house of the late Horace Vernon was a modern villa of prosperous appearance; but, on this sunny September morning, a palpable atmosphere of gloom seemed to overlie it. This made itself perceptible even to the toughened and unimpressionable nerves of Inspector Dunbar. As he mounted the five steps leading up to the door, glancing meanwhile at the lowered blinds at the windows, he wondered if, failing these evidences and his own private knowledge of the facts, he should have recognized that the hand of tragedy had placed its mark upon this house. But when the door was opened by a white-faced servant, he told himself that he should, for a veritable miasma of death seemed to come out to meet him, to envelop him.

Within, proceeded a subdued activity: somber figures moved upon the staircase; and Inspector Dunbar, having presented his card, presently found himself in a well-appointed library.

At the table, whereon were spread a number of documents, sat a lean, clean-shaven, sallow-faced man, wearing gold-rimmed pince-nez; a man whose demeanor of business-like gloom was most admirably adapted to that place and occasion. This was Mr. Debnam, the solicitor. He gravely waved the detective to an armchair, adjusted his pince-nez, and coughed, introductorily.

"Your communication, Inspector," he began (he had the kind of voice which seems to be buried in sawdust packing), "was brought to me this morning, and has disturbed me immeasurably, unspeakably."

"You have been to view the body, sir?"

"One of my clerks, who knew Mrs. Vernon, has just returned to this house to report that he has identified her."

"I should have preferred you to have gone yourself, sir," began Dunbar, taking out his notebook.

"My state of health, Inspector," said the solicitor, "renders it undesirable that I should submit myself to an ordeal so unnecessary—so wholly unnecessary."

"Very good!" muttered Dunbar, making an entry in his book; "your clerk, then, whom I can see in a moment, identifies the murdered woman as Mrs. Vernon. What was her Christian name?"

"Iris—Iris Mary Vernon."

Inspector Dunbar made a note of the fact.

"And now," he said, "you will have read the copy of that portion of my report which I submitted to you this morning—acting upon information supplied by Miss Helen Cumberly?"

"Yes, yes, Inspector, I have read it—but, by the way, I do not know Miss Cumberly."

"Miss Cumberly," explained the detective, "is the daughter of Dr. Cumberly, the Harley Street physician. She lives with her father in the flat above that of Mr. Leroux. She saw the body by accident—and recognized it as that of a lady who had been named to her at the last Arts Ball."

"Ah!" said Debnam, "yes—I see—at the Arts Ball, Inspector. This is a mysterious and a very ghastly case."

"It is indeed, sir," agreed Dunbar. "Can you throw any light upon the presence of Mrs. Vernon at Mr. Leroux's flat on the very night of her husband's death?"

"I can—and I cannot," answered the solicitor, leaning back in the chair and again adjusting his pince-nez, in the manner of a man having important matters—and gloomy, very gloomy, matters—to communicate.

"Good!" said the inspector, and prepared to listen.

"You see," continued Debnam, "the late Mrs. Vernon was not actually residing with her husband at the date of his death."

"Indeed!"

"Ostensibly"—the solicitor shook a lean forefinger at his *vis-à-vis*—"ostensibly, Inspector, she was visiting her sister in Scotland."

Inspector Dunbar sat up very straight, his brows drawn down over the tawny eyes.

"These visits were of frequent occurrence, and usually of about a week's duration. Mr. Vernon, my late client, a man—I'll not deny it—of inconstant affections (you understand me, Inspector?), did not greatly concern himself with his wife's movements. She belonged to a smart Bohemian set, and—to use a popular figure of speech—burnt the candle at both ends; late dances, night clubs, bridge parties, and other feverish pursuits, possibly taken up as a result of the—shall I say cooling?—of her husband's affections."

"There was another woman in the case?"

"I fear so, Inspector; in fact, I am sure of it: but to return to Mrs. Vernon. My client provided her with ample funds; and I, myself, have expressed to him astonishment respecting her expenditures in Scotland. I understand that her sister was in comparatively poor circumstances, and I went so far as to point out to Mr. Vernon that one hundred pounds was—shall I say an excessive?—outlay upon a week's sojourn in Auchterander, Perth."

"A hundred pounds!"

"One hundred pounds!"

"Was it queried by Mr. Vernon?"

"Not at all."

"Was Mr. Vernon personally acquainted with this sister in Perth?"

"He was not, Inspector. Mrs. Vernon, at the time of her marriage, did not enjoy that social status to which my late client elevated her. For many years she held no open communication with any member of her family, but latterly, as I have explained, she acquired the habit of recuperating—recuperating from the effects of her febrile pleasures—at this obscure place in Scotland. And Mr. Vernon, his interest in her movements having considerably—shall I say abated?—offered no objection: even suffered it gladly, counting the cost but little against . . ."

"Freedom?" suggested Dunbar, scribbling in his notebook.

"Rather crudely expressed, perhaps," said the solicitor, peering over the top of his glasses, "but you have the idea. I come now to my client's awakening. Four days ago, he learned the truth; he learned that he was being deceived!"

"Deceived!"

"Mrs. Vernon, thoroughly exhausted with irregular living, announced that she was about to resort once more to the healing breezes of the heather-land"—Mr. Debnam was thoroughly warming to his discourse and thoroughly enjoying his own dusty phrases.

"Interrupting you for a moment," said the inspector, "at what intervals did these visits take place?"

"At remarkably regular intervals, Inspector: something like six times a year."

"For how long had Mrs. Vernon made a custom of these visits?"

"Roughly, for two years."

"Thank you. Will you go on, sir?"

"She requested Mr. Vernon, then, on the last occasion to give her a check for eighty pounds; and this he did, unquestioningly. On Thursday, the second of September, she left for Scotland . . ."

"Did she take her maid?"

"Her maid always received a holiday on these occasions; Mrs. Vernon wired her respecting the date of her return."

"Did any one actually see her off?"

"No, not that I am aware of, Inspector."

"To put the whole thing quite bluntly, Mr. Debnam," said Dunbar, fixing his tawny eyes upon the solicitor, "Mr. Vernon was thoroughly glad to get rid of her for a week?"

Mr. Debnam shifted uneasily in his chair; the truculent directness of the detective was unpleasing to his tortuous mind. However—

"I fear you have hit upon the truth," he confessed, "and I must admit that we have no legal evidence of her leaving for Scotland on this, or on any other occasion. Letters were received from Perth, and letters sent to Auchterander from London were answered. But the truth, the painful truth came to light, unexpectedly, dramatically, on Monday last . . ."

"Four days ago?"

"Exactly; three days before the death of my client." Mr. Debnam wagged his finger at the inspector again. "I maintain," he said, "that this painful discovery, which I am about to mention, precipitated my client's end; although it is a fact that there was—hereditary heart trouble. But I admit that his neglect of his wife (to give it no harsher name) contributed to the catastrophe."

He paused to give dramatic point to the revelation.

"Walking homeward at a late hour on Monday evening from a flat in Victoria Street—the flat of—shall I employ the term a particular friend?—Mr. Vernon was horrified—horrified beyond measure, to perceive, in a large and well-appointed car—a limousine—his wife!"

"The inside lights of the car were on, then?"

"No; but the light from a street lamp shone directly into the car. A temporary block in the traffic compelled the driver of the car, whom my client described to me as an Asiatic—to pull up for a moment. There, within a few yards of her husband, Mrs. Vernon reclined in the car—or rather in the arms of a male companion!"

"What!"

"Positively!" Mr. Debnam was sedately enjoying himself. "Positively, my dear Inspector, in the arms of a man of extremely dark complexion. Mr. Vernon was unable to perceive more than this, for the man had his back toward him. But the light shone fully upon the face of Mrs. Vernon, who appeared pale and exhausted. She wore a conspicuous motor-coat of civet fur, and it was this which first attracted Mr. Vernon's attention. The blow was a very severe one to a man in my client's state of health; and although I cannot claim that his own conscience was clear, this open violation of the marriage vows outraged the husband— outraged him. In fact he was so perturbed, that he stood there shaking, quivering, unable to speak or act, and the car drove away before he had recovered sufficient presence of mind to note the number."

"In which direction did the car proceed?"

"Toward Victoria Station."

"Any other particulars?"

"Not regarding the car, its driver, or its occupants; but early on the following morning, Mr. Vernon, very much shaken, called upon me and instructed me to despatch an agent to Perth immediately. My agent's report reached me at practically the same time as the news of my client's death . . ."

"And his report was. . . ?"

"His report, Inspector, telegraphic, of course, was this: that no sister of Mrs. Vernon resided at the address; that the place was a cottage occupied by a certain Mrs. Fry and her husband; that the husband was of no occupation, and had no visible means of support"—he ticked off the points on the long forefinger—"that the Frys lived better than any of their neighbors; and—most important of all—that Mrs. Fry's maiden name, which my agent discovered by recourse to the parish register of marriages—was Ann Fairchild."

"What of that?"

"Ann Fairchild was a former maid of Mrs. Vernon!"

"In short, it amounts to this, then: Mrs. Vernon, during these various absences, never went to Scotland at all? It was a conspiracy?"

"Exactly—exactly, Inspector! I wired instructing my agent to extort from the woman, Fry, the address to which she forwarded letters received by her for Mrs. Vernon. The lady's death, news of which will now have reached him, will no doubt be a lever, enabling my representative to obtain the desired information."

"When do you expect to hear from him?"

"At any moment. Failing a full confession by the Frys, you will of course know how to act, Inspector?"

"Damme!" cried Dunbar, "can your man be relied upon to watch them? They mustn't slip away! Shall I instruct Perth to arrest the couple?"

"I wired my agent this morning, Inspector, to communicate with the local police respecting the Frys."

Inspector Dunbar tapped his small, widely-separated teeth with the end of his fountain-pen.

"I have had one priceless witness slip through my fingers," he muttered. "I'll hand in my resignation if the Frys go!"

"To whom do you refer?"

Inspector Dunbar rose.

"It is a point with which I need not trouble you, sir," he said. "It was not included in the extract of report sent to you. This is going to be the biggest case of my professional career, or my name is not Robert Dunbar!"

Closing his notebook, he thrust it into his pocket, and replaced his fountain-pen in the little leather wallet.

"Of course," said the solicitor, rising in turn, and adjusting the troublesome pince-nez, "there was some intrigue with Leroux? So much is evident."

"You will be thinking that, eh?"

"My dear Inspector—" Mr. Debnam, the wily, was seeking information. "My dear Inspector, Leroux's own wife was absent in Paris—quite a safe distance; and Mrs. Vernon (now proven to be a woman conducting a love intrigue) is found dead under most compromising circumstances—*most* compromising circumstances—in his flat! His servants, even, are got safely out of the way for the evening . . ."

"Quite so," said Dunbar, shortly, "quite so, Mr. Debnam." He opened the door. "Might I see the late Mrs. Vernon's maid?"

"She is at her home. As I told you, Mrs. Vernon habitually released her for the period of these absences."

The notebook reappeared.

"The young woman's address?"

"You can get it from the housekeeper. Is there anything else you wish to know?"

"Nothing beyond that, thank you."

Three minutes later, Inspector Dunbar had written in his book— *Clarice Goodstone, c/o Mrs. Herne, 134a Robert Street, Hampstead Road, N. W.*

He departed from the house whereat Death the Gleaner had twice knocked with his Scythe.

VIII

CABMAN TWO

Returning to Scotland Yard, Inspector Dunbar walked straight up to his own room. There he found Sowerby, very red faced and humid, and a taximan who sat stolidly surveying the Embankment from the window.

"Hullo!" cried Dunbar; "he's turned up, then?"

"No, he hasn't," replied Sowerby with a mild irritation. "But we know where to find him, and he ought to lose his license."

The taximan turned hurriedly. He wore a muffler so tightly packed between his neck and the collar of his uniform jacket, that it appeared materially to impair his respiration. His face possessed a bluish tinge, suggestive of asphyxia, and his watery eyes protruded remarkably; his breathing was noisily audible.

"No, chuck it, mister!" he exclaimed. "I'm only tellin' you 'cause it ain't my line to play tricks on the police. You'll find my name in the books downstairs more'n any other driver in London! I reckon I've brought enough umbrellas, cameras, walkin' sticks, hopera cloaks, watches and sicklike in 'ere, to set up a blarsted pawnbroker's!"

"That's all right, my lad!" said Dunbar, holding up his hand to silence the voluble speaker. "There's going to be no license-losing. You did not hear that you were wanted before?"

The watery eyes of the cabman protruded painfully; he respired like a horse.

"*Me*, guv'nor!" he exclaimed. "Gor'blime! I ain't the bloke! I was drivin' back from takin' the Honorable 'Erbert 'Arding 'ome—same as I does almost every night, when the 'ouse is a-sittin'—when I see old Tom Brian drawin' away from the door o' Palace Man—"

Again Dunbar held up his hand.

"No doubt you mean well," he said; "but damme! begin at the beginning! Who are you, and what have you come to tell us?"

"'Oo are I?—'Ere's 'oo I ham!" Wheezed the cabman, proffering a greasy license. "Richard 'Amper, number 3 Breams Mews, Dulwich Village."

"That's all right," said Dunbar, thrusting back the proffered document; "and last night you had taken Mr. Harding the member of Parliament, to his residence in?"—

"In Peers' Chambers, Westminister—that's it, guv'nor! Comin' back, I 'ave to pass along the north side o' the Square, an' just a'ead o' me, I see old Tom Brian a-pullin' round the Johnny 'Orner,—'im comin' from Palace Mansions."

"Mr. Exel only mentioned seeing *one* cab," muttered Dunbar, glancing keenly aside at Sowerby.

"Wotcher say, guv'nor?" asked the cabman.

"I say—did you see a gentleman approaching from the corner?" asked Dunbar.

"Yus," declared the man; "I see 'im, but 'e 'adn't got as far as the Johnny 'Orner. As I passed outside old Tom Brian, wot's changin' 'is gear, I see a bloke blowin' along on the pavement—a bloke in a high 'at, an' wearin' a heye-glass."

"At this time, then," pursued Dunbar, "you had actually passed the other cab, and the gentleman on the pavement had not come up with it?"

"'E couldn't see it, guv'nor! I'm tellin' you 'e 'adn't got to the Johnny 'Orner!"

"I see," muttered Sowerby. "It's possible that Mr. Exel took no notice of the first cab—especially as it did not come out of the Square."

"Wotcher say, guv'nor?" queried the cabman again, turning his bleared eyes upon Sergeant Sowerby.

"He said," interrupted Dunbar, "was Brian's cab empty?"

"'Course it was," rapped Mr. Hamper. "'E'd just dropped 'is fare at Palace Mansions."

"How do you know?" snapped Dunbar, suddenly, fixing his fierce eyes upon the face of the speaker.

The cabman glared in beery truculence.

"I got me blarsted senses, ain't I?" he inquired. "There's only two lots o' flats on that side o' the Square—Palace Mansions, an' St. Andrew's Mansions."

"Well?"

"St. Andrew's Mansions," continued Hamper, "is all away!"

"All away?"

"All away! I know, 'cause I used to have a reg'lar fare there. 'E's in Egyp'; flat shut up. Top floor's to let. Bottom floor's two old unmarried maiden ladies what always travels by 'bus. So does all their blarsted friends an' relations. Where can old Tom Brian 'ave been comin' from, if it wasn't Palace Mansions?"

"H'm!" said Dunbar, "you are a loss to the detective service, my lad! And how do you account for the fact that Brian has not got to hear of the inquiry?"

Hamper bent to Dunbar and whispered, beerily, in his ear: "P'r'aps 'e don't want to 'ear, guv'nor!"

"Oh! Why not?"

"Well, 'e knows there's something up there!"

"Therefore it's his plain duty to assist the police."

"Same as what I does?" cried Hamper, raising his eyebrows. "Course it is! but 'ow d'you know 'e ain't been got at?"

"Our friend, here, evidently has one up against Mr. Tom Brian!"

41

muttered Dunbar aside to Sowerby.

"Wotcher say, guv'nor?" inquired the cabman, looking from one to the other.

"I say, no doubt you can save us the trouble of looking out Brian's license, and give us his private address?" replied Dunbar.

"Course I can. 'E lives hat num'er 36 Forth Street, Brixton, and 'e's out o' the big Brixton depot."

"Oh!" said Dunbar, dryly. "Does he owe you anything?"

"Wotcher say, guv'nor?"

"I say, it's very good of you to take all this trouble and whatever it has cost you in time, we shall be pleased to put right."

Mr. Hamper spat in his right palm, and rubbed his hands together, appreciatively.

"Make it five bob!" he said.

"Wait downstairs," directed Dunbar, pressing a bell-push beside the door. "I'll get it put through for you."

"Right-o!" rumbled the cabman, and went lurching from the room as a constable in uniform appeared at the door. "Good mornin', guv'nor. Good mornin'!"

The cabman having departed, leaving in his wake a fragrant odor of fourpenny ale—

"Here you are, Sowerby!" cried Dunbar. "We are moving at last! This is the address of the late Mrs. Vernon's maid. See her; feel your ground, carefully, of course; get to know what clothes Mrs. Vernon took with her on her periodical visits to Scotland."

"What clothes?"

"That's the idea; it is important. I don't think the girl was in her mistress's confidence, but I leave it to you to find out. If circumstances point to my surmise being inaccurate—you know how to act."

"Just let me glance over your notes, bearing on the matter," said Sowerby, "and I'll be off."

Dunbar handed him the bulging notebook, and Sergeant Sowerby lowered his inadequate eyebrows, thoughtfully, whilst he scanned the evidence of Mr. Debnam. Then, returning the book to his superior, and adjusting the peculiar bowler firmly upon his head, he set out.

Dunbar glanced through some papers—apparently reports—which lay upon the table, penciled comments upon two of them, and then, consulting his notebook once more in order to refresh his memory, started off for Forth Street, Brixton.

Forth Street, Brixton, is a depressing thoroughfare. It contains small, cheap flats, and a number of frowsy looking houses which give one the impression of having run to seed. A hostelry of sad aspect occupies a commanding position midway along the street, but inspires the traveler not with cheer, but with lugubrious reflections upon the horrors of inebriety. The odors, unpleasantly mingled, of fried bacon and paraffin oil, are wafted to the wayfarer from the porches of these family residences.

Number 36 proved to be such a villa, and Inspector Dunbar contemplated it from a distance, thoughtfully. As he stood by the door of the public house, gazing across the street, a tired looking woman, lean and anxious-eyed, a poor, dried up bean-pod of a woman, appeared from the door of number 36, carrying a basket. She walked along in the direction of the neighboring highroad, and Dunbar casually followed her.

For some ten minutes he studied her activities, noting that she went from shop to shop until her basket was laden with provisions of all sorts. When she entered a wine-and-spirit merchant's, the detective entered close behind her, for the place was also a post-office. Whilst he purchased a penny stamp and fumbled in his pocket for an imaginary letter, he observed, with interest, that the woman had purchased, and was loading into the hospitable basket, a bottle of whisky, a bottle of rum, and a bottle of gin.

He left the shop ahead of her, sure, now, of his ground, always provided that the woman proved to be Mrs. Brian. Dunbar walked along Forth Street slowly enough to enable the woman to overtake him. At the door of number 36, he glanced up at the number, questioningly, and turned in the gate as she was about to enter.

He raised his hat.

"Have I the pleasure of addressing Mrs. Brian?"

Momentarily, a hard look came into the tired eyes, but Dunbar's gentleness of manner and voice, together with the kindly expression upon his face, turned the scales favorably.

"I am Mrs. Brian," she said; "yes. Did you want to see me?"

"On a matter of some importance. May I come in?"

She nodded and led the way into the house; the door was not closed.

In a living-room whereon was written a pathetic history—a history of decline from easy circumstance and respectability to poverty and utter disregard of appearances—she confronted him, setting down her basket on a table from which the remains of a fish breakfast were not yet removed.

"Is your husband in?" inquired Dunbar with a subtle change of manner.

"He's lying down."

The hard look was creeping again into the woman's eyes.

"Will you please awake him, and tell him that I have called in regard to his license?"

He thrust a card into her hand—

DETECTIVE-INSPECTOR DUNBAR, C. I. D.
NEW SCOTLAND YARD. S. W.

IX

THE MAN IN BLACK

Mrs. Brian started back, with a wild look, a trapped look, in her eyes.

"What's he done?" she inquired. "What's he done? Tom's not done anything!"

"Be good enough to waken him," persisted the inspector. "I wish to speak to him."

Mrs. Brian walked slowly from the room and could be heard entering one further along the passage. An angry snarling, suggesting that of a wild animal disturbed in its lair, proclaimed the arousing of Taximan Thomas Brian. A thick voice inquired, brutally, why the sanguinary hell he (Mr. Brian) had had his bloodstained slumbers disturbed in this gory manner and who was the vermilion blighter responsible.

Then Mrs. Brian's voice mingled with that of her husband, and both became subdued. Finally, a slim man, who wore a short beard, or had omitted to shave for some days, appeared at the door of the living-room. His face was another history upon the same subject as that which might be studied from the walls, the floor, and the appointments of the room. Inspector Dunbar perceived that the shadow of the neighboring hostelry overlay this home.

"What's up?" inquired the new arrival.

The tone of his voice, thickened by excess, was yet eloquent of the gentleman. The barriers passed, your pariah gentleman can be the completest blackguard of them all. He spoke coarsely, and the infectious Cockney accent showed itself in his vowels; but Dunbar, a trained observer, summed up his man in a moment and acted accordingly.

"Come in and shut the door!" he directed. "No"—as Mrs. Brian sought to enter behind her husband—"I wish to speak with you, privately."

"Hop it!" instructed Brian, jerking his thumb over his shoulder—and Mrs. Brian obediently disappeared, closing the door.

"Now," said Dunbar, looking the man up and down, "have you been into the depot, today?"

"No."

"But you have heard that there's an inquiry?"

"I've heard nothing. I've been in bed."

"We won't argue about that. I'll simply put a question to you: Where did you pick up the fare that you dropped at Palace Mansions at twelve o'clock last night?"

"Palace Mansions!" muttered Brian, shifting uneasily beneath the unflinching stare of the tawny eyes. "What d'you mean? What Palace Mansions?"

"Don't quibble!" warned Dunbar, thrusting out a finger at him. "This is not a matter of a loss of license; it's a life job!"

"Life job!" whispered the man, and his weak face suddenly relaxed, so that, oddly, the old refinement shone out through the new, vulgar veneer.

"Answer my questions straight and square and I'll take your word that you have not seen the inquiry!" said Dunbar.

"Dick Hamper's done this for me!" muttered Brian. "He's a dirty, low swine! Somebody'll do for him one night!"

"Leave Hamper out of the question," snapped Dunbar. "You put down a fare at Palace Mansions at twelve o'clock last night?"

For one tremendous moment, Brian hesitated, but the good that was in him, or the evil—a consciousness of wrongdoing, or of retribution pending—respect for the law, or fear of its might—decided his course.

"I did."

"It was a man?"

Again Brian, with furtive glance, sought to test his opponent; but his opponent was too strong for him. With Dunbar's eyes upon his face, he chose not to lie.

"It was a woman."

"How was she dressed?"

"In a fur motor-coat—civet fur."

The man of culture spoke in those two words, "civet fur"; and Dunbar nodded quickly, his eyes ablaze at the importance of the evidence.

"Was she alone?"

"She was."

"What fare did she pay you?"

"The meter only registered eightpence, but she gave me half-a-crown."

"Did she appear to be ill?"

"Very ill. She wore no hat, and I supposed her to be in evening dress. She almost fell as she got out of the cab, but managed to get into the hall of Palace Mansions quickly enough, looking behind her all the time."

Inspector Dunbar shot out the hypnotic finger again.

"She told you to wait!" he asserted, positively. Brian looked to right and left, up and down, thrusting his hands into his coat pockets, and taking them out again to stroke his collarless neck. Then—

"She did—yes," he admitted.

"But you were bribed to drive away? Don't deny it! Don't dare to trifle with me, or by God! you'll spend the night in Brixton Jail!"

"It was made worth my while," muttered Brian, his voice beginning to break, "to hop it."

"Who paid you to do it?"

"A man who had followed all the way in a big car."

"That's it! Describe him!"

"I can't! No, no! you can threaten as much as you like, but I can't describe him. I never saw his face. He stood behind me on the near side of the cab, and just reached forward and pushed a flyer under my nose."

Inspector Dunbar searched the speaker's face closely—and concluded that he was respecting the verity.

"How was he dressed?"

"In black, and that's all I can tell you about him."

"You took the money?"

"I took the money, yes . . ."

"What did he say to you?"

"Simply: 'Drive off.'"

"Did you take him to be an Englishman from his speech?"

"No; he was not an Englishman. He had a foreign accent."

"French? German?"

"No," said Brian, looking up and meeting the glance of the fierce eyes. "Asiatic!"

Inspector Dunbar, closely as he held himself in hand, started slightly.

"Are you sure?"

"Certainly. Before I—when I was younger—I traveled in the East, and I know the voice and intonation of the cultured Oriental."

"Can you place him any closer than that?"

"No, I can't venture to do so." Brian's manner was becoming, momentarily, more nearly that of a gentleman. "I might be leading you astray if I ventured a guess, but if you asked me to do so, I should say he was a Chinaman."

"A *Chinaman?*" Dunbar's voice rose excitedly.

"I think so."

"What occurred next?"

"I turned my cab and drove off out of the Square."

"Did you see where the man went?"

"I didn't. I saw nothing of him beyond his hand."

"And his hand?"

"He wore a glove."

"And now," said Dunbar, speaking very slowly, "where did you pick up your fare?"

"In Gillingham Street, near Victoria Station."

"From a house?"

"Yes, from Nurse Proctor's."

"Nurse Proctor's! Who is Nurse Proctor?"

Brian shrugged his shoulders in a nonchalant manner, which obviously belonged to an earlier phase of existence.

"She keeps a nursing home," he said—"for ladies."

"Do you mean a maternity home?"

"Not exactly; at least I don't think so. Most of her clients are society ladies, who stay there periodically."

"What are you driving at?" demanded Dunbar. "I have asked you if it is a maternity home."

"And I have replied that it isn't. I am only giving you facts; you don't want my surmises."

"Who hailed you?"

"The woman did—the woman in the fur coat. I was just passing the door very slowly when it was flung open with a bang, and she rushed out as though hell were after her. Before I had time to pull up, she threw herself into my cab and screamed: 'Palace Mansions! Westminster!' I reached back and shut the door, and drove right away."

"When did you see that you were followed?"

"We were held up just outside the music hall, and looking back, I saw that my fare was dreadfully excited. It didn't take me long to find out that the cause of her excitement was a big limousine, three or four back in the block of traffic. The driver was some kind of an Oriental, too, although I couldn't make him out very clearly."

"Good!" snapped Dunbar; "that's important! But you saw nothing more of this car?"

"I saw it follow me into the Square."

"Then where did it wait?"

"I don't know; I didn't see it again."

Inspector Dunbar nodded rapidly.

"Have you ever driven women to or from this Nurse Proctor's before?"

"On two other occasions, I have driven ladies who came from there. I knew they came from there, because it got about amongst us that the tall woman in nurse's uniform who accompanied them was Nurse Proctor."

"You mean that you didn't take these women actually from the door of the house in Gillingham Street, but from somewhere adjacent?"

"Yes; they never take a cab from the door. They always walk to the corner of the street with a nurse, and a porter belonging to the house brings their luggage along."

"The idea is secrecy?"

"No doubt. But as I have said, the word was passed round."

"Did you know either of these other women?"

"No; but they were obviously members of good society."

"And you drove them?"

"One to St. Pancras, and one to Waterloo," said Brian, dropping back somewhat into his coarser style, and permitting a slow grin to overspread his countenance.

"To catch trains, no doubt?"

"Not a bit of it! To *meet* trains!"

"You mean?"

"I mean that their own private cars were waiting for them at the *arrival* platform as I drove 'em up to the *departure* platform, and that they simply marched through the station and pretended to have arrived by train!"

Inspector Dunbar took out his notebook and fountain-pen, and began to tap his teeth with the latter, nodding his head at the same time.

"You are sure of the accuracy of your last statement?" he said, raising his eyes to the other.

"I followed one of them," was the reply, "and saw her footman gravely take charge of the luggage which I had just brought from Victoria; and a pal of mine followed the other—the Waterloo one, that was."

Inspector Dunbar scribbled busily. Then—

"You have done well to make a clean breast of it," he said. "Take a straight tip from me. Keep off the drink!"

X

THE GREAT UNDERSTANDING

It was in the afternoon of this same day—a day so momentous in the lives of more than one of London's millions—that two travelers might have been seen to descend from a first-class compartment of the Dover boat-train at Charing Cross.

They had been the sole occupants of the compartment, and, despite the wide dissimilarity of character to be read upon their countenances, seemed to have struck up an acquaintance based upon mutual amiability and worldly common sense. The traveler first to descend and gallantly to offer his hand to his companion in order to assist her to the platform, was the one whom a casual observer would first have noted.

He was a man built largely, but on good lines; a man past his youth, and somewhat too fleshy; but for all his bulk, there was nothing unwieldy, and nothing ungraceful in his bearing or carriage. He wore a French traveling-coat, conceived in a style violently Parisian, and composed of a wonderful check calculated to have blinded any cutter in Savile Row. From beneath its gorgeous folds protruded the extremities of severely creased cashmere trousers, turned up over white spats which nestled coyly about a pair of glossy black boots. The traveler's hat was of velour, silver gray and boasting a partridge feather thrust in its silken band. One glimpse of the outfit must have brought the entire staff of the Tailor and Cutter to an untimely grave.

But if ever man was born who could carry such a make-up, this traveler was he. The face was cut on massive lines, on fleshy lines, clean-shaven, and inclined to pallor. The hirsute blue tinge about the jaw and lips helped to accentuate the virile strength of the long, flexible mouth, which could be humorous, which could be sorrowful, which could be grim. In the dark eyes of the man lay a wealth of experience, acquired in a lifelong pilgrimage among many peoples, and to many lands. His dark brows were heavily marked, and his close-cut hair was splashed with gray.

Let us glance at the lady who accepted his white-gloved hand, and who sprang alertly onto the platform beside him.

She was a woman bordering on the forties, with a face of masculine vigor, redeemed and effeminized, by splendid hazel eyes, the kindliest imaginable. Obviously, the lady was one who had never married, who despised, or affected to despise, members of the other sex, but who had never learned to hate them; who had never grown soured, but who found the world a garden of heedless children—of children who called for mothering. Her athletic figure was clothed in a "sensible" tweed traveling dress, and she wore a tweed hat pressed well on to her head, and brown boots with the flattest heels conceivable. Add to this a Scotch woolen muffler, and a pair of woolen gloves, and you have a mental picture of the second traveler—a truly incongruous companion for the first.

Joining the crowd pouring in the direction of the exit gates, the two chatted together animatedly, both speaking English, and the man employing that language with a perfect ease and command of words which nevertheless failed to disguise his French nationality. He spoke with an American accent; a phenomenon sometimes observable in one who has learned his English in Paris.

The irritating formalities which beset the returning traveler—and the lady distinctly was of the readily irritated type—were smoothed away by the magic personality of her companion. Porters came at the beck of his gloved hand; guards, catching his eye, saluted and were completely his servants; ticket inspectors yielded to him the deference ordinarily reserved for directors of the line.

Outside the station, then, her luggage having been stacked upon a cab, the lady parted from her companion with assurances, which were returned, that she should hope to improve the acquaintance.

The address to which the French gentleman politely requested the cabman to drive, was that of a sound and old-established hotel in the neighborhood of the Strand, and at no great distance from the station.

Then, having stood bareheaded until the cab turned out into the traffic stream of that busy thoroughfare, the first traveler, whose baggage consisted of a large suitcase, hailed a second cab and drove to the Hotel Astoria—the usual objective of Americans.

Taking leave of him for the moment, let us follow the lady.

Her arrangements were very soon made at the hotel, and having removed some of the travel-stains from her person and partaken of one cup of China tea, respecting the quality whereof she delivered herself of some caustic comments, she walked down into the Strand and mounted to the top of a Victoria bound 'bus.

That she was not intimately acquainted with London, was a fact readily observable by her fellow passengers; for as the 'bus went rolling westward, from the large pocket of her Norfolk jacket she took out a guide-book provided with numerous maps, and began composedly to consult its complexities.

When the conductor came to collect her fare, she had made up her mind, and was replacing the guidebook in her pocket.

"Put me down by the Storis, Victoria Street, conductor," she directed, and handed him a penny—the correct fare.

It chanced that at about the time, within a minute or so, of the American lady's leaving the hotel, and just as red rays, the harbingers of dusk, came creeping in at the latticed widow of her cozy work-room, Helen Cumberly laid down her pen with a sigh. She stood up, mechanically rearranging her hair as she did so, and crossed the corridor to her bedroom, the window whereof overlooked the Square.

She peered down into the central garden. A common-looking man sat upon a bench, apparently watching the labors of the gardener, which consisted at the moment of the spiking of scraps of paper which disfigured the green carpet of the lawn.

Helen returned to her writing-table and reseated herself. Kindly twilight veiled her, and a chatty sparrow who perched upon the window-ledge pretended that he had not noticed two tears which trembled, quivering, upon the girl's lashes. Almost unconsciously, for it was an established custom, she sprinkled crumbs from the tea-tray beside her upon the ledge, whilst the tears dropped upon a written page and two more appeared in turn upon her lashes.

The sparrow supped enthusiastically, being joined in his repast by two talkative companions. As the last fragments dropped from the girl's white fingers, she withdrew her hand, and slowly—very slowly—her head sank down, pillowed upon her arms.

For some five minutes she cried silently; the sparrows, unheeded, bade her good night, and flew to their nests in the trees of the Square. Then, very resolutely, as if inspired by a settled purpose, she stood up and recrossed the corridor to her bedroom.

She turned on the lamp above the dressing-table and rapidly removed the traces of her tears, contemplating in dismay a redness of her pretty nose which did not prove entirely amenable to treatment with the powder-puff. Finally, however, she switched off the light, and, going out on to the landing, descended to the door of Henry Leroux's flat.

In reply to her ring, the maid, Ferris, opened the door. She wore her hat and coat, and beside her on the floor stood a tin trunk.

"Why, Ferris!" cried Helen—"are you leaving?"

"I am indeed, miss!" said the girl, independently.

"But why? whatever will Mr. Leroux do?"

"He'll have to do the best he can. Cook's goin' too!"

"What! cook is going?"

"I am!" announced a deep, female voice.

And the cook appeared beside the maid.

"But whatever—" began Helen; then, realizing that she could achieve no good end by such an attitude: "Tell Mr. Leroux," she instructed the maid, quietly, "that I wish to see him."

Ferris glanced rapidly at her companion, as a man appeared on the landing, to inquire in an abysmal tone, if "them boxes was ready to be took?" Helen Cumberly forestalled an insolent refusal which the cook, by furtive wink, counseled to the housemaid.

"Don't trouble," she said, with an easy dignity reminiscent of her father. "I will announce myself."

She passed the servants, crossed the lobby, and rapped upon the study door.

"Come in," said the voice of Henry Leroux.

Helen opened the door. The place was in semidarkness, objects being but dimly discernible. Leroux sat in his usual seat at the writing-table. The room was in the utmost disorder, evidently having received no attention since its overhauling by the police. Helen pressed the switch, lighting the two lamps.

Leroux, at last, seemed in his proper element: he exhibited an unhealthy pallor, and it was obvious that no razor had touched his chin for at least three days. His dark blue eyes the eyes of a dreamer—were heavy and dull, with shadows pooled below them. A biscuit-jar, a decanter and a syphon stood half buried in papers on the table.

"Why, Mr. Leroux!" said Helen, with a deep note of sympathy in her voice—"you don't mean to say . . ."

Leroux rose, forcing a smile to his haggard face.

"You see—much too good," he said. "Altogether—too good."

"I thought I should find you here," continued the girl, firmly; "but I did not anticipate—"she indicated the chaos about—"this! The insolence, the disgraceful, ungrateful insolence, of those women!"

"Dear, dear, dear!" murmured Leroux, waving his hand vaguely; "never mind—never mind! They—er—they . . . I don't want them to stop . . . and, believe me, I am—er—perfectly comfortable!"

"You should not be in—*this* room, at all. In fact, you should go right away."

"I cannot . . . my wife may—return—at any moment." His voice shook. "I—am expecting her return—hourly."

His gaze sought the table-clock; and he drew his lips very tightly together when the pitiless hands forced upon his mind the fact that the day was marching to its end.

Helen turned her head aside, inhaling deeply, and striving for composure.

"Garnham shall come down and tidy up for you," she said, quietly; "and you must dine with us."

The outer door was noisily closed by the departing servants.

"You are much too good," whispered Leroux, again; and the weary eyes glistened with a sudden moisture. "Thank you! Thank you! But—er—I could not dream of disturbing . . ."

"Mr. Leroux," said Helen, with all her old firmness—"Garnham is coming down *immediately* to put the place in order! And, whilst he is doing so, you are going to prepare yourself for a decent, Christian dinner!"

Henry Leroux rested one hand upon the table, looking down at the carpet. He had known for a long time, in a vague fashion, that he lacked something; that his success—a wholly inartistic one—had yielded him little gratification; that the comfort of his home was a purely monetary product and not in any sense atmospheric. He had schooled himself to believe that he liked loneliness—loneliness physical and mental, and that in marrying a pretty, but pleasure-loving girl, he had insured an ideal menage. Furthermore, he honestly believed that he worshiped his wife; and with his present grief at her unaccountable silence was mingled no atom of reproach.

But latterly he had begun to wonder—in his peculiarly indefinite way he had begun to doubt his own philosophy. Was the void in his soul a product of thwarted ambition?—for, whilst he slaved, scrupulously, upon "Martin Zeda," he loathed every deed and every word of that Old Man of the Sea. Or could it be that his own being—his nature of Adam—lacked something which wealth, social position, and Mira, his wife, could not yield to him?

Now, a new tone in the voice of Helen Cumberly—a tone different from that compound of good-fellowship and raillery, which he knew—a tone which had entered into it when she had exclaimed upon the state of the room—set his poor, anxious heart thrumming like a lute. He felt a hot flush creeping upon him; his forehead grew damp. He feared to raise his eyes.

"Is that a bargain?" asked Helen, sweetly.

Henry Leroux found a lump in his throat; but he lifted his untidy head and took the hand which the girl had extended to him. She smiled a bit unnaturally; then every tinge of color faded from her cheeks, and Henry Leroux, unconsciously holding the white hand in a vice-like grip, looked hungrily into the eyes grown suddenly tragic whilst into his own came the light of a great and sorrowful understanding.

"God bless you," he said. "I will do anything you wish."

Helen released her hand, turned, and ran from the study. Not until she was on the landing did she dare to speak. Then—

"Garnham shall come down immediately. Don't be late for dinner!" she called—and there was a hint of laughter and of tears in her voice, of the restraint of culture struggling with rebellious womanhood.

XI

PRESENTING M. GASTON MAX

Not venturing to turn on the light, not daring to look upon her own face in the mirror, Helen Cumberly sat before her dressing-table, trembling wildly. She wanted to laugh, and wanted to cry; but the daughter of Seton Cumberly knew what those symptoms meant and knew how to deal with them. At the end of an interval of some four or five minutes, she rang.

The maid opened the door.

"Don't light up, Merton," she said, composedly. "I want you to tell Garnham to go down to Mr. Leroux's and put the place in order. Mr. Leroux is dining with us."

The girl withdrew; and Helen, as the door closed, pressed the electric switch. She stared at her reflection in the mirror as if it were the face of an enemy, then, turning her head aside, sat deep in reflection, biting her lip and toying with the edge of the white doily.

"You little traitor!" she whispered, through clenched teeth. "You little traitor—and hypocrite"—sobs began to rise in her throat—"and fool!"

Five more minutes passed in a silent conflict. A knock announced the return of the maid; and the girl reentered, placing upon the table a visiting-card—

DENISE RYLAND
ATELIER 4, RUE DU COQ D'OR,
MONTMARTRE,
PARIS.

Helen Cumberly started to her feet with a stifled exclamation and turned to the maid; her face, to which the color slowly had been returning, suddenly blanched anew.

"Denise Ryland!" she muttered, still holding the card in her hand, "why—that's Mrs. Leroux's friend, with whom she had been staying in Paris! Whatever can it mean?"

"Shall I show her in here, please?" asked the maid.

"Yes, in here," replied Helen, absently; and, scarcely aware that she had given instructions to that effect, she presently found herself confronted by the lady of the boat-train!

"Miss Cumberly?" said the new arrival in a pleasant American voice.

"Yes—I am Helen Cumberly. Oh! I am so glad to know you at last! I have often pictured you; for Mira—Mrs. Leroux—is always talking about you, and about the glorious times you have together! I have sometimes longed to join you in beautiful Paris. How good of you to come back with her!"

Miss Ryland unrolled the Scotch muffler from her throat, swinging her head from side to side in a sort of spuriously truculent manner, quite peculiarly her own. Her keen hazel eyes were fixed upon the face of the girl before her. Instinctively and immediately she liked Helen Cumberly; and Helen felt that this strong-looking, vaguely masculine woman, was an old, intimate friend, although she had never before set eyes upon her.

"H'm!" said Miss Ryland. "I have come from Paris"—she punctuated many of her sentences with wags of the head as if carefully weighing her words—"especially" (pause) "to see you" (pause and wag of head) "I am glad . . . to find that . . . you are the thoroughly sensible . . . kind of girl that I . . . had imagined, from the accounts which . . . I have had of you."

She seated herself in an armchair.

"Had of me from Mira?" asked Helen.

"Yes . . . from Mrs. Leroux."

"How delightful it must be for you to have her with you so often! Marriage, as a rule, puts an end to that particular sort of good-time, doesn't it?"

"It does . . . very properly . . . too. No *man* . . . no *man* in his . . . right senses . . . would permit . . . his wife . . . to gad about in Paris with another . . . girl" (she presumably referred to herself) whom *he* had only met . . . casually . . . and did not like . . ."

"What! do you mean that Mr. Leroux doesn't like you? I can't believe that!"

"Then the sooner . . . you believe it . . . the better."

"It can only be that he does not know you, properly?"

"He has no wish . . . to know me . . . properly; and I have no desire . . . to cultivate . . . the . . . friendship of such . . . a silly being."

Helen Cumberly was conscious that a flush was rising from her face to her brow, and tingling in the very roots of her hair. She was indignant with herself and turned, aside, bending over her table in order to conceal this ill-timed embarrassment from her visitor.

"Poor Mr. Leroux!" she said, speaking very rapidly; "I think it awfully good of him, and sporty, to allow his wife so much liberty."

"Sporty!" said Miss Ryland, head wagging and nostrils distended in scorn. "Idi-otic . . . I should call it."

"Why?"

Helen Cumberly, perfectly composed again, raised her clear eyes to her visitor.

"You seem so . . . thoroughly sensible, except in regard to . . . Harry Leroux;—and *all* women, with a few . . . exceptions, are *fools* where the true . . . character of a *man* is concerned—that I will take you right into my confidence."

Her speech lost its quality of syncopation; the whole expression of her face changed; and in the hazel eyes a deep concern might be read.

"My dear," she stood up, crossed to Helen's side, and rested her artistic looking hands upon the girl's shoulder. "Harry Leroux stands upon the brink of a great tragedy—a life's tragedy!"

Helen was trembling slightly again.

"Oh, I know!" she whispered—"I know—"

"You know?"

There was surprise in Miss Ryland's voice.

"Yes, I have seen them—watched them—and I know that the police think . . ."

"Police! What are you talking about—the police?"

Helen looked up with a troubled face.

"The murder!" she began.

Miss Ryland dropped into a chair which, fortunately, stood close behind her, with a face suddenly set in an expression of horror. She began to understand, now, a certain restraint, a certain ominous shadow, which she had perceived, or thought she had perceived, in the atmosphere of this home, and in the manner of its occupants.

"My dear girl," she began, and the old nervous, jerky manner showed itself again, momentarily,—"remember that . . . I left Paris by . . . the first train, this morning, and have simply been . . . traveling right up to the present moment. . . ."

"Then you have not heard? You don't know that a—murder—has been committed?"

"*Murder*! Not—not . . ."

"Not any one connected with Mr. Leroux; no, thank God! but it was done in his flat."

Miss Ryland brushed a whisk of straight hair back from her brow with a rough and ungraceful movement.

"My dear," she began, taking a French telegraphic form from her pocket, "you see this message? It's one which reached me at an unearthly hour this morning from Harry Leroux. It was addressed to his wife at my studio; therefore, as her friend, I opened it. Mira Leroux has actually visited me there twice since her marriage—"

"Twice!" Helen rose slowly to her feet, with horrified eyes fixed upon the speaker.

"Twice I said! I have not seen her, and have rarely heard from her, for nearly twelve months, now! Therefore I packed up post-haste and here I am! I came to you, because, from what little I have heard of you, and of your father, I judged you to be the right kind of friends to consult."

"You have not seen her for twelve months?"

Helen's voice was almost inaudible, and she was trembling dreadfully.

"That's a fact, my dear. And now, what are we going to tell Harry Leroux?"

It was a question, the answer to which was by no means evident at a glance; and leaving Helen Cumberly face to face with this new and horrible truth which had brought Denise Ryland hotfoot from Paris to London, let us glance, for a moment, into the now familiar room of Detective-Inspector Dunbar at Scotland Yard.

He had returned from his interrogation of Brian; and he received the report of Sowerby, respecting the late Mrs. Vernon's maid. The girl, Sergeant Sowerby declared, was innocent of complicity, and could only depose to the fact that her late mistress took very little luggage with her on the occasions of her trips to Scotland. With his notebook open before him upon the table, Dunbar was adding this slight item to his notes upon the case, when the door opened, and the uniformed constable entered, saluted, and placed an envelope in the Inspector's hand.

"From the commissioner!" said Sowerby, significantly.

With puzzled face, Dunbar opened the envelope and withdrew the commissioner's note. It was very brief—

"M. Gaston Max, of the Paris Police, is joining you in the Palace Mansions murder case. You will cooperate with him from date above."

"*Max!*" said Dunbar, gazing astoundedly at his subordinate.

Certainly it was a name which might well account for the amazement written upon the inspector's face; for it was the name of admittedly the greatest criminal investigator in Europe!

"What the devil has the case to do with the French police?" muttered Sowerby, his ruddy countenance exhibiting a whole history of wonderment.

The constable, who had withdrawn, now reappeared, knocking deferentially upon the door, throwing it open, and announcing:

"Mr. Gaston Max, to see Detective-Inspector Dunbar."

Bowing courteously upon the threshold, appeared a figure in a dazzling check traveling-coat—a figure very novel, and wholly unforgettable.

"I am honored to meet a distinguished London colleague," he said in perfect English, with a faint American accent.

Dunbar stepped across the room with outstretched hand, and cordially shook that of the famous Frenchman.

"I am the more honored," he declared, gallantly playing up to the other's courtesy. "This is Detective-Sergeant Sowerby, who is acting with me in the case."

M. Gaston Max bowed low in acknowledgment of the introduction.

"It is a pleasure to meet Detective-Sergeant Sowerby," he declared.

These polite overtures being concluded then, and the door being closed, the three detectives stood looking at one another in momentary silence. Then Dunbar spoke with blunt directness:

"I am very pleased to have you with us, Mr. Max," he said; "but might I ask what your presence in London means?"

M. Gaston Max shrugged in true Gallic fashion.

"It means, monsieur," he said, "—murder—and *Mr. King!*"

XII

MR. GIANAPOLIS

It will prove of interest at this place to avail ourselves of an opportunity denied to the police, and to inquire into the activities of Mr. Soames, whilom employee of Henry Leroux.

Luke Soames was a man of unpleasant character; a man ever seeking advancement—advancement to what he believed to be an ideal state, viz.: the possession of a competency; and to this ambition he subjugated all conflicting interests—especially the interests of others. From narrow but honest beginnings, he had developed along lines ever growing narrower until gradually honesty became squeezed out. He formed the opinion that wealth was unobtainable by dint of hard work; and indeed in a man of his limited intellectual attainments, this was no more than true.

At the period when he becomes of interest, he had just discovered himself a gentleman-at-large by reason of his dismissal from the services of a wealthy bachelor, to whose establishment in Piccadilly he had been attached in the capacity of valet. There was nothing definite against his character at this time, save that he had never remained for long in any one situation.

His experience was varied, if his references were limited; he had served not only as valet, but also as chauffeur, as steward on an ocean liner, and, for a limited period, as temporary butler in an American household at Nice.

Soames' banking account had increased steadily, but not at a rate commensurate with his ambitions; therefore, when entering his name and qualifications in the books of a certain exclusive employment agency in Mayfair he determined to avail himself, upon this occasion, of his comparative independence by waiting until kindly Fate should cast something really satisfactory in his path.

Such an opening occurred very shortly after his first visit to the agent. He received a card instructing him to call at the office in order to meet a certain Mr. Gianapolis. Quitting his rooms in Kennington, Mr. Soames, attired in discreet black, set out to make the acquaintance of his hypothetical employer.

He found Mr. Gianapolis to be a little and very swarthy man, who held his head so low as to convey the impression of having a pronounced stoop; a man whose well-cut clothes and immaculate linen could not redeem his appearance from a constitutional dirtiness. A jet black mustache, small, aquiline features, an engaging smile, and very dark brown eyes, viciously crossed, made up a personality incongruous with his sheltering silk hat, and calling aloud for a tarboosh and a linen suit, a shop in a bazaar, or a part in the campaign of commercial brigandage which, based in the Levant, spreads its ramifications throughout the Orient, Near and Far.

Mr. Gianapolis had the suave speech and smiling manner. He greeted Soames not as one greets a prospective servant, but as one welcomes an esteemed acquaintance. Following a brief chat, he proposed an adjournment to a neighboring saloon bar; and there, over cocktails, he conversed with Mr. Soames as one crook with another.

Soames was charmed, fascinated, yet vaguely horrified; for this man smilingly threw off the cloak of hypocrisy from his companion's shoulders, and pretended, with the skill of his race, equally to nudify his own villainy.

"My dear Mr. Soames!" he said, speaking almost perfect English, but with the sing-song intonation of the Greek, and giving all his syllables an equal value—"you are the man I am looking for; and I can make your fortune."

This was entirely in accordance with Mr. Soames' own views, and he nodded, respectfully.

"I know," continued Gianapolis, proffering an excellent Egyptian cigarette, "that you were cramped in your last situation—that you were misunderstood . . ."

Soames, cigarette in hand, suppressed a start, and wondered if he were turning pale. He selected a match with nervous care.

"The little matter of the silver spoons," continued Gianapolis, smiling fraternally, "was perhaps an error of judgment. Although—" patting the startled Soames upon the shoulder—"they were a legitimate perquisite; I am not blaming you. But it takes so long to accumulate a really useful balance in that petty way. Now"—he glanced cautiously about him—"I can offer you a post under conditions which will place you above the consideration of silver spoons!"

Soames, hastily finishing his cocktail, sought for words; but Gianapolis, finishing his own, blandly ordered two more, and, tapping Soames upon the knee, continued:

"Then that matter of the petty cash, and those trifling irregularities in the wine-bill, you remember?—when you were with Colonel Hewett in Nice?"

Soames gripped the counter hard, staring at the newly arrived cocktail as though it were hypnotizing him.

"These little matters," added Gianapolis, appreciatively sipping from his own glass, "which would weigh heavily against your other references, in the event of their being mentioned to any prospective employer . . ."

Soames knew beyond doubt that his face was very pale indeed.

"These little matters, then," pursued Gianapolis, "all go to prove to *me* that you are a man of enterprise and spirit—that you are the very man I require. Now I can offer you a post in the establishment of Mr. Henry Leroux, the novelist. The service will be easy. You will be required to attend to callers and to wait at table upon special occasions. There will be no valeting, and you will have undisputed charge of the pantry and wine-cellar. In short, you will enjoy unusual liberty. The salary, you would say? It will be the same as that which you received from Mr. Mapleson . . ."

Soames raised his head drearily; he felt himself in the toils; he felt himself a mined man.

"It isn't a salary," he began, "which . . ."

"My dear Mr. Soames," said Gianapolis, tapping him confidentially upon the knee again—"my dear Soames, it isn't the salary, I admit, which you enjoyed whilst in the services of Colonel Hewett in a similar capacity. But this is not a large establishment, and the duties are light. Furthermore, there will be—extras."

"Extras?"

Mr. Soames' eye brightened, and under the benignant influence of the cocktails his courage began to return.

"I do not refer," smiled Mr. Gianapolis, "to perquisites! The extras will be monetary. Another two pounds per week . . ."

"Two pounds!"

"Bringing your salary up to a nice round figure; the additional amount will be paid to you from another source. You will receive the latter payment quarterly . . ."

"From—from . . ."

"From me!" said Mr. Gianapolis, smiling radiantly. "Now, I know you are going to accept; that is understood between us. I will give you the address—Palace Mansions, Westminster—at which you must apply; and I will tell you what little services will be required from you in return for this additional emolument."

Mr. Soames hurriedly finished his second cocktail. Mr. Gianapolis, in true sporting fashion, kept pace with him and repeated the order.

"You will take charge of the mail!" he whispered softly, one irregular eye following the movements of the barmaid, and the other fixed almost fiercely upon the face of Soames. "At certain times—of which you will be notified in advance—Mrs. Leroux will pay visits to Paris. At such times, all letters addressed to her, or re-addressed to her, will not be posted! You will ring me up when such letters come into your possession—they must *all* come into your possession!—and I will arrange to meet you, say at the corner of Victoria Street, to receive them. You understand?"

Mr. Soames understood, and thus far found his plastic conscience marching in step with his inclinations.

"Then," resumed Gianapolis, "prior to her departure on these occasions, Mrs. Leroux will hand you a parcel. This also you will bring to me at the place arranged. Do you find anything onerous in these conditions?"

"Not at all," muttered Soames, a trifle unsteadily; "it seems all right"—the cocktails were beginning to speak now, and his voice was a duet—"simply perfectly all right—all square."

"Good!" said Mr. Gianapolis with his radiant smile; and the gaze of his left eye, crossing that of its neighbor, observed the entrance of a stranger into the bar. He drew his stool closer and lowered his voice:

"Mrs. Leroux," he continued, "will be in your confidence. Mr. Leroux and every one else—*every one* else—must not suspect the arrangement . . ."

"Certainly—I quite understand . . ."

"Mrs. Leroux will engage you this afternoon—her husband is a mere cipher in the household—and you will commence your duties on Monday. Later in the week, Wednesday or Thursday, we will meet by appointment, and discuss further details."

"Where can I see you?"

"Ring up this number: 18642 East, and ask for Mr. King. No! don't write it down; remember it! I will come to the telephone, and arrange a meeting."

Shortly after this, then, the interview concluded; and later in the afternoon of that day Mr. Soames presented himself at Palace Mansions.

He was received by Mrs. Leroux—a pretty woman with a pathetically weak mouth. She had fair hair, not very abundant, and large eyes; which, since they exhibited the unusual phenomenon, in a blonde, of long dark lashes (Mr. Soames judged their blackness to be natural), would have been beautiful had they not been of too light a color, too small in the pupils, and utterly expressionless. Indeed, her whole face lacked color, as did her personality, and the exquisite tea-gown which she wore conveyed that odd impression of slovenliness, which is often an indication of secret vice. She was quite young and indisputably pretty, but this malproprete, together with a certain aimlessness of manner, struck an incongruous note; for essentially she was of a type which for its complement needs vivacity.

Mr. Soames, a man of experience, scented an intrigue and a neglectful husband. Since he was engaged on the spot without reference to the invisible Leroux, he was immediately confirmed in the latter part of his surmise. He departed well satisfied with his affairs, and with the promise of the future, over which Mr. Gianapolis, the cherubic, radiantly presided.

XIII

THE DRAFT ON PARIS

For close upon a month Soames performed the duties imposed upon him in the household of Henry Leroux. He was unable to discover, despite a careful course of inquiry from the cook and the housemaid, that Mrs. Leroux frequently absented herself. But the servants were newly engaged, for the flat in Palace Mansions had only recently been leased by the Leroux. He gathered that they had formerly lived much abroad, and that their marriage had taken place in Paris. Mrs. Leroux had been to visit a friend in the French capital once, he understood, since the housemaid had been in her employ.

The mistress (said the housemaid) did not care twopence-ha'penny for her husband; she had married him for his money, and for nothing else. She had had an earlier love (declared the cook) and was pining away to a mere shadow because of her painful memories. During the last six months (the period of the cook's service) Mrs. Leroux had altered out of all recognition. The cook was of opinion that she drank secretly.

Of Mr. Leroux, Soames formed the poorest opinion. He counted him a spiritless being, whose world was bounded by his book-shelves, and whose wife would be a fool if she did not avail herself of the liberty which his neglect invited her to enjoy. Soames felt himself, not a snake in the grass, but a benefactor—a friend in need—a champion come to the defense of an unhappy and persecuted woman.

He wondered when an opportunity should arise which would enable him to commence his chivalrous operations; almost daily he anticipated instructions to the effect that Mrs. Leroux would be leaving for Paris immediately. But the days glided by and the weeks glided by, without anything occurring to break the monotony of the Leroux household.

Mr. Soames sought an opportunity to express his respectful readiness to Mrs. Leroux; but the lady was rarely visible outside her own apartments until late in the day, when she would be engaged in preparing for the serious business of the evening: one night a dance, another, a bridge-party; so it went. Mr. Leroux rarely joined her upon these festive expeditions, but clung to his study like Diogenes to his tub.

Great was Mr. Soames' contempt; bitter were the reproaches of the cook; dark were the predictions of the housemaid.

At last, however, Soames, feeling himself neglected, seized an opportunity which offered to cement the secret bond (the *too* secret bond) existing between himself and the mistress of the house.

Meeting her one afternoon in the lobby, which she was crossing on the way from her bedroom to the drawing-room, he stood aside to let her pass, whispering:

"At your service, whenever you are ready, madam!"

It was a non-committal remark, which, if she chose to keep up the comedy, he could explain away by claiming it to refer to the summoning of the car from the garage—for Mrs. Leroux was driving out that afternoon.

She did not endeavor to evade the occult meaning of the words, however. In the wearily dreamy manner which, when first he had seen her, had aroused Soames' respectful interest, she raised her thin hand to her hair, slowly pressing it back from her brow, and directed her big eyes vacantly upon him.

"Yes, Soames," she said (her voice had a faraway quality in keeping with the rest of her personality), "Mr. King speaks well of you. But please do not refer again to"—she glanced in a manner at once furtive and sorrowful, in the direction of the study-door—"to the . . . little arrangement of . . ."

She passed on, with the slow, gliding gait, which, together with her fragility, sometimes lent her an almost phantomesque appearance.

This was comforting, in its degree; since it proved that the smiling Gianapolis had in no way misled him (Soames). But as a man of business, Mr. Soames was not fully satisfied. He selected an evening when Mrs. Leroux was absent—and indeed she was absent almost every evening, for Leroux entertained but little. The cook and the housemaid were absent, also; therefore, to all intents and purposes, Soames had the flat to himself; since Henry Leroux counted in that establishment, not as an entity, but rather as a necessary, if unornamental, portion of the fittings.

Standing in the lobby, Soames raised the telephone receiver, and having paused with closed eyes preparing the exact form of words in which he should address his invisible employer, he gave the number: East 18642.

Following a brief delay—

"Yes," came a nasal voice, "who is it?"

"Soames! I want to speak to Mr. King!"

The words apparently surprised the man at the other end of the wire, for he hesitated ere inquiring—

"What did you say your name was?"

"Soames—Luke Soames."

"Hold on!"

Soames, with closed eyes, and holding the receiver to his ear, silently rehearsed again the exact wording of his speech. Then—

"Hullo!" came another voice—"is that Mr. Soames?"

"Yes! Is that Mr. Gianapolis speaking?"

"It is, my dear Soames!" replied the sing-song voice; and Soames, closing his eyes again, had before him a mental picture of the radiantly smiling Greek.

"Yes, my dear Soames," continued Gianapolis; "here I am. I hope you are quite well—perfectly well?"

"I am perfectly well, thank you; but as a man of business, it has occurred to me that failing a proper agreement—which in this case I know would be impossible—a trifling advance on the first quarter's . . ."

"On your salary, my dear Soames! On your salary? Payment for the first quarter shall be made to you tomorrow, my dear Soames! Why ever did you not express the wish before? Certainly, certainly!"

"Will it be sent to me?"

"My dear fellow! How absurd you are! Can you get out tomorrow evening about nine o'clock?"

"Yes, easily."

"Then I will meet you at the corner of Victoria Street, by the hotel, and hand you your first quarter's salary. Will that be satisfactory?"

"Perfectly," said Soames, his small eyes sparkling with avarice. "Most decidedly, Mr. Gianapolis. Many thanks."

"And by the way," continued the other, "it is rather fortunate that you rang me up this evening, because it has saved me the trouble of ringing you up."

"What?" Soames' eyes half closed, from the bottom lids upwards. "There is something . . ."

"There is a trifling service which I require of you—yes, my dear Soames."

"Is it?"

"We will discuss the matter tomorrow evening. Oh! it is a mere trifle. So good-by for the present."

Soames, with the fingers of his two hands interlocked before him, and his thumbs twirling rapidly around one another, stood in the lobby, gazing reflectively at the rug-strewn floor. He was working out in his mind how handsomely this first payment would show up on the welcome side of his passbook. Truly, he was fortunate in having met the generous Gianapolis. . . .

He thought of a trifling indiscretion committed at the expense of one Mr. Mapleson, and of the wine-bill of Colonel Hewett; and he thought of the apparently clairvoyant knowledge of the Greek. A cloud momentarily came between his perceptive and the rosy horizon.

But nearer to the foreground of the mental picture, uprose a left-hand page of his pass book; and its tidings of great joy, written in clerkly hand, served to dispel the cloud.

Soames sighed in gentle rapture, and, soft-footed, passed into his own room.

Certainly his duties were neither difficult nor unpleasant. The mistress of the house lived apparently in a hazy dream-world of her own, and Mr. Leroux was the ultimate expression of the non-commercial. Mr. Soames could have robbed him every day had he desired to do so; but he had refrained from availing himself even of those perquisites which he considered justly his; for it was evident, to his limited intelligence, that greater profit was to be gained by establishing himself in this household than by weeding-out five shillings here, and half-a-sovereign there, at the risk of untimely dismissal.

Yet—it was a struggle! All Mr. Soames' commercial instincts were up in arms against this voice of a greater avarice which counseled abstention. For instance: he could have added half-a-sovereign a week to his earnings by means of a simple arrangement with the local wine merchant. Leroux's cigars he could have sold by the hundreds; for Leroux, when a friend called, would absently open a new box, entirely forgetful of the fact that a box from which but two—or at most three—cigars had been taken, lay already on the bureau.

Mr. Soames, in order to put his theories to the test, had temporarily abstracted half-a-dozen such boxes from the study and the dining-room and had hidden them. Leroux, finding, as he supposed, that he was out of cigars, had simply ordered Soames to get him some more.

"Er—about a dozen boxes—er—Soames," he had said; "of the same sort!"

Was ever a man of business submitted to such an ordeal? After receiving those instructions, Soames had sat for close upon an hour in his own room, contemplating the six broken boxes, containing in all some five hundred and ninety cigars; but the voice within prevailed; he must court no chance of losing his situation; therefore, he "discovered" these six boxes in a cupboard—much to Henry Leroux's surprise!

Then, Leroux regularly sent him to the Charing Cross branch of the London County and Suburban Bank with open checks! Sometimes, he would be sent to pay in, at other times to withdraw; the amounts involved varying from one guinea to 150 pounds! But, as he told himself, on almost every occasion that he went to Leroux's bank, he was deliberately throwing money away, deliberately closing his eyes to the good fortune which this careless and gullible man cast in his path. He observed a scrupulous honesty in all these dealings, with the result that the bank manager came to regard him as a valuable and trustworthy servant, and said as much to the assistant manager, expressing his wonder that Leroux—whose account occasioned the bank more anxiety, and gave it more work, than that of any other two depositors—had at last engaged a man who would keep his business affairs in order!

And these were but a few of the golden apples which Mr. Soames permitted to slip through his fingers, so steadfast was he in his belief that Gianapolis would be as good as his word, and make his fortune.

Leroux employed no secretary; and his MSS. were typed at his agent's office. A most slovenly man in all things, and in business matters especially, he was the despair, not only of his banker, but of his broker; he was a man who, in professional parlance, "deserved to be robbed." It is improbable that he had any but the haziest ideas, at any particular time, respecting the state of his bank balance and investments. He detested the writing of business letters, and was always at great pains to avoid anything in the nature of a commercial rendezvous. He would sign any document which his lawyer or his broker cared to send him, with simple, unquestioned faith.

His bank he never visited, and his appearance was entirely unfamiliar to the staff. True, the manager knew him slightly, having had two interviews with him: one when the account was opened, and the second when Leroux introduced his solicitor and broker—in order that in the future he might not be troubled in any way with business affairs.

Mr. Soames perceived more and more clearly that the mild deception projected was unlikely to be discovered by its victim; and, at the appointed time, he hastened to the corner of Victoria Street, to his appointment with Gianapolis. The latter was prompt, for Soames perceived his radiant smile afar off.

The saloon bar of the Red Lion was affably proposed by Mr. Gianapolis as a suitable spot to discuss the business. Soames agreed, not without certain inward qualms; for the proximity of the hostelry to New Scotland Yard was a disquieting circumstance.

However, since Gianapolis affected to treat their negotiations in the light of perfectly legitimate business, he put up no protest, and presently found himself seated in a very cozy corner of the saloon bar, with a glass of whisky-and-soda on a little table before him, bubbling in a manner which rendered it an agreeable and refreshing sight in the eyes of Mr. Soames.

"You know," said Gianapolis, the gaze of his left eye bisecting that of his right in a most bewildering manner, "they call this 'the 'tec's tabernacle!'"

"Indeed," said Soames, without enthusiasm; "I suppose some of the Scotland Yard men do drop in now and then?"

"Beyond doubt, my dear Soames."

Soames responded to his companion's radiant smile with a smile of his own by no means so pleasant to look upon. Soames had the type of face which, in repose, might be the face of an honest man; but his smile would have led to his instant arrest on any racecourse in Europe: it was the smile of a pick-pocket.

"Now," continued Gianapolis, "here is a quarter's salary in advance."

From a pocket-book, he took a little brown paper envelope and from the brown paper envelope counted out four five-pound notes, five golden sovereigns, one half-sovereign, and ten shillings' worth of silver. Soames' eyes glittered, delightedly.

"A little informal receipt?" smiled Gianapolis, raising his eyebrows, satanically. "Here on this page of my notebook I have written: 'Received from Mr. King for service rendered, 26 pounds, being payment, in advance, of amount due on 31st October 19—' I have attached a stamp to the page, as you will see," continued Gianapolis, "and here is a fountain-pen. Just sign across the stamp, adding today's date."

Soames complied with willing alacrity; and Gianapolis having carefully blotted the signature, replaced the notebook in his pocket, and politely acknowledged the return of the fountain-pen. Soames, glancing furtively about him, replaced the money in the envelope, and thrust the latter carefully into a trouser pocket.

"Now," resumed Gianapolis, "we must not permit our affairs of business to interfere with our amusements."

He stepped up to the bar and ordered two more whiskies with soda. These being sampled, business was resumed.

"To-morrow," said Gianapolis, leaning forward across the table so that his face almost touched that of his companion, "you will be entrusted by Mr. Leroux with a commission."

Soames nodded eagerly, his eyes upon the speaker's face.

"You will accompany Mrs. Leroux to the bank," continued Gianapolis, "in order that she may write a specimen signature, in the presence of the manager, for transmission to the Credit Lyonnais in Paris."

Soames nearly closed his little eyes in his effort to comprehend.

"A draft in her favor," continued the Greek, "has been purchased by Mr. Leroux's bank from the Paris bank, and, on presentation of this, a checkbook will be issued to Mrs. Leroux by the Credit Lyonnais in Paris to enable her to draw at her convenience upon that establishment against the said order. Do you follow me?"

Soames nodded rapidly, eager to exhibit an intelligent grasp of the situation.

"Now"—Gianapolis lowered his voice impressively—"no one at the Charing Cross branch of the London County and Suburban Bank has ever seen Mrs. Leroux!—Oh! we have been careful of that, and we shall be careful in the future. You are known already as an accredited agent of Leroux; therefore"—he bent yet closer to Soames' ear—"you will direct the chauffeur to drop you, not at the Strand entrance, but at the side entrance. You follow?"

Soames, almost holding his breath, nodded again.

"At the end of the court, in which the latter entrance is situated, a lady dressed in the same manner as Mrs. Leroux (this is arranged) will be waiting. Mrs. Leroux will walk straight up the court, into the corridor of Bank Chambers by the back entrance, and from thence out into the Strand. *You* will escort the second lady into the manager's office, and she will sign 'Mira Leroux' instead of the real Mira Leroux."

Soames became aware that he was changing color. This was a superior felony, and as such it awed his little mind. It was tantamount to burning his boats. Missing silver spoons and cooked petty cash were trivialities usually expiable at the price of a boot-assisted dismissal; but this—!

"You understand?" Gianapolis was not smiling, now. "There is not the slightest danger. The signature of the lady whom you will meet will be an exact duplicate of the real one; that is, exact enough to deceive a man who is not looking for a forgery. But it would not be exact enough to deceive the French banker—he *will* be looking for a forgery. You follow me? The signature on the checks drawn against the Credit Lyonnais will be the *same* as the specimen forwarded by the London County and Suburban, since they will be written by the same lady—the duplicate Mrs. Leroux. Therefore, the French bank will have no means of detecting the harmless little deception practised upon them, and the English bank, if it should ever see those checks, will raise no question, since the checks will have been honored by the Credit Lyonnais."

Soames finished his whisky-and-soda at a gulp.

"Finally," concluded Gianapolis, "you will escort the lady out by the front entrance to the Strand. She will leave you and walk in an easterly direction—making some suitable excuse if the manager should insist upon seeing her to the door; and the real Mrs. Leroux will come out by the Strand end of Bank Chambers' corridor, and walk back with you around the corner to where the car will be waiting. Perfect?"

"Quite," said Soames, huskily. . . .

But when, some twenty minutes later, he returned to Palace Mansions, he was a man lost in thought; and he did not entirely regain his wonted composure, and did not entirely shake off the incubus, Doubt, until in his own room he had re-counted the contents of the brown paper envelope. Then—

"It's safe enough," he muttered; "and it's worth it!"

Thus it came about that, on the following morning, Leroux called him into the study and gave him just such instructions as Gianapolis had outlined the evening before.

"I am—er—too busy to go myself, Soames," said Leroux, "and—er—Mrs. Leroux will shortly be paying a visit to friends in—er—in Paris. So that I am opening a credit there for her. Save so much trouble—and—such a lot of—correspondence—international money orders—and such worrying things. Mr. Smith, the manager, knows you and you will take this letter of authority. The draft I understand has already been purchased."

Mr. Soames was bursting with anxiety to learn the amount of this draft, but could find no suitable opportunity to inquire. The astonishing deception, then, was carried out without anything resembling a hitch. Mrs. Leroux went through with her part in the comedy, in the dreamy manner of a somnambulist; and the duplicate Mrs. Leroux, who waited at the appointed spot, had achieved so startling a resemblance to her prototype, that Mr. Soames became conscious of a craving for a peg of brandy at the moment of setting eyes upon her. However, he braced himself up and saw the business through.

As was to be expected, no questions were raised and no doubts entertained. The bank manager was very courteous and very reserved, and the fictitious Mrs. Leroux equally reserved, indeed, cold. She avoided raising her motor veil, and, immediately the business was concluded, took her departure, Mr. Smith escorting her as far as the door.

She walked away toward Fleet Street, and the respectful attendant, Soames, toward Charing Cross; he rejoined Mrs. Leroux at the door of Bank Chambers, and the two turned the corner and entered the waiting car. Soames was rather nervous; Mrs. Leroux quite apathetic.

Shortly after this event, Soames learnt that the date of Mrs. Leroux's departure to Paris was definitely fixed. He received from her hands a large envelope.

"For Mr. King," she said, in her dreamy fashion; and he noticed that she seemed to be in poorer health than usual. Her mouth twitched strangely; she was a nervous wreck.

Then came her departure, attended by a certain bustle, an appointment with Mr. Gianapolis; and the delivery of the parcel into that gentleman's keeping.

Mrs. Leroux was away for six days on this occasion. Leroux sent her three postcards during that time, and re-addressed some ten or twelve letters which arrived for her. The address in all cases was:

c/o Miss Denise Ryland,
Atelier 4, Rue du Coq d'Or,
Montmartre,
Paris.

East 18642 was much in demand that week; and there were numerous meetings between Soames and Gianapolis at the corner of Victoria Street, and numerous whiskies-and-sodas in the Red Lion; for Gianapolis persisted in his patronage of that establishment, apparently for no other reason than because it was dangerously near to Scotland Yard, and an occasional house of call for members of the Criminal Investigation Department.

Thus did Mr. Soames commence his career of duplicity at the flat of Henry Leroux; and for some twelve months before the events which so dramatically interfered with the delightful scheme, he drew his double salary and performed his perfidious work with great efficiency and contentment. Mrs. Leroux paid four other visits to Paris during that time, and always returned in much better spirits, although pale and somewhat haggard looking. It fell to the lot of Soames always to meet her at Charing Cross; but never once, by look or by word, did she proffer, or invite, the slightest exchange of confidence. She apathetically accepted his aid in conducting this intrigue as she would have accepted his aid in putting on her opera-cloak.

The curious Soames had read right through the telephone directory from A to Z in quest of East 18642—only to learn that no such number was published. His ingenuity not being great, he could think of no means to learn the address of the mysterious Mr. King. So keenly had he been impressed with the omniscience of that shadowy being who knew all his past, that he feared to inquire of the Eastern Exchange. His banking account was growing handsomely, and, above all things, he dreaded to kill the goose that laid the golden eggs.

Then came the night which shattered all. Having rung up East 18642 and made an appointment with Gianapolis in regard to some letters for Mrs. Leroux, he had been surprised, on reaching the corner of Victoria Street, to find that Gianapolis was not there! He glanced up at the face of Big Ben. Yes—for the first time during their business acquaintance, Mr. Gianapolis was late!

For close upon twenty minutes, Soames waited, walking slowly up and down. When, at last, coming from the direction of Westminster, he saw the familiar spruce figure.

Eagerly he hurried forward to meet the Greek; but Gianapolis—to the horror and amazement of Soames—affected not to know him! He stepped aside to avoid the stupefied butler, and passed. But, in passing, he hissed these words at Soames—

"Follow to Victoria Street Post Office! Pretend to post letters at next box to me and put them in my hand!"

He was gone!

Soames, dazed at this new state of affairs, followed him at a discreet distance. Gianapolis ran up the Post Office steps briskly, and Soames, immediately afterwards, ascended also—furtively. Gianapolis was taking out a number of letters from his pocket.

Soames walked across to the "Country" box on his right, and affected to scrutinize the addresses on the envelopes of Mrs. Leroux's correspondence.

Gianapolis, on the pretense of posting a country letter, reached out and snatched the correspondence from Soames' hand. The gaze of his left eye crookedly sought the face of the butler.

"Go home!" whispered Gianapolis; "be cautious!"

XIV

EAST 18642

In a pitiable state of mind, Soames walked away from the Post Office. Gianapolis had hurried off in the direction of Victoria Station. Something was wrong! Some part of the machine, of the dimly divined machine whereof he formed a cog, was out of gear. Since the very nature of this machine—its construction and purpose, alike—was unknown to Soames, he had no basis upon which to erect surmises for good or ill.

His timid inquiries into the identity of East 18642 had begun and terminated with his labored perusal of the telephone book, a profitless task which had occupied him for the greater part of an evening.

The name, Gianapolis, did not appear at all; whereas there proved to be some two hundred and ninety Kings. But, oddly, only four of these were on the Eastern Exchange; one was a veterinary surgeon; one a boat-builder; and a third a teacher of dancing. The fourth, an engineer, seemed a "possible" to Soames, although his published number was not 18642; but a brief—a very brief—conversation, convinced the butler that this was not his man.

He had been away from the flat for over an hour, and he doubted if even the lax sense of discipline possessed by Mr. Leroux would enable that gentleman to overlook this irregularity. Soames had a key of the outer door, and he built his hopes upon the possibility that Leroux had not noticed his absence and would not hear his return.

He opened the door very quietly, but had scarcely set his foot in the lobby ere the dreadful, unforgettable scene met his gaze.

For more years than he could remember, he had lived in dread of the law; and, in Luke Soames' philosophy, the words Satan and Detective were interchangeable. Now, before his eyes, was a palpable, unmistakable police officer; and on the floor . . .

Just one glimpse he permitted himself—and, in a voice that seemed to reach him from a vast distance, the detective was addressing *him*!

Slinking to his room, with his craven heart missing every fourth beat, and his mind in chaos, Soames sank down upon the bed, locked his hands together and hugged them, convulsively, between his knees.

It was come! He had overstepped that almost invisible boundary-line which divides indiscretion from crime. He knew now that the voice within him, the voice which had warned him against Gianapolis and against becoming involved in what dimly he had perceived to be an elaborate scheme, had been, not the voice of cowardice (as he had supposed) but that of prudence.

And it was too late. The dead woman, he told himself—he had been unable to see her very clearly—undoubtedly was Mrs. Leroux. What in God's name had happened! Probably her husband had killed her . . . which meant? It meant that proofs—*proofs*—were come into his possession; and who should be involved, entangled in the meshes of this fallen conspiracy, but himself, Luke Soames!

As must be abundantly evident, Soames was not a criminal of the daring type; he did not believe in reaching out for anything until he was well assured that he could, if necessary, draw back his hand. This last venture, this regrettable venture—this ruinous venture—had been a mistake. He had entered into it under the glamour of Gianapolis' personality. Of what use, now, to him was his swelling bank balance?

But in justice to the mental capacity of Soames, it must be admitted that he had not entirely overlooked such a possibility as this; he had simply refrained, for the good of his health, from contemplating it.

Long before, he had observed, with interest, that, should an emergency arise (such as a fire), a means of egress had been placed by the kindly architect adjacent to his bedroom window. Thus, his departure on the night of the murder was not the fruit of a sudden scheme, but of one well matured.

Closing and locking his bedroom door, Soames threw out upon the bed the entire contents of his trunk; selected those things which he considered indispensable, and those which might constitute clues. He hastily packed his grip, and, with a last glance about the room and some seconds of breathless listening at the door, he attached to the handle a long piece of cord, which at some time had been tied about his trunk, and, gently opening the window, lowered the grip into the courtyard beneath. The light he had already extinguished, and with the conviction dwelling in his bosom that in some way he was become accessory to a murder—that he was a man shortly to be pursued by the police of the civilized world—he descended the skeleton lift-shaft, picked up his grip, and passed out under the archway into the lane at the back of Palace Mansions and St. Andrew's Mansions.

He did not proceed in the direction which would have brought him out into the Square, but elected to emerge through the other end. At exactly the moment that Inspector Dunbar rushed into his vacated room, Mr. Soames, grip in hand, was mounting to the top of a southward bound 'bus at the corner of Parliament Street!

He was conscious of a need for reflection. He longed to sit in some secluded spot in order to think. At present, his brain was a mere whirligig, and all things about him seemingly danced to the same tune. Stationary objects were become unstable in the eyes of Soames, and the solid earth, burst free of its moorings, no longer afforded him a safe foothold. There was a humming in his ears; and a mist floated before his eyes. By the time that the motor-'bus was come to the south side of the bridge, Soames had succeeded in slowing down his mental roundabout in some degree; and now he began grasping at the flying ideas which the diminishing violence of his brain storm enabled him, vaguely, to perceive.

The first fruits of his reflections were bitter. He viewed the events of the night in truer focus; he saw that by his flight he had sealed his fate—had voluntarily outlawed himself. It became frightfully evident to him that he dared not seek to draw from his bank, that he dared not touch even his modest Post Office account. With the exception of some twenty-five shillings in his pocket, he was penniless!

How could he hope to fly the country, or even to hide himself, without money?

He glanced suspiciously about the 'bus; for he perceived that an old instinct had prompted him to mount one which passed the Oval—a former point of debarkation when he lived in rooms near Kennington Park. Someone might recognize him!

Furtively, he scanned his fellow passengers, but perceived no acquaintance.

What should he do—where should he go? It was a desperate situation.

The inspector who had cared to study that furtive, isolated figure, could not have failed to mark it for that of a hunted man.

At Kennington Gate the 'bus made a halt. Soames glanced at the clock on the corner. It was close upon one A. M. Where in heaven's name should he go? What a fool he had been to come to this district where he was known!

Stay! There was one man in London, surely, who must be almost as keenly interested in the fate of Luke Soames as Luke Soames himself . . . Gianapolis!

Soames sprang up and hurried off the 'bus. No public telephone box would be available at that hour, but dire need spurred his slow mind and also lent him assurance. He entered the office of the taxicab depot on the next corner, and, from the man whom he found in charge, solicited and obtained the favor of using the telephone. Lifting the receiver, he asked for East 18642.

The seconds that elapsed, now, were as hours of deathly suspense to the man at the telephone. If the number should be engaged . . . if the exchange could get no reply!

"Hullo!" said a nasal voice—"who is it?"

"It is Soames—and I want to speak to Mr. King!"

He lowered his tone as much as possible, almost whispering his own name. He knew the voice which had answered him; it was the same that he always heard when ringing up East 18642. But would Gianapolis come to the telephone? Suddenly—

"Is that Soames?" spoke the sing-song voice of the Greek.

"Yes, yes!"

"Where are you?"

"At Kennington."

"Are they following you?"

"No—I don't think so, at least; what am I to do? Where am I to go?"

"Get to Globe Road—near Stratford Bridge, East, without delay. But whatever you do, see that you are not followed! Globe Road is the turning immediately beyond the Railway Station. It is not too late, perhaps, to get a 'bus or tram, for some part of the way, at any rate. But even if the last is gone, don't take a cab; walk. When you get to Globe Road, pass down on the left-hand side, and, if necessary, right to the end. Make sure you are not followed, then walk back again. You will receive a signal from an open door. Come right in. Good-by."

Soames replaced the receiver on the hook, uttering a long-drawn sigh of relief. The arbiter of his fortunes had not failed him!

"Thank you very much!" he said to the man in charge of the office, who had been bending over his books and apparently taking not the slightest interest in the telephone conversation. Soames placed twopence, the price of the call, on the desk. "Good night."

"Good night."

He hastened out of the gate and across the road. An electric tramcar which would bear him as far as the Elephant-and-Castle was on the point of starting from the corner. Grip in hand, Soames boarded the car and mounted to the top deck. He was in some doubt respecting his mode of travel from the next point onward, but the night was fine, even if he had to walk, and his reviving spirits would cheer him with visions of a golden future!

His money!—That indeed was a bitter draught: the loss of his hardly earned savings! But he was now established—linked by a common secret—in partnership with Gianapolis; he was one of that mysterious, obviously wealthy group which arranged drafts on Paris—which could afford to pay him some hundreds of pounds per annum for such a trifling service as juggling the mail!

Mr. King!—If Gianapolis were only the servant, what a magnificent man of business must be hidden beneath the cognomen, Mr. King! And he was about to meet that lord of mystery. Fear and curiosity were oddly blended in the anticipation.

By great good fortune, Soames arrived at the Elephant-and-Castle in time to catch an eastward bound motor-'bus, a 'bus which would actually carry him to the end of Globe Road. He took his seat on top, and with greater composure than he had known since his dramatic meeting with Gianapolis in Victoria Street, lighted one of Mr. Leroux's cabanas (with which he invariably kept his case filled) and settled down to think about the future.

His reflections served apparently to shorten the journey; and Soames found himself proceeding along Globe Road—a dark and uninviting highway—almost before he realized that London Bridge had been traversed. It was now long past one o'clock; and that part of the east-end showed dreary and deserted. Public houses had long since ejected their late guests, and even those argumentative groups, which, after closing-time, linger on the pavements, within the odor Bacchanalian, were dispersed. The jauntiness was gone, now, from Soames' manner, and aware of a marked internal depression, he passed furtively along the pavement with its long shadowy reaches between the islands of light formed by the street lamps. From patch to patch he passed, and each successive lamp that looked down upon him found him more furtive, more bent in his carriage.

Not a shop nor a house exhibited any light. Sleeping Globe Road, East, served to extinguish the last poor spark of courage within Soames' bosom. He came to the extreme end of the road without having perceived a beckoning hand, without having detected a sound to reveal that his advent was observed. In the shadow of a wall he stopped, resting his grip upon the pavement and looking back upon his tracks.

No living thing moved from end to end of Globe Road.

Shivering slightly, Soames picked up the bag and began to walk back. Less than half-way along, an icy chill entered into his veins, and his nerves quivered like piano wires, for a soft crying of his name came, eerie, through the silence, and terrified the hearer.

"Soames . . . ! Soames . . . !"

Soames stopped dead, breathing very rapidly, and looking about him right and left. He could hear the muted pulse of sleeping London. Then, in the dark doorway of the house before which he stood, he perceived, dimly, a motionless figure. His first sensation was not of relief, but of fear. The figure raised a beckoning hand. Soames, conscious that his course was set and that he must navigate it accordingly, opened the iron gate, passed up the path and entered the house to which he thus had been summoned. . . .

He found himself surrounded by absolute darkness, and the door was closed behind him.

"Straight ahead, Soames!" said the familiar voice of Gianapolis out of the darkness.

Soames, with a gasp of relief, staggered on. A hand rested upon his shoulder, and he was guided into a room on the right of the passage. Then an electric lamp was lighted, and he found himself confronting the Greek.

But Gianapolis was no longer radiant; all the innate evil of the man shone out through the smirking mask.

"Sit down, Soames!" he directed.

Soames, placing his bag upon the floor, seated himself in a cane armchair. The room was cheaply furnished as an office, with a roll-top desk, a revolving chair, and a filing cabinet. On a side-table stood a typewriter, and about the room were several other chairs, whilst the floor was covered with cheap linoleum. Gianapolis sat in the revolving chair, staring at the lowered blinds of the window, and brushing up the points of his black mustache.

With a fine white silk handkerchief Soames gently wiped the perspiration from his forehead and from the lining of his hat-band. Gianapolis began abruptly—

"There has been an—accident" (he continued to brush his mustache, with increasing rapidity). "Tell me all that took place after you left the Post Office."

Soames nervously related his painful experiences of the evening, whilst Gianapolis drilled his mustache to a satanic angle. The story being concluded:

"Whatever has happened?" groaned Soames; "and what am I to do?"

"What you are to do," replied Gianapolis, "will be arranged, my dear Soames, by—Mr. King. Where you are to go, is a problem shortly settled: you are to go nowhere; you are to stay here."

"Here!"

Soames gazed drearily about the room.

"Not exactly here—this is merely the office; but at our establishment proper in Limehouse."

"Limehouse!"

"Certainly. Although you seem to be unaware of the fact, Soames, there are some charming resorts in Limehouse; and your duties, for the present, will confine you to one of them."

"But—but," hesitated Soames, "the police . . ."

"Unless my information is at fault," said Gianapolis, "the police have no greater chance of paying us a visit, now, than they had formerly."

"But Mrs. Leroux . . ."

"Mrs. Leroux!"

Gianapolis twirled around in the chair, his eyes squinting demoniacally—"Mrs. Leroux!"

"She—she . . ."

"What about Mrs. Leroux?"

"Isn't she dead?"

"Dead! Mrs. Leroux! You are laboring under a strange delusion, Soames. The lady whom you saw was not Mrs. Leroux."

Soames' brain began to fail him again.

"Then who," he began. . . .

"That doesn't concern you in the least, Soames. But what does concern you is this: your connection, and my connection, with the matter cannot possibly be established by the police. The incident is regrettable, but the emergency was dealt with—in time. It represents a serious deficit, unfortunately, and your own usefulness, for the moment, becomes nil; but we shall have to look after you, I suppose, and hope for better things in the future."

He took up the telephone.

"East 39951," he said, whilst Soames listened, attentively. Then—

"Is that Kan-Suh Concessions?" he asked. "Yes—good! Tell Said to bring the car past the end of the road at a quarter-to-two. That's all."

He hung up the receiver.

"Now, my dear Soames," he said, with a faint return to his old manner, "you are about to enter upon new duties. I will make your position clear to you. Whilst you do your work, and keep yourself to yourself, you are in no danger; but one indiscretion—just one—apart from what it may mean for others, will mean, for *you*, immediate arrest as accessory to a murder!"

Soames shuddered, coldly.

"You can rely upon me, Mr. Gianapolis," he protested, "to do absolutely what you wish—absolutely. I am a ruined man, and I know it—I know it. My only hope is that you will give me a chance."

"You shall have every chance, Soames," replied Gianapolis—"every chance."

XV

CAVE OF THE GOLDEN DRAGON

When the car stopped at the end of a short drive, Soames had not the slightest idea of his whereabouts. The blinds at the window of the limousine had been lowered during the whole journey, and now he descended from the step of the car on to the step of a doorway. He was in some kind of roofed-in courtyard, only illuminated by the headlamps of the car. Mr. Gianapolis pushed him forward, and, as the door was closed, he heard the gear of the car reversed; then—silence fell.

"My grip!" he began, nervously.

"It will be placed in your room, Soames."

The voice of the Greek answered him from the darkness.

Guided by the hand of Gianapolis, he passed on and descended a flight of stone steps. Ahead of him a light shone out beneath a door, and, as he stumbled on the steps, the door was thrown suddenly open.

He found himself looking into a long, narrow apartment. . . . He pulled up short with a smothered, gasping cry.

It was a cavern!—but a cavern the like of which he had never seen, never imagined. The walls had the appearance of being rough-hewn from virgin rock—from black rock—from rock black as the rocks of Shellal—black as the gates of Erebus.

Placed at regular intervals along the frowning walls, to right and left, were spiral, slender pillars, gilded and gleaming. They supported an archwork of fancifully carven wood, which curved gently outward to the center of the ceiling, forming, by conjunction with a similar, opposite curve, a pointed arch.

In niches of the wall were a number of grotesque Chinese idols. The floor was jet black and polished like ebony. Several tiger-skin rugs were strewn about it. But, dominating the strange place, in the center of the floor stood an ivory pedestal, supporting a golden dragon of exquisite workmanship; and before it, as before a shrine, an enormous Chinese vase was placed, of the hue, at its base, of deepest violet, fading, upward, through all the shades of rose pink seen in an Egyptian sunset, to a tint more elusive than a maiden's blush. It contained a mass of exotic poppies of every shade conceivable, from purple so dark as to seem black, to poppies of the whiteness of snow.

Just within the door, and immediately in front of Soames, stood a slim man of about his own height, dressed with great nicety in a perfectly fitting morning-coat, his well-cut cashmere trousers falling accurately over glossy boots having gray suede uppers. His linen was immaculate, and he wore a fine pearl in his black poplin cravat. Between two yellow fingers smoldered a cigarette.

Soames, unconsciously, clenched his fists: this slim man embodied the very spirit of the outre. The fantastic surroundings melted from the ken of Soames, and he seemed to stand in a shadow-world, alone with an incarnate shadow.

For this was a Chinaman! His jet black lusterless hair was not shaven in the national manner, but worn long, and brushed back from his slanting brow with no parting, so that it fell about his white collar behind, lankly. He wore gold-rimmed spectacles, which magnified his oblique eyes and lent him a terrifying beetle-like appearance. His mephistophelean eyebrows were raised interrogatively, and he was smiling so as to exhibit a row of uneven yellow teeth.

Soames, his amazement giving place to reasonless terror, fell back a step—into the arms of Gianapolis.

"This is our friend from Palace Mansions," said the Greek. He squeezed Soames' arm, reassuringly. "Your new principal, Soames, Mr. Ho-Pin, from whom you will take your instructions."

"I have these instructions for Mr. Soames," said Ho-Pin, in a metallic, monotonous voice. (He gave to "r" half the value of "w," with a hint of the presence of "l.") "He will wremain here as valet until the search fowr him becomes less wrigowrous."

Soames, scarce believing that he was awake, made no reply. He found himself unable to meet the glittering eyes of the Chinaman; he glanced furtively about the room, prepared at any moment to wake up from what seemed to him an absurd, a ghostly dream.

"Said will change his appeawrance," continued Ho-Pin, smoothly, "so that he will not wreadily be wrecognized. Said will come now."

Ho-Pin clapped his hands three times.

The door at the end of the room immediately opened, and a thickset man of a pronounced Arabian type, entered. He wore a chauffeur's livery of dark blue; and Soames recognized him for the man who had driven the car.

"Said," said Ho-Pin very deliberately, turning to face the new arrival, "ahu hina—Lucas Effendi—Mr. Lucas. Waddi el—shenta ila beta oda. Fehimt?"

Said bowed his head.

"Fahim, effendi," he muttered rapidly.

"Ma fihsh."

Again Said bowed his head, then, glancing at Soames—

"Ta'ala wayyaya!" he said.

Soames, looking helplessly at Gianapolis—who merely pointed to the door—followed Said from the room.

He was conducted along a wide passage, thickly carpeted and having its walls covered with a kind of matting kept in place by strips of bamboo. Its roof was similarly concealed. A door near to the end, and on the right, proved to open into a square room quite simply furnished in the manner of a bed-sitting room. A little bathroom opened out of it in one corner. The walls were distempered white, and there was no window. Light was furnished by an electric lamp, hanging from the center of the ceiling.

Soames, glancing at his bag, which Said had just placed beside the white-enameled bedstead, turned to his impassive guide.

"This is a funny go!" he began, with forced geniality. "Am I to live here?"

"Ma'lesh!" muttered Said—"ma'lesh!"

He indicated, by gestures, that Soames should remove his collar; he was markedly unemotional. He crossed to the bathroom, and could be heard filling the hand-basin with water.

"Kursi!" he called from within.

Soames, seriously doubting his own sanity, and so obsessed with a sense of the unreal that his senses were benumbed, began to take off his collar; he could not feel the contact of his fingers with his neck in the act. Collarless, he entered the little bathroom. . . .

"Kursi!" repeated Said; then: "Ah! ana nesit! ma'lesh!"

Said—whilst Soames, docile in his stupor, watched him—went back, picked up the solitary cane chair which the apartment boasted, and brought it into the bathroom. Soames perceived that he was to be treated to something in the nature of a shampoo; for Said had ranged a number of bottles, a cake of soap, and several towels, along a shelf over the bath.

In a curious state of passivity, Soames submitted to the operation. His hair was vigorously toweled, then fanned in the most approved fashion; but this was no more than the beginning of the operation. As he leaned back in the chair:

"Am I dreaming?" he said aloud. "What's all this about?"

"Uskut!" muttered Said—"Uskut!"

Soames, at no time an aggressive character, resigned himself to the incredible.

Some lotion, which tingled slightly upon the scalp, was next applied by Said from a long-necked bottle. Then, fresh water having been poured into the basin, a dark purple liquid was added, and Soames' head dipped therein by the operating Eastern. This time no rubbing followed, but after some minutes of vigorous fanning, he was thrust back into the chair, and a dry towel tucked firmly into his collar-band. He anticipated that he was about to be shaved, and in this was not disappointed.

Said, filling a shaving-mug from the hot-water tap, lathered Soames' chin and the abbreviated whiskers upon which he had prided himself. Then the razor was skilfully handled, and Soames' face shaved until his chin was as smooth as satin.

Next, a dark brown solution was rubbed over the skin, and even upon his forehead and right into the roots of the hair; upon his throat, his ears, and the back of his neck. He was now past the putting of questions or the raising of protest; he was as clay in the hands of the silent Oriental. Having fanned his wet face again for some time, Said, breaking the long silence, muttered:

"Ikfil'iyyun!"

Soames stared. Said indicated, by pantomime, that he desired him to close his eyes, and Soames obeyed mechanically. Thereupon the Oriental busied himself with the ex-butler's not very abundant lashes for five minutes or more. Then the busy fingers were at work with his inadequate eyebrows: finally—

"Khalas!" muttered Said, tapping him on the shoulder.

Soames wearily opened his eyes, wondering if his strange martyrdom were nearly at its end. He discovered his hair to be still rather damp, but, since it was sparse, it was rapidly drying. His eyes smarted painfully.

Removing all trace of his operations, Said, with no word of farewell, took up his towels, bottles and other paraphernalia and departed.

Soames watched the retreating figure crossing the outer room, but did not rise from the chair until the door had closed behind Said. Then, feeling strangely like a man who has drunk too heavily, he stood up and walked into the bedroom. There was a small shaving-glass upon the chest-of-drawers, and to this he advanced, filled with the wildest apprehensions.

One glance he ventured, and started back with a groan.

His apprehensions had fallen short of the reality. With one hand clutching the bedrail, he stood there swaying from side to side, and striving to screw up his courage to the point whereat he might venture upon a second glance in the mirror. At last he succeeded, looking long and pitifully.

"Oh, Lord!" he groaned, "what a guy!"

Beyond doubt he was strangely changed. By nature, Luke Soames had hair of a sandy color; now it was of so dark a brown as to seem black in the lamplight. His thin eyebrows and scanty lashes were naturally almost colorless; but they were become those of a pronounced brunette. He was of pale complexion, but tonight had the face of a mulatto, or of one long in tropical regions. In short, he was another man—a man whom he detested at first sight!

This was the price, or perhaps only part of the price, of his indiscretion. Mr. Soames was become Mr. Lucas. Clutching the top of the chest-of-drawers with both hands, he glared at his own reflection, dazedly.

In that pose, he was interrupted. Said, silently opening the door behind him, muttered:

"Ta'ala wayyaya!"

Soames whirled around in a sudden panic, his heart leaping madly. The immobile brown face peered in at the door.

"Ta'ala wayyaya!" repeated Said, his face expressionless as a mask. He pointed along the corridor. "Ho-Pin Effendi!" he explained.

Soames, raising his hands to his collarless neck, made a swallowing noise, and would have spoken; but:

"Ta'ala wayyaya!" reiterated the Oriental.

Soames hesitated no more. Reentering the corridor, with its straw-matting walls, he made a curious discovery. Away to the left it terminated in a blank, matting-covered wall. There was no indication of the door by which he had entered it. Glancing hurriedly to the right, he failed also to perceive any door there. The bespectacled Ho-Pin stood halfway along the passage, awaiting him. Following Said in that direction, Soames was greeted with the announcement:

"Mr. King will see you."

The words taught Soames that his capacity for emotion was by no means exhausted. His endless conjectures respecting the mysterious Mr. King were at last to be replaced by facts; he was to see him, to speak with him. He knew now that it was a fearful privilege which gladly he would have denied himself.

Ho-Pin opened a door almost immediately behind him, a door the existence of which had not hitherto been evident to Soames. Beyond, was a dark passage.

"You will follow me, closely," said Ho-Pin with one of his piercing glances.

Soames, finding his legs none too steady, entered the passage behind Ho-Pin. As he did so, the door was closed by Said, and he found himself in absolute darkness.

"Keep close behind me," directed the metallic voice.

Soames could not see the speaker, since no ray of light penetrated into the passage. He stretched out a groping hand, and, although he was conscious of an odd revulsion, touched the shoulder of the man in front of him and maintained that unpleasant contact whilst they walked on and on through apparently endless passages, extensive as a catacomb. Many corners they turned; they turned to the right, they turned to the left. Soames was hopelessly bewildered. Then, suddenly, Ho-Pin stopped.

"Stand still," he said.

Soames became vaguely aware that a door was being closed somewhere near to him. A lamp lighted up directly over his head . . . he found himself in a small library!

Its four walls were covered with book-shelves from floor to ceiling, and the shelves were packed to overflowing with books in most unusual and bizarre bindings. A red carpet was on the floor and a red-shaded lamp hung from the ceiling, which was conventionally white-washed. Although there was no fireplace, theroom was immoderately hot, and heavy with the perfume of roses. On three little tables were great bowls filled with roses, and there were other bowls containing roses in gaps between the books on the open shelves.

A tall screen of beautifully carved sandalwood masked one corner of the room, but beyond it protruded the end of a heavy writing-table upon which lay some loose papers, and, standing amid them, an enormous silver rose-bowl, brimming with sulphur-colored blooms.

Soames, obeying a primary instinct, turned, as the light leaped into being, to seek the door by which he had entered. As he did so, the former doubts of his own sanity returned with renewed vigor.

The book-lined wall behind him was unbroken by any opening.

Slowly, as a man awaking from a stupor, Soames gazed around the library.

It contained no door.

He rested his hand upon one of the shelves and closed his eyes. Beyond doubt he was going mad! The tragic events of that night had proved too much for him; he had never disguised from himself the fact that his mental capacity was not of the greatest. He was assured, now, that his brain had lost its balance shortly after his flight from Palace Mansions, and that the events of the past two hours had been phantasmal. He would presently return to sanity (or, blasphemously, he dared to petition heaven that he would) and find himself . . . ? Perhaps in the hands of the police!

"Oh, God!" he groaned—"Oh, God!"

He opened his eyes . . .

A woman stood before the sandalwood screen! She had the pallidly dusky skin of a Eurasian, but, by virtue of nature or artifice, her cheeks wore a peachlike bloom. Her features were flawless in their chiseling, save for the slightly distended nostrils, and her black eyes were magnificent.

She was divinely petite, slender and girlish; but there was that in the lines of her figure, so seductively defined by her clinging Chinese dress, in the poise of her small head, with the blush rose nestling amid the black hair—above all in the smile of her full red lips—which discounted the youth of her body; which whispered "Mine is a soul old in strange sins—a soul for whom dead Alexandria had no secrets, that learnt nothing of Athenean Thais and might have tutored Messalina . . ."

In her fanciful robe of old gold, with her tiny feet shod in ridiculously small, gilt slippers, she stood by the screen watching the stupefied man—an exquisite, fragrantly youthful casket of ancient, unnameable evils.

"Good evening, Soames!" she said, stumbling quaintly with her English, but speaking in a voice musical as a silver bell. "You will here be known as Lucas. Mr. King he wishing me to say that you to receive two pounds, at each week."

Soames, glassy-eyed, stood watching her. A horror, the horror of insanity, had descended upon him—a clammy, rose-scented mantle. The room, the incredible, book-lined room, was a red blur, surrounding the black, taunting eyes of the Eurasian. Everything was out of focus; past, present, and future were merged into a red, rose-haunted nothingness . . .

"You will attend to Block A," resumed the girl, pointing at him with a little fan. "You will also attend to the gentlemen. . . ."

She laughed softly, revealing tiny white teeth; then paused, head tilted coquettishly, and appeared to be listening to someone's conversation—to the words of some person seated behind the screen. This fact broke in upon Soames' disordered mind and confirmed him in his opinion that he was a man demented. For only one slight sound broke the silence of the room. The red carpet below the little tables was littered with rose petals, and, in the super-heated atmosphere, other petals kept falling—softly, with a gentle rustling. Just that sound there was . . . and no other. Then:

"Mr. King he wishing to point out to you," said the girl, "that he hold receipts of you, which bind you to him. So you will be free man, and have liberty to go out sometimes for your own business. Mr. King he wishing to hear you say you thinking to agree with the conditions and be satisfied."

She ceased speaking, but continued to smile; and so complete was the stillness, that Soames, whose sense of hearing had become nervously stimulated, heard a solitary rose petal fall upon the corner of the writing-table.

"I . . . agree," he whispered huskily; "and . . . I am . . . satisfied."

He looked at the carven screen as a lost soul might look at the gate of Hades; he felt now that if a sound should come from beyond it he would shriek out, he would stop up his ears; that if the figure of the Unseen should become visible, he must die at the first glimpse of it.

The little brown girl was repeating the uncanny business of listening to that voice of silence; and Soames knew that he could not sustain his part in this eerie comedy for another half-minute without breaking out into hysterical laughter. Then:

"Mr. King he releasing you for tonight," announced the silver bell voice.

The light went out.

Soames uttered a groan of terror, followed by a short, bubbling laugh, but was seized firmly by the arm and led on into the blackness—on through the solid, book-laden walls, presumably; and on—on—on, along those interminable passages by which he had come. Here the air was cooler, and the odor of roses no longer perceptible, no longer stifling him, no longer assailing his nostrils, not as an odor of sweetness, but as a perfume utterly damnable and unholy.

With his knees trembling at every step, he marched on, firmly supported by his unseen companion.

"Stop!" directed a metallic, guttural voice.

Soames pulled up, and leaned weakly against the wall. He heard the clap of hands close behind him; and a door opened within twelve inches of the spot whereat he stood.

He tottered out into the matting-lined corridor from which he had started upon that nightmare journey; Ho-Pin appeared at his elbow, but no door appeared behind Ho-Pin!

"This is your wroom," said the Chinaman, revealing his yellow teeth in a mirthless smile.

He walked across the corridor, threw open a door—a real, palpable door . . . and there was Soames' little white room!

Soames staggered across, for it seemed a veritable haven of refuge—entered, and dropped upon the bed. He seemed to see the rose-petals fall—fall—falling in that red room in the labyrinth—the room that had no door; he seemed to see the laughing eyes of the beautiful Eurasian.

"Good night!" came the metallic voice of Ho-Pin.

The light in the corridor went out.

XVI

HO-PIN'S CATACOMBS

The newly-created Mr. Lucas entered upon a sort of cave-man existence in this fantastic abode where night was day and day was night; where the sun never shone.

He was awakened on the first morning of his sojourn in the establishment of Ho-Pin by the loud ringing of an electric bell immediately beside his bed. He sprang upright with a catching of the breath, peering about him at the unfamiliar surroundings and wondering, in the hazy manner of a sleeper newly awakened, where he was, and how come there. He was fully dressed, and his strapped-up grip lay beside him on the floor; for he had not dared to remove his clothes, had not dared to seek slumber after that terrifying interview with Mr. King. But outraged nature had prevailed, and sleep had come unbeckoned, unbidden.

The electric light was still burning in the room, as he had left it, and as he sat up, looking about him, a purring whistle drew his attention to a speaking-tube which protruded below the bell.

Soames rolled from the bed, head throbbing, and an acrid taste in his mouth, and spoke into the tube:

"Hullo!"

"You will pwrepare for youwr duties," came the metallic gutturals of Ho-Pin. "Bwreakfast will be bwrought to you in a quawrter-of-an-hour."

He made no reply, but stood looking about him dully. It had not been a dream, then, nor was he mad. It was a horrible reality; here, in London, in modern, civilized London, he was actually buried in some incredible catacomb; somewhere near to him, very near to him, was the cave of the golden dragon, and, also adjacent—terrifying thought—was the doorless library, the rose-scented haunt where the beautiful Eurasian spoke, oracularly, the responses of Mr. King!

Soames could not understand it all; he felt that such things could not be; that there must exist an explanation of those seeming impossibilities other than that they actually existed. But the instructions were veritable enough, and would not be denied.

Rapidly he began to unpack his grip. His watch had stopped, since he had neglected to wind it, and he hurried with his toilet, fearful of incurring the anger of Ho-Pin—of Ho-Pin, the beetlesque.

He observed, with passive interest, that the operation of shaving did not appreciably lighten the stain upon his skin, and, by the time that he was shaved, he had begun to know the dark-haired, yellow-faced man grimacing in the mirror for himself; but he was far from being reconciled to his new appearance.

Said peeped in at the door. He no longer wore his chauffeur's livery, but was arrayed in a white linen robe, red-sashed, and wore loose, red slippers; a tarboosh perched upon his shaven skull.

Pushing the door widely open, he entered with a tray upon which was spread a substantial breakfast.

"Hurryup!" he muttered, as one word; wherewith he departed again.

Soames seated himself at the little table upon which the tray rested, and endeavored to eat. His usual appetite had departed with his identity; Mr. Lucas was a poor, twitching being of raw nerves and internal qualms. He emptied the coffee-pot, however, and smoked a cigarette which he found in his case.

Said reappeared.

"Ta'ala!" he directed.

Soames having learnt that that term was evidently intended as an invitation to follow Said, rose and followed, dumbly.

He was conducted along the matting-lined corridor to the left; and now, where formerly he had seen a blank wall, he saw an open door! Passing this, he discovered himself in the cave of the golden dragon. Ho-Pin, dressed in a perfectly fitting morning coat and its usual accompaniments, received him with a mirthless smile.

"Good mowrning!" he said; "I twrust your bwreakfast was satisfactowry?"

"Quite, sir," replied Soames, mechanically, and as he might have replied to Mr. Leroux.

"Said will show you to a wroom," continued Ho-Pin, "where you will find a gentleman awaiting you. You will valet him and perfowrm any other services which he may wrequire of you. When he departs, you will clean the wroom and adjoining bath-wroom, and put it into thowrough order for an incoming tenant. In short, your duties in this wrespect will be identical to those which formerly you perfowrmed at sea. There is one important diffewrence: your name is Lucas, and you will answer no questions."

The metallic voice seemed to reach Soames' comprehension from some place other than the room of the golden dragon—from a great distance, or as though he were fastened up in a box and were being addressed by someone outside it.

"Yes, sir," he replied.

Said opened the yellow door upon the right of the room, and Soames followed him into another of the matting-lined corridors, this one running right and left and parallel with the wall of the apartment which he had just quitted. Six doors opened out of this corridor; four of them upon the side opposite to that by which he had entered, and one at either end.

These doors were not readily to be detected; and the wall, at first glance, presented an unbroken appearance. But from experience, he had learned that where the strips of bamboo which overlay the straw matting formed a rectangular panel, there was a door, and by the light of the electric lamp hung in the center of the corridor, he counted six of these.

Said, selecting a key from a bunch which he carried, opened one of the doors, held it ajar for Soames to enter, and permitted it to reclose behind him.

Soames entered nervously. He found himself in a room identical in size with his own private apartment; a bathroom, etc., opened out of it in one corner after the same fashion. But there similarity ended.

The bed in this apartment was constructed more on the lines of a modern steamer bunk; that is, it was surrounded by a rail, and was raised no more than a foot from the floor. The latter was covered with a rich carpet, worked in many colors, and the wall was hung with such paper as Soames had never seen hitherto in his life. The scheme of this mural decoration was distinctly Chinese, and consisted in an intricate design of human and animal figures, bewilderingly mingled; its coloring was brilliant, and the scheme extended, unbroken, over the entire ceiling. Cushions, most fancifully embroidered, were strewn about the floor, and the bed coverlet was a piece of heavy Chinese tapestry. A lamp, shaded with silk of a dull purple, swung in the center of the apartment, and an ebony table, inlaid with ivory, stood on one side of the bed; on the other was a cushioned armchair figured with the eternal, chaotic Chinese design, and being littered, at the moment, with the garments of the man in the bed. The air of the room was disgusting, unbreathable; it caught Soames by the throat and sickened him. It was laden with some kind of fumes, entirely unfamiliar to his nostrils. A dainty Chinese tea-service stood upon the ebony table.

For fully thirty seconds Soames, with his back to the door, gazed at the man in the bed, and fought down the nausea which the air of the place had induced in him.

This sleeper was a man of middle age, thin to emaciation and having lank, dark hair. His face was ghastly white, and he lay with his head thrown back and with his arms hanging out upon either side of the bunk, so that his listless hands rested upon the carpet. It was a tragic face; a high, intellectual brow and finely chiseled features; but it presented an indescribable aspect of decay; it was as the face of some classic statue which has long lain buried in humid ruins.

Soames shook himself into activity, and ventured to approach the bed. He moistened his dry lips and spoke:

"Good morning, sir"—the words sounded wildly, fantastically out of place. "Shall I prepare your bath?"

The sleeper showed no signs of awakening.

Soames forced himself to touch one of the thrown-back shoulders. He shook it gently.

The man on the bed raised his arms and dropped them back again into their original position, without opening his eyes.

"They . . . are hiding," he murmured thickly . . . "in the . . . orange grove . . . . If the felucca sails . . . closer . . . they will . . ."

Soames, finding something very horrifying in the broken words, shook the sleeper more urgently.

"Wake up, sir!" he cried; "I am going to prepare your bath."

"Don't let them . . . escape," murmured the man, slowly opening his eyes—"I have not . . ."

He struggled upright, glaring madly at the intruder. His light gray eyes had a glassiness as of long sickness, and his pupils, which were unnaturally dilated, began rapidly to contract; became almost invisible. Then they expanded again—and again contracted.

"Who—the deuce are you?" he murmured, passing his hand across his unshaven face.

"My name is—Lucas, sir," said Soames, conscious that if he remained much longer in the place he should be physically sick. "At your service—shall I prepare the bath?"

"The bath?" said the man, sitting up more straightly—"certainly, yes—of course . . ."

He looked at Soames, with a light of growing sanity creeping into his eyes; a faint flush tinged the pallid face, and his loose mouth twitched sensitively.

"Then, Said," he began, looking Soames up and down . . . "let me see, whom did you say you were?"

"Lucas, sir—at your service."

"Ah," muttered the man, lowering his eyes in unmistakable shame. "Yes, yes, of course. You are new here?"

"Yes, sir. Shall I prepare your bath?"

"Yes, please. This is Wednesday morning?"

"Wednesday morning, sir; yes."

"Of course—it is Wednesday. You said your name was?"

"Lucas, sir," reiterated Soames, and, crossing the fantastic apartment, he entered the bathroom beyond.

This contained the most modern appointments and was on an altogether more luxurious scale than that attached to his own quarters. He noted, without drawing any deduction from the circumstance, that the fittings were of American manufacture. Here, as in the outer room, there was no window; an electric light hung from the center of the ceiling. Soames busied himself in filling the bath, and laying out the towels upon the rack.

"Fairly warm, sir?" he asked.

"Not too warm, thank you," replied the other, now stumbling out of bed and falling into the armchair—"not too warm."

"If you will take your bath, sir," said Soames, returning to the outer room, "I will brush your clothes and be ready to shave you."

"Yes, yes," said the man, rubbing his hands over his face wearily. "You are new here?"

Soames, who was becoming used to answering this question, answered it once more without irritation.

"Yes, sir, will you take your bath now? It is nearly full, I think."

The man stood up unsteadily and passed into the bathroom, closing the door behind him. Soames, seeking to forget his surroundings, took out from a small hand-bag which he found beneath the bed, a razor-case and a shaving stick. The clothes-brush he had discovered in the bathroom; and now he set to work to brush the creased garments stacked in the armchair. He noted that they were of excellent make, and that the linen was of the highest quality. He was thus employed when the outer door silently opened and the face of Said looked in.

"Gazm," said the Oriental; and he placed inside, upon the carpet, a pair of highly polished boots.

The door was reclosed.

Soames had all the garments in readiness by the time that the man emerged from the bathroom, looking slightly less ill, and not quite so pallid. He wore a yellow silk kimono; and, with greater composure than he had yet revealed, he seated himself in the armchair that Soames might shave him.

This operation Soames accomplished, and the subject, having partially dressed, returned to the bathroom to brush his hair. When his toilet was practically completed:

"Shall I pack the rest of the things in the bag, sir?" asked Soames.

The man nodded affirmatively.

Five minutes later he was ready to depart, and stood before the ex-butler a well-dressed, intellectual, but very debauched-looking gentleman. Being evidently well acquainted with the regime of the establishment, he pressed an electric bell beside the door, presented Soames with half-a-sovereign, and, as Said reappeared, took his departure, leaving Soames more reconciled to his lot than he could ever have supposed possible.

The task of cleaning the room was now commenced by Soames. Said returned, bringing him the necessary utensils; and for fifteen minutes or so he busied himself between the outer apartment and the bathroom. During this time he found leisure to study the extraordinary mural decorations; and, as he looked at them, he learned that they possessed a singular property.

If one gazed continuously at any portion of the wall, the intertwined figures thereon took shape—nay, took life; the intricate, elaborate design ceased to be a design, and became a procession, a saturnalia; became a sinister comedy, which, when first visualized, shocked Soames immoderately. The horrors presented by these devices of evil cunning, crowding the walls, appalled the narrow mind of the beholder, revolted him in an even greater degree than they must have revolted a man of broader and cleaner mind. He became conscious of a quality of evil which pervaded the room; the entire place seemed to lie beneath a spell, beneath the spell of an invisible, immeasurably wicked intelligence.

His reflections began to terrify him, and he hastened to complete his duties. The stench of the place was sickening him anew, and when at last Said opened the door, Soames came out as a man escaping from some imminent harm.

"Di," muttered Said.

He pointed to the opened door of a second room, identical in every respect with the first; and Soames started back with a smothered groan. Had his education been classical he might have likened himself to Hercules laboring for Augeus; but his mind tending scripturally, he wondered if he had sold his soul to Satan in the person of the invisible Mr. King!

XVII

KAN-SUH CONCESSIONS

Soames' character was of a pliable sort, and ere many days had passed he had grown accustomed to this unnatural existence among the living corpses in the catacombs of Ho-Pin.

He rarely saw Ho-Pin, and desired not to see him at all; as for Mr. King, he even endeavored to banish from his memory the name of that shadowy being. The memory of the Eurasian he could not banish, and was ever listening for the silvery voice, but in vain. He had no particular duties, apart from the care of the six rooms known as Block A, and situated in the corridor to the left of the cave of the golden dragon; this, and the valeting of departing occupants. But the hours at which he was called upon to perform these duties varied very greatly. Sometimes he would attend to four human wrecks in the same morning; whilst, perhaps on the following day, he would not be called upon to officiate until late in the evening. One fact early became evident to him. There was a ceaseless stream of these living dead men pouring into the catacombs of Ho-Pin, coming he knew not whence, and issuing forth again, he knew not whither.

Twice in the first week of his new and strange service he recognized the occupants of the rooms as men whom he had seen in the upper world. On entering the room of one of these (at ten o'clock at night) he almost cried out in his surprise; for the limp, sallow-faced creature extended upon the bed before him was none other than Sir Brian Malpas—the brilliant politician whom his leaders had earmarked for office in the next Cabinet!

As Soames stood contemplating him stretched there in his stupor, he found it hard to credit the fact that this was the same man whom political rivals feared for his hard brilliance, whom society courted, and whose engagement to the daughter of a peer had been announced only a few months before.

Throughout this time, Soames had made no attempt to seek the light of day: he had not seen a newspaper; he knew nothing of the hue and cry raised throughout England, of the hunt for the murderer of Mrs. Vernon. He suffered principally from lack of companionship. The only human being with whom he ever came in contact was Said, the Egyptian; and Said, at best, was uncommunicative. A man of very limited intellect, Luke Soames had been at a loss for many days to reconcile Block A and its temporary occupants with any comprehensible scheme of things. Whereas some of the rooms would be laden with nauseating fumes, others would be free of these; the occupants, again, exhibited various symptoms.

That he was a servant of an opium-den de luxe did not for some time become apparent to him; then, when first the theory presented itself, he was staggered by a discovery so momentous.

But it satisfied his mind only partially. Some men whom he valeted might have been doped with opium, certainly, but all did not exhibit those indications which, from hearsay, he associated with the resin of the white poppy.

Knowing nothing of the numerous and exotic vices which have sprung from the soil of the Orient, he was at a loss for a full explanation of the facts as he saw them.

Finding himself unmolested, and noting, in the privacy of his own apartment, how handsomely his tips were accumulating, Soames was rapidly becoming reconciled to his underground existence, more especially as it spelt safety to a man wanted by the police. His duties thus far had never taken him beyond the corridor known as Block A; what might lie on the other side of the cave of the golden dragon he knew not. He never saw any of the habitues arrive, or actually leave; he did not know whether the staff of the place consisted of himself, Said, Ho-Pin, the Eurasian girl—and . . . the other, or if there were more servants of this unseen master. But never a day passed by that the clearance of at least one apartment did not fall to his lot, and never an occupant quitted those cells without placing a golden gratuity in the valet's palm.

His appetite returned, and he slept soundly enough in his clean white bedroom, content to lose the upper world, temporarily, and to become a dweller in the catacombs—where tips were large and plentiful. His was the mind of a domestic animal, neither learning from the past nor questioning the future; but dwelling only in the well-fed present.

No other type of European, however lowly, could have supported existence in such a place.

Thus the days passed, and the nights passed, the one merged imperceptibly in the other. At the end of the first week, two sovereigns appeared upon the breakfast tray which Said brought to Soames' room; and, some little time later, Said reappeared with his bottles and paraphernalia to renew the ex-butler's make-up. As he was leaving the room:

"Ahu hina—G'nap'lis effendi!" he muttered, and went out as Mr. Gianapolis entered.

At sight of the Greek, Soames realized, in one emotional moment, how really lonely he had been and how in his inmost heart he longed for a sight of the sun, for a breath of unpolluted air, for a glimpse of gray, homely London.

All the old radiance had returned to Gianapolis; his eyes were crossed in an amiable smile.

"My dear Soames!" he cried, greeting the really delighted man. "How well your new complexion suits you! Sit down, Soames, sit down, and let us talk."

Soames placed a chair for Gianapolis, and seated himself upon the bed, twirling his thumbs in the manner which was his when under the influence of excitement.

"Now, Soames," continued Gianapolis—"I mean Lucas!—my anticipations, which I mentioned to you on the night of—the accident . . . you remember?"

"Yes," said Soames rapidly, "yes."

"Well, they have been realized. Our establishment, here, continues to flourish as of yore. Nothing has come to light in the press calculated to prejudice us in the eyes of our patrons, and although your own name, Soames . . ."

Soames started and clutched at the bedcover.

"Although your own name has been freely mentioned on all sides, it is not generally accepted that you perpetrated the deed."

Soames discovered his hair to be bristling; his skin tingled with a nervous apprehension.

"That I," he began dryly, paused and swallowed—"that I perpetrated . . . . Has it been . . ."

"It has been hinted at by one or two Fleet Street theorists—yes, Soames! But the post-mortem examination of—the victim, revealed the fact that she was addicted to drugs . . ."

"Opium?" asked Soames, eagerly.

Gianapolis smiled.

"What an observant mind you have, Soames!" he said. "So you have perceived that these groves are sacred to our Lady of the Poppies? Well, in part that is true. Here, under the auspices of Mr. Ho-Pin, fretful society seeks the solace of the brass pipe; yes, Soames, that is true. Have you ever tried opium?"

"Never!" declared Soames, with emphasis, "never!"

"Well, it is a delight in store for you! But the reason of our existence as an institution, Soames, is not far to seek. Once the joys of Chandu become perceptible to the neophyte, a great need is felt—a crying need. One may drink opium or inject morphine; these, and other crude measures, may satisfy temporarily, but if one would enjoy the delights of that fairyland, of that enchanted realm which bountiful nature has concealed in the heart of the poppy, one must retire from the ken of goths and vandals who do not appreciate such exquisite delights; one must dedicate, not an hour snatched from grasping society, but successive days and nights to the goddess."

Soames, barely understanding this discourse, listened eagerly to every word of it, whilst Gianapolis, waxing eloquent upon his strange thesis, seemed to be addressing, not his solitary auditor, but an invisible concourse.

"In common with the lesser deities," he continued, "our Lady of the Poppies is exacting. After a protracted sojourn at her shrine, so keen are the delights which she opens up to her worshipers, that a period of lassitude, of exhaustion, inevitably ensues. This precludes the proper worship of the goddess in the home, and necessitates—I say *necessitates* the presence, in such a capital as London, of a suitable Temple. You have the honor, Soames, to be a minor priest of that Temple!"

Soames brushed his dyed hair with his fingers and endeavored to look intelligent.

"A branch establishment—merely a sacred caravanserai where votaries might repose ere reentering the ruder world," continued Gianapolis—"has unfortunately been raided by the police!"

With that word, *police*, he seemed to come to earth again.

"Our arrangements, I am happy to say, were such that not one of the staff was found on the premises and no visible link existed between that establishment and this. But now let us talk about yourself. You may safely take an evening off, I think . . ."

He scrutinized Soames attentively.

"You will be discreet as a matter of course, and I should not recommend your visiting any of your former haunts. I make this proposal, of course, with the full sanction of Mr. King."

The muscles of Soames' jaw tightened at sound of the name, and he avoided the gaze of the crossed eyes.

"And the real purpose of my visit here this morning is to acquaint you with the little contrivance by which we ensure our privacy here. Once you are acquainted with it, you can take the air every evening at suitable hours, on application to Mr. Ho-Pin."

Soames coughed dryly.

"Very good," he said in a strained voice; "I am glad of that."

"I knew you would be glad, Soames," declared the smiling Gianapolis; "and now, if you will step this way, I will show you the door by which you must come and go." He stood up, then bent confidentially to Soames' ear. "Mr. King, very wisely," he whispered, "has retained you on the premises hitherto, because some doubt, some little doubt, remained respecting the information which had come into the possession of the police."

Again that ominous word! But ere Soames had time to reflect, Gianapolis led the way out of the room and along the matting-lined corridor into the apartment of the golden dragon. Soames observed, with a nervous tremor, that Mr. Ho-Pin sat upon one of the lounges, smoking a cigarette, and arrayed in his usual faultless manner. He did not attempt to rise, however, as the pair entered, but merely nodded to Gianapolis and smiled mirthlessly at Soames.

They quitted the room by the door opening on the stone steps—the door by which Soames had first entered into that evil Aladdin's cave. Gianapolis went ahead, and Soames, following him, presently emerged through a low doorway into a concrete-paved apartment, having walls of Portland stone and a white-washed ceiling. One end consisted solely of a folding gate, evidently designed to admit the limousine.

Gianapolis turned, as Soames stepped up beside him.

"If you will glance back," he said, "you will see exactly where the door is situated."

Soames did as directed, and suppressed a cry of surprise. Four of the stone blocks were fictitious—were, in verity, a heavy wooden door, faced in some way with real, or imitation granite—a door communicating with the steps of the catacombs.

"Observe!" said Gianapolis.

He closed the door, which opened outward, and there remained nothing to show the keenest observer—unless he had resorted to sounding—that these four blocks differed in any way from their fellows.

"Ingenious, is it not?" said Gianapolis, genially. "And now, my dear Soames, observe again!"

He rolled back the folding gates; and beyond was a garage, wherein stood the big limousine.

"I keep my car here, Soames, for the sake of—convenience! And now, my dear Soames, when you go out this evening, Said will close this entrance after you. When you return, which, I understand, you must do at ten o'clock, you will enter the garage by the side door yonder, which will not be locked, and you will press the electric button at the back of the petrol cans here—look! you can see it!—the inner door will then be opened for you. Step this way."

He passed between the car and the wall of the garage, opened the door at the left of the entrance gates, and, Soames following, came out into a narrow lane. For the first time in many days Soames scented the cleaner air of the upper world, and with it he filled his lungs gratefully.

Behind him was the garage, before him the high wall of a yard, and, on his right, for a considerable distance, extended a similar wall; in the latter case evidently that of a wharf—for beyond it flowed the Thames.

Proceeding along beside this wall, the two came to the gates of a warehouse. They passed these, however, and entered a small office. Crossing the office, they gained the interior of the warehouse, where chests bearing Chinese labels were stacked in great profusion.

"Then this place," began Soames.

"Is a ginger warehouse, Soames! There is a very small office staff, but sufficiently large to cope with the limited business done—in the import and export of ginger! The firm is known as Kan-Suh Concessions and imports preserved Chinese ginger from its own plantations in that

97

province of the Celestial Empire. There is a small wharf attached, as you may have noted. Oh! it is a going concern and perfectly respectable!"

Soames looked about him with wide-opened eyes.

"The ginger staff," said Gianapolis, "is not yet arrived. Mr. Ho-Pin is the manager. The lane, in which the establishment is situated, communicates with Limehouse Causeway, and, being a *cul-de-sac*, is little frequented. Only this one firm has premises actually opening into it and I have converted the small corner building at the extremity of the wharf into a garage for my car. There are no means of communication between the premises of Kan-Suh Concessions and those of the more important enterprise below—and I, myself, am not officially associated with the ginger trade. It is a precaution which we all adopt, however, never to enter or leave the garage if anyone is in sight."

Soames became conscious of a new security. He set about his duties that morning with a greater alacrity than usual, valeting one of the living dead men—a promising young painter whom he chanced to know by sight—with a return to the old affable manner which had rendered him so popular during his career as cabin steward.

He felt that he was now part and parcel of Kan-Suh Concessions; that Kan-Suh Concessions and he were at one. He had yet to learn that his sense of security was premature, and that his added knowledge might be an added danger.

When Said brought his lunch into his room, he delivered also a slip of paper bearing the brief message:

"Go out 6.30—return 10."

Mr. Soames uncorked his daily bottle of Bass almost gaily, and attacked his lunch with avidity.

XVIII

THE WORLD ABOVE

The night had set in grayly, and a drizzle of fine rain was falling. West India Dock Road presented a prospect so uninviting that it must have damped the spirits of anyone but a cave-dweller.

Soames, buttoned up in a raincoat kindly lent by Mr. Gianapolis, and of a somewhat refined fit, with a little lagoon of rainwater forming within the reef of his hat-brim, trudged briskly along. The necessary ingredients for the manufacture of mud are always present (if invisible during dry weather) in the streets of East-end London, and already Soames' neat black boots were liberally bedaubed with it. But what cared Soames? He inhaled the soot-laden air rapturously; he was glad to feel the rain beating upon his face, and took a childish pleasure in ducking his head suddenly and seeing the little stream of water spouting from his hat-brim. How healthy they looked, these East-end workers, these Italian dock-hands, these Jewish tailors, these nondescript, greasy beings who sometimes saw the sun. Many of them, he knew well, labored in cellars; but he had learnt that there are cellars and cellars. Ah! it was glorious, this gray, murky London!

Yet, now that temporarily he was free of it, he realized that there was that within him which responded to the call of the catacombs; there was a fascination in the fume-laden air of those underground passages; there was a charm, a mysterious charm, in the cave of the golden dragon, in that unforgettable place which he assumed to mark the center of the labyrinth; in the wicked, black eyes of the Eurasian. He realized that between the abstraction of silver spoons and deliberate, organized money-making at the expense of society, a great chasm yawned; that there may be romance even in felony.

Soames at last felt himself to be a traveler on the highroad to fortune; he had become almost reconciled to the loss of his bank balance, to the loss of his place in the upper world. His was the constitution of a born criminal, and, had he been capable of subtle self-analysis, he must have known now that fear, and fear only, hitherto had held him back, had confined him to the ranks of the amateurs. Well, the plunge was taken.

Deep in such reflections, he trudged along through the rain, scarce noting where his steps were leading him, for all roads were alike tonight. His natural inclinations presently dictated a halt at a brilliantly lighted public house; and, taking off his hat to shake some of the moisture from it, he replaced it on his head and entered the saloon lounge.

The place proved to be fairly crowded, principally with local tradesmen whose forefathers had toiled for Pharaoh; and conveying his glass of whisky to a marble-topped table in a corner comparatively secluded, Soames sat down for a consideration of past, present, and future; an unusual mental exercise. Curiously enough, he had lost something of his old furtiveness; he no longer examined, suspiciously, every stranger who approached his neighborhood; for as the worshipers of old came by the gate of Fear into the invisible presence of Moloch, so he—of equally untutored mind—had entered the presence of Mr. King! And no devotee of the Ammonite god had had greater faith in his potent protection than Soames had in that of his unseen master. What should a servant of Mr. King fear from the officers of the law? How puny a thing was the law in comparison with the director of that secret, powerful, invulnerable organization whereof today he (Soames) formed an unit!

Then, oddly, the old dormant cowardice of the man received a sudden spurring, and leaped into quickness. An evening paper lay upon the marble top of the table, and carelessly taking it up, Soames, hitherto lost in imaginings, was now reminded that for more than a week he had lain in ignorance of the world's doings. Good Heavens! how forgetful he had been! It was the nepenthe of the catacombs. He must make up for lost time and get in touch again with passing events: especially he must post himself up on the subject of . . . the murder. . . .

The paper dropped from his hands, and, feeling himself blanch beneath his artificial tan, Soames, in his old furtive manner, glanced around the saloon to learn if he were watched. Apparently no one was taking the slightest notice of him, and, with an unsteady hand, he raised his glass and drained its contents. There, at the bottom of the page before him, was the cause of this sudden panic; a short paragraph conceived as follows—

REPORTED ARREST OF SOAMES

It is reported that a man answering to the description of Soames, the butler wanted in connection with the Palace Mansions outrage, has been arrested in Birmingham. He was found sleeping in an outhouse belonging to Major Jennings, of Olton, and as he refused to give any account of himself, was handed over, by the gentleman's gardener, to the local police. His resemblance to the published photograph being observed, he was closely questioned, and although he denies being Luke Soames, he is being held for further inquiry.

Soames laid down the paper, and, walking across to the bar, ordered a second glass of whisky. With this he returned to the table and began more calmly to re-read the paragraph. From it he passed to the other news. He noted that little publicity was given to the Palace Mansions affair, from which he judged that public interest in the matter was already growing cold. A short summary appeared on the front page, and this he eagerly devoured. It read as follows—

PALACE MANSIONS MYSTERY

The police are following up an important clue to the murderer of Mrs. Vernon, and it is significant in this connection that a man answering to the description of Soames was apprehended at Olton (Birmingham) late last night. (See Page 6). The police are very reticent in regard to the new information which they hold, but it is evident that at last they are confident of establishing a case. Mr. Henry Leroux, the famous novelist, in whose flat the mysterious outrage took place, is suffering from a nervous breakdown, but is reported to be progressing favorably by Dr. Cumberly, who is attending him. Dr. Cumberly, it will be remembered, was with Mr. Leroux, and Mr. John Exel, M. P., at the time that the murder was discovered. The executors of the late Mr. Horace Vernon are faced with extraordinary difficulties in administering the will of the deceased, owing to the tragic coincidence of his wife's murder within twenty-four hours of his own demise.

Public curiosity respecting the nursing home in Gillingham Street, with its electric baths and other modern appliances, has by no means diminished, and groups of curious spectators regularly gather outside the former establishment of Nurse Proctor, and apparently derive some form of entertainment from staring at the windows and questioning the constable on duty. The fact that Mrs. Vernon undoubtedly came from this establishment on the night of the crime, and that the proprietors of the nursing home fled immediately, leaving absolutely no clue behind them, complicates the mystery which Scotland Yard is engaged in unraveling.

It is generally believed that the woman, Proctor, and her associates had actually no connection with the crime, and that realizing that the inquiry might turn in their direction, they decamped. The obvious inference, of course, is that the nursing home was conducted on lines which would not bear official scrutiny.

The flight of the butler, Soames, presents a totally different aspect, and in this direction the police are very active.

Soames searched the remainder of the paper scrupulously, but failed to find any further reference to the case. The second Scottish stimulant had served somewhat to restore his failing courage; he congratulated himself upon taking the only move which could have saved him from arrest; he perceived that he owed his immunity entirely to the protective wings of Mr. King. He trembled to think that his fate might indeed have been that of the man arrested at Olton; for, without money and without friends, he would have become, ere this, just such an outcast and natural object of suspicion.

He noted, as a curious circumstance, that throughout the report there was no reference to the absence of Mrs. Leroux; therefore—a primitive reasoner—he assumed that she was back again at Palace Mansions. He was mentally incapable of fitting Mrs. Leroux into the secret machine engineered by Mr. King through the visible agency of Ho-Pin. On the whole, he was disposed to believe that her several absences—ostensibly on visits to Paris—had nothing to do with the catacombs of Ho-Pin, but were to be traced to the amours of the radiant Gianapolis. Taking into consideration his reception by the Chinaman in the cave of the golden dragon, he determined, to his own satisfaction, that this had been dictated by prudence, and by Mr. Gianapolis. In short he believed that the untimely murder of Mrs. Vernon had threatened to direct attention to the commercial enterprise of the Greek, and that he, Soames, had become incorporated in the latter in this accidental fashion. He believed himself to have been employed in a private intrigue during the time that he was at Palace Mansions, and counted it a freak of fate that Mr. Gianapolis' affairs of the pocket had intruded upon his affairs of the heart.

It was all very confusing, and entirely beyond Soames' mental capacity to unravel.

He treated himself to a third scotch whisky, and sallied out into the rain. A brilliantly lighted music hall upon the opposite side of the road attracted his attention. The novelty of freedom having worn off, he felt no disposition to spend the remainder of the evening in the street, for the rain was now falling heavily, but determined to sample the remainder of the program offered by the "first house," and presently was reclining in a plush-covered, tip-up seat in the back row of the stalls.

The program was not of sufficient interest wholly to distract his mind, and during the performance of a very tragic comedian, Soames found his thoughts wandering far from the stage. His seat was at the extreme end of the back row, and, quite unintentionally, he began to listen to the conversation of two men, who, standing just inside the entrance door and immediately behind him to the right, were talking in subdued voices.

"There are thousands of Kings in London," said one.

Soames slowly lowered his hands to the chair-arms on either side of him and clutched them tightly. Every nerve in his body seemed to be strung up to the ultimate pitch of tensity. He was listening, now, as a man arraigned might listen for the pronouncement of a judgment.

"That's the trouble," replied a second voice; "but you know Max's ideas on the subject? He has his own way of going to work; but my idea, Sowerby, is that if we can find the one Mr. Soames—and I am open to bet he hasn't left London—we shall find the right Mr. King."

The comedian finished, and the orchestra noisily chorded him off. Soames, his forehead wet with perspiration, began to turn his head, inch by inch. The lights in the auditorium were partially lowered, and he prayed, devoutly, that they would remain so; for now, glancing out of the corner of his right eye, he saw the speakers.

The taller of the two, a man wearing a glistening brown overall and rain-drenched tweed cap, was the detective who had been in Leroux's study and who had ordered him to his room on the night of the murder!

Then commenced for Soames such an ordeal as all his previous life had not offered him; an ordeal beside which even the interview with Mr. King sank into insignificance. His one hope was in the cunning of Said's disguise; but he knew that Scotland Yard men judged likenesses, not by complexions, which are alterable, not by the color of the hair, which can be dyed, but by certain features which are measurable, and which may be memorized because nature has fashioned them immutable.

What should he do?—What should he do? In the silence:

"No good stopping any longer," came the whispered voice of the shorter detective; "I have had a good look around the house, and there is nobody here."

Soames literally held his breath.

"We'll get along down to the Dock Gate," was the almost inaudible reply; "I am meeting Stringer there at nine o'clock."

Walking softly, the Scotland Yard men passed out of the theater.

XIX

THE LIVING DEAD

The night held yet another adventure in store for Soames. His encounter with the two Scotland Yard men had finally expelled all thoughts of pleasure from his mind. The upper world, the free world, was beset with pitfalls; he realized that for the present, at any rate, there could be no security for him, save in the catacombs of Ho-Pin. He came out of the music-hall and stood for a moment just outside the foyer, glancing fearfully up and down the rain-swept street. Then, resuming the drenched raincoat which he had taken off in the theater, and turning up its collar about his ears, he set out to return to the garage adjoining the warehouse of Kan-Suh Concessions.

He had fully another hour of leave if he cared to avail himself of it, but, whilst every pedestrian assumed, in his eyes, the form of a detective, whilst every dark corner seemed to conceal an ambush, whilst every passing instant he anticipated feeling a heavy hand upon his shoulder, and almost heard the words—"Luke Soames, I arrest you . . ." Whilst this was his case, freedom had no joys for him.

No light guided him to the garage door, and he was forced to seek for the handle by groping along the wall. Presently, his hand came in contact with it, he turned it—and the way was open before him.

Being far from familiar with the geography of the place, he took out a box of matches, and struck one to light him to the shelf above which the bell-push was concealed.

Its feeble light revealed, not only the big limousine near which he was standing and the usual fixtures of a garage, but, dimly penetrating beyond into the black places, it also revealed something else. . . .

The door in the false granite blocks was open!

Soames, who had advanced to seek the bell-push, stopped short. The match burnt down almost to his fingers, whereupon he blew it out and carefully crushed it under his foot. A faint reflected light rendered perceptible the stone steps below. At the top, Soames stood looking down. Nothing stirred above, below, or around him. What did it mean? Dimly to his ears came the hooting of some siren from the river—evidently that of a large vessel. Still he hesitated; why he did so, he scarce knew, save that he was afraid—vaguely afraid.

Then, he asked himself what he had to fear, and conjuring up a mental picture of his white bedroom below, he planted his foot firmly upon the first step, and from thence, descended to the bottom, guided by the faint light which shone out from the doorway beneath.

But the door proved to be only partly opened, and Soames knocked deferentially. No response came to his knocking, and he so greatly ventured as to push the door fully open.

The cave of the golden dragon was empty. Half frightfully, Soames glanced about the singular apartment, in amid the mountainous cushions of the leewans, behind the pedestal of the dragon; to the right and to the left of the doorway wherein he stood.

There was no one there; but the door on the right—the door inlaid with ebony and green stone, which he had never yet seen open was open now, widely opened. He glided across the floor, his wet boots creaking unmusically, and peeped through. He saw a matting-lined corridor identical with that known as Block A. The door of one apartment, that on the extreme left, was opened. Sickly fumes were wafted out to him, and these mingled with the incense-like odor which characterized the temple of the dragon.

A moment he stood so, then started back, appalled.

An outcry—the outcry of a woman, of a woman whose very soul is assailed—split the stillness. Not from the passageway before him, but from somewhere behind him—from the direction of Block A—it came.

"For God's sake—oh! for God's sake, have mercy! Let me go! Let me go!" Higher, shriller, more fearful and urgent, grew the voice. "Let me go!"

Soames' knees began to tremble beneath him; he clutched at the black wall for support; then turned, and with unsteady footsteps crossed to the door communicating with the corridor which contained his room. It had a lever handle of the Continental pattern, and, trembling with apprehension that it might prove to be locked, Soames pressed down this handle.

The door opened . . .

"Hina, effendi!—hina!"

The voice sounded like that of Said. . . .

"Oh! God in Heaven help me! Help—help!"

"Imsik!"

Footsteps were pattering upon the stone stairs; someone was descending from the warehouse! The frenzied shrieks of the woman continued. Soames broke into a cold perspiration; his heart, which had leaped wildly, seemed now to have changed to a cold stone in his breast. Just at the entrance to the corridor he stood, frozen with horror at those cries.

"Ikfil el-bab!" came now, in the voice of Ho-Pin,—and nearer.

"Let me go! Only let me go, and I will never breathe a word. . . . Ah! Ah! Oh! God of mercy! not the needle again! You are killing me! Not the needle!"

Soames staggered on to his own room and literally fell within—as across the cave of the golden dragon, behind him, *someone*—one whom he did not see but only heard, one whom with all his soul he hoped had not seen *him*—passed rapidly.

Another shriek, more frightful than any which had preceded it, struck the trembling man as an arrow might have struck him. He dropped upon his knees at the side of the bed and thrust his fingers firmly into his ears. He had never swooned in his life, and was unfamiliar with the symptoms, but now he experienced a sensation of overpowering nausea; a blood-red mist floated before his eyes, and the floor seemed to rock beneath him like the deck of a ship. . . .

That soul-appalling outcry died away, merged into a sobbing, moaning sound which defied Soames' efforts to exclude it . . . . He rose to his feet, feeling physically ill, and turned to close his door. . . .

They were dragging someone—someone who sighed, shudderingly, and whose sighs sank to moans, and sometimes rose to sobs,—across the apartment of the dragon. In a faint, dying voice, the woman spoke again—

"Not Mr. King! *Not Mr. King!* —Is there no God in Heaven! . . . *ah!* spare me . . . spare . . ."

Soames closed the door and stood propped up against it, striving to fight down the deathly sickness which assailed him. His clothes were sticking to his clammy body, and a cold perspiration was trickling down his forehead and into his eyes. The sensation at his heart was unlike anything that he had ever known; he thought that he must be dying.

The awful sounds died away . . . then a muffled disturbance drew his attention to a sort of square trap which existed high up on one wall of the room, but which admitted no light, and which hitherto had never admitted any sound. Now, in the utter darkness, he found himself listening—listening . . .

He had learnt, during his duties in Block A, that each of the minute suites was rendered sound-proof in some way, so that what took place in one would be inaudible to the occupant of the next, provided that both doors were closed. He perceived, now, that some precaution hitherto exercised continuously had been omitted tonight, and that the sounds which he could hear came from the room next to his own—the room which opened upon the corridor that he had never entered, and which now he classified, mentally, as Block B.

What did it mean?

Obviously there had been some mishap in the usually smooth conduct of Ho-Pin's catacombs. There had been a hurried outgoing in several directions . . . a search?

And by the accident of his returning an hour earlier than he was expected, he was become a witness of this incident, or of its dreadful, concluding phases. He had begun to move away from the door, but now he returned, and stood leaning against it.

That stifling room where roses shed their petals, had been opened tonight; a chill touched the very center of his being and told him so. The occupant of that room—the Minotaur of this hideous labyrinth—was at large tonight, was roaming the passages about him, was perhaps outside his very door. . . .

Dull moaning sounds reached him through the trap. He realized that if he had the courage to cross the room, stand upon a chair and place his ear to the wall, he might be able to detect more of what was passing in the next apartment. But craven fear held him in its grip, and in vain he strove to shake it off. Trembling wildly, he stood with his back to the door, whilst muttered words, and moans, ever growing fainter, reached him from beyond. A voice, a harsh, guttural voice—surely not that of Ho-Pin—was audible, above the moaning.

For two minutes—three minutes—four minutes—he stood there, tottering on the brink of insensibility, then . . . a faint sound—a new sound,—drew his gaze across the room, and up to the corner where the trap was situated.

A very dim light was dawning there; he could just detect the outline of an opening—a half-light breaking the otherwise impenetrable darkness.

He felt that his capacity for fear was strained to its utmost; that he could support nothing more, yet a new horror was in store for him; for, as he watched that gray patch, in it, as in a frame, a black silhouette appeared—the silhouette of a human head . . . a woman's head!

Soames convulsively clenched his jaws, for his teeth were beginning to chatter.

A whistle, an eerie, minor whistle, subscribed the ultimate touch of terror to the night. The silhouette disappeared, and, shortly afterwards, the gray luminance. A faint click told of some shutter being fastened; complete silence reigned.

Soames groped his way to the bed and fell weakly upon it, half lying down and burying his face in the pillow. For how long, he had no idea, but for some considerable time, he remained so, fighting to regain sufficient self-possession to lie to Ho-Pin, who sooner or later must learn of his return.

At last he managed to sit up. He was not trembling quite so wildly, but he still suffered from a deathly sickness. A faint streak of light from the corridor outside shone under his door. As he noted it, it was joined by a second streak, forming a triangle.

There was a very soft rasping of metal. Someone was opening the door!

Soames lay back upon the bed. This time he was past further panic and come to a stage of sickly apathy. He lay, now, because he could not sit upright, because stark horror had robbed him of physical strength, and had drained the well of his emotions dry.

Gradually—so that the operation seemed to occupy an interminable time, the door opened, and in the opening a figure appeared.

The switch clicked, and the room was flooded with electric light.

Ho-Pin stood watching him.

Soames—in his eyes that indescribable expression seen in the eyes of a bird placed in a cobra's den—met the Chinaman's gaze. This gaze was no different from that which habitually he directed upon the people of the catacombs. His yellow face was set in the same mirthless smile, and his eyebrows were raised interrogatively. For the space of ten seconds, he stood watching the man on the bed. Then—

"You wreturn vewry soon, Mr. Soames?" he said, softly.

Soames groaned like a dying man, whispering:

"I was . . . taken ill—very ill."

"So you wreturn befowre the time awranged for you?"

His metallic voice was sunk in a soothing hiss. He smiled steadily: he betrayed no emotion.

"Yes . . . sir," whispered Soames, his hair clammily adhering to his brow and beads of perspiration trickling slowly down his nose.

"And when you wreturn, you see and you hear—stwrange things, Mr. Soames?"

Soames, who was in imminent danger of becoming physically ill, gulped noisily.

"No, sir," he whispered,—tremulously, "I've been—in here all the time."

Ho-Pin nodded, slowly and sympathetically, but never removed the glittering eyes from the face of the man on the bed.

"So you hear nothing, and see nothing?"

The words were spoken even more softly than he had spoken hitherto.

"Nothing," protested Soames. He suddenly began to tremble anew, and his trembling rattled the bed. "I have been—very ill indeed, sir."

Ho-Pin nodded again slowly, and with deep sympathy.

"Some medicine shall be sent to you, Mr. Soames," he said.

He turned and went out slowly, closing the door behind him.

XX

ABRAHAM LEVINSKY BUTTS IN

At about the time that this conversation was taking place in Ho-Pin's catacombs, Detective-Inspector Dunbar and Detective-Sergeant Sowerby were joined by a third representative of New Scotland Yard at the appointed spot by the dock gates. This was Stringer, the detective to whom was assigned the tracing of the missing Soames; and he loomed up through the rain-mist, a glistening but dejected figure.

"Any luck?" inquired Sowerby, sepulchrally.

Stringer, a dark and morose looking man, shook his head.

"I've beaten up every 'Chink' in Wapping and Limehouse, I should reckon," he said, plaintively. "They're all as innocent as babes unborn. You can take it from me: Chinatown hasn't got a murder on its conscience at present. *Brr*! it's a beastly night. Suppose we have one?"

Dunbar nodded, and the three wet investigators walked back for some little distance in silence, presently emerging via a narrow, dark, uninviting alleyway into West India Dock Road. A brilliantly lighted hostelry proved to be their objective, and there, in a quiet corner of the deserted billiard room, over their glasses, they discussed this mysterious case, which at first had looked so simple of solution if only because it offered so many unusual features, but which, the deeper they probed, merely revealed fresh complications.

"The business of those Fry people, in Scotland, was a rotten disappointment," said Dunbar, suddenly. "They were merely paid by the late Mrs. Vernon to re-address letters to a little newspaper shop in Knightsbridge, where an untraceable boy used to call for them! Martin has just reported this evening. Perth wires for instructions, but it's a dead-end, I'm afraid."

"You know," said Sowerby, fishing a piece of cork from the brown froth of a fine example by Guinness, "to my mind our hope's in Soames; and if we want to find Soames, to my mind we want to look, not east, but west."

"Hear, hear!" concorded Stringer, gloomily sipping hot rum.

"It seems to me," continued Sowerby, "that Limehouse is about the last place in the world a man like Soames would think of hiding in."

"It isn't where he'll be *thinking* of hiding," snapped Dunbar, turning his fierce eyes upon the last speaker. "You can't seem to get the idea out of your head, Sowerby, that Soames is an independent agent. He *isn't* an independent agent. He's only the servant; and through the servant we hope to find the master."

"But why in the east-end?" came the plaintive voice of Stringer; "for only one reason, that I can see—because Max says that there's a Chinaman in the case."

"There's opium in the case, isn't there?" said Dunbar, adding more water to his whisky, "and where there's opium there is pretty frequently a Chinaman."

"But to my mind," persisted Sowerby, his eyebrows drawn together in a frown of concentration, "the place where Mrs. Vernon used to get the opium was the place we raided in Gillingham Street."

"Nurse Proctor's!" cried Stringer, banging his fist on the table. "Exactly my idea! There may have been a Chinaman concerned in the management of the Gillingham Street stunt, or there may not, but I'll swear that was where the opium was supplied. In fact I don't think that there's any doubt about it. Medical evidence (opinions differed a bit, certainly) went to show that she had been addicted to opium for some years. Other evidence—you got it yourself, Inspector—went to show that she came from Gillingham Street on the night of the murder. Gillingham Street crowd vanished like a beautiful dream before we had time to nab them! What more do you want? What are we up to, messing about in Limehouse and Wapping?"

Sowerby partook of a long drink and turned his eyes upon Dunbar, awaiting the inspector's reply.

"You both have the wrong idea!" said Dunbar, deliberately; "you are all wrong! You seem to be under the impression that if we could lay our hands upon the missing staff of the so-called Nursing Home, we should find the assassin to be one of the crowd. It doesn't follow at all. For a long time, you, Sowerby,"—he turned his tawny eyes upon the sergeant—"had the idea that Soames was the murderer, and I'm not sure that you have got rid of it yet! You, Stringer, appear to think that Nurse Proctor is responsible. Upon my word, you are a hopeless pair! Suppose Soames had nothing whatever to do with the matter, but merely realized that he could not prove an alibi? Wouldn't *you* bolt? I put it to you."

Sowerby stared hard, and Stringer scratched his chin, reflectively.

"The same reasoning applies to the Gillingham Street people," continued Dunbar. "We haven't the slightest idea of *their* whereabouts because we don't even know who they were; but we do know something about Soames, and we're looking for him, not because we think he did the murder, but because we think he can tell us who did."

"Which brings us back to the old point," interrupted Stringer, softly beating his fist upon the table at every word; "why are we looking for Soames in the east-end?"

"Because," replied Dunbar, "we're working on the theory that Soames, though actually not accessory to the crime, was in the pay of those who were . . ."

"Well?"—Stringer spoke the word eagerly, his eyes upon the inspector's face.

"And those who *were* accessory,"—continued Dunbar, "were servants of Mr. King."

"Ah!" Stringer brought his fist down with a bang—"Mr. King! That's where I am in the dark, and where Sowerby, here, is in the dark." He bent forward over the table. "Who the devil is Mr. King?"

Dunbar twirled his whisky glass between his fingers.

"We don't know," he replied quietly, "but Soames does, in all probability; and that's why we're looking for Soames."

"Is it why we're looking in Limehouse?" persisted Stringer, the argumentative.

"It is," snapped Dunbar. "We have only got one Chinatown worthy of the name, in London, and that's not ten minutes' walk from here."

"Chinatown—yes," said Sowerby, his red face glistening with excitement; "but why look for Mr. King in Chinatown?"

"Because," replied Dunbar, lowering his voice, "Mr. King in all probability is a Chinaman."

"Who says so?" demanded Stringer.

"Max says so . . ."

"Max!"—again Stringer beat his fist upon the table. "Now we have got to it! We're working, then, not on our own theories, but on those of Max?"

Dunbar's sallow face flushed slightly, and his eyes seemed to grow brighter.

"Mr. Gaston Max obtained information in Paris," he said, "which he placed, unreservedly, at my disposal. We went into the matter thoroughly, with the result that our conclusions were identical. A certain Mr. King is at the bottom of this mystery, and, in all probability, Mr. King is a Chinaman. Do I make myself clear?"

Sowerby and Stringer looked at one another, perplexedly. Each man finished his drink in silence. Then:

"What took place in Paris?" began Sowerby.

There was an interruption. A stooping figure in a shabby, black frock-coat, the figure of a man who wore a dilapidated bowler pressed down upon his ears, who had a greasy, Semitic countenance, with a scrubby, curling, sandy colored beard, sparse as the vegetation of a desert, appeared at Sowerby's elbow.

He carried a brimming pewter pot. This he set down upon a corner of the table, depositing himself in a convenient chair and pulling out a very dirty looking letter from an inside pocket. He smoothed it carefully. He peered, little-eyed, from the frowning face of Dunbar to the surprised countenance of Sowerby, and smiled with native amiability at the dangerous-looking Stringer.

"Excuthe me," he said, and his propitiatory smile was expansive and dazzling, "excuthe me buttin' in like thith. It theemth rude, I know—it doth theem rude; but the fact of the matter ith I'm a tailor—thath's my pithneth, a tailor. When I thay a tailor, I really mean a breecheth-maker—tha'th what I mean, a breecheth-maker. Now thethe timeth ith very hard timeth for breecheth-makerth."

Dunbar finished his whisky, and quietly replaced the glass upon the table, looking from Sowerby to Stringer with unmistakable significance. Stringer emptied his glass of rum, and Sowerby disposed of his stout.

"I got thith letter lath night," continued the breeches-maker, bending forward confidentially over the table. (The document looked at least twelve months old.) "I got thith letter latht night with thethe three fiverth in it; and not havin' no friendth in London—I'm an American thitithen, by birth,—Levinthky, my name ith—Abraham Levinthky—I'm a Noo Englander. Well, not havin' no friendth in London, and theein' you three gentlemen thittin' here, I took the liberty . . ."

Dunbar stood up, glared at Levinsky, and stalked out of the billiard-room, followed by his equally indignant satellites. Having gained the outer door:

"Of all the blasted impudence!" he said, turning to Sowerby and Stringer; but there was a glint of merriment in the fierce eyes. "Can you beat that? Did you tumble to his game?"

Sowerby stared at Stringer, and Stringer stared at Sowerby.

"Except," began the latter in a voice hushed with amazement, "that he's got the coolest cheek of any mortal being I ever met."

Dunbar's grim face relaxed, and he laughed boyishly, his square shoulders shaking.

"He was leading up to the confidence trick!" he said, between laughs. "Damn it all, man, it was the old confidence trick! The idea of a confidence-merchant spreading out his wares before three C. I. D. men!"

He was choking with laughter again; and now, Sowerby and Stringer having looked at one another for a moment, the surprised pair joined him in his merriment. They turned up their collars and went out into the rain, still laughing.

"That man," said Sowerby, as they walked across to the stopping place of the electric trains, "is capable of calling on the Commissioner and asking him to 'find the lady'!"

XXI

THE STUDIO IN SOHO

Certainly, such impudence as that of Mr. Levinsky is rare even in east-end London, and it may be worth while to return to the corner of the billiard-room and to study more closely this remarkable man.

He was sitting where the detectives had left him, and although their departure might have been supposed to have depressed him, actually it had had a contrary effect; he was chuckling with amusement, and, between his chuckles, addressing himself to the contents of the pewter with every mark of appreciation. Three gleaming golden teeth on the lower row, and one glittering canine, made a dazzling show every time that he smiled; he was a very greasy and a very mirthful Hebrew.

Finishing his tankard of ale, he shuffled out into the street, the line of his bent shoulders running parallel with that of his hat-brim. His hat appeared to be several sizes too large for his head, and his skull was only prevented from disappearing into the capacious crown by the intervention of his ears, which, acting as brackets, supported the whole weight of the rain-sodden structure. He mounted a tram proceeding in the same direction as that which had borne off the Scotland Yard men. Quitting this at Bow Road, he shuffled into the railway station, and from Bow Road proceeded to Liverpool Street. Emerging from the station at Liverpool Street, he entered a motor-'bus bound westward.

His neighbors, inside, readily afforded him ample elbow room; and, smiling agreeably at every one, including the conductor (who resented his good-humor) and a pretty girl in the corner seat (who found it embarrassing) he proceeded to Charing Cross. Descending from the 'bus, he passed out into Leicester Square and plunged into the network of streets which complicates the map of Soho. It will be of interest to follow him.

In a narrow turning off Greek Street, and within hail of the popular Bohemian restaurants, he paused before a doorway sandwiched between a Continental newsagent's and a tiny French cafe; and, having fumbled in his greasy raiment he presently produced a key, opened the door, carefully closed it behind him, and mounted the dark stair.

On the top floor he entered a studio, boasting a skylight upon which the rain was drumming steadily and drearily. Lighting a gas burner in one corner of the place which bore no evidence of being used for its legitimate purpose—he entered a little adjoining dressing-room. Hot and cold water were laid on there, and a large zinc bath stood upon the floor. With the aid of an enamel bucket, Mr. Abraham Levinsky filled the bath.

Leaving him to his ablutions, let us glance around the dressing-room. Although there was no easel in the studio, and no indication of artistic activity, the dressing-room was well stocked with costumes. Two huge dress-baskets were piled in one corner, and their contents hung upon hooks around the three available walls. A dressing table, with a triplicate mirror and a suitably shaded light, presented a spectacle reminiscent less of a model's dressing-room than of an actor's.

At the expiration of some twenty-five minutes, the door of this dressing-room opened; and although Abraham Levinsky had gone in, Abraham Levinsky did not come out!

Carefully flicking a particle of ash from a fold of his elegant, silk-lined cloak, a most distinguished looking gentleman stepped out onto the bleak and dirty studio. He wore, in addition to a graceful cloak, which was lined with silk of cardinal red, a soft black hat, rather wide brimmed and dented in a highly artistic manner, and irreproachable evening clothes; his linen was immaculate; and no valet in London could have surpassed the perfect knotting of his tie. His pearl studs were elegant and valuable; and a single eyeglass was swung about his neck by a thin, gold chain. The white gloves, which fitted perfectly, were new; and if the glossy boots were rather long in the toe-cap from an English point of view, the gold-headed malacca cane which the newcomer carried was quite de rigueur.

The strong clean-shaven face calls for no description here; it was the face of M. Gaston Max.

M. Max, having locked the study door, and carefully tried it to make certain of its security, descended the stairs. He peeped out cautiously into the street ere setting foot upon the pavement; but no one was in sight at the moment, and he emerged quickly, closing the door behind him, and taking shelter under the newsagent's awning. The rain continued its steady downpour, but M. Max stood there softly humming a little French melody until a taxi-cab crawled into view around the Greek Street corner.

He whistled shrilly through his teeth—the whistle of a gamin; and the cabman, glancing up and perceiving him, pulled around into the turning, and drew up by the awning.

M. Max entered the cab.

"To Frascati's," he directed.

The cabman backed out into Greek Street and drove off. This was the hour when the theaters were beginning to eject their throngs, and outside one of them, where a popular comedy had celebrated its three-hundred-and-fiftieth performance, the press of cabs and private cars was so great that M. Max found himself delayed within sight of the theater foyer.

Those patrons of the comedy who had omitted to order vehicles or who did not possess private conveyances, found themselves in a quandary tonight, and amongst those thus unfortunately situated, M. Max, watching the scene with interest, detected a lady whom he knew—none other than the delightful American whose conversation had enlivened his recent journey from Paris—Miss Denise Ryland. She was accompanied by a charming companion, who, although she was wrapped up in a warm theater cloak, seemed to be shivering disconsolately as she and her friend watched the interminable stream of vehicles filing up before the theater, and cutting them off from any chance of obtaining a cab for themselves.

M. Max acted promptly.

"Drive into that side turning!" he directed the cabman, leaning out of the window. The cabman followed his directions, and M. Max, heedless of the inclement weather, descended from the cab, dodged actively between the head lamps of a big Mercedes and the tail-light of a taxi, and stood bowing before the two ladies, his hat pressed to his bosom with one gloved hand, the other, ungloved, resting upon the gold knob of the malacca.

"Why!" cried Miss Ryland, "if it isn't . . . M. Gaston! My dear . . . M. Gaston! Come under the awning, or"—her head was wagging furiously—"you will be . . . simply drowned."

M. Max smilingly complied.

"This is M. Gaston," said Denise Ryland, turning to her companion, "the French gentleman . . . whom I met . . . in the train from . . . Paris. This is Miss Helen Cumberly, and I know you two will get on . . . famously."

M. Max acknowledged the presentation with a few simple words which served to place the oddly met trio upon a mutually easy footing. He was, par excellence, the polished cosmopolitan man of the world.

"Fortunately I saw your dilemma," he explained. "I have a cab on the corner yonder, and it is entirely at your service."

"Now that . . . is real good of you," declared Denise Ryland. "I think you're . . . a brick."

"But, my dear Miss Ryland!" cried Helen, "we cannot possibly deprive M. Gaston of his cab on a night like this!"

"I had hoped," said the Frenchman, bowing gallantly, "that this most happy reunion might not be allowed to pass uncelebrated. Tell me if I intrude upon other plans, because I am speaking selfishly; but I was on my way to a lonely supper, and apart from the great pleasure which your company would afford me, you would be such very good Samaritans if you would join me."

Helen Cumberly, although she was succumbing rapidly to the singular fascination of M. Max, exhibited a certain hesitancy. She was no stranger to Bohemian customs, and if the distinguished Frenchman had been an old friend of her companion's, she should have accepted without demur; but she knew that the acquaintance had commenced in a Continental railway train, and her natural prudence instinctively took up a brief for the prosecution. But Denise Ryland had other views.

"My dear girl," she said, "you are not going to be so . . . crack-brained . . . as to stand here . . . arguing and contracting . . . rheumatism, lumbago . . . and other absurd complaints . . . when you know *perfectly* well that we had already arranged to go . . . to supper!" She turned to the smiling Max. "This girl needs . . . *dragging* out of . . . her morbid self . . . M. Gaston! We'll accept . . . your cab, on the distinct . . . understanding that *you* are to accept *our* invitation . . . to supper."

M. Max bowed agreeably.

"By all means let *my* cab take us to *your* supper," he said, laughing.

XXII

M. MAX MOUNTS CAGLIOSTRO'S STAIRCASE

At a few minutes before midnight, Helen Cumberly and Denise Ryland, escorted by the attentive Frenchman, arrived at Palace Mansions. Any distrust which Helen had experienced at first was replaced now by the esteem which every one of discrimination (criminals excluded) formed of M. Max. She perceived in him a very exquisite gentleman, and although the acquaintance was but one hour old, counted him a friend. Denise Ryland was already quite at home in the Cumberly household, and she insisted that Dr. Cumberly would be deeply mortified should M. Gaston take his departure without making his acquaintance. Thus it came about that M. Gaston Max was presented (as "M. Gaston") to Dr. Cumberly.

Cumberly, who had learned to accept men and women upon his daughter's estimate, welcomed the resplendent Parisian hospitably; the warm, shaded lights made convivial play in the amber deeps of the decanters, and the cigars had a fire-side fragrance which M. Max found wholly irresistible.

The ladies being momentarily out of ear-shot, M. Gaston glancing rapidly about him, said: "May I beg a favor, Dr. Cumberly?"

"Certainly, M. Gaston," replied the physician—he was officiating at the syphon. "Say when."

"When!" said Max. "I should like to see you in Harley Street tomorrow morning."

Cumberly glanced up oddly. "Nothing wrong, I hope?"

"Oh, not professionally," smiled Max; "or perhaps I should say only semi-professionally. Can you spare me ten minutes?"

"My book is rather full in the morning, I believe," said Cumberly, frowning thoughtfully, "and without consulting it—which, since it is in Harley Street, is impossible—I scarcely know when I shall be at liberty. Could we not lunch together?"

Max blew a ring of smoke from his lips and watched it slowly dispersing.

"For certain reasons," he replied, and his odd American accent became momentarily more perceptible, "I should prefer that my visit had the appearance of being a professional one."

Cumberly was unable to conceal his surprise, but assuming that his visitor had good reason for the request, he replied after a moment's reflection:

"I should propose, then, that you come to Harley Street at, shall we say, 9.30? My earliest professional appointment is at 10. Will that inconvenience you?"

"Not at all," Max assured him; "it will suit me admirably."

With that the matter dropped for the time, since Helen and her new friend now reentered; and although Helen's manner was markedly depressed, Miss Ryland energetically turned the conversation upon the subject of the play which they had witnessed that evening.

M. Max, when he took his departure, found that the rain had ceased, and accordingly he walked up Whitehall, interesting himself in those details of midnight London life so absorbing to the visitor, though usually overlooked by the resident.

Punctually at half-past nine, a claret-colored figure appeared in sedate Harley Street. M. Gaston Max pressed the bell above which appeared:

DR. BRUCE CUMBERLY.

He was admitted by Garnham, who attended there daily during the hours when Dr. Cumberly was visible to patients, and presently found himself in the consulting room of the physician.

"Good morning, M. Gaston!" said Cumberly, rising and shaking his visitor by the hand. "Pray sit down, and let us get to business. I can give you a clear half-hour."

Max, by way of reply, selected a card from one of the several divisions of his card-case, and placed it on the table. Cumberly glanced at it and started slightly, turning and surveying his visitor with a new interest.

"You are M. Gaston Max!" he said, fixing his gray eyes upon the face of the man before him. "I understood my daughter to say . . ."

Max waved his hands, deprecatingly.

"It is in the first place to apologize," he explained, "that I am here. I was presented to your daughter in the name of Gaston—which is at least part of my own name—and because other interests were involved I found myself in the painful position of being presented to you under the same false colors . . ."

"Oh, dear, dear!" began Cumberly. "But—"

"Ah! I protest, it is true," continued Max with an inimitable movement of the shoulder; "and I regret it; but in my profession . . ."

"Which you adorn, monsieur," injected Cumberly.

"Many thanks—but in my profession these little annoyances sometimes occur. At the earliest suitable occasion, I shall reveal myself to Miss Cumberly and Miss Ryland, but at present,"—he spread his palms eloquently, and raised his eyebrows—"morbleu! it is impossible."

"Certainly; I quite understand that. Your visit to London is a professional one? I am more than delighted to have met you, M. Max; your work on criminal anthroposcopy has an honored place on my shelves."

Again M. Max delivered himself of the deprecatory wave.

"You cover me with confusion," he protested; "for I fear in that book I have intruded upon sciences of which I know nothing, and of which you know much."

"On the contrary, you have contributed to those sciences, M. max," declared the physician; "and now, do I understand that the object of your call this morning?"

"In the first place it was to excuse myself—but in the second place, I come to ask your help."

He seated himself in a deep armchair—bending forward, and fixing his dark, penetrating eyes upon the physician. Cumberly, turning his own chair slightly, evinced the greatest interest in M. Max's disclosures.

"If you have been in Paris lately," continued the detective, "you will possibly have availed yourself of the opportunity—since another may not occur—of visiting the house of the famous magician, Cagliostro, on the corner of Rue St. Claude, and Boulevard Beaumarchais . . ."

"I have not been in Paris for over two years," said Cumberly, "nor was I aware that a house of that celebrated charlatan remained extant."

"Ah! Dr. Cumberly, your judgment of Cagliostro is a harsh one. We have no time for such discussion now, but I should like to debate with you this question: was Cagliostro a charlatan? However, the point is this: Owing to alterations taking place in the Boulevard Beaumarchais, some of the end houses in Rue St. Claude are being pulled down, among them Number 1, formerly occupied by the Comte de Cagliostro. At the time that the work commenced, I availed myself of a little leisure to visit that house, once so famous. I was very much interested, and found it fascinating to walk up the Grande Staircase where so many historical personages once walked to consult the seer. But great as was my interest in the apartments of Cagliostro, I was even more interested in one of the apartments in a neighboring house, into which—quite accidentally, you understand—I found myself looking."

XXIII

RAID IN THE RUE ST. CLAUDE

"I perceived," said M. Gaston Max, "that owing to the progress of the work of demolition, and owing to the carelessness of the people in charge—nom d'un nom! they were careless, those!—I was able, from a certain point, to look into a small room fitted up in a way very curious. There was a sort of bunk somewhat similar to that in a steamer berth, and the walls were covered with paper of a Chinese pattern most bizarre. No one was in the room when I first perceived it, but I had not been looking in for many moments before a Chinaman entered and closed the shutters. He was hasty, this one.

"Eh bien! I had seen enough. I perceived that my visit to the house of Cagliostro had been dictated by a good little angel. It happened that for many months I had been in quest of the headquarters of a certain group which I knew, beyond any tiny doubt, to have its claws deep in Parisian society. I refer to an opium syndicate . . ."

Dr. Cumberly started and seemed about to speak; but he restrained himself, bending forward and awaiting the detective's next words with even keener interest than hitherto.

"I had been trying—all vainly—to trace the source from which the opium was obtained, and the place where it was used. I have devoted much attention to the subject, and have spent some twelve months in the opium provinces of China, you understand. I know how insidious a thing it is, this opium, and how dreadful a curse it may become when it gets a hold upon a community. I was formerly engaged upon a most sensational case in San Francisco; and the horrors of the discoveries which we made there—the American police and myself—have remained with me ever since. Pardieu! I cannot forget them! Therefore when I learnt that an organized attempt was being made to establish elaborate opium dens upon a most up-to-date plan, in Paris, I exerted myself to the utmost to break up this scheme in its infancy . . ."

Dr. Cumberly was hanging upon every word.

"Apart from the physical and moral ruin attendant upon the vice," continued Max, "the methods of this particular organization have brought financial ruin to many." He shook his finger at Dr. Cumberly as if to emphasize his certainty upon this point. "I will not go into particulars now, but there is a system of wholesale robbery—sapristi! of most ingenious brigandage—being practised by this group. Therefore I congratulated myself upon the inspiration which had led me to mount Cagliostro's staircase. The way in which these people had conducted their sinister trade from so public a spot as this was really wonderful, but I had already learned to respect the ingenuity of the group, or of the man at the head of it. I wasted no time; not I! We raided the house that evening . . ."

"And what did you find?" asked Dr. Cumberly, eagerly.

"We found this establishment elaborately fitted, and the whole of the fittings were American. Eh bien! This confirmed me in my belief that the establishment was a branch of the wealthy concern I have mentioned in San Francisco. There was also a branch in New York, apparently. We found six or eight people in the place in various stages of coma; and I cannot tell you their names because—among them, were some well-known in the best society . . ."

"Good Heavens, M. Max, you surprise and shock me!"

"What I tell you is but the truth. We apprehended two low fellows who acted as servants sometimes in the place. We had records of both of them at the Bureau. And there was also a woman belonging to the same class. None of these seemed to me very important, but we were fortunate enough to capture, in addition, a Chinaman—Sen—and a certain Madame Jean—the latter the principal of the establishment!"

"What! a woman?"

"Morbleu! a woman—exactly! You are surprised? Yes; and I was surprised, but full inquiry convinced me that Madame Jean was the chief of staff. We had conducted the raid at night, of course, and because of the big names, we hushed it up. We can do these things in Paris so much more easily than is possible here in London." He illustrated, delivering a kick upon the person of an imaginary malefactor. "Cochon! Va!" he shrugged. "It is finished!

"The place was arranged with Oriental magnificence. The reception-room—if I can so term that apartment—was like the scene of Rimsky Korsakov's Sheherezade; I could see that very heavy charges were made at this establishment. I will not bore you with further particulars, but I will tell you of my disappointment."

"Your disappointment?"

"Yes, I was disappointed. True, I had brought about the closing of that house, but of the huge sums of money fraudulently obtained from victims, I could find no trace in the accounts of Madame Jean. She defied me with silence, simply declining to give any account of herself beyond admitting that she conducted an hotel at which opium might be smoked if desired. Blagueur! Sen, the Chinaman, who professed to speak nothing but Chinese—ah! cochon!—was equally a difficult case, Nom d'un nom! I was in despair, for apart from frauds connected with the concern, I had more than small suspicions that at least one death— that of a wealthy banker—could be laid at the doors of the establishment in Rue St. Claude."

Dr. Cumberly bent yet lower, watching the speaker's face.

"A murder!" he whispered.

"I do not say so," replied Max, "but it certainly might have been. The case then must, indeed, have ended miserably, as far as I was concerned, if I had not chanced upon a letter which the otherwise prudent Madame Jean had forgotten to destroy. Triomphe! It was a letter of instruction, and definitely it proved that she was no more than a kind of glorified concierge, and that the chief of the opium group was in London."

"Undoubtedly in London. There was no address on the letter, and no date, and it was curiously signed: Mr. King."

"Mr. King!"

Dr. Cumberly rose slowly from his chair, and took a step toward M. Max.

"You are interested?" said the detective, and shrugged his shoulders, whilst his mobile mouth shaped itself in a grim smile. "Pardieu! I knew you would be! Acting upon another clue which the letter—priceless letter—contained, I visited the Credit Lyonnais. I discovered that an account had been opened there by Mr. Henry Leroux of London on behalf of his wife, Mira Leroux, to the amount of a thousand pounds."

"A thousand pounds—really!" cried Dr. Cumberly, drawing his heavy brows together—"as much as that?"

"Certainly. It was for a thousand pounds," repeated Max, "and the whole of that amount had been drawn out."

"The whole thousand?"

"The whole thousand; nom d'un p'tit bonhomme! The whole thousand! Acting, as I have said, upon the information in this always priceless letter, I confronted Madame Jean and the manager of the bank with each other. Morbleu! 'This,' he said, 'is Mira Leroux of London!'"

"What!" cried Cumberly, seemingly quite stupefied by this last revelation.

Max spread wide his palms, and the flexible lips expressed sympathy with the doctor's stupefaction.

"It is as I tell you," he continued. "This Madame Jean had been posing as Mrs. Leroux, and in some way, which I was unable to understand, her signature had been accepted by the Credit Lyonnais. I examined the specimen signature which had been forwarded to them by the London County and Suburban Bank, and I perceived, at once, that it was not a case of common forgery. The signatures were identical . . ."

"Therefore," said Cumberly, and he was thinking of Henry Leroux, whom Fate delighted in buffeting—"therefore, the Credit Lyonnais is not responsible?"

"Most decidedly not responsible," agreed Max. "So you see I now have two reasons for coming to London: one, to visit the London County and Suburban Bank, and the other to find . . . Mr. King. The first part of my mission I have performed successfully; but the second . . ." again he shrugged, and the lines of his mouth were humorous.

Dr. Cumberly began to walk up and down the carpet.

"Poor Leroux!" he muttered—"poor Leroux."

"Ah! poor Leroux, indeed," said Max. "He is so typical a victim of this most infernal group!"

"What!" Dr. Cumberly turned in his promenade and stared at the detective—"he's not the only one?"

"My dear sir," said Max, gently, "the victims of Mr. King are truly as the sands of Arabia."

"Good heavens!" muttered Dr. Cumberly; "good heavens!"

"I came immediately to London," continued Max, "and presented myself at New Scotland Yard. There I discovered that my inquiry was complicated by a ghastly crime which had been committed in the flat of Mr. Leroux; but I learned, also, that Mr. King was concerned in this crime—his name had been found upon a scrap of paper clenched in the murdered woman's hand!"

"I was present when it was found," said Dr. Cumberly.

"I know you were," replied Max. "In short, I discovered that the Palace Mansions murder case was my case, and that my case was the Palace Mansions case. Eh bien! the mystery of the Paris draft did not detain me long. A call upon the manager of the London County and Suburban Bank at Charing Cross revealed to me the whole plot. The real Mrs. Leroux had never visited that bank; it was Madame Jean, posing as Mrs. Leroux, who went there and wrote the specimen signature, accompanied by a certain Soames, a butler . . ."

"I know him!" said Dr. Cumberly, grimly, "the blackguard!"

"Truly a blackguard, truly a big, dirty blackguard! But it is such canaille as this that Mr. King discovers and uses for his own ends. Paris society, I know for a fact; has many such a cankerworm in its heart. Oh! it is a big case, a very big case. Poor Mr. Leroux being confined to his bed—ah! I pity him—I took the opportunity to visit his flat in Palace Mansions with Inspector Dunbar, and I obtained further evidence showing how the conspiracy had been conducted; yes. For instance, Dunbar's notebook showed me that Mr. Leroux was accustomed to receive letters from Mrs. Leroux whilst she was supposed to be in Paris. I actually discovered some of those letters, and they bore no dates. This, if they came from a woman, was not remarkable, but, upon one of them I found something that *was* remarkable. It was still in its envelope, you must understand, this letter, its envelope bearing the Paris post-mark. But impressed upon the paper I discovered a second post-mark, which, by means of a simple process, and the use of a magnifying glass, I made out to be Bow, East!"

"What!"

"Do you understand? This letter, and others doubtless, had been enclosed in an envelope and despatched to Paris from Bow, East? In short, Mrs. Leroux wrote those letters before she left London; Soames never posted them, but handed them over to some representative of Mr. King; this other, in turn, posted them to Madame Jean in Paris! Morbleu! these are clever rogues! This which I was fortunate enough to discover had been on top, you understand, this billet, and the outer envelope being very heavily stamped, that below retained the impress of the post-mark."

"Poor Leroux!" said Cumberly again, with suppressed emotion. "That unsuspecting, kindly soul has been drawn into the meshes of this conspiracy. How they have been wound around him, until . . ."

"He knows the truth about his wife?" asked Max, suddenly glancing up at the physician, "that she is not in Paris?"

"I, myself, broke the painful news to him," replied Cumberly—"after a consultation with Miss Ryland and my daughter. I considered it my duty to tell him, but I cannot disguise from myself that it hastened, if it did not directly occasion, his breakdown."

"Yes, yes," said Max; "we have been very fortunate however in diverting the attention of the press from the absence of Mrs. Leroux throughout this time. Nom d'un nom! Had they got to know about the scrap of paper found in the dead woman's hand, I fear that this would have been impossible."

"I do not doubt that it would have been impossible, knowing the London press," replied Dr. Cumberly, "but I, too, am glad that it has been achieved; for in the light of your Paris discoveries, I begin at last to understand."

"You were not Mrs. Leroux's medical adviser?"

"I was not," replied Cumberly, glancing sharply at Max. "Good heavens, to think that I had never realized the truth!"

"It is not so wonderful at all. Of course, as I have seen from the evidence which you gave to the police, you knew that Mrs. Vernon was addicted to the use of opium?"

"It was perfectly evident," replied Cumberly; "painfully evident. I will not go into particulars, but her entire constitution was undermined by the habit. I may add, however, that I did not associate the vice with her violent end, except . . ."

"Ah!" interrupted Max, shaking his finger at the physician, "you are coming to the point upon which you disagreed with the divisional surgeon! Now, it is an important point. You are of opinion that the injection in Mrs. Vernon's shoulder—which could not have been self-administered . . ."

"She was not addicted to the use of the needle," interrupted Cumberly; "she was an opium *smoker*."

"Quite so, quite so," said Max: "it makes the point all the more clear. You are of opinion that this injection was made at least eight hours before the woman's death?"

"At least eight hours—yes."

"Eh bien!" said Max; "and have you had extensive experience of such injections?"

Dr. Cumberly stared at him in some surprise.

"In a general way," he said, "a fair number of such cases have come under my notice; but it chances that one of my patients, a regular patient—is addicted to the vice."

"Injections?"

"Only as a makeshift. He has periodical bouts of opium smoking—what I may term deliberate debauches."

"Ah!" Max was keenly interested. "This patient is a member of good society?"

"He's a member of Parliament," replied Cumberly, a faint, humorous glint creeping into his gray eyes; "but, of course, that is not an answer to your question! Yes, he is of an old family, and is engaged to the daughter of a peer."

"Dr. Cumberly," said Max, "in a case like the present—apart from the fact that the happiness—pardieu! the life—of one of your own friends is involved . . . should you count it a breach of professional etiquette to divulge the name of that patient?"

It was a disturbing question; a momentous question for a fashionable physician to be called upon to answer thus suddenly. Dr. Cumberly, who had resumed his promenade of the carpet, stopped with his back to M. Max, and stared out of the window into Harley Street.

M. Max, a man of refined susceptibilities, came to his aid, diplomatically.

"It is perhaps overmuch to ask you," he said. "I can settle the problem in a more simple manner. Inspector Dunbar will ask you for this gentleman's name, and you, as witness in the case, cannot refuse to give it."

"I can refuse until I stand in the witness-box!" replied Cumberly, turning, a wry smile upon his face.

"With the result," interposed Max, "that the ends of justice might be defeated, and the wrong man hanged!"

"True," said Cumberly; "I am splitting hairs. It is distinctly a breach of professional etiquette, nevertheless, and I cannot disguise the fact from myself. However, since the knowledge will never go any further, and since tremendous issues are at stake, I will give you the name of my opium patient. It is Sir Brian Malpas!"

"I am much indebted to you, Dr. Cumberly," said Max; "a thousand thanks;" but in his eyes there was a far-away look. "Malpas—Malpas! Where in this case have I met with the name of Malpas?"

"Inspector Dunbar may possibly have mentioned it to you in reference to the evidence of Mr. John Exel, M. P. Mr. Exel, you may remember . . ."

"I have it!" cried Max; "Nom d'un nom! I have it! It was from Sir Brian Malpas that he had parted at the corner of Victoria Street on the night of the murder, is it not so?"

"Your memory is very good, M. Max!"

"Then Mr. Exel is a personal friend of Sir Brian Malpas?

"Excellent! Kismet aids me still! I come to you hoping that you may be acquainted with the constitution of Mrs. Leroux, but no! behold me disappointed in this. Then—morbleu! among your patients I find a possible client of the opium syndicate!"

"What! Malpas? Good God! I had not thought of that! Of course, he must retire somewhere from the ken of society to indulge in these opium orgies . . ."

"Quite so. I have hopes. Since it would never do for Sir Brian Malpas to know who I am and what I seek, a roundabout introduction is provided by kindly Providence—Ah! that good little angel of mine!—in the person of Mr. John Exel, M. P."

"I will introduce you to Mr. Exel with pleasure."

"Eh bien! Let it be arranged as soon as possible," said M. Max. "To Mr. John Exel I will be, as to Miss Ryland (morbleu! I hate me!) and Miss Cumberly (pardieu! I loathe myself!), M. Gaston! It is ten o'clock, and already I hear your first patient ringing at the front-door bell. Good morning, Dr. Cumberly."

Dr. Cumberly grasped his hand cordially.

"Good morning, M. Max!"

The famous detective was indeed retiring, when:

"M. Max!"

He turned and looked into the troubled gray eyes of Dr. Cumberly.

"You would ask me where is she—Mrs. Leroux?" he said. "My friend—I may call you my friend, may I not?—I cannot say if she is living or is dead. Some little I know of the Chinese, quite a little; nom de dieu! I hope she is dead!"

XXIV

OPIUM

Denise Ryland was lunching that day with Dr. Cumberly and his daughter at Palace Mansions; and as was usually the case when this trio met, the conversation turned upon the mystery.

"I have just seen Leroux," said the physician, as he took his seat, "and I have told him that he must go for a drive tomorrow. I have released him from his room, and given him the run of the place again, but until he can get right away, complete recovery is impossible. A little cheerful company might be useful, though. You might look in and see him for a while, Helen?"

Helen met her father's eyes, gravely, and replied, with perfect composure, "I will do so with pleasure. Miss Ryland will come with me."

"Suppose," said Denise Ryland, assuming her most truculent air, "you leave off . . . talking in that . . . frigid manner . . . my dear. Considering that Mira . . . Leroux and I were . . . old friends, and that you . . . are old friends of hers, too, and considering that I spend . . . my life amongst . . . people who very sensibly call . . . one another . . . by their Christian names, forget that my name is Ryland, and call me . . . Denise!"

"I should love to!" cried Helen Cumberly; "in fact, I wanted to do so the very first time I saw you; perhaps because Mira Leroux always referred to you as Denise . . ."

"May I also avail myself of the privilege?" inquired Dr. Cumberly with gravity, "and may I hope that you will return the compliment?"

"I cannot . . . do it!" declared Denise Ryland, firmly. "A doctor . . . should never be known by any other name than . . . Doctor. If I heard any one refer to my own . . . physician as Jack or . . . Bill, or Dick . . . I should lose *all* faith in him at once!"

As the lunch proceeded, Dr. Cumberly gradually grew more silent, seeming to be employed with his own thoughts; and although his daughter and Denise Ryland were discussing the very matter that engaged his own attention, he took no part in the conversation for some time. Then:

"I agree with you!" he said, suddenly, interrupting Helen; "the greatest blow of all to Leroux was the knowledge that his wife had been deceiving him."

"He invited . . . deceit!" proclaimed Denise Ryland, "by his . . . criminal neglect."

"Oh! how can you say so!" cried Helen, turning her gray eyes upon the speaker reproachfully; "he deserves—"

"He certainly deserves to know the real truth," concluded Dr. Cumberly; "but would it relieve his mind or otherwise?"

Denise Ryland and Helen looked at him in silent surprise.

"The truth?" began the latter—"Do you mean that you know— where she is . . ."

"If I knew that," replied Dr. Cumberly, "I should know everything; the mystery of the Palace Mansions murder would be a mystery no longer. But I know one thing: Mrs. Leroux's absence has nothing to do with any love affair."

"What!" exclaimed Denise Ryland. "There isn't another man . . . in the case? You can't tell me . . ."

"But I *do* tell you!" said Dr. Cumberly; "I *assure* you."

"And you have not told—Mr. Leroux?" said Helen incredulously. "You have *not* told him—although you know that the thought—of *that* is . . . ?"

"Is practically killing him? No, I have not told him yet. For—would my news act as a palliative or as an irritant?"

"That depends," pronounced Denise Ryland, "on the nature of . . . your news."

"I suppose I have no right to conceal it from him. Therefore, we will tell him today. But although, beyond doubt, his mind will be relieved upon one point, the real facts are almost, if not quite, as bad."

"I learnt, this morning," he continued, lighting a cigarette, "certain facts which, had I been half as clever as I supposed myself, I should have deduced from the data already in my possession. I was aware, of course, that the unhappy victim—Mrs. Vernon—was addicted to the use of opium, and if a tangible link were necessary, it existed in the form of the written fragment which I myself took from the dead woman's hand."

"A link!" said Denise Ryland.

"A link between Mrs. Vernon and Mrs. Leroux," explained the physician. "You see, it had never occurred to me that they knew one another."

"And did they?" questioned his daughter, eagerly.

"It is almost certain that they were acquainted, at any rate; and in view of certain symptoms, which, without giving them much consideration, I nevertheless had detected in Mrs. Leroux, I am disposed to think that the bond of sympathy which existed between them was . . ."

He seemed to hesitate, looking at his daughter, whose gray eyes were fixed upon him intently, and then at Denise Ryland, who, with her chin resting upon her hands, and her elbows propped upon the table, was literally glaring at him.

"Opium!" he said.

A look of horror began slowly to steal over Helen Cumberly's face; Denise Ryland's head commenced to sway from side to side. But neither women spoke.

"By the courtesy of Inspector Dunbar," continued Dr. Cumberly, "I have been enabled to keep in touch with the developments of the case, as you know; and he had noted as a significant fact that the late Mrs. Vernon's periodical visits to Scotland corresponded, curiously, with those of Mrs. Leroux to Paris. I don't mean in regard to date; although in one or two instances (notably Mrs. Vernon's last journey to Scotland, and that of Mrs. Leroux to Paris), there was similarity even in this particular. A certain Mr. Debnam—the late Horace Vernon's solicitor—placed an absurd construction upon this . . ."

"Do you mean," interrupted Helen in a strained voice, "that he insinuated that Mrs. Vernon . . ."

"He had an idea that she visited Leroux—yes," replied her father hastily. "It was one of those absurd and irritating theories, which, instinctively, we know to be wrong, but which, if asked for evidence, we cannot hope to *prove* to be wrong."

"It is outrageous!" cried Helen, her eyes flashing indignantly; "Mr. Debnam should be ashamed of himself!"

Dr. Cumberly smiled rather sadly.

"In this world," he said, "we have to count with the Debnams. One's own private knowledge of a man's character is not worth a brass farthing as legal evidence. But I am happy to say that Dunbar completely pooh-poohed the idea."

"I like Inspector Dunbar!" declared Helen; "he is so strong—a splendid man!"

Denise Ryland stared at her cynically, but made no remark.

"The inspector and myself," continued Dr. Cumberly, "attached altogether a different significance to the circumstances. I am pleased to tell you that Debnam's unpleasant theories are already proved fallacious; the case goes deeper, far deeper, than a mere intrigue of that kind. In short, I am now assured—I cannot, unfortunately, name the source of my new information—but I am assured, that Mrs. Leroux, as well as Mrs. Vernon, was addicted to the opium vice. . . ."

"Oh, my God! how horrible!" whispered Helen.

"A certain notorious character," resumed Dr. Cumberly.

"Soames!" snapped Denise Ryland. "Since I heard . . . that man's name I knew him for . . . a villain . . . of the worst possible . . . description . . . imaginable."

"Soames," replied Dr. Cumberly, smiling slightly, "was one of the group, beyond doubt—for I may as well explain that we are dealing with an elaborate organization; but the chief member, to whom I have referred, is a greater one than Soames. He is a certain shadowy being, known as Mr. King."

"The name on the paper!" said Helen, quickly. "But of course the police have been looking for Mr. King all along?"

"In a general way—yes; but as we have thousands of Kings in London alone, the task is a stupendous one. The information which I received this morning narrows down the search immensely; for it points to Mr. King being the chief, or president, of a sort of opium syndicate, and, furthermore, it points to his being a Chinaman."

"A Chinaman!" cried Denise and Helen together.

"It is not absolutely certain, but it is more than probable. The point is that Mrs. Leroux has not eloped with some unknown lover; she is in one of the opium establishments of Mr. King."

"Do you mean that she is detained there?" asked Helen.

"It appears to me, now, to be certain that she is. My hypothesis is that she was an habitue of this place, as also was Mrs. Vernon. These unhappy women, by means of elaborate plans, made on their behalf by the syndicate, indulged in periodical opium orgies. It was a game well worth the candle, as the saying goes, from the syndicates standpoint; for Mrs. Leroux, alone, has paid no less than a thousand pounds to the opium group!"

"A thousand pounds!" cried Denise Ryland. "You don't mean to tell me that that . . . silly fool . . . of a man, Harry Leroux . . . has allowed himself to be swindled of . . . all that money?"

"There is not the slightest doubt about it," Dr. Cumberly assured her; "he opened a credit to that amount in Paris, and the entire sum has been absorbed by Mr. King!"

"It's almost incredible! " said Helen.

"I quite agree with you," replied her father. "Of course, most people know that there are opium dens in London, as in almost every other big city, but the existence of these palatial establishments, conducted by Mr. King, although undoubtedly a fact, is a fact difficult to accept. It doesn't seem possible that such a place can be conducted secretly; whereas I am assured that all the efforts of Scotland Yard thus far have failed to locate the site of the London branch."

"But surely," cried Denise Ryland, nostrils dilated indignantly, "some of the . . . customers of this . . . disgusting place . . . can be followed?"

"The difficulty is to identify them," explained Cumberly. "Opium smoking is essentially a secret vice; a man does not visit an opium den openly as he would visit his club; and the elaborate precautions adopted by the women are illustrated in the case of Mrs. Vernon, and in the case of Mrs. Leroux. It is a pathetic fact almost daily brought home to me, that women who acquire a drug habit become more rapidly and more entirely enslaved by it than does a man. It becomes the center of the woman's existence; it becomes her god: all other claims, social and domestic, are disregarded. Upon this knowledge, Mr. King has established his undoubtedly extensive enterprise."

Dr. Cumberly stood up.

"I will go down and see Leroux," he announced quietly. "His sorrow hitherto has been secondary to his indignation. Possibly ignorance in this case is preferable to the truth, but nevertheless I am determined to tell him what I know. Give me ten minutes or so, and then join me. Are you agreeable?"

"Quite," said Helen.

Dr. Cumberly departed upon his self-imposed mission.

XXV

FATE'S SHUTTLECOCK

Some ten minutes later, Helen Cumberly and Denise Ryland were in turn admitted to Henry Leroux's flat. They found him seated on a couch in his dining-room, wearing the inevitable dressing-gown. Dr. Cumberly, his hands clasped behind him, stood looking out of the window.

Leroux's pallor now was most remarkable; his complexion had assumed an ivory whiteness which lent his face a sort of statuesque beauty. He was cleanly shaven (somewhat of a novelty), and his hair was brushed back from his brow. But the dark blue eyes were very tragic.

He rose at sight of his new visitors, and a faint color momentarily tinged his cheeks. Helen Cumberly grasped his outstretched hand, then looked away quickly to where her father was standing.

"I almost thought," said Leroux, "that you had deserted me."

"No," said Helen, seeming to speak with an effort—"we—my father, thought—that you needed quiet."

Denise Ryland nodded grimly.

"But now," she said, in her most truculent manner, "we are going to . . . drag you out of . . . your morbid . . . self . . . for a change . . . which you need . . . if ever a man . . . needed it."

"I have just prescribed a drive," said Dr. Cumberly, turning to them, "for tomorrow morning; with lunch at Richmond and a walk across the park, rejoining the car at the Bushey Gate, and so home to tea."

Henry Leroux looked eagerly at Helen in silent appeal. He seemed to fear that she would refuse.

"Do you mean that you have included us in the prescription, father?" she asked.

"Certainly; you are an essential part of it."

"It will be fine," said the girl quietly; "I shall enjoy it."

"Ah!" said Leroux, with a faint note of contentment in his voice; and he reseated himself.

There was an interval of somewhat awkward silence, to be broken by Denise Ryland.

"Dr. Cumberly has told you the news?" she asked, dropping for the moment her syncopated and pugnacious manner.

Leroux closed his eyes and leant back upon the couch.

"Yes," he replied. "And to think that I am a useless wreck—a poor parody of a man—whilst—Mira is . . . Oh, God! help me!—God help *her!*"

He was visibly contending with his emotions; and Helen Cumberly found herself forced to turn her head aside.

"I have been blind," continued Leroux, in a forced, monotonous voice. "That Mira has not—deceived me, in the worst sense of the word, is in no way due to my care of her. I recognize that, and I accept my punishment; for I deserved it. But what now overwhelms me is the knowledge, the frightful knowledge, that in a sense I have misjudged her, that I have remained here inert, making no effort, thinking her absence voluntary, whilst—God help her!—she has been . . ."

"Once again, Leroux," interrupted Dr. Cumberly, "I must ask you not to take too black a view. I blame myself more than I blame you, for having failed to perceive what as an intimate friend I had every opportunity to perceive; that your wife was acquiring the opium habit. You have told me that you count her as dead"—he stood beside Leroux, resting both hands upon the bowed shoulders—"I have not encouraged you to change that view. One who has cultivated—the—vice, to a point where protracted absences become necessary—you understand me?—is, so far as my experience goes . . ."

"Incurable! I quite understand," jerked Leroux. "A thousand times better dead, indeed."

"The facts as I see them," resumed the physician, "as I see them, are these: by some fatality, at present inexplicable, a victim of the opium syndicate met her death in this flat. Realizing that the inquiries brought to bear would inevitably lead to the cross-examination of Mrs. Leroux, the opium syndicate has detained her; was forced to detain her."

"Where is the place," began Leroux, in a voice rising higher with every syllable—"where is the infamous den to which—to which . . ."

Dr. Cumberly pressed his hands firmly upon the speaker's shoulders.

"It is only a question of time, Leroux," he said, "and you will have the satisfaction of knowing that—though at a great cost to yourself—this dreadful evil has been stamped out, that this yellow peril has been torn from the heart of society. Now, I must leave you for the present; but rest assured that everything possible is being done to close the nets about Mr. King."

"Ah!" whispered Leroux, *"Mr. King!"*

"The circle is narrowing," continued the physician. "I may not divulge confidences; but a very clever man—the greatest practical criminologist in Europe—is devoting the whole of his time, night and day, to this object."

Helen Cumberly and Denise Ryland exhibited a keen interest in the words, but Leroux, with closed eyes, merely nodded in a dull way.

Shortly, Dr. Cumberly took his departure, and, Helen looking at her companion interrogatively—

"I think," said Denise Ryland, addressing Leroux, "that you should not over-tax your strength at present." She walked across to where he sat, and examined some proofslips lying upon the little table beside the couch. "'Martin Zeda,'" she said, with a certain high disdain. "Leave 'Martin Zeda' alone for once, and read a really cheerful book!"

Leroux forced a smile to his lips.

"The correction of these proofs," he said diffidently, "exacts no great mental strain, but is sufficient to—distract my mind. Work, after all, is nature's own sedative."

"I rather agree with Mr. Leroux, Denise," said Helen;—"and really you must allow him to know best."

"Thank you," said Leroux, meeting her eyes momentarily. "I feared that I was about to be sent to bed like a naughty boy!"

"I hope it's fine tomorrow," said Helen rapidly. "A drive to Richmond will be quite delightful."

"I think, myself," agreed Leroux, "that it will hasten my recovery to breathe the fresh air once again."

Knowing how eagerly he longed for health and strength, and to what purpose, the girl found something very pathetic in the words.

"I wish you were well enough to come out this afternoon," she said; "I am going to a private view at Olaf van Noord's studio. It is sure to be an extraordinary afternoon. He is the god of the Soho futurists, you know. And his pictures are the weirdest nightmares imaginable. One always meets such singular people there, too, and I am honored in receiving an invitation to represent the Planet!"

"I consider," said Denise Ryland, head wagging furiously again, "that the man is . . . mad. He had an exhibition . . . in Paris . . . and everybody . . . laughed at him . . . simply *laughed* at him."

"But financially, he is very successful," added Helen.

"Financially!" exclaimed Denise Ryland. "*Financially!* To criticize a man's work . . . financially, is about as . . . sensible as . . . to judge the Venus . . . de Milo . . . by weight!—or to sell the works . . . of Leonardo . . . da Vinci by the . . . yard! Olaf van Noord is nothing but . . . a fool . . . of the worst possible . . . description . . . imaginable."

"He is at least an entertaining fool!" protested Helen, laughingly.

"A mountebank!" cried Denise Ryland; "a clown . . . a pantaloon . . . a whole family of . . . idiots . . . rolled into one!"

"It seems unkind to run away and leave you here—in your loneliness," said Helen to Leroux; "but really I must be off to the wilds of Soho."

"To-morrow," said Leroux, standing up and fixing his eyes upon her lingeringly, "will be a red-letter day. I have no right to complain, whilst such good friends remain to me—such true friends."

XXVI

"OUR LADY OF THE POPPIES"

A number of visitors were sprinkled about Olaf van Noord's large and dirty studio, these being made up for the most part of those weird and nondescript enthusiasts who seek to erect an apocryphal Montmartre in the plains of Soho. One or two ordinary mortals, representing the Press, leavened the throng, but the entire gathering—"advanced" and unenlightened alike—seemed to be drawn to a common focus: a large canvas placed advantageously in the southeast corner of the studio, where it enjoyed all the benefit of a pure and equably suffused light.

Seated apart from his worshipers upon a little sketching stool, and handling a remarkably long, amber cigarette-holder with much grace, was Olaf van Noord. He had hair of so light a yellow as sometimes to appear white, worn very long, brushed back from his brow and cut squarely all around behind, lending him a medieval appearance. He wore a slight mustache carefully pointed; and his scanty vandyke beard could not entirely conceal the weakness of his chin. His complexion had the color and general appearance of drawing-paper, and in his large blue eyes was an eerie hint of sightlessness. He was attired in a light tweed suit cut in an American pattern, and out from his low collar flowed a black French knot.

Olaf van Noord rose to meet Helen Cumberly and Denise Ryland, advancing across the floor with the measured gait of a tragic actor. He greeted them aloofly, and a little negro boy proffered tiny cups of China tea. Denise Ryland distended her nostrils as her gaze swept the picture-covered walls; but she seemed to approve of the tea.

The artist next extended to them an ivory box containing little yellow-wrapped cigarettes. Helen Cumberly smilingly refused, but Denise Ryland took one of the cigarettes, sniffed at it superciliously—and then replaced it in the box.

"It has a most . . . egregiously horrible . . . odor," she commented.

"They are a special brand," explained Olaf van Noord, distractedly, "which I have imported for me from Smyrna. They contain a small percentage of opium."

"Opium!" exclaimed Denise Ryland, glaring at the speaker and then at Helen Cumberly, as though the latter were responsible in some way for the vices of the painter.

"Yes," he said, reclosing the box, and pacing somberly to the door to greet a new arrival.

"Did you ever in all your life," said Denise Ryland, glancing about her, "see such an exhibition . . . of nightmares?"

Certainly, the criticism was not without justification; the dauby-looking oil-paintings, incomprehensible water-colors, and riotous charcoal sketches which formed the mural decoration of the studio were distinctly "advanced." But, since the center of interest seemed to be the large canvas on the easel, the two moved to the edges of the group of spectators and began to examine this masterpiece. A very puzzled newspaperman joined them, bending and whispering to Helen Cumberly:

"Are you going to notice the thing seriously? Personally, I am writing it up as a practical joke! We are giving him half a column—Lord knows what for!—but I can't see how to handle it except as funny stuff."

"But, for heaven's sake . . . what does he . . . *call* it?" muttered Denise Ryland, holding a pair of gold rimmed pince-nez before her eyes, and shifting them to and fro in an endeavor to focus the canvas.

"'Our Lady of the Poppies,'" replied the journalist. "Do you think it's intended to mean anything in particular?"

The question was no light one; it embodied a problem not readily solved. The scene depicted, and depicted with a skill, with a technical mastery of the bizarre that had in it something horrible—was a long narrow room—or, properly, cavern. The walls apparently were hewn from black rock, and at regular intervals, placed some three feet from these gleaming walls, uprose slender golden pillars supporting a kind of fretwork arch which entirely masked the ceiling. The point of sight adopted by the painter was peculiar. One apparently looked down into this apartment from some spot elevated fourteen feet or more above the floor level. The floor, which was black and polished, was strewn with tiger skins; and little, inlaid tables and garishly colored cushions were spread about in confusion, whilst cushioned divans occupied the visible corners of the place. The lighting was very "advanced": a lamp, having a kaleidoscopic shade, swung from the center of the roof low into the room and furnished all the illumination.

Three doors were visible; one, directly in line at the further end of the place, apparently of carved ebony inlaid with ivory; another, on the right, of lemon wood or something allied to it, and inlaid with a design in some emerald hued material; with a third, corresponding door, on the left, just barely visible to the spectator.

Two figures appeared. One was that of a Chinaman in a green robe scarcely distinguishable from the cushions surrounding him, who crouched upon the divan to the left of the central door, smoking a long bamboo pipe. His face was the leering face of a yellow satyr. But, dominating the composition, and so conceived in form, in color, and in lighting, as to claim the attention centrally, so that the other extravagant details became but a setting for it, was another figure.

Upon a slender ivory pedestal crouched a golden dragon, and before the pedestal was placed a huge Chinese vase of the indeterminate pink seen in the heart of a rose, and so skilfully colored as to suggest an internal luminousness. The vase was loaded with a mass of exotic poppies, a riotous splash of color; whilst beside this vase, and slightly in front of the pedestal, stood the figure presumably intended to represent the Lady of the Poppies who gave title to the picture.

The figure was that of an Eastern girl, slight and supple, and possessing a devilish and forbidding grace. Her short hair formed a black smudge upon the canvas, and cast a dense shadow upon her face. The composition was infinitely daring; for out of this shadow shone the great black eyes, their diablerie most cunningly insinuated; whilst with a brilliant exclusion of detail—by means of two strokes of the brush steeped in brightest vermilion, and one seemingly haphazard splash of dead white—an evil and abandoned smile was made to greet the spectator.

To the waist, the figure was a study in satin nudity, whence, from a jeweled girdle, light draperies swept downward, covering the feet and swinging, a shimmering curve out into the foreground of the canvas, the curve being cut off in its apogee by the gold frame.

Above her head, this girl of demoniacal beauty held a bunch of poppies seemingly torn from the vase: this, with her left hand; with her right she pointed, tauntingly, at her beholder.

In comparison with the effected futurism of the other pictures in the studio, "Our Lady of the Poppies," beyond question was a great painting. From a point where the entire composition might be taken in by the eye, the uncanny scene glowed with highly colored detail; but, exclude the scheme of the composition, and focus the eye upon any one item—the golden dragon—the seated Chinaman—the ebony door—the silk-shaded lamp; it had no detail whatever: one beheld a meaningless mass of colors. Individually, no one section of the canvas had life, had meaning; but, as a whole, it glowed, it lived—it was genius. Above all, it was uncanny.

This, Denise Ryland fully realized, but critics had grown so used to treating the work of Olaf van Noord as a joke, that "Our Lady of the Poppies" in all probability would never be judged seriously.

"What does it mean, Mr. van Noord?" asked Helen Cumberly, leaving the group of worshipers standing hushed in rapture before the canvas and approaching the painter. "Is there some occult significance in the title?"

"It is a priestess," replied the artist, in his dreamy fashion . . . .

"A priestess?"

"A priestess of the temple."

Helen Cumberly glanced again at the astonishing picture.

"Do you mean," she began, "that there is a living original?"

Olaf van Noord bowed absently, and left her side to greet one who at that moment entered the studio. Something magnetic in the personality of the newcomer drew all eyes from the canvas to the figure on the threshold. The artist was removing garish tiger skin furs from the shoulders of the girl—for the new arrival was a girl, a Eurasian girl.

She wore a tiger skin motor-coat, and a little, close-fitting, turban-like cap of the same. The coat removed, she stood revealed in a clinging gown of silk; and her feet were shod in little amber colored slippers with green buckles. The bodice of her dress opened in a surprising V, displaying the satin texture of her neck and shoulders, and enhancing the barbaric character of her appearance. Her jet black hair was confined by no band or comb, but protruded Bishareen-like around the shapely head. Without doubt, this was the Lady of the Poppies—the original of the picture.

"Dear friends," said Olaf van Noord, taking the girl's hand, and walking into the studio, "permit me to present my model!"

Following, came a slightly built man who carried himself with a stoop; an olive faced man, who squinted frightfully, and who dressed immaculately.

"What a most . . . *extraordinary*-looking creature!" whispered Denise Ryland to Helen. "She has undoubted attractions of . . . a hellish sort . . . if I may use . . . the term."

"She is the strangest looking girl I have ever seen in my life," replied Helen, who found herself unable to turn her eyes away from Olaf van Noord's model. "Surely she is not a professional model!"

The chatty reporter (his name was Crockett) confided to Helen Cumberly:

"She is not exactly a professional model, I think, Miss Cumberly, but she is one of the van Noord set, and is often to be seen in the more exclusive restaurants, and sometimes in the Cafe Royal."

"She is possibly a member of the theatrical profession?"

"I think not. She is the only really strange figure (if we exclude Olaf) in this group of poseurs. She is half Burmese, I believe, and a native of Moulmein."

"Most *extraordinary* creature!" muttered Denise Ryland, focussing upon the Eurasian her gold rimmed glasses—"*Most* extraordinary." She glanced around at the company in general. "I really begin to feel . . . more and more as though I were . . . in a private lunatic . . . asylum. That picture . . . beyond doubt is the work . . . of a madman . . . a perfect . . . madman!"

"I, also, begin to be conscious of an uncomfortable sensation," said Helen, glancing about her almost apprehensively. "Am I dreaming, or did *some one else* enter the studio, immediately behind that girl?"

"A squinting man . . . yes!"

"But a *third* person?"

"No, my dear . . . look for yourself. As you say . . . you are . . . dreaming. It's not to be wondered . . . at!"

Helen laughed, but very uneasily. Evidently it had been an illusion, but an unpleasant illusion; for she should have been prepared to swear that not two, but *three* people had entered! Moreover, although she was unable to detect the presence of any third stranger in the studio, the persuasion that this third person actually was present remained with her, unaccountably, and uncannily.

The lady of the tiger skins was surrounded by an admiring group of unusuals, and Helen, who had turned again to the big canvas, suddenly became aware that the little cross-eyed man was bowing and beaming radiantly before her.

"May I be allowed," said Olaf van Noord who stood beside him, "to present my friend Mr. Gianapolis, my dear Miss Cumberly?"

Helen Cumberly found herself compelled to acknowledge the introduction, although she formed an immediate, instinctive distaste for Mr. Gianapolis. But he made such obvious attempts to please, and was so really entertaining a talker, that she unbent towards him a little. His admiration, too, was unconcealed; and no pretty woman, however great her common sense, is entirely admiration-proof.

"Do you not think 'Our Lady of the Poppies' remarkable?" said Gianapolis, pleasantly.

"I think," replied Denise Ryland,—to whom, also, the Greek had been presented by Olaf van Noord, "that it indicates . . . a disordered . . . imagination on the part of . . . its creator."

"It is a technical masterpiece," replied the Greek, smiling, "but hardly a work of imagination; for you have seen the original of the principal figure, and"—he turned to Helen Cumberly—"one need not go very far East for such an interior as that depicted."

"What!" Helen knitted her brows, prettily—"you do not suggest that such an apartment actually exists either East or West?"

Gianapolis beamed radiantly.

"You would, perhaps, like to see such an apartment?" he suggested.

"I should, certainly," replied Helen Cumberly. "Not even in a stage setting have I seen anything like it."

"You have never been to the East?"

"Never, unfortunately. I have desired to go for years, and hope to go some day."

"In Smyrna you may see such rooms; possibly in Port Said—certainly in Cairo. In Constantinople—yes! But perhaps in Paris; and—who knows?—Sir Richard Burton explored Mecca, but who has explored London?"

Helen Cumberly watched him curiously.

"You excite my curiosity," she said. "Don't you think"—turning to

Denise Ryland—"he is most tantalizing?"

Denise Ryland distended her nostrils scornfully.

"He is telling . . . fairy tales," she declared. "He thinks . . . we are . . . silly!"

"On the contrary," declared Gianapolis; "I flatter myself that I am too good a judge of character to make that mistake."

Helen Cumberly absorbed his entire attention; in everything he sought to claim her interest; and when, ere taking their departure, the girl and her friend walked around the studio to view the other pictures, Gianapolis was the attendant cavalier, and so well as one might judge, in his case, his glance rarely strayed from the piquant beauty of Helen.

When they departed, it was Gianapolis, and not Olaf van Noord, who escorted them to the door and downstairs to the street. The red lips of the Eurasian smiled upon her circle of adulators, but her eyes—her unfathomable eyes—followed every movement of the Greek.

XXVII

GROVE OF A MILLION APES

Four men sauntered up the grand staircase and entered the huge smoking-room of the Radical Club as Big Ben was chiming the hour of eleven o'clock. Any curious observer who had cared to consult the visitor's book in the hall, wherein the two lines last written were not yet dry, would have found the following entries:

VISITOR	RESIDENCE	INTROD'ING MEMBER
Dr. Bruce Cumberly	London	John Exel
M. Gaston	Paris	Brian Malpas

The smoking-room was fairly full, but a corner near the big open grate had just been vacated, and here, about a round table, the four disposed themselves. Our French acquaintance being in evening dress had perforce confined himself in his sartorial eccentricities to a flowing silk knot in place of the more conventional, neat bow. He was already upon delightfully friendly terms with the frigid Exel and the aristocratic Sir Brian Malpas. Few natures were proof against the geniality of the brilliant Frenchman.

Conversation drifted, derelict, from one topic to another, now seized by this current of thought, now by that; and M. Gaston Max made no perceptible attempt to steer it in any given direction. But presently:

"I was reading a very entertaining article," said Exel, turning his monocle upon the physician, "in the Planet today, from the pen of Miss Cumberly; Ah! dealing with Olaf van Noord."

Sir Brian Malpas suddenly became keenly interested.

"You mean in reference to his new picture, 'Our Lady of the Poppies'?" he said.

"Yes," replied Exel, "but I was unaware that you knew van Noord?"

"I do not know him," said Sir Brian, "I should very much like to meet him. But directly the picture is on view to the public I shall certainly subscribe my half-crown."

"My own idea," drawled Exel, "was that Miss Cumberly's article probably was more interesting than the picture or the painter. Her description of the canvas was certainly most vivid; and I, myself, for a moment, experienced an inclination to see the thing. I feel sure, however, that I should be disappointed."

"I think you are wrong," interposed Cumberly. "Helen is enthusiastic about the picture, and even Miss Ryland, whom you have met and who is a somewhat severe critic, admits that it is out of the ordinary."

Max, who covertly had been watching the face of Sir Brian Malpas, said at this point:

"I would not miss it for anything, after reading Miss Cumberly's account of it. When are you thinking of going to see it, Sir Brian? I might arrange to join you."

"Directly the exhibition is opened," replied the baronet, lapsing again into his dreamy manner. "Ring me up when you are going, and I will join you."

"But you might be otherwise engaged?"

"I never permit business," said Sir Brian, "to interfere with pleasure."

The words sounded absurd, but, singularly, the statement was true. Sir Brian had won his political position by sheer brilliancy. He was utterly unreliable and totally indifferent to that code of social obligations which ordinarily binds his class. He held his place by force of intellect, and it was said of him that had he possessed the faintest conception of his duties toward his fellow men, nothing could have prevented him from becoming Prime Minister. He was a puzzle to all who knew him. Following a most brilliant speech in the House, which would win admiration and applause from end to end of the Empire, he would, perhaps on the following day, exhibit something very like stupidity in debate. He would rise to address the House and take his seat again without having uttered a word. He was eccentric, said his admirers, but there were others who looked deeper for an explanation, yet failed to find one, and were thrown back upon theories.

M. Max, by strategy, masterful because it was simple, so arranged matters that at about twelve o'clock he found himself strolling with Sir Brian Malpas toward the latter's chambers in Piccadilly.

A man who wore a raincoat with the collar turned up and buttoned tightly about his throat, and whose peculiar bowler hat seemed to be so tightly pressed upon his head that it might have been glued there, detached himself from the shadows of the neighboring cab rank as M. Gaston Max and Sir Brian Malpas quitted the Club, and followed them at a discreet distance.

It was a clear, fine night, and both gentlemen formed conspicuous figures, Sir Brian because of his unusual height and upright military bearing, and the Frenchman by reason of his picturesque cloak and hat. Up Northumberland Avenue, across Trafalgar Square and so on up to Piccadilly Circus went the two, deep in conversation; with the tireless man in the raincoat always dogging their footsteps. So the procession proceeded on, along Piccadilly. Then Sir Brian and M. Max turned into the door of a block of chambers, and a constable, who chanced to be passing at the moment, touched his helmet to the baronet.

As the two were entering the lift, the follower came up level with the doorway and abreast of the constable; the top portion of a very red face showed between the collar of the raincoat and the brim of the hat, together with a pair of inquiring blue eyes.

"Reeves!" said the follower, addressing the constable.

The latter turned and stared for a moment at the speaker; then saluted hurriedly.

"Don't do that!" snapped the proprietor of the bowler; "you should know better! Who was that gentleman?"

"Sir Brian Malpas, sir."

"Sir Brian Malpas?"

"Yes, sir."

"And the other?"

"I don't know, sir. I have never seen him before."

"H'm!" grunted Detective-Sergeant Sowerby, walking across the road toward the Park with his hands thrust deep in his pockets; "I have! What the deuce is Max up to? I wonder if Dunbar knows about this move?"

He propped himself up against the railings, scarcely knowing what he expected to gain by remaining there, but finding the place as well suited to reflection as any other. He shared with Dunbar a dread that the famous Frenchman would bring the case to a successful conclusion unaided by Scotland Yard, thus casting professional discredit upon Dunbar and himself.

His presence at that spot was largely due to accident. He had chanced to be passing the Club when Sir Brian and M. Max had come out, and, fearful that the presence of the tall stranger portended some new move on the Frenchman's part, Sowerby had followed, hoping to glean something by persistency when clues were unobtainable by other means. He had had no time to make inquiries of the porter of the Club respecting the identity of M. Max's companion, and thus, as has appeared, he did not obtain the desired information until his arrival in Piccadilly.

Turning over these matters in his mind, Sowerby stood watching the block of buildings across the road. He saw a light spring into being in a room overlooking Piccadilly, a room boasting a handsome balcony. This took place some two minutes after the departure of the lift bearing Sir Brian and his guest upward; so that Sowerby permitted himself to conclude that the room with the balcony belonged to Sir Brian Malpas.

He watched the lighted window aimlessly and speculated upon the nature of the conversation then taking place up there above him. Had he possessed the attributes of a sparrow, he thought, he might have flown up to that balcony and have "got level" with this infernally clever Frenchman who was almost certainly going to pull off the case under the very nose of Scotland Yard.

In short, his reflections were becoming somewhat bitter; and persuaded that he had nothing to gain by remaining there any longer he was about to walk off, when his really remarkable persistency received a trivial reward.

One of the windows communicating with the balcony was suddenly thrown open, so that Sowerby had a distant view of the corner of a picture, of the extreme top of a book-case, and of a patch of white ceiling in the room above; furthermore he had a clear sight of the man who had opened the window, and who now turned and reentered the room. The man was Sir Brian Malpas.

Heedless of the roaring traffic stream, upon the brink of which he stood, heedless of all who passed him by, Sowerby gazed aloft, seeking to project himself, as it were, into that lighted room. Not being an accomplished clairvoyant, he remained in all his component parts upon the pavement of Piccadilly; but ours is the privilege to succeed where Sowerby failed, and the comedy being enacted in the room above should prove well deserving of study.

To the tactful diplomacy of M. Gaston Max, the task of securing from Sir Brian an invitation to step up into his chambers in order to smoke a final cigar was no heavy one. He seated himself in a deep armchair, at the baronet's invitation, and accepted a very fine cigar, contentedly, sniffing at the old cognac with the appreciation of a connoisseur, ere holding it under the syphon.

He glanced around the room, noting the character of the ornaments, and looked up at the big bookshelf which was near to him; these rapid inquiries dictated the following remark: "You have lived in China, Sir Brian?"

Sir Brian surveyed him with mild surprise.

"Yes," he replied; "I was for some time at the Embassy in Pekin."

His guest nodded, blowing a ring of smoke from his lips and tracing its hazy outline with the lighted end of his cigar.

"I, too, have been in China," he said slowly.

"What, really! I had no idea."

"Yes—I have been in China . . . I . . ."

M. Gaston grew suddenly deathly pale and his fingers began to twitch alarmingly. He stared before him with wide-opened eyes and began to cough and to choke as if suffocating—dying.

Sir Brian Malpas leapt to his feet with an exclamation of concern. His visitor weakly waved him away, gasping: "It is nothing . . . it will . . . pass off. Oh! *mon dieu!*"

Sir Brian ran and opened one of the windows to admit more air to the apartment. He turned and looked back anxiously at the man in the armchair.

M. Gaston, twitching in a pitiful manner and still frightfully pale, was clutching the chair-arms and glaring straight in front of him. Sir Brian started slightly and advanced again to his visitor's side.

The burning cigar lay upon the carpet beside the chair, and Sir Brian took it up and tossed it into the grate. As he did so he looked searchingly into the eyes of M. Gaston. The pupils were extraordinary dilated . . . .

"Do you feel better?" asked Sir Brian.

"Much better," muttered M. Gaston, his face twitching nervously— "much better."

"Are you subject to these attacks?"

"Since—I was in China—yes, unfortunately."

Sir Brian tugged at his fair mustache and seemed about to speak, then turned aside, and, walking to the table, poured out a peg of brandy and offered it to his guest.

"Thanks," said M. Gaston; "many thanks indeed, but already I recover. There is only one thing that would hasten my recovery, and that, I fear, is not available."

"What is that?"

He looked again at M. Gaston's eyes with their very dilated pupils.

"Opium!" whispered M. Gaston.

"What! you . . . you . . ."

"I acquired the custom in China," replied the Frenchman, his voice gradually growing stronger; "and for many years, now, I have regarded opium, as essential to my well-being. Unfortunately business has detained me in London, and I have been forced to fast for an unusually long time. My outraged constitution is protesting—that is all."

He shrugged his shoulders and glanced up at his host with an odd smile.

"You have my sympathy," said Sir Brian . . . .

"In Paris," continued the visitor, "I am a member of a select and cozy little club; near the Boulevard Beaumarchais . . . ."

"I have heard of it," interjected Malpas—"on the Rue St. Claude?"

"That indeed is its situation," replied the other with surprise. "You know someone who is a member?"

Sir Brian Malpas hesitated for ten seconds or more; then, crossing the room and reclosing the window, he turned, facing his visitor across the large room.

"I was a member, myself, during the time that I lived in Paris," he said, in a hurried manner which did not entirely serve to cover his confusion.

"My dear Sir Brian! We have at least one taste in common!"

Sir Brian Malpas passed his hand across his brow with a weary gesture well-known to fellow Members of Parliament, for it often presaged the abrupt termination of a promising speech.

"I curse the day that I was appointed to Pekin," he said; "for it was in Pekin that I acquired the opium habit. I thought to make it my servant; it has made me . . ."

"What! you would give it up?"

Sir Brian surveyed the speaker with surprise again.

"Do you doubt it?"

"My dear Sir Brian!" cried the Frenchman, now completely restored, "my real life is lived in the land of the poppies; my other life is but a shadow! Morbleu! to be an outcast from that garden of bliss is to me torture excruciating. For the past three months I have regularly met in my trances."

Sir Brian shuddered coldly.

"In my explorations of that wonderland," continued the Frenchman, "a most fascinating Eastern girl. Ah! I cannot describe her; for when, at a time like this, I seek to conjure up her image,—nom d'um nom! do you know, I can think of nothing but a serpent!"

"A serpent!"

"A serpent, exactly. Yet, when I actually meet her in the land of the poppies, she is a dusky Cleopatra in whose arms I forget the world—even the world of the poppy. We float down the stream together, always in an Indian bark canoe, and this stream runs through orange groves. Numberless apes—millions of apes, inhabit these groves, and as we two float along, they hurl orange blossoms—orange blossoms, you understand—until the canoe is filled with them. I assure you, monsieur, that I perform these delightful journeys regularly, and to be deprived of the key which opens the gate of this wonderland, is to me like being exiled from a loved one. Pardieu! that grove of the apes! Morbleu! my witch of the dusky eyes! Yet, as I have told you, owing to some trick of my brain, whilst I can experience an intense longing for that companion of my dreams, my waking attempts to visualize her provide nothing but the image . . ."

"Of a serpent," concluded Sir Brian, smiling pathetically. "You are indeed an enthusiast, M. Gaston, and to me a new type. I had supposed that every slave of the drug cursed his servitude and loathed and despised himself. . . ."

"Ah, monsieur! to me those words sound almost like a sacrilege!"

"But," continued Sir Brian, "your remarks interest me strangely; for two reasons. First, they confirm your assertion that you are, or were, an habitue of the Rue St. Claude, and secondly, they revive in my mind an old fancy—a superstition."

"What is that, Sir Brian?" inquired M. Max, whose opium vision was a faithful imitation of one related to him by an actual frequenter of the establishment near the Boulevard Beaumarchais.

"Only once before, M. Gaston, have I compared notes with a fellow opium-smoker, and he, also, was a patron of Madame Jean; he, also, met in his dreams that Eastern Circe, in the grove of apes, just as I . . ."

"Morbleu! Yes?"

"As I meet her!"

"But this is astounding!" cried Max, who actually thought it so. "Your fancy—your superstition—was this: that only habitues of Rue St. Claude met, in poppyland, this vision? And in your fancy you are now confirmed?"

"It is singular, at least."

"It is more than that, Sir Brian! Can it be that some intelligence presides over that establishment and exercises—shall I call it a hypnotic influence upon the inmates?"

M. Max put the question with sincere interest.

"One does not *always* meet her," murmured Sir Brian. "But—yes, it is possible. For I have since renewed those experiences in London."

"What! in London?"

"Are you remaining for some time longer in London?"

"Alas! for several weeks yet."

"Then I will introduce you to a gentleman who can secure you admission to an establishment in London—where you may even hope sometimes to find the orange grove—to meet your dream-bride!"

"What!" cried M. Gaston, rising to his feet, his eyes bright with gratitude, "you will do that?"

"With pleasure," said Sir Brian Malpas, wearily; "nor am I jealous! But—no! do not thank me, for I do not share your views upon the subject, monsieur. You are a devout worshiper; I, an unhappy slave!"

XXVIII

THE OPIUM AGENT

Into the Palm Court of the Hotel Astoria, Mr. Gianapolis came, radiant and bowing. M. Gaston rose to greet his visitor. M. Gaston was arrayed in a light gray suit and wore a violet tie of very chaste design; his complexion had assumed a quality of sallowness, and the pupils of his eyes had acquired (as on the occasion of his visit to the chambers of Sir Brian Malpas) a chatoyant quality; they alternately dilated and contracted in a most remarkable manner—in a manner which attracted the immediate attention of Mr. Gianapolis.

"My dear sir," he said, speaking in French, "you suffer. I perceive how grievously you suffer; and you have been denied that panacea which beneficent nature designed for the service of mankind. A certain gentleman known to both of us (we brethren of the poppy are all nameless) has advised me of your requirements—and here I am."

"You are welcome," declared M. Gaston.

He rose and grasped eagerly the hand of the Greek, at the same time looking about the Palm Court suspiciously. "You can relieve my sufferings?"

Mr. Gianapolis seated himself beside the Frenchman.

"I perceive," he said, "that you are of those who abjure the heresies of De Quincey. How little he knew, that De Quincey, of the true ritual of the poppy! He regarded it as the German regards his lager, whereas we know—you and I—that it is an Eleusinian mystery; that true communicants must retreat to the temple of the goddess if they would partake of Paradise with her."

"It is perhaps a question of temperament," said M. Gaston, speaking in a singularly tremulous voice. "De Quincey apparently possessed the type of constitution which is cerebrally stimulated by opium. To such a being the golden gates are closed; and the Easterners, whom he despised for what he termed their beastly lethargies, have taught me the real secret of the poppy. I do not employ opium as an aid to my social activities; I regard it as nepenthe from them and as a key to a brighter realm. It has been my custom, M. Gianapolis, for many years, periodically to visit that fairyland. In Paris I regularly arranged my affairs in such a manner that I found myself occasionally at liberty to spend two or three days, as the case might be, in the company of my bright friends who haunted the Boulevard Beaumarchais."

"Ah! Our acquaintance has mentioned something of this to me, Monsieur. You knew Madame Jean?"

"The dear Madame Jean! Name of a name! She was the hierophant of my Paris Temple . . ."

"And Sen?"

"Our excellent Sen! Splendid man! It was from the hands of the worthy Sen, the incomparable Sen, that I received the key to the gate! Ah! how I have suffered since the accursed business has exiled me from the . . ."

"I feel for you," declared Gianapolis, warmly; "I, too, have worshiped at the shrine; and although I cannot promise that the London establishment to which I shall introduce you is comparable with that over which Madame Jean formerly presided . . ."

"Formerly?" exclaimed M. Gaston, with lifted eyebrows. "You do not tell me . . ."

"My friend," said Gianapolis, "in Europe we are less enlightened upon certain matters than in Smyrna, in Constantinople—in Cairo. The impertinent police have closed the establishment in the Rue St. Claude!"

"Ah!" exclaimed M. Gaston, striking his brow, "misery! I shall return to Paris, then, only to die?"

"I would suggest, monsieur," said Gianapolis, tapping him confidentially upon the breast, "that you periodically visit London in future. The journey is a short one, and already, I am happy to say, the London establishment (conducted by Mr. Ho-Pin of Canton—a most accomplished gentleman, and a graduate of London)—enjoys the patronage of several distinguished citizens of Paris, of Brussels, of Vienna, and elsewhere."

"You offer me life!" declared M. Gaston, gratefully. "The commoner establishments, for the convenience of sailors and others of that class, at Dieppe, Calais,"—he shrugged his shoulders, comprehensively—"are impossible as resorts. In catering for the true devotees—for those who, unlike De Quincey, plunge and do not dabble—for those who seek to explore the ultimate regions of poppyland, for those who have learnt the mystery from the real masters in Asia and not in Europe—the enterprise conducted by Madame Jean supplied a want long and bitterly experienced. I rejoice to know that London has not been neglected . . ."

"My dear friend!" cried Gianapolis enthusiastically, "no important city has been neglected! A high priest of the cult has arisen, and from a parent lodge in Pekin he has extended his offices to kindred lodges in most of the capitals of Europe and Asia; he has not neglected the Near East, and America owes him a national debt of gratitude."

"Ah! the great man!" murmured M. Gaston, with closed eyes. "As an old habitue of the Rue St. Claude, I divine that you refer to Mr. King?"

"Beyond doubt," whispered Gianapolis, imparting a quality of awe to his voice. "From you, my friend, I will have no secrets; but"—he glanced about him crookedly, and lowered his voice to an impressive whisper—"the police, as you are aware . . ."

"Curse their interference!" said M. Gaston.

"Curse it indeed; but the police persist in believing, or in pretending to believe, that any establishment patronized by lovers of the magic resin must necessarily be a resort of criminals."

"Pah!"

"Whilst this absurd state of affairs prevails, it is advisable, it is more than advisable, it is imperative, that all of us should be secret. The . . . raid—unpleasant word!—upon the establishment in Paris—was so unexpected that there was no time to advise patrons; but the admirable tact of the French authorities ensured the suppression of all names. Since—always as a protective measure—no business relationship exists between any two of Mr. King's establishments (each one being entirely self-governed) some difficulty is being experienced, I believe, in obtaining the names of those who patronized Madame Jean. But I am doubly glad to have met you, M. Gaston, for not only can I put you in touch with the London establishment, but I can impress upon you the necessity of preserving absolute silence . . ."

M. Gaston extended his palms eloquently.

"To me," he declared, "the name of Mr. King is a sacred symbol."

"It is to all of us!" responded the Greek, devoutly.

M. Gaston in turn became confidential, bending toward Gianapolis so that, as the shadow of the Greek fell upon his face, his pupils contracted catlike.

"How often have I prayed," he whispered, "for a sight of that remarkable man!"

A look of horror, real or simulated, appeared upon the countenance of Gianapolis.

"To see—Mr. King!" he breathed. "My clear friend, I declare to you by all that I hold sacred that I—though one of the earliest patrons of the first establishment, that in Pekin—have never seen Mr. King!"

"He is so cautious and so clever as that?"

"Even as cautious and even as clever—yes! Though every branch of the enterprise in the world were destroyed, no man would ever see Mr. King; he would remain but a *name!*"

"You will arrange for me to visit the house of—Ho-Pin, did you say?—immediately?"

"To-day, if you wish," said Gianapolis, brightly.

"My funds," continued M. Gaston, shrugging his shoulders, "are not limitless at the moment; and until I receive a remittance from Paris . . ."

The brow of Mr. Gianapolis darkened slightly.

"Our clientele here," he replied, "is a very wealthy one, and the fees are slightly higher than in Paris. An entrance fee of fifty guineas is charged, and an annual subscription of the same amount . . ."

"But," exclaimed M. Gaston, "I shall not be in London for so long as a year! In a week or a fortnight from now, I shall be on my way to America!"

"You will receive an introduction to the New York representative, and your membership will be available for any of the United States establishments."

"But I am going to South America."

"At Buenos Aires is one of the largest branches."

"But I am not going to Buenos Aires! I am going with a prospecting party to Yucatan."

"You must be well aware, monsieur, that to go to Yucatan is to exile yourself from all that life holds for you."

"I can take a supply . . ."

"You will die, monsieur! Already you suffer abominably . . ."

"I do not suffer because of any lack of the specific," said M. Gaston wearily; "for if I were entirely unable to obtain possession of it, I should most certainly die. But I suffer because, living as I do at present in a public hotel, I am unable to embark upon a protracted voyage into those realms which hold so much for me . . ."

"I offer you the means . . ."

"But to charge me one hundred guineas, since I cannot possibly avail myself of the full privileges, is to rob me—is to trade upon my condition!" M. Gaston was feebly indignant.

"Let it be twenty-five guineas, monsieur," said the Greek, reflectively, "entitling you to two visits."

"Good! good!" cried M. Gaston. "Shall I write you a check?"

"You mistake me," said Gianapolis. "I am in no way connected with the management of the establishment. You will settle this business matter with Mr. Ho-Pin . . ."

"Yes, yes!"

"To whom I will introduce you this evening. Checks, as you must be aware, are unacceptable. I will meet you at Piccadilly Circus, outside the entrance to the London Pavilion, at nine o'clock this evening, and you will bring with you the twenty-five guineas in cash. You will arrange to absent yourself during the following day?"

"Of course, of course! At nine o'clock at Piccadilly Circus?"

"Exactly."

M. Gaston, this business satisfactorily completed, made his way to his own room by a somewhat devious route, not wishing to encounter anyone of his numerous acquaintances whilst in an apparent state of ill-health so calculated to excite compassion. He avoided the lift and ascended the many stairs to his small apartment.

Here he rectified the sallowness of his complexion, which was due, not to outraged nature, but to the arts of make-up. His dilated pupils (a phenomenon traceable to drops of belladonna) he was compelled to suffer for the present; but since their condition tended temporarily to impair his sight, he determined to remain in his room until the time for the appointment with Gianapolis.

"So!" he muttered—"we have branches in Europe, Asia, Africa and America! Eh, bien! to find all those would occupy five hundred detectives for a whole year. I have a better plan: crush the spider and the winds of heaven will disperse his web!"

XXIX

M. MAX OF LONDON AND M. MAX OF PARIS

He seated himself in a cane armchair and, whilst the facts were fresh in his memory, made elaborate notes upon the recent conversation with the Greek. He had achieved almost more than he could have hoped for; but, knowing something of the elaborate organization of the opium group, he recognized that he owed some part of his information to the sense of security which this admirably conducted machine inspired in its mechanics. The introduction from Sir Brian Malpas had worked wonders, without doubt; and his own intimate knowledge of the establishment adjoining the Boulevard Beaumarchais, far from arousing the suspicions of Gianapolis, had evidently strengthened the latter's conviction that he had to deal with a confirmed opium slave.

The French detective congratulated himself upon the completeness of his Paris operation. It was evident that the French police had succeeded in suppressing all communication between the detained members of the Rue St. Claude den and the head office—which he shrewdly suspected to be situated in London. So confident were the group in the self-contained properties of each of their branches that the raid of any one establishment meant for them nothing more than a temporary financial loss. Failing the clue supplied by the draft on Paris, the case, so far as he was concerned, indeed, must have terminated with the raiding of the opium house. He reflected that he owed that precious discovery primarily to the promptness with which he had conducted the raid—to the finding of the letter (the *one* incriminating letter) from Mr. King.

Evidently the group remained in ignorance of the fact that the little arrangement at the Credit Lyonnais had been discovered. He surveyed—and his eyes twinkled humorously—a small photograph which was contained in his writing-case.

It represented a very typical Parisian gentleman, with a carefully trimmed square beard and well brushed mustache, wearing pince-nez and a white silk knot at his neck. The photograph was cut from a French magazine, and beneath it appeared the legend:

"M. Gaston Max, Service de Surete."

There was marked genius in the conspicuous dressing of M. Gaston Max, who, as M. Gaston, was now patronizing the Hotel Astoria. For whilst there was nothing furtive, nothing secret, about this gentleman, the closest scrutiny (and because he invited it, he was never subjected to it) must have failed to detect any resemblance between M. Gaston of the Hotel Astoria and M. Gaston Max of the Service de Surete.

And which was the original M. Gaston Max? Was the M. Max of the magazine photograph a disguised M. Max? or was that the veritable M. Max, and was the patron of the Astoria a disguised M. Max? It is quite possible that M. Gaston Max, himself, could not have answered that question, so true an artist was he; and it is quite certain that had the occasion arisen he would have refused to do so.

He partook of a light dinner in his own room, and having changed into evening dress, went out to meet Mr. Gianapolis. The latter was on the spot punctually at nine o'clock, and taking the Frenchman familiarly by the arm, he hailed a taxi-cab, giving the man the directions, "To Victoria-Suburban." Then, turning to his companion, he whispered: "Evening dress? And you must return in daylight."

M. Max felt himself to be flushing like a girl. It was an error of artistry that he had committed; a heinous crime! "So silly of me!" he muttered.

"No matter," replied the Greek, genially.

The cab started. M. Max, though silently reproaching himself, made mental notes of the destination. He had not renewed his sallow complexion, for reasons of his own, and his dilated pupils were beginning to contract again, facts which were not very evident, however, in the poor light. He was very twitchy, nevertheless, and the face of the man beside him was that of a sympathetic vulture, if such a creature can be imagined. He inquired casually if the new patron had brought his money with him, but for the most part his conversation turned upon China, with which country he seemed to be well acquainted. Arrived at Victoria, Mr. Gianapolis discharged the cab, and again taking the Frenchman by the arm, walked with him some twenty paces away from the station. A car suddenly pulled up almost beside them.

Ere M. Max had time to note those details in which he was most interested, Gianapolis had opened the door of the limousine, and the Frenchman found himself within, beside Gianapolis, and behind drawn blinds, speeding he knew not in what direction!

"I suppose I should apologize, my dear M. Gaston," said the Greek; and, although unable to see him, for there was little light in the car, M. Max seemed to *feel* him smiling—"but this little device has proved so useful hitherto. In the event of any of those troubles—wretched police interferences—arising, and of officious people obtaining possession of a patron's name, he is spared the necessity of perjuring himself in any way . . ."

"Perhaps I do not entirely understand you, monsieur?" said M. Max.

"It is so simple. The police are determined to raid one of our establishments: they adopt the course of tracking an habitue. This is not impossible. They question him; they ask, 'Do you know a Mr. King?' He replies that he knows no such person, has never seen, has never spoken with him! I assure you that official inquiries have gone thus far already, in New York, for example; but to what end? They say, 'Where is the establishment of a Mr. King to which you have gone on such and such an occasion?' He replies with perfect truth, 'I do not know.' Believe me this little device is quite in your own interest, M. Gaston."

"But when again I feel myself compelled to resort to the solace of the pipe, how then?"

"So simple! You will step to the telephone and ask for this number: East 18642. You will then ask for Mr. King, and an appointment will be made; I will meet you as I met you this evening—and all will be well."

M. Max began to perceive that he had to deal with a scheme even more elaborate than hitherto he had conjectured. These were very clever people, and through the whole complicated network, as through the petal of a poppy one may trace the veins, he traced the guiding will—the power of a tortuous Eastern mind. The system was truly Chinese in its elaborate, uncanny mystifications.

In some covered place that was very dark, the car stopped, and Gianapolis, leaping out with agility, assisted M. Max to descend.

This was a covered courtyard, only lighted by the head-lamps of the limousine.

"Take my hand," directed the Greek.

M. Max complied, and was conducted through a low doorway and on to descending steps.

Dimly, he heard the gear of the car reversed, and knew that the limousine was backing out from the courtyard. The door behind him was closed, and he heard no more. A dim light shone out below.

He descended, walking more confidently now that the way was visible. A moment later he stood upon the threshold of an apartment which calls for no further description at this place; he stood in the doorway of the incredible, unforgettable cave of the golden dragon; he looked into the beetle eyes of Ho-Pin!

Ho-Pin bowed before him, smiling his mirthless smile. In his left hand he held an amber cigarette tube in which a cigarette smoldered gently, sending up a gray pencil of smoke into the breathless, perfumed air.

"Mr. Ho-Pin," said Gianapolis, indicating the Chinaman, "who will attend to your requirements. This is our new friend from Paris, M. Gaston."

"You are vewry welcome," said the Chinaman in his monotonous, metallic voice. "I understand that a fee of twenty-five guineas—" He bowed again, still smiling.

The visitor took out his pocket-book and laid five notes, one sovereign, and two half-crowns upon a little ebony table beside him. Ho-Pin bowed again and waved his hand toward the lemon-colored door on the left.

"Good night, M. Gaston!" said Gianapolis, in radiant benediction.

"Au revoir, monsieur!"

M. Max followed Ho-Pin to Block A and was conducted to a room at the extreme right of the matting-lined corridor. He glanced about it curiously.

"If you will pwrepare for your flight into the subliminal," said Ho-Pin, bowing in the doorway, "I shall pwresently wreturn with your wings."

In the cave of the golden dragon, Gianapolis sat smoking upon one of the divans. The silence of the place was extraordinary; unnatural, in the very heart of busy commercial London. Ho-Pin reappeared and standing in the open doorway of Block A sharply clapped his hands three times.

Said, the Egyptian, came out of the door at the further end of the place, bearing a brass tray upon which were a little brass lamp of Oriental manufacture wherein burned a blue spirituous flame, a Japanese, lacquered box not much larger than a snuff-box, and a long and most curiously carved pipe of wood inlaid with metal and having a metal bowl. Bearing this, he crossed the room, passed Ho-Pin, and entered the corridor beyond.

"You have, of course, put him in the observation room?" said Gianapolis.

Ho-Pin regarded the speaker unemotionally.

"Assuwredly," he replied; "for since he visits us for the first time, Mr. King will wish to see him . . ."

A faint shadow momentarily crossed the swarthy face of the Greek at mention of that name—*Mr. King*. The servants of Mr. King, from the highest to the lowest, served him for gain . . . and from fear.

XXX

MAHARA

Utter silence had claimed again the cave of the golden dragon. Gianapolis sat alone in the place, smoking a cigarette, and gazing crookedly at the image on the ivory pedestal. Then, glancing at his wrist-watch, he stood up, and, stepping to the entrance door, was about to open it . . .

"Ah, so! You go—already?"—

Gianapolis started back as though he had put his foot upon a viper, and turned.

The Eurasian, wearing her yellow, Chinese dress, and with a red poppy in her hair, stood watching him through half-shut eyes, slowly waving her little fan before her face. Gianapolis attempted the radiant smile, but its brilliancy was somewhat forced tonight.

"Yes, I must be off," he said hurriedly; "I have to see someone—a future client, I think!"

"A future client—yes!"—the long black eyes were closed almost entirely now. "Who is it—this future client, that you have to see?"

"My dear Mahara! How odd of you to ask that . . ."

"It is odd of me?—so! It is odd of me that I thinking to wonder why you alway running away from me now?"

"Run away from you! My dear little Mahara!"—He approached the dusky beauty with a certain timidity as one might seek to caress a tiger-cat—"Surely you know . . ."

She struck down his hand with a sharp blow of her closed fan, darting at him a look from the brilliant eyes which was a living flame.

Resting one hand upon her hip, she stood with her right foot thrust forward from beneath the yellow robe and pivoting upon the heel of its little slipper. Her head tilted, she watched him through lowered lashes.

"It was not so with you in Moulmein," she said, her silvery voice lowered caressingly. "Do you remember with me a night beside the Irawaddi?—where was that I wonder? Was it in Prome?—Perhaps, yes? You threatened me to leap in, if . . . and I think to believe you!—I believing you!"

"Mahara!" cried Gianapolis, and sought to seize her in his arms.

Again she struck down his hand with the little fan, watching him continuously and with no change of expression. But the smoldering fire in those eyes told of a greater flame which consumed her slender body and was potent enough to consume many a victim upon its altar. Gianapolis' yellow skin assumed a faintly mottled appearance.

"Whatever is the matter?" he inquired plaintively.

"So you must be off—yes? I hear you say it; I asking you who to meet?"

"Why do you speak in English?" said Gianapolis with a faint irritation. "Let us talk . . ."

She struck him lightly on the face with her fan; but he clenched his teeth and suppressed an ugly exclamation.

"Who was it?" she asked, musically, "that say to me, 'to hear you speaking English—like rippling water'?"

"You are mad!" muttered Gianapolis, beginning to drill the points of his mustache as was his manner in moments of agitation. His crooked eyes were fixed upon the face of the girl. "You go too far."

"Be watching, my friend, that you also go not too far."

The tones were silvery as ever, but the menace unmistakable. Gianapolis forced a harsh laugh and brushed up his mustache furiously.

"What are you driving at?" he demanded, with some return of self-confidence. "Am I to be treated to another exhibition of your insane jealousies?"

"*Ah!*" The girl's eyes opened widely; she darted another venomous glance at him. "I am sure now, I am *sure!*"

"My dear Mahara, you talk nonsense!"

"*Ah!*"

She glided sinuously toward him, still with one hand resting upon her hip, stood almost touching his shoulder and raised her beautiful wicked face to his, peering at him through half-closed eyes, and resting the hand which grasped the fan lightly upon his arm.

"You think I do not see? You think I do not watch?"—softer and softer grew the silvery voice—"at Olaf van Noord's studio you think I do not hear? Perhaps you not thinking to care if I see and hear—for it seem you not seeing nor hearing *me*. I watch and I see. Is it her so soft brown hair? That color of hair is so more prettier than ugly black! Is it her English eyes? Eyes that born in the dark forests of Burma so hideous and so like the eyes of the apes! Is it her white skin and her red cheeks? A brown skin—though someone, there was, that say it is satin of heaven—is so tiresome; when no more it is a new toy it does not interest . . ."

"Really," muttered Gianapolis, uneasily, "I think you must be mad! I don't know what you are talking about."

"*Liar!*"

One lithe step forward the Eurasian sprang, and, at the word, brought down the fan with all her strength across Gianapolis' eyes!

He staggered away from her, uttering a hoarse cry and instinctively raising his arms to guard himself from further attack; but the girl stood poised again, her hand upon her hip; and swinging her right toe to and fro. Gianapolis, applying his handkerchief to his eyes, squinted at her furiously.

"Liar!" she repeated, and her voice had something of a soothing whisper. "I say to you, be so careful that you go not too far—with me! I do what I do, not because I am a poor fool . . ."

"It's funny," declared Gianapolis, an emotional catch in his voice. "It's damn funny for you—for *you*—to adopt these airs with me! Why, you went to Olaf van . . ."

"Stop!" cried the girl furiously, and sprang at him panther-like so that he fell back again in confusion, stumbled and collapsed upon a divan, with upraised, warding arms. "You Greek rat! you skinny Greek rat! Be careful what you think to say to me—to *me*! to *me*! Olaf van Noord—the poor, white-faced corpse-man! He is only one of Said's mummies! Be careful what you think to say to me . . . Oh! be careful—be very careful! It is dangerous of any friend of—*Mr. King* . . ."

Gianapolis glanced at her furtively.

"It is dangerous of anyone in a house of—*Mr. King* to think to make attachments,"—she hissed the words beneath her breath—"outside of ourselves. *Mr. King* would not be glad to hear of it . . . I do not like to tell it to *Mr. King* . . ."

Gianapolis rose to his feet, unsteadily, and stretched out his arms in supplication.

"Mahara!" he said, "don't treat me like this! dear little Mahara! what have I done to you? Tell me!—only tell me!"

"Shall I tell it in English?" asked the Eurasian softly. Her eyes now were nearly closed; "or does it worry you that I speak so ugly . . ."

"Mahara!"

"I only say, be so very careful."

He made a final, bold attempt to throw his arms about her, but she slipped from his grasp and ran lightly across the room.

"Go! hurry off!" she said, bending forward and pointing at him with her fan, her eyes widely opened and blazing—"but remember—there is danger! There is Said, who creeps silently, like the jackal . . ."

She opened the ebony door and darted into the corridor beyond, closing the door behind her.

Gianapolis looked about him in a dazed manner, and yet again applied his handkerchief to his stinging eyes. Whoever could have seen him now must have failed to recognize the radiant Gianapolis so well-known in Bohemian society, the Gianapolis about whom floated a halo of mystery, but who at all times was such a good fellow and so debonair. He took up his hat and gloves, turned, and resolutely strode to the door. Once he glanced back over his shoulder, but shrugged with a sort of self-contempt, and ascended to the top of the steps.

With a key which he selected from a large bunch in his pocket, he opened the door, and stepped out into the garage, carefully closing the door behind him. An electric pocket-lamp served him with sufficient light to find his way out into the lane, and very shortly he was proceeding along Limehouse Causeway. At the moment, indignation was the major emotion ruling his mind; he resented the form which his anger assumed, for it was a passion of rebellion, and rebellion is only possible in servants. It is the part of a slave resenting the lash. He was an unscrupulous, unmoral man, not lacking in courage of a sort; and upon the conquest of Mahara, the visible mouthpiece of Mr. King, he had entered in much the same spirit as that actuating a Kanaka who dives for pearls in a shark-infested lagoon. He had sought a slave, and lo! the slave was become the master! Otherwise whence this spirit of rebellion . . . this fear?

He occupied himself with such profitless reflections up to the time that he came to the electric trains; but, from thence onward, his mind became otherwise engaged. On his way to Piccadilly Circus that same evening, he had chanced to find himself upon a crowded pavement walking immediately behind Denise Ryland and Helen Cumberly. His esthetic, Greek soul had been fired at first sight of the beauty of the latter; and now, his heart had leaped ecstatically. His first impulse, of course, had been to join the two ladies; but Gianapolis had trained himself to suspect all impulses.

Therefore he had drawn near—near enough to overhear their conversation without proclaiming himself. What he had learned by this eavesdropping he counted of peculiar value.

Helen Cumberly was arranging to dine with her friend at the latter's hotel that evening. "But I want to be home early," he had heard the girl say, "so if I leave you at about ten o'clock I can walk to Palace Mansions. No! you need not come with me; I enjoy a lonely walk through the streets of London in the evening . . ."

Gianapolis registered a mental vow that Helen's walk should not be a lonely one. He did not flatter himself upon the possession of a pleasing exterior, but, from experience, he knew that with women he had a winning way.

Now, his mind aglow with roseate possibilities, he stepped from the tram in the neighborhood of Shoreditch, and chartered a taxi-cab. From this he descended at the corner of Arundel Street and strolled along westward in the direction of the hotel patronized by Miss Ryland. At a corner from which he could command a view of the entrance, he paused and consulted his watch.

It was nearly twenty minutes past ten. Mentally, he cursed Mahara, who perhaps had caused him to let slip this golden opportunity. But his was not a character easily discouraged; he lighted a cigarette and prepared himself to wait, in the hope that the girl had not yet left her friend.

Gianapolis was a man capable of the uttermost sacrifices upon either of two shrines; that of Mammon, or that of Eros. His was a temperament (truly characteristic of his race) which can build up a structure painfully, year by year, suffering unutterable privations in the cause of its growth, only to shatter it at a blow for a woman's smile. He was a true member of that brotherhood, represented throughout the bazaars of the East, of those singular shopkeepers who live by commercial rapine, who, demanding a hundred piastres for an embroidered shawl from a plain woman, will exchange it with a pretty one for a perfumed handkerchief. Externally of London, he was internally of the Levant.

His vigil lasted but a quarter of an hour. At twenty-five minutes to eleven, Helen Cumberly came running down the steps of the hotel and hurried toward the Strand. Like a shadow, Gianapolis, throwing away a half-smoked cigarette, glided around the corner, paused and so timed his return that he literally ran into the girl as she entered the main thoroughfare.

He started back.

"Why!" he cried, "Miss Cumberly!"

Helen checked a frown, and hastily substituted a smile.

"How odd that I should meet you here, Mr. Gianapolis," she said.

"Most extraordinary! I was on my way to visit a friend in Victoria Street upon a rather urgent matter. May I venture to hope that your path lies in a similar direction?"

Helen Cumberly, deceived by his suave manner (for how was she to know that the Greek had learnt her address from Crockett, the reporter?), found herself at a loss for an excuse. Her remarkably pretty mouth was drawn down to one corner, inducing a dimple of perplexity in her left cheek. She had that breadth between the eyes which, whilst not an attribute of perfect beauty, indicates an active mind, and is often found in Scotch women; now, by the slight raising of her eyebrows, this space was accentuated. But Helen's rapid thinking availed her not at all.

"Had you proposed to walk?" inquired Gianapolis, bending deferentially and taking his place beside her with a confidence which showed that her opportunity for repelling his attentions was past.

"Yes," she said, hesitatingly; "but—I fear I am detaining you . . ."

Of two evils she was choosing the lesser; the idea of being confined in a cab with this ever-smiling Greek was unthinkable.

"Oh, my dear Miss Cumberly!" cried Gianapolis, beaming radiantly, "it is a greater pleasure than I can express to you, and then for two friends who are proceeding in the same direction to walk apart would be quite absurd, would it not?"

The term "friend" was not pleasing to Helen's ears; Mr. Gianapolis went far too fast. But she recognized her helplessness, and accepted this cavalier with as good a grace as possible.

He immediately began to talk of Olaf van Noord and his pictures, whilst Helen hurried along as though her life depended upon her speed. Sometimes, on the pretense of piloting her at crossings, Gianapolis would take her arm; and this contact she found most disagreeable; but on the whole his conduct was respectful to the point of servility.

A pretty woman who is not wholly obsessed by her personal charms, learns more of the ways of mankind than it is vouchsafed to her plainer sister ever to know; and in the crooked eyes of Gianapolis, Helen Cumberly read a world of unuttered things, and drew her own conclusions. These several conclusions dictated a single course; avoidance of Gianapolis in future.

Fortunately, Helen Cumberly's self-chosen path in life had taught her how to handle the nascent and undesirable lover. She chatted upon the subject of art, and fenced adroitly whenever the Greek sought to introduce the slightest personal element into the conversation. Nevertheless, she was relieved when at last she found herself in the familiar Square with her foot upon the steps of Palace Mansions.

"Good night, Mr. Gianapolis!" she said, and frankly offered her hand.

The Greek raised it to his lips with exaggerated courtesy, and retained it, looking into her eyes in his crooked fashion.

"We both move in the world of art and letters; may I hope that this meeting will not be our last?"

"I am always wandering about between Fleet Street and Soho," laughed Helen. "It is quite certain we shall run into each other again before long. Good night, and thank you so much!"

She darted into the hallway, and ran lightly up the stairs. Opening the flat door with her key, she entered and closed it behind her, sighing with relief to be free of the over-attentive Greek. Some impulse prompted her to enter her own room, and, without turning up the light, to peer down into the Square.

Gianapolis was descending the steps. On the pavement he stood and looked up at the windows, lingeringly; then he turned and walked away.

Helen Cumberly stifled an exclamation.

As the Greek gained the corner of the Square and was lost from view, a lithe figure—kin of the shadows which had masked it—became detached from the other shadows beneath the trees of the central garden and stood, a vague silhouette seemingly looking up at her window as Gianapolis had looked.

Helen leaned her hands upon the ledge and peered intently down. The figure was a vague blur in the darkness, but it was moving away along by the rails . . . following Gianapolis. No clear glimpse she had of it, for bat-like, it avoided the light, this sinister shape—and was gone.

XXXI

MUSK AND ROSES

It is time to rejoin M. Gaston Max in the catacombs of Ho-Pin. Having prepared himself for drugged repose in the small but luxurious apartment to which he had been conducted by the Chinaman, he awaited with interest the next development. This took the form of the arrival of an Egyptian attendant, white-robed, red-slippered, and wearing the inevitable tarboosh. Upon the brass tray which he carried were arranged the necessities of the opium smoker. Placing the tray upon a little table beside the bed, he extracted from the lacquered box a piece of gummy substance upon the end of a long needle. This he twisted around, skilfully, in the lamp flame until it acquired a blue spirituous flame of its own. He dropped it into the bowl of the carven pipe and silently placed the pipe in M. Max's hand.

Max, with simulated eagerness, rested the mouthpiece between his lips and *exhaled* rapturously.

Said stood watching him, without the slightest expression of interest being perceptible upon his immobile face. For some time the Frenchman made pretense of inhaling, gently, the potent vapor, lying propped upon one elbow; then, allowing his head gradually to droop, he closed his eyes and lay back upon the silken pillow.

Once more he exhaled feebly ere permitting the pipe to drop from his listless grasp. The mouthpiece yet rested between his lips, but the lower lip was beginning to drop. Finally, the pipe slipped through his fingers on to the rich carpet, and he lay inert, head thrown back, and revealing his lower teeth. The nauseating fumes of opium loaded the atmosphere.

Said silently picked up the pipe, placed it upon the tray and retired, closing the door in the same noiseless manner that characterized all his movements.

For a time, M. Max lay inert, glancing about the place through the veil of his lashes. He perceived no evidence of surveillance, therefore he ventured fully to open his eyes; but he did not move his head.

With the skill in summarizing detail at a glance which contributed largely to make him the great criminal investigator that he was, he noted those particulars which at an earlier time had occasioned the astonishment of Soames.

M. Max was too deeply versed in his art to attempt any further investigations, yet; he contented himself with learning as much as was possible without moving in any way; and whilst he lay there awaiting whatever might come, the door opened noiselessly—to admit Ho-Pin.

He was about to be submitted to a supreme test, for which, however, he was not unprepared. He lay with closed eyes, breathing nasally.

Ho-Pin, his face a smiling, mirthless mask, bent over the bed. Adeptly, he seized the right eyelid of M. Max, and rolled it back over his forefinger, disclosing the eyeball. M. Max, anticipating this test of the genuineness of his coma, had rolled up his eyes at the moment of Ho-Pin's approach, so that now only the white of the sclerotic showed. His trained nerves did not betray him. He lay like a dead man, never flinching.

Ho-Pin, releasing the eyelid, muttered something gutturally, and stole away from the bed as silently as he had approached it. Very methodically he commenced to search through M. Max's effects, commencing with the discarded garments. He examined the maker's marks upon these, and scrutinized the buttons closely. He turned out all the pockets, counted the contents of the purse, and of the notecase, examined the name inside M. Max's hat, and explored the lining in a manner which aroused the detective's professional admiration. Watch and pocket-knife, Ho-Pin inspected with interest. The little hand-bag which M. Max had brought with him, containing a few toilet necessaries, was overhauled religiously. So much the detective observed through his lowered lashes.

Then Ho-Pin again approached the bed and M. Max became again a dead man.

The silken pyjamas which the detective wore were subjected to gentle examination by the sensitive fingers of the Chinaman, and those same fingers crept beetle-like beneath the pillow.

Silently, Ho-Pin stole from the room and silently closed the door.

M. Max permitted himself a long breath of relief. It was an ordeal through which few men could have passed triumphant.

The *silence* of the place next attracted the inquirer's attention. He had noted this silence at the moment that he entered the cave of the golden dragon, but here it was even more marked; so that he divined, even before he had examined the walls, that the apartment was rendered sound-proof in the manner of a public telephone cabinet. It was a significant circumstance to which he allotted its full value.

But the question uppermost in his mind at the moment was this: Was the time come yet to commence his explorations?

Patience was included in his complement, and, knowing that he had the night before him, he preferred to wait. In this he did well. Considerable time elapsed, possibly half-an-hour . . . and again the door opened.

M. Max was conscious of a momentary nervous tremor; for now a *woman* stood regarding him. She wore a Chinese costume; a huge red poppy was in her hair. Her beauty was magnificently evil; she had the grace of a gazelle and the eyes of a sorceress. He had deceived Ho-Pin, but could he deceive this Eurasian with the witch-eyes wherein burnt ancient wisdom?

He felt rather than saw her approach; for now he ventured to peep no more. She touched him lightly upon the mouth with her fingers and laughed a little low, rippling laugh, the sound of which seemed to trickle along his sensory nerves, icily. She bent over him—lower—lower—and lower yet; until, above the nauseating odor of the place he could smell the musk perfume of her hair. Yet lower she bent; with every nerve in his body he could feel her nearing presence . . . .

She kissed him on the lips.

Again she laughed, in that wicked, eerie glee.

M. Max was conscious of the most singular, the maddest impulses; it was one of the supreme moments of his life. He knew that all depended upon his absolute immobility; yet something in his brain was prompting him—prompting him—to gather the witch to his breast; to return that poisonous, that vampirish kiss, and then to crush out life from the small lithe body.

Sternly he fought down these strange promptings, which he knew to emanate hypnotically from the brain of the creature bending over him.

"Oh, my beautiful dead-baby," she said, softly, and her voice was low, and weirdly sweet. "Oh, my new baby, how I love you, my dead one!" Again she laughed, a musical peal. "I will creep to you in the poppyland where you go . . . and you shall twine your fingers in my hair and pull my red mouth down to you, kissing me . . . kissing me, until you stifle and you die of my love . . . . Oh! my beautiful mummy-baby . . . my baby."

The witch-crooning died away into a murmur; and the Frenchman became conscious of the withdrawal of that presence from the room. No sound came to tell of the reclosing of the door; but the obsession was removed, the spell raised.

Again he inhaled deeply the tainted air, and again he opened his eyes.

He had no warranty to suppose that he should remain unmolested during the remainder of the night. The strange words of the Eurasian he did not construe literally; yet could he be certain that he was secure? Nay! he could be certain that he was *not!*

The shaded lamp was swung in such a position that most of the light was directed upon him where he lay, whilst the walls of the room were bathed in a purple shadow. Behind him and above him, directly over the head of the bunk, a faint sound—a sound inaudible except in such a dead silence as that prevailing—told of some shutter being raised or opened. He had trained himself to watch beneath lowered lids without betraying that he was doing so by the slightest nervous twitching. Now, as he watched the purple shaded lamp above him, he observed that it was swaying and moving very gently, whereas hitherto it had floated motionless in the still air.

No other sound came to guide him, and to have glanced upward would have been to betray all.

For the second time that night he became aware of one who watched him, became conscious of observation without the guaranty of his physical senses. And beneath this new surveillance, there grew up such a revulsion of his inner being as he had rarely experienced. The perfume of *roses* became perceptible; and for some occult reason, its fragrance *disgusted*.

It was as though a faint draught from the opened shutter poured into the apartment an impalpable cloud of evil; the very soul of the Eurasian, had it taken vapory form and enveloped him, could not have created a greater turmoil of his senses than this!

Some sinister and definitely malignant intelligence was focussed upon him; or was this a chimera of his imagination? Could it be that now he was become en rapport with the thought-forms created in that chamber by its successive occupants?

Scores, perhaps hundreds of brains had there partaken of the unholy sacrament of opium; thousands, millions of evil carnivals had trailed in impish procession about that bed. He knew enough of the creative power of thought to be aware that a sensitive mind coming into contact with such an atmosphere could not fail to respond in some degree to the suggestions, to the elemental hypnosis, of the place.

Was he, owing to his self-induced receptivity of mind, redreaming the evil dreams of those who had occupied that bed before him?

It might be so, but, whatever the explanation, he found himself unable to shake off that uncanny sensation of being watched, studied, by a powerful and inimical intelligence.

Mr. King! Mr. King was watching him!

The director of that group, whose structure was founded upon the wreckage of human souls, was watching him! Because of a certain sympathy which existed between his present emotions and those which had threatened to obsess him whilst the Eurasian was in the room, he half believed that it was she who peered down at him, now . . . or she, and another.

The lamp swung gently to and fro, turning slowly to the right and then revolving again to the left, giving life in its gyrations to the intermingled figures on the walls. The atmosphere of the room was nauseating; it was beginning to overpower him . . . .

Creative power of thought . . . what startling possibilities it opened up. Almost it seemed, if Sir Brian Malpas were to be credited, that the collective mind-force of a group of opium smokers had created the "glamor" of a woman—an Oriental woman—who visited them regularly in their trances. Or had that vision a prototype in the flesh—whom he had seen?

Creative power of thought . . . *Mr. King*! He was pursuing Mr. King; whilst Mr. King might be nothing more than a thought-form—a creation of cumulative thought—an elemental spirit which became visible to his subjects, his victims, which had power over them; which could slay them as the "shell" slew Frankenstein, his creator; which could materialize: . . . Mr. King might be the Spirit of Opium . . . .

The faint clicking sound was repeated.

Beads of perspiration stood upon M. Max's forehead; his imagination had been running away with him. God! this was a house of fear! He controlled himself, but only by dint of a tremendous effort of will.

Stealthily watching the lamp, he saw that the arc described by its gyrations was diminishing with each successive swing, and, as he watched, its movements grew slighter and slighter, until finally it became quite stationary again, floating, purple and motionless, upon the stagnant air.

Very slowly, he ventured to change his position, for his long ordeal was beginning to induce cramp. The faint creaking of the metal bunk seemed, in the dead stillness and to his highly-tensed senses, like the rattling of castanets.

For ten minutes he lay in his new position; then moved slightly again and waited for fully three-quarters of an hour. Nothing happened, and he now determined to proceed with his inquiries.

Sitting upon the edge of the bunk, he looked about him, first directing his attention to that portion of the wall immediately above. So cunningly was the trap contrived that he could find no trace of its existence. Carefully balancing himself upon the rails on either side of the bunk, he stood up, and peered closely about that part of the wall from which the sound had seemed to come. He even ran his fingers lightly over the paper, up as high as he could reach; but not the slightest crevice was perceptible. He began to doubt the evidence of his own senses.

Unless his accursed imagination had been playing him tricks, a trap of some kind had been opened above his head and someone had looked in at him; yet—and his fingers were trained to such work—he was prepared to swear that the surface of the Chinese paper covering the wall was perfectly continuous. He drummed upon it lightly with his finger-tips, here and there over the surface above the bed. And in this fashion he became enlightened.

A portion, roughly a foot in height and two feet long, yielded a slightly different note to his drumming; whereby he knew that that part of the paper was not *attached* to the wall. He perceived the truth. The trap, when closed, fitted flush with the back of the wall-paper, and this paper (although when pasted upon the walls it showed no evidence of the fact) must be *transparent*.

From some dark place beyond, it was possible to peer in *through* the rectangular patch of paper as through a window, at the occupant of the bunk below, upon whom the shaded lamp directly poured its rays!

He examined more closely a lower part of the wall, which did not fall within the shadow of the purple lamp-shade; for he was thinking of the draught which had followed the opening of the trap. By this examination he learnt two things: The explanation of the draught, and that of a peculiar property possessed by the mural decorations. These (as Soames had observed before him) assumed a new form if one stared at them closely; other figures, figures human and animal, seemed to take shape and to peer out from *behind* the more obvious designs which were perceptible at a glance. The longer and the closer one studied these singular walls, the more evident the *under* design became, until it usurped the field of vision entirely. It was a bewildering delusion; but M. Max had solved the mystery.

There were *two* designs; the first, an intricate Chinese pattern, was painted or printed upon material like the finest gauze. This was attached over a second and vividly colored pattern upon thick parchment-like paper—as he learnt by the application of the point of his pocket-knife.

The observation trap was covered with this paper, and fitted so nicely in the opening that his fingers had failed to detect, through the superimposed gauze, the slightest irregularity there. But, the trap opened, a perfectly clear view of the room could be obtained through the gauze, which, by reason of its texture, also admitted a current of air.

This matter settled, M. Max proceeded carefully to examine the entire room foot by foot. Opening the door in one corner, he entered the bathroom, in which, as in the outer apartment, an electric light was burning. No window was discoverable, and not even an opening for ventilation purposes. The latter fact he might have deduced from the stagnation of the atmosphere.

Half an hour or more he spent in this fashion, without having discovered anything beyond the secret of the observation trap. Again he took out his pocket-knife, which was a large one with a handsome mother-o'-pearl handle. Although Mr. Ho-Pin had examined this carefully, he had solved only half of its secrets. M. Max extracted a little pair of tweezers from the slot in which they were lodged—as Ho-Pin had not neglected to do; but Ho-Pin, having looked at the tweezers, had returned them to their place: M. Max did not do so. He opened the entire knife as though it had been a box, and revealed within it a tiny set of appliances designed principally for the desecration of locks!

Selecting one of these, he took up his watch from the table upon which it lay, and approached the door. It possessed a lever handle of the Continental pattern, and M. Max silently prayed that this might not be a snare and a delusion, but that the lock below might be of the same manufacture.

In order to settle the point, he held the face of his watch close to the keyhole, wound its knob in the wrong direction, and lo! it became an electric lamp!

One glance he cast into the tiny cavity, then dropped back upon the bunk, twisting his mobile mouth in that half smile at once humorous and despairful.

"Nom d'un p'tit bonhomme!—a Yale!" he muttered. "To open that without noise is impossible! Damn!"

M. Max threw himself back upon the pillow, and for an hour afterward lay deep in silent reflection.

He had cigarettes in his case and should have liked to smoke, but feared to take the risk of scenting the air with a perfume so unorthodox.

He had gained something by his exploit, but not all that he had hoped for; clearly his part now was to await what the morning should bring.

XXXII

BLUE BLINDS

Morning brought the silent opening of the door, and the entrance of Said, the Egyptian, bearing a tiny Chinese tea service upon a lacquered tray.

But M. Max lay in a seemingly deathly stupor, and from this the impassive Oriental had great difficulty in arousing him. Said, having shaken some symptoms of life into the limp form of M. Max, filled the little cup with fragrant China tea, and, supporting the dazed man, held the beverage to his lips. With his eyes but slightly opened, and with all his weight resting upon the arm of the Egyptian, he gulped the hot tea, and noted that it was of exquisite quality.

Theine is an antidote to opium, and M. Max accordingly became somewhat restored, and lay staring at the Oriental, and blinking his eyes foolishly.

Said, leaving the tea service upon the little table, glided from the room. Something else the Egyptian had left upon the tray in addition to the dainty vessels of porcelain; it was a steel ring containing a dozen or more keys. Most of these keys lay fanwise and bunched together, but one lay isolated and pointing in an opposite direction. It was a Yale key—the key of the door!

Silently as a shadow, M. Max glided into the bathroom, and silently, swiftly, returned, carrying a cake of soap. Three clear, sharp impressions, he secured of the Yale, the soap leaving no trace of the operation upon the metal. He dropped the precious soap tablet into his open bag.

In a state of semi-torpor, M. Max sprawled upon the bed for ten minutes or more, during which time, as he noted, the door remained ajar. Then there entered a figure which seemed wildly out of place in the establishment of Ho-Pin. It was that of a butler, most accurately dressed and most deferential in all his highly-trained movements. His dark hair was neatly brushed, and his face, which had a pinched appearance, was composed in that "if-it-is-entirely-agreeable-to-you-Sir" expression, typical of his class.

The unhealthy, yellow skin of the new arrival, which harmonized so ill with the clear whites of his little furtive eyes, interested M. Max extraordinarily. M. Max was blinking like a week-old kitten, and one could have sworn that he was but hazily conscious of his surroundings; whereas in reality he was memorizing the cranial peculiarities of the new arrival, the shape of his nose, the disposition of his ears; the exact hue of his eyes; the presence of a discolored tooth in his lower jaw, which a fish-like, nervous trick of opening and closing the mouth periodically revealed.

"Good morning, sir!" said the valet, gently rubbing his palms together and bending over the bed.

M. Max inhaled deeply, stared in glassy fashion, but in no way indicated that he had heard the words.

The valet shook him gently by the shoulder.

"Good morning, sir. Shall I prepare your bath?"

"She is a serpent!" muttered M. Max, tossing one arm weakly above his head . . . "all yellow . . . . But roses are growing in the mud . . . of the river!"

"If you will take your bath, sir," insisted the man in black, "I shall be ready to shave you when you return."

"Bath . . . shave me!"

M. Max began to rub his eyes and to stare uncomprehendingly at the speaker.

"Yes, sir; good morning, sir,"—there was another bow and more rubbing of palms.

"Ah!"—of course! Morbleu! This is Paris . . . ."

"No, sir, excuse me, sir, London. Bath hot or cold, sir?"

"Cold," replied M. Max, struggling upright with apparent difficulty; "yes,—cold."

"Very good, sir. Have you brought your own razor, sir?"

"Yes, yes," muttered Max—"in the bag—in that bag."

"I will fill the bath, sir."

The bath being duly filled, M. Max, throwing about his shoulders a magnificent silk kimono which he found upon the armchair, steered a zigzag course to the bathroom. His tooth-brush had been put in place by the attentive valet; there was an abundance of clean towels, soaps, bath salts, with other necessities and luxuries of the toilet. M. Max, following his bath, saw fit to evidence a return to mental clarity; and whilst he was being shaved he sought to enter into conversation with the valet. But the latter was singularly reticent, and again M. Max changed his tactics. He perceived here a golden opportunity which he must not allow to slip through his fingers.

"Would you like to earn a hundred pounds?" he demanded abruptly, gazing into the beady eyes of the man bending over him.

Soames almost dropped the razor. His state of alarm was truly pitiable; he glanced to the right, he glanced to the left, he glanced over his shoulder, up at the ceiling and down at the floor.

"Excuse me, sir," he said, nervously; "I don't think I quite understand you, sir?"

"It is quite simple," replied M. Max. "I asked you if you had some use for a hundred pounds. Because if you have, I will meet you at any place you like to mention and bring with me cash to that amount!"

"Hush, sir!—for God's sake, hush, sir!" whispered Soames.

A dew of perspiration was glistening upon his forehead, and it was fortunate that he had finished shaving M. Max, for his hand was trembling furiously. He made a pretense of hurrying with towels, bay rum, and powder spray, but the beady eyes were ever glancing to right and left and all about.

M. Max, who throughout this time had been reflecting, made a second move.

"Another fifty, or possibly another hundred, could be earned as easily," he said, with assumed carelessness. "I may add that this will not be offered again, and . . . that you will shortly be out of employment, with worse to follow."

Soames began to exhibit signs of collapse.

"Oh, my God!" he muttered, "what shall I do? I can't promise—I can't promise; but I might—I *might* look in at the 'Three Nuns' on Friday evening about nine o'clock."

He hastily scooped up M. Max's belongings, thrust them into the handbag and closed it. M. Max was now fully dressed and ready to depart. He placed a sovereign in the valet's ready palm.

"That's an appointment," he said softly.

Said entered and stood bowing in the doorway.

"Good morning, sir, good morning," muttered Soames, and covertly he wiped the perspiration from his brow with the corner of a towel—"good morning, and thank you very much."

M. Max, buttoning his light overcoat in order to conceal the fact that he wore evening dress, entered the corridor, and followed the Egyptian into the cave of the golden dragon. Ho-Pin, sleek and smiling, received him there. Ho-Pin was smoking the inevitable cigarette in the long tube, and, opening the door, he silently led the way up the steps into the covered courtyard, Said following with the hand bag. The limousine stood there, dimly visible in the darkness. Said placed the handbag upon the seat inside, and Ho-Pin assisted M. Max to enter, closing the door upon him, but leaning through the open window to shake his hand. The Chinaman's hand was icily cold and limp.

"Au wrevoir, my dear fwriend," he said in his metallic voice. "I hope to have the pleasure of gwreeting you again vewry shortly."

With that he pulled up the window from the outside, and the occupant of the limousine found himself in impenetrable darkness; for dark blue blinds covered all the windows. He lay back, endeavoring to determine what should be his next move. The car started with a perfect action, and without the slightest jolt or jar. By reason of the light which suddenly shone in through the chinks of the blinds, he knew that he was outside the covered courtyard; then he became aware that a sharp turning had been taken to the left, followed almost immediately, by one to the right.

He directed his attention to the blinds.

"Ah! nom d'un nom! they are clever—these!"

The blinds worked in little vertical grooves and had each a tiny lock. The blinds covering the glass doors on either side were attached to the adjustable windows; so that when Ho-Pin had raised the window, he had also closed the blind! And these windows operated automatically, and defied all M. Max's efforts to open them!

He was effectively boxed in and unable to form the slightest impression of his surroundings. He threw himself back upon the soft cushions with a muttered curse of vexation; but the mobile mouth was twisted into that wryly humorous smile. Always, M. Max was a philosopher.

At the end of a drive of some twenty-five minutes or less, the car stopped—the door was opened, and the radiant Gianapolis extended both hands to the occupant.

"My dear M. Gaston!" he cried, "how glad I am to see you looking so well! Hand me your bag, I beg of you!"

M. Max placed the bag in the extended hand of Gianapolis, and leapt out upon the pavement.

"This way, my dear friend!" cried the Greek, grasping him warmly by the arm.

The Frenchman found himself being led along toward the head of the car; and, at the same moment, Said reversed the gear and backed away. M. Max was foiled in his hopes of learning the number of the limousine.

He glanced about him wonderingly.

"You are in Temple Gardens, M. Gaston," explained the Greek, "and here, unless I am greatly mistaken, comes a disengaged taxi-cab. You will drive to your hotel?"

"Yes, to my hotel," replied M. Max.

"And whenever you wish to avail yourself of your privilege, and pay a second visit to the establishment presided over by Mr. Ho-Pin, you remember the number?"

"I remember the number," replied M. Max.

The cab hailed by Gianapolis drew up beside the two, and M. Max entered it.

"Good morning, M. Gaston."

"Good morning, Mr. Gianapolis."

XXXIII

LOGIC VS. INTUITION

And now, Henry Leroux, Denise Ryland and Helen Cumberly were speeding along the Richmond Road beneath a sky which smiled upon Leroux's convalescence; for this was a perfect autumn morning which ordinarily had gladdened him, but which saddened him today.

The sun shone and the sky was blue; a pleasant breeze played upon his cheeks; whilst Mira, his wife, was . . .

He knew that he had come perilously near to the borderland beyond which are gibbering, mowing things: that he had stood upon the frontier of insanity; and realizing the futility of such reflections, he struggled to banish them from his mind, for his mind was not yet healed—and he must be whole, be sane, if he would take part in the work, which, now, strangers were doing, whilst he—whilst he was a useless hulk.

Denise Ryland had been very voluble at the commencement of the drive, but, as it progressed, had grown gradually silent, and now sat with her brows working up and down and with a little network of wrinkles alternately appearing and disappearing above the bridge of her nose. A self-reliant woman, it was irksome to her to know herself outside the circle of activity revolving around the mysterious Mr. King. She had had one interview with Inspector Dunbar, merely in order that she might give personal testimony to the fact that Mira Leroux had not visited her that year in Paris. Of the shrewd Scotsman she had formed the poorest opinion; and indeed she never had been known to express admiration for, or even the slightest confidence in, any man breathing. The amiable M. Gaston possessed virtues which appealed to her, but whilst she admitted that his conversation was entertaining and his general behavior good, she always spoke with the utmost contempt of his sartorial splendor.

Now, with the days and the weeks slipping by, and with the spectacle before her of poor Leroux, a mere shadow of his former self, with the case, so far as she could perceive, at a standstill, and with the police (she firmly believed) doing "absolutely . . . nothing . . . whatever"—Denise Ryland recognized that what was lacking in the investigation was that intuition and wit which only a clever woman could bring to bear upon it, and of which she, in particular, possessed an unlimited reserve.

The car sped on toward the purer atmosphere of the riverside, and even the clouds of dust, which periodically enveloped them, with the passing of each motor-'bus, and which at the commencement of the drive had inspired her to several notable and syncopated outbursts, now left her unmoved.

She thought that at last she perceived the secret working of that Providence which ever dances attendance at the elbow of accomplished womankind. Following the lead set by "H. C." in the Planet ("H. C." was Helen Cumberly's nom de plume) and by Crocket in the Daily Monitor, the London Press had taken Olaf van Noord to its bosom; and his exhibition in the Little Gallery was an established financial success, whilst "Our Lady of the Poppies" (which had, of course, been rejected by the Royal Academy) promised to be the picture of the year.

Mentally, Denise Ryland was again surveying that remarkable composition; mentally she was surveying Olaf van Noord's model, also. Into the scheme slowly forming in her brain, the yellow-wrapped cigarette containing "a small percentage of opium" fitted likewise. Finally, but not last in importance, the Greek gentleman, Mr. Gianapolis, formed a unit of the whole.

Denise Ryland had always despised those detective creations which abound in French literature; perceiving in their marvelous deductions a tortured logic incompatible with the classic models. She prided herself upon her logic, possibly because it was a quality which she lacked, and probably because she confused it with intuition, of which, to do her justice, she possessed an unusual share. Now, this intuition was at work, at work well and truly; and the result which this mental contortionist ascribed to pure reason was nearer to the truth than a real logician could well have hoped to attain by confining himself to legitimate data. In short, she had determined to her own satisfaction that Mr. Gianapolis was the clue to the mystery; that Mr. Gianapolis was not (as she had once supposed) enacting the part of an amiable liar when he declared that there were, in London, such apartments as that represented by Olaf van Noord; that Mr. Gianapolis was acquainted with the present whereabouts of Mrs. Leroux; that Mr. Gianapolis knew who murdered Iris Vernon; and that Scotland Yard was a benevolent institution for the support of those of enfeebled intellect.

These results achieved, she broke her long silence at the moment that the car was turning into Richmond High Street.

"My dear!" she exclaimed, clutching Helen's arm, "I see it all!"

"Oh!" cried the girl, "how you startled me! I thought you were ill or that you had seen something frightful."

"I HAVE . . . seen something . . . frightful," declared Denise Ryland. She glared across at the haggard Leroux. "Harry . . . Leroux," she continued, "it is very fortunate . . . that I came to London . . . very fortunate."

"I am sincerely glad that you did," answered the novelist, with one of his kindly, weary smiles.

"My dear," said Denise Ryland, turning again to Helen Cumberly, "you say you met that . . . cross-eyed . . . being . . . Gianapolis, again?"

"Good Heavens!" cried Helen; "I thought I should never get rid of him; a most loathsome man!"

"My dear . . . child"—Denise squeezed her tightly by the arm, and peered into her face, intently—"cultivate . . . *deliberately* cultivate that man's acquaintance!"

Helen stared at her friend as though she suspected the latter's sanity.

"I am afraid I do not understand at all," she said, breathlessly.

"I am positive that I do not," declared Leroux, who was as much surprised as Helen. "In the first place I am not acquainted with this cross-eyed being."

"You are . . . out of this!" cried Denise Ryland with a sweeping movement of the left hand; "entirely . . . out of it! This is no *man's* . . . business."

"But my dear Denise!" exclaimed Helen . . . .

"I beseech you; I entreat you; . . . I *order* . . . you to cultivate . . . that . . . execrable . . . being."

"Perhaps," said Helen, with eyes widely opened, "you will condescend to give me some slight reason why I should do anything so extraordinary and undesirable?"

"Undesirable!" cried Denise. "On the contrary; . . . it is *most* . . . desirable! It is essential. The wretched . . . cross-eyed . . . creature has presumed to fall in love . . . with you."

"Oh!" cried Helen, flushing, and glancing rapidly at Leroux, who now was thoroughly interested, "please do not talk nonsense!"

"It is no . . . nonsense. It is the finger . . . of Providence. Do you know where you can find . . . him?"

"Not exactly; but I have a shrewd suspicion," again she glanced in an embarrassed way at Leroux, "that he will know where to find *me*."

"Who is this presumptuous person?" inquired the novelist, leaning forward, his dark blue eyes aglow with interest.

"Never mind," replied Denise Ryland, "you will know . . . soon enough. In the meantime . . . as I am simply . . . starving, suppose we see about . . . lunch?"

Moved by some unaccountable impulse, Helen extended her hand to Leroux, who took it quietly in his own and held it, looking down at the slim fingers as though he derived strength and healing from their touch.

"Poor boy," she said softly.

XXXIV

M. MAX REPORTS PROGRESS

Detective-Sergeant Sowerby was seated in Dunbar's room at New Scotland Yard. Some days had elapsed since that critical moment when, all unaware of the fact, they had stood within three yards of the much-wanted Soames, in the fauteuils of the east-end music-hall. Every clue thus far investigated had proved a *cul-de-sac*. Dunbar, who had literally been working night and day, now began to show evidence of his giant toils. The tawny eyes were as keen as ever, and the whole man as forceful as of old, but in the intervals of conversation, his lids would droop wearily; he would only arouse himself by a perceptible effort.

Sowerby, whose bowler hat lay upon Dunbar's table, was clad in the familiar raincoat, and his ruddy cheerfulness had abated not one whit.

"Have you ever read 'The Adventures of Martin Zeda'?" he asked suddenly, breaking a silence of some minutes' duration.

Dunbar looked up with a start, as . . .

"Never!" he replied; "I'm not wasting my time with magazine trash."

"It's not trash," said Sowerby, assuming that unnatural air of reflection which sat upon him so ill. "I've looked up the volumes of the *Ludgate Magazine* in our local library, and I've read all the series with much interest."

Dunbar leaned forward, watching him frowningly.

"I should have thought," he replied, "that you had enough to do without wasting your time in that way!"

"*Is* it a waste of time?" inquired Sowerby, raising his eyebrows in a manner which lent him a marked resemblance to a famous comedian. "I tell you that the man who can work out plots like those might be a second Jack-the-Ripper and not a soul the wiser!"

"Ah!"

"I've never met a more innocent *looking* man, I'll allow; but if you'll read the 'Adventures of Martin Zeda,' you'll know that . . ."

"Tosh!" snapped Dunbar, irritably; "your ideas of psychology would make a Manx cat laugh! I suppose, on the same analogy, you think the leader-writers of the dailies could run the Government better than the Cabinet does it?"

"I think it very likely . . ."

"Tosh! Is there anybody in London knows more about the inside workings of crime than the Commissioner? You will admit there isn't;

very good. Accordingly to your ideas, the Commissioner must be the biggest blackguard in the Metropolis! I have said it twice before, and I'll be saying it again, Sowerby: *Tosh!*"

"Well," said Sowerby with an offended air, "has anybody ever seen Mr. King?"

"What are you driving at?"

"I am driving at this: somebody known in certain circles as Mr. King is at the bottom of this mystery. It is highly probable that Mr. King himself murdered Mrs. Vernon. On the evidence of your own notes, nobody left Palace Mansions between the time of the crime and the arrival of witnesses. Therefore, *one* of your witnesses must be a liar; and the liar is Mr. King!"

Inspector Dunbar glared at his subordinate. But the latter continued undaunted—

"You won't believe it's Leroux; therefore it must be either Mr. Exel, Dr. Cumberly, or Miss Cumberly."

Inspector Dunbar stood up very suddenly, thrusting his chair from him with much violence.

"Do you recollect the matter of Soames leaving Palace Mansions?" he snapped.

Sowerby's air of serio-comic defiance began to leave him. He scratched his head reflectively.

"Soames got away like that because no one was expecting him to do it. In the same way, neither Leroux, Exel, nor Dr. Cumberly knew that there was any one else *in* the flat at the very time when the murderer was making his escape. The cases are identical. They were not looking for a fugitive. He had gone before the search commenced. A clever man could have slipped out in a hundred different ways unobserved. Sowerby, you are . . ."

What Sowerby was, did not come to light at the moment; for, the door quietly opened and in walked M. Gaston Max arrayed in his inimitable traveling coat, and holding his hat of velour in his gloved hand. He bowed politely.

"Good morning, gentlemen," he said.

"Good morning," said Dunbar and Sowerby together.

Sowerby hastened to place a chair for the distinguished visitor. M. Max, thanking him with a bow, took his seat, and from an inside pocket extracted a notebook.

"There are some little points," he said with a deprecating wave of the hand, "which I should like to confirm." He opened the book, sought the wanted page, and continued: "Do either of you know a person answering to the following description: Height, about four feet eight-and-a-half inches, medium build and carries himself with a nervous stoop. Has a habit of rubbing his palms together when addressing anyone. Has plump hands with rather tapering fingers, and a growth of reddish down upon the backs thereof, indicating that he has red or reddish hair. His chin recedes slightly and is pointed, with a slight cleft parallel with the mouth and situated equidistant from the base of the chin and the lower lip. A nervous mannerism of the latter periodically reveals the lower teeth, one of which, that immediately below the left canine, is much discolored. He is clean-shaven, but may at some time have worn whiskers. His eyes are small and ferret-like, set very closely together and of a ruddy brown color. His nose is wide at the bridge, but narrows to an unusual point at the end. In profile it is irregular, or may have been broken at some time. He has scanty eyebrows set very high, and a low forehead with two faint, vertical wrinkles starting from the inner points of the eyebrows. His natural complexion is probably sallow, and his hair (as hitherto mentioned) either red or of sandy color. His ears are set far back, and the lobes are thin and pointed. His hair is perfectly straight and sparse, and there is a depression of the cheeks where one would expect to find a prominence: that is—at the cheekbone. The cranial development is unusual. The skull slopes back from the crown at a remarkable angle, there being no protuberance at the back, but instead a straight slope to the spine, sometimes seen in the Teutonic races, and in this case much exaggerated. Viewed from the front the skull is narrow, the temples depressed, and the crown bulging over the ears, and receding to a ridge on top. In profile the forehead is almost apelike in size and contour . . . ."

"*Soames!*" exclaimed Inspector Dunbar, leaping to his feet, and bringing both his palms with a simultaneous bang upon the table before him—"Soames, by God!"

M. Max, shrugging and smiling slightly, returned his notebook to his pocket, and, taking out a cigar-case, placed it, open, upon the table, inviting both his confreres, with a gesture, to avail themselves of its contents.

"I thought so," he said simply. "I am glad."

Sowerby selected a cigar in a dazed manner, but Dunbar, ignoring the presence of the cigar-case, leant forward across the table, his eyes blazing, and his small, even, lower teeth revealed in a sort of grim smile.

"M. Max," he said tensely—"you are a clever man! Where have you got him?"

"I have not got him," replied the Frenchman, selecting and lighting one of his own cigars. "He is much too useful to be locked up."

"But . . ."

"But yes, my dear Inspector—he is safe; oh! he is quite safe. And on Tuesday night he is going to introduce us to Mr. King!"

"*Mr. King!*" roared Dunbar; and in three strides of the long legs he was around the table and standing before the Frenchman.

In passing he swept Sowerby's hat on to the floor, and Sowerby, picking it up, began mechanically to brush it with his left sleeve, smoking furiously the while.

"Soames," continued M. Max, quietly—"he is now known as Lucas, by the way—is a man of very remarkable character; a fact indicated by his quite unusual skull. He has no more will than this cigar"—he held the cigar up between his fingers, illustratively—"but of stupid pig obstinacy, that canaille—saligaud!—has enough for all the cattle in Europe! He is like a man who knows that he stands upon a sinking ship, yet, who whilst promising to take the plunge every moment, hesitates and will continue to hesitate until someone pushes him in. Pardieu! I push! Because of his pig obstinacy I am compelled to take risks most unnecessary. He will not consent, that Soames, to open the door for us . . ."

"What door?" snapped Dunbar.

"The door of the establishment of Mr. King," explained Max, blandly.

"But where is it?"

"It is somewhere between Limehouse Causeway—is it not called so?—and the riverside. But although I have been there, myself, I can tell you no more. . . ."

"What! you have been there yourself?"

"But yes—most decidedly. I was there some nights ago. But they are ingenious, ah! they are so ingenious!—so Chinese! I should not have known even the little I do know if it were not for the inquiries which I made last week. I knew that the letters to Mr. Leroux which were supposed to come from Paris were handed by Soames to some one who posted them to Paris from Bow, East. You remember how I found the impression of the postmark?"

Dunbar nodded, his eyes glistening; for that discovery of the Frenchman's had filled him with a sort of envious admiration.

"Well, then," continued Max, "I knew that the inquiry would lead me to your east-end, and I suspected that I was dealing with Chinamen; therefore, suitably attired, of course, I wandered about in those interesting slums on more than one occasion; and I concluded that the only district in which a Chinaman could live without exciting curiosity was that which lies off the West India Dock Road."

Dunbar nodded significantly at Sowerby, as who should say: "What did I tell you about this man?"

"On one of these visits," continued the Frenchman, and a smile struggled for expression upon his mobile lips, "I met you two gentlemen with a Mr.—I think he is called Stringer—"

"You met *us*!" exclaimed Sowerby.

"My sense of humor quite overcoming me," replied M. Max, "I even tried to swindle you. I think I did the trick very badly!"

Dunbar and Sowerby were staring at one another amazedly.

"It was in the corner of a public house billiard-room," added the Frenchman, with twinkling eyes; "I adopted the ill-used name of Levinsky on that occasion."

Dunbar began to punch his left palm and to stride up and down the floor; whilst Sowerby, his blue eyes opened quite roundly, watched M. Max as a schoolboy watches an illusionist.

"Therefore," continued M. Max, "I shall ask you to have a party ready on Tuesday night in Limehouse Causeway—suitably concealed, of course; and as I am almost sure that the haunt of Mr. King is actually upon the riverside (I heard one little river sound as I was coming away) a launch party might cooperate with you in affecting the raid."

"The raid!" said Dunbar, turning from a point by the window, and looking back at the Frenchman. "Do you seriously tell me that we are going to raid Mr. King's on Tuesday night?"

"Most certainly," was the confident reply. "I had hoped to form one of the raiding party; but nom d'un nom!"—he shrugged, in his graceful fashion—"I must be one of the rescued!"

"Of the rescued!"

"You see I visited that establishment as a smoker of opium . . ."

"You took that risk?"

"It was no greater risk than is run by quite a number of people socially well known in London, my dear Inspector Dunbar! I was introduced by an habitue and a member of the best society; and since nobody knows that Gaston Max is in London—that Gaston Max has any business in hand likely to bring him to London—pardieu, what danger did I incur? But, excepting the lobby—the cave of the dragon (a stranger apartment even than that in the Rue St. Claude) and the Chinese cubiculum where I spent the night—mon dieu! what a night!—I saw nothing of the establishment . . ."

"But you must know where it is!" cried Dunbar.

"I was driven there in a closed limousine, and driven away in the same vehicle . . ."

"You got the number?"

"It was impossible. These are clever people! But it must be a simple matter, Inspector, to trace a fine car like that which regularly appears in those east-end streets?"

"Every constable in the division must be acquainted with it," replied Dunbar, confidently. "I'll know all about that car inside the next hour!"

"If on Tuesday night you could arrange to have it followed," continued M. Max, "it would simplify matters. What I have done is this: I have bought the man, Soames—up to a point. But so deadly is his fear of the mysterious Mr. King that although he has agreed to assist me in my plans, he will not consent to divulge an atom of information until the raid is successfully performed."

"Then for heaven's sake what *is he* going to do?"

"Visitors to the establishment (it is managed by a certain Mr. Ho-Pin; make a note of him, that Ho-Pin) having received the necessary dose of opium are locked in for the night. On Tuesday, Soames, who acts as valet to poor fools using the place, has agreed—for a price—to unlock the door of the room in which I shall be . . ."

"What!" cried Dunbar, "you are going to risk yourself alone in that place *again?*"

"I have paid a very heavy fee," replied the Frenchman with his odd smile, "and it entitles me to a second visit; I shall pay that second visit on Tuesday night, and my danger will be no greater than on the first occasion."

"But Soames may betray you!"

"Fear nothing; I have measured my Soames, not only anthropologically, but otherwise. I fear only his folly, not his knavery. He will not betray me. Morbleu! he is too much a frightened man. I do not know what has taken place; but I could see that, assured of escaping the police for complicity in the murder, he would turn King's evidence immediately . . ."

"And you gave him that assurance?"

"At first I did not reveal myself. I weighed up my man very carefully; I measured that Soames-pig. I had several stories in readiness, but his character indicated which I should use. Therefore, suddenly I arrested him!"

"Arrested him?"

"Pardieu! I arrested him very quietly in a corner of the bar of 'Three Nuns' public house. My course was justified. He saw that the reign of his mysterious Mr. King was nearing its close, and that I was his only hope . . ."

"But still he refused . . ."

"His refusal to reveal anything whatever under those circumstances impressed me more than all. It showed me that in Mr. King I had to deal with a really wonderful and powerful man; a man who ruled by means of *fear*; a man of gigantic force. I had taken the pattern of the key fitting the Yale lock of the door of my room, and I secured a duplicate immediately. Soames has not access to the keys, you understand. I must rely upon my diplomacy to secure the same room again—all turns upon that; and at an hour after midnight, or later if advisable, Soames has agreed to let me out. Beyond this, I could induce him to do nothing—nothing whatever. Cochon! Therefore, having got out of the locked room, I must rely upon my own wits—and the Browning pistol which I have presented to Soames together with the duplicate key . . ."

"Why not go armed?" asked Dunbar.

"One's clothes are searched, my dear Inspector, by an expert! I have given the key, the pistol, and the implements of the house-breaker (a very neat set which fits easily into the breast-pocket) to Soames, to conceal in his private room at the establishment until Tuesday night. All turns upon my securing the same apartment. If I am unable to do so, the arrangements for the raid will have to be postponed. Opium smokers are faddists essentially, however, and I think I can manage to pretend that I have formed a strange penchant for this particular cubiculum . . ."

"By whom were you introduced to the place?" asked Dunbar, leaning back against the table and facing the Frenchman.

"That I cannot in honor divulge," was the reply; "but the representative of Mr. King who actually admitted me to the establishment is one Gianapolis; address unknown, but telephone number 18642 East. Make a note of him, that Gianapolis."

"I'll arrest him in the morning," said Sowerby, writing furiously in his notebook.

"Nom d'un p'tit bonhomme! M. Sowerby, you will do nothing of that foolish description, my dear friend," said Max; and Dunbar glared at the unfortunate sergeant. "Nothing whatever must be done to arouse suspicion between now and the moment of the raid. You must be circumspect—ah, morbleu! so circumspect. By all means trace this Mr. Gianapolis; yes. But do not let him *suspect* that he is being traced . . ."

XXXV

TRACKER TRACKED

Helen Cumberly and Denise Ryland peered from the window of the former's room into the dusk of the Square, until their eyes ached with the strain of an exercise so unnatural.

"I tell you," said Denise with emphasis, "that . . . sooner or later . . . he will come prowling . . . around. The mere fact that he did not appear . . . last night . . . counts for nothing. His own crooked . . . plans no doubt detain him . . . very often . . . at night."

Helen sighed wearily. Denise Ryland's scheme was extremely distasteful to her, but whenever she thought of the pathetic eyes of Leroux she found new determination. Several times she had essayed to analyze the motives which actuated her; always she feared to pursue such inquiries beyond a certain point. Now that she was beginning to share her friend's views upon the matter, all social plans sank into insignificance, and she lived only in the hope of again meeting Gianapolis, of tracing out the opium group, and of finding Mrs. Leroux. In what state did she hope and expect to find her? This was a double question which kept her wakeful through the dreary watches of the night . . . .

"Look!"

Denise Ryland grasped her by the arm, pointing out into the darkened Square. A furtive figure crossed from the northeast corner into the shade of some trees and might be vaguely detected coming nearer and nearer.

"There he is!" whispered Denise Ryland, excitedly; "I told you he couldn't . . . keep away. I know that kind of brute. There is nobody at home, so listen: I will watch . . . from the drawing-room, and you . . . light up here and move about . . . as if preparing to go out."

Helen, aware that she was flushed with excitement, fell in with the proposal readily; and having switched on the lights in her room and put on her hat so that her moving shadow was thrown upon the casement curtain, she turned out the light again and ran to rejoin her friend. She found the latter peering eagerly from the window of the drawing-room.

"He thinks you are coming out!" gasped Denise. "He has slipped . . . around the corner. He will pretend to be . . . passing . . . this way . . . the cross-eyed . . . hypocrite. Do you feel capable . . . of the task?"

"Quite," Helen declared, her cheeks flushed and her eyes sparkling. "You will follow us as arranged; for heaven's sake, don't lose us!"

"If the doctor knew of this," breathed Denise, "he would never . . . forgive me. But no woman . . . no true woman . . . could refuse to undertake . . . so palpable . . . a duty . . ."

Helen Cumberly, wearing a warm, golfing jersey over her dress, with a woolen cap to match, ran lightly down the stairs and out into the Square, carrying a letter. She walked along to the pillar-box, and having examined the address upon the envelope with great care, by the light of an adjacent lamp, posted the letter, turned—and there, radiant and bowing, stood Mr. Gianapolis!

"Kismet is really most kind to me!" he cried. "My friend, who lives, as I think I mentioned once before, in Peer's Chambers, evidently radiates good luck. I last had the good fortune to meet you when on my way to see him, and I now meet you again within five minutes of leaving him! My dear Miss Cumberly, I trust you are quite well?"

"Quite," said Helen, holding out her hand. "I am awfully glad to see you again, Mr. Gianapolis!"

He was distinctly encouraged by her tone. He bent forward confidentially.

"The night is young," he said; and his smile was radiant. "May I hope that your expedition does not terminate at this post-box?"

Helen glanced at him doubtfully, and then down at her jersey. Gianapolis was unfeignedly delighted with her naivete.

"Surely you don't want to be seen with me in this extraordinary costume!" she challenged.

"My dear Miss Cumberly, it is simply enchanting! A girl with such a figure as yours never looks better than when she dresses sportily!"

The latent vulgarity of the man was escaping from the bondage in which ordinarily he confined it. A real passion had him in its grip, and the real Gianapolis was speaking. Helen hesitated for one fateful moment; it was going to be even worse than she had anticipated. She glanced up at Palace Mansions.

Across a curtained window moved a shadow, that of a man wearing a long gown and having his hands clasped behind him, whose head showed as an indistinct blur because the hair was wildly disordered. This shadow passed from side to side of the window and was lost from view. It was the shadow of Henry Leroux.

"I am afraid I have a lot of work to do," said Helen, with a little catch in her voice.

"My dear Miss Cumberly," cried Gianapolis, eagerly, placing his hand upon her arm, "it is precisely of your work that I wish to speak to you! Your work is familiar to me—I never miss a line of it; and knowing how you delight in the outre and how inimitably you can describe scenes of Bohemian life, I had hoped, since it was my privilege to meet you, that you would accept my services as cicerone to some of the lesser-known resorts of Bohemian London. Your article, 'Dinner in Soho,' was a delightful piece of observation, and the third—I think it was the third—of the same series: 'Curiosities of the Cafe Royal,' was equally good. But your powers of observation would be given greater play in any one of the three establishments to which I should be honored to escort you."

Helen Cumberly, though perfectly self-reliant, as only the modern girl journalist can be, was fully aware that, not being of the flat-haired, bespectacled type, she was called upon to exercise rather more care in her selection of companions for copy-hunting expeditions than was necessary in the case of certain fellow-members of the Scribes' Club. No power on earth could have induced her to accept such an invitation from such a man, under ordinary circumstances; even now, with so definite and important an object in view, she hesitated. The scheme might lead to nothing; Denise Ryland (horrible thought!) might lose the track; the track might lead to no place of importance, so far as her real inquiry was concerned.

In this hour of emergency, new and wiser ideas were flooding her brain. For instance, they might have admitted Inspector Dunbar to the plot. With Inspector Dunbar dogging her steps, she should have felt perfectly safe; but Denise—she had every respect for Denise's reasoning powers, and force of character—yet Denise nevertheless might fail her.

She glanced into the crooked eyes of Gianapolis, then up again at Palace Mansions.

The shadow of Henry Leroux recrossed the cream-curtained window.

"So early in the evening," pursued the Greek, rapidly, "the more interesting types will hardly have arrived; nevertheless, at the Memphis Cafe . . ."

"Memphis Cafe!" muttered Helen, glancing at him rapidly; "what an odd name."

"Ah! my dear Miss Cumberly!" cried Gianapolis, with triumph—'I knew that you had never heard of the true haunts of Bohemia! The Memphis Cafe—it is actually a club—was founded by Olaf van Noord two years ago, and at present has a membership including some of the most famous artistic folk of London; not only painters, but authors, composers, actors, actresses. I may add that the peerage, male and female, is represented."

"It is actually a gaming-house, I suppose?" said Helen, shrewdly.

"A gaming-house? Not at all! If what you wish to see is play for high stakes, it is not to the Memphis Cafe you must go. I can show you Society losing its money in thousands, if the spectacle would amuse you. I only await your orders . . ."

"You certainly interest me," said Helen; and indeed this half-glimpse into phases of London life hidden from the world—even from the greater part of the ever-peering journalistic world—was not lacking in fascination.

The planning of a scheme in its entirety constitutes a mental effort which not infrequently blinds us to the shortcomings of certain essential details. Denise's plan, a good one in many respects, had the fault of being over-elaborate. Now, when it was too late to advise her friend of any amendment, Helen perceived that there was no occasion for her to suffer the society of Gianapolis.

To bid him good evening, and then to follow him, herself, was a plan much superior to that of keeping him company whilst Denise followed both!

Moreover, he would then be much more likely to go home, or to some address which it would be useful to know. What a *very* womanish scheme theirs had been, after all; Helen told herself that the most stupid man imaginable could have placed his finger upon its weak spot immediately.

But her mind was made up. If it were possible, she would warn Denise of the change of plan; if it were not, then she must rely upon her friend to see through the ruse which she was about to practise upon the Greek.

"Good night, Mr. Gianapolis!" she said abruptly, and held out her hand to the smiling man. His smile faded. "I should love to join you, but really you must know that it's impossible. I will arrange to make up a party, with pleasure, if you will let me know where I can 'phone you?"

"But," he began.

"Many thanks, it's really impossible; there are limits even to the escapades allowed under the cloak of 'Copy'! Where can I communicate with you?"

"Oh! how disappointed I am! But I must permit you to know your own wishes better than I can hope to know them, Miss Cumberly. Therefore"—Helen was persistently holding out her hand—"good night! Might I venture to telephone to *you* in the morning? We could then come to some arrangement, no doubt . . ."

"You might not find me at home . . ."

"But at nine o'clock!"

"It allows me no time to make up my party!"

"But such a party must not exceed three: yourself and two others . . ."

"Nevertheless, it has to be arranged."

"I shall ring up tomorrow evening, and if you are not at home, your maid will tell me when you are expected to return."

Helen quite clearly perceived that no address and no telephone number were forthcoming.

"You are committing yourself to endless and unnecessary trouble, Mr. Gianapolis, but if you really wish to do as you suggest, let it be so.

Good night!"

She barely touched his extended hand, turned, and ran fleetly back toward the door of Palace Mansions. Ere reaching the entrance, however, she dropped a handkerchief, stooped to recover it, and glanced back rapidly.

Gianapolis was just turning the corner.

Helen perceived the unmistakable form of Denise Ryland lurking in the Palace Mansions doorway, and, waving frantically to her friend, who was nonplussed at this change of tactics, she hurried back again to the corner and peeped cautiously after the retreating Greek.

There was a cab rank some fifty paces beyond, with three taxis stationed there. If Gianapolis chartered a cab, and she were compelled to follow in another, would Denise come upon the scene in time to take up the prearranged role of sleuth-hound?

Gianapolis hesitated only for a few seconds; then, shrugging his shoulders, he stepped out into the road and into the first cab on the rank. The man cranked his engine, leapt into his seat and drove off. Helen Cumberly, ignoring the curious stares of the two remaining taximen, ran out from the shelter of the corner and jumped into the next cab, crying breathlessly:

"Follow that cab! Don't let the man in it suspect, but follow, and don't lose sight of it!"

They were off!

Helen glanced ahead quickly, and was just in time to see Gianapolis' cab disappear; then, leaning out of the window, she indulged in an extravagant pantomime for the benefit of Denise Ryland, who was hurrying after her.

"Take the next cab and follow *me!*" she cried, whilst her friend raised her hand to her ear the better to detect the words. "I cannot wait for you or the track will be lost . . ."

Helen's cab swung around the corner—and she was not by any means certain that Denise Ryland had understood her; but to have delayed would have been fatal, and she must rely upon her friend's powers of penetration to form a third in this singular procession.

Whilst these thoughts were passing in the pursuer's mind, Gianapolis, lighting a cigarette, had thrown himself back in a corner of the cab and was mentally reviewing the events of the evening—that is, those events which were associated with Helen Cumberly. He was disappointed but hopeful: at any rate he had suffered no definite repulse. Without doubt, his reflections had been less roseate had he known that he was followed, not only by two, but by *three* trackers.

He had suspected for some time now, and the suspicion had made him uneasy, that his movements were being watched. Police surveillance he did not fear; his arrangements were too complete, he believed, to occasion him any ground for anxiety even though half the Criminal

Investigation Department were engaged in dogging his every movement. He understood police methods very thoroughly, and all his experience told him that this elusive shadow which latterly had joined him unbidden, and of whose presence he was specially conscious whenever his steps led toward Palace Mansions, was no police officer.

He had two theories respecting the shadow—or, more properly, one theory which was divisible into two parts; and neither part was conducive to peace of mind. Many years, crowded with many happenings, some of which he would fain forget, had passed since the day when he had entered the service of Mr. King, in Pekin. The enterprises of Mr. King were always of a secret nature, and he well remembered the fate of a certain Burmese gentleman of Rangoon who had attempted to throw the light of publicity into the dark places of these affairs.

From a confidant of the doomed man, Gianapolias had learned, fully a month before a mysterious end had come to the Burman, how the latter (by profession a money-lender) had complained of being shadowed night and day by someone or something, of whom or of which he could never succeed in obtaining so much as a glimpse.

Gianapolis shuddered. These were morbid reflections, for, since he had no thought of betraying Mr. King, he had no occasion to apprehend a fate similar to that of the unfortunate money-lender of Rangoon. It was a very profitable service, that of Mr. King, yet there were times when the fear of his employer struck a chill to his heart; there were times when almost he wished to be done with it all . . .

By Whitechapel Station he discharged the cab, and, standing on the pavement, lighted a new cigarette from the glowing stump of the old one. A fair amount of traffic passed along the Whitechapel Road, for the night was yet young; therefore Gianapolis attached no importance to the fact that almost at the moment when his own cab turned and was driven away, a second cab swung around the corner of Mount Street and disappeared.

But, could he have seen the big limousine drawn up to the pavement some fifty yards west of London Hospital, his reflections must have been terrible, indeed.

Fate willed that he should know nothing of this matter, and, his thoughts automatically reverting again to Helen Cumberly, he enjoyed that imaginary companionship throughout the remainder of his walk, which led him along Cambridge Road, and from thence, by a devious route, to the northern end of Globe Road.

It may be enlightening to leave Gianapolis for a moment and to return to Mount Street.

Helen Cumberly's cabman, seeing the cab ahead pull up outside the railway station, turned around the nearest corner on the right (as has already appeared), and there stopped. Helen, who also had observed the maneuver of the taxi ahead, hastily descended, and giving the man half-a-sovereign, said rapidly:

"I must follow on foot now, I am afraid! but as I don't know this district at all, could you bring the cab along without attracting attention, and manage to keep me in sight?"

"I'll try, miss," replied the man, with alacrity; "but it won't be an easy job."

"Do your best," cried Helen, and ran off rapidly around the corner, and into Whitechapel Road.

She was just in time to see Gianapolis throw away the stump of his first cigarette and stroll off, smoking a second. She rejoiced that she was inconspicuously dressed, but, simple as was her attire, it did not fail to attract coarse comment from some whom she jostled on her way. She ignored all this, however, and, at a discreet distance followed the Greek, never losing sight of him for more than a moment.

When, leaving Cambridge Road—a considerable thoroughfare—he plunged into a turning, crooked and uninviting, which ran roughly at right angles with the former, she hesitated, but only for an instant. Not another pedestrian was visible in the street, which was very narrow and ill-lighted, but she plainly saw Gianapolis passing under a street-lamp some thirty yards along. Glancing back in quest of the cabman, but failing to perceive him, she resumed the pursuit.

She was nearly come to the end of the street (Gianapolis already had disappeared into an even narrower turning on the left) when a bright light suddenly swept from behind and cast her shadow far out in front of her upon the muddy road. She heard the faint thudding of a motor, but did not look back, for she was confident that this was the taximan following. She crept to the corner and peered around it; Gianapolis had disappeared.

The light grew brighter—brighter yet; and, with the engine running very silently, the car came up almost beside her. She considered this unwise on the man's part, yet welcomed his presence, for in this place not a soul was visible, and for the first time she began to feel afraid . . .

A shawl, or some kind of silken wrap, was suddenly thrown over her head!

She shrieked frenziedly, but the arm of her captor was now clasped tightly about her mouth and head. She felt herself to be suffocating. The silken thing which enveloped her was redolent of the perfume of roses; it was stifling her. She fought furiously, but her arms were now seized in an irresistible grasp, and she felt herself lifted—and placed upon a cushioned seat.

Instantly there was a forward movement of the vehicle which she had mistaken for a taxi-cab, and she knew that she was speeding through those unknown east-end streets—God! to what destination?

She could not cry out, for she was fighting for air—she seemed to be encircled by a swirling cloud of purplish mist. On—and on—and on, she was borne; she knew that she must have been drugged in some way, for consciousness was slipping—slipping . . .

Helpless as a child in that embrace which never faltered, she was lifted again and carried down many steps. Insensibility was very near now, but with all the will that was hers she struggled to fend it off. She felt herself laid down upon soft cushions . . .

A guttural voice was speaking, from a vast distance away:

"What is this that you bwring us, Mahara?"

Answered a sweet, silvery voice:

"Does it matter to you what I bringing? It is one I hate—hate—hate! There will be *two* cases of 'ginger' to go away some day instead of *one*—that is all! Said, yalla!"

"Your pwrimitive passions will wruin us . . ."

The silvery voice grew even more silvery:

"Do you quarrel with me, Ho-Pin, my friend?"

"This is England, not Burma! Gianapolis . . ."

"Ah! Whisper—*whisper* it to *him*, and . . ."

Oblivion closed in upon Helen Cumberly; she seemed to be sinking into the heart of a giant rose.

XXXVI

IN DUNBAR'S ROOM

Dr. Cumberly, his face unusually pale, stood over by the window of Inspector Dunbar's room, his hands locked behind him. In the chair nearest to the window sat Henry Leroux, so muffled up in a fur-collared motor-coat that little of his face was visible; but his eyes were tragic as he leant forward resting his elbows upon his knees and twirling his cap between his thin fingers. He was watching Inspector Dunbar intently; only glancing from the gaunt face of the detective occasionally to look at Denise Ryland, who sat close to the table. At such times his gaze was pathetically reproachful, but always rather sorrowful than angry.

As for Miss Ryland, her habitual self-confidence seemed somewhat to have deserted her, and it was almost with respectful interest that she followed Dunbar's examination of a cabman who, standing cap in hand, completed the party so strangely come together at that late hour.

"This is what you have said," declared Dunbar, taking up an official form, and, with a movement of his hand warning the taxi-man to pay attention: "'I, Frederick Dean, motor-cab driver, was standing on the rank in Little Abbey Street tonight at about a quarter to nine. My cab was the second on the rank. A young lady who wore, I remember, a woolen cap and jersey, with a blue serge skirt, ran out from the corner of the Square and directed me to follow the cab in front of me, which had just been chartered by a dark man wearing a black overcoat and silk hat. She ordered me to keep him in sight; and as I drove off I heard her calling from the window of my cab to another lady who seemed to be following her. I was unable to see this other lady, but my fare addressed her as "Denise." I followed the first cab to Whitechapel Station; and as I saw it stop there, I swung into Mount Street. The lady gave me half-a-sovereign, and told me that she proposed to follow the man on foot. She asked me if I could manage to keep her in sight, without letting my cab be seen by the man she was following. I said I would try, and I crept along at some distance behind her, going as slowly as possible until she went into a turning branching off to the right of Cambridge Road; I don't know the name of this street. She was some distance ahead of me, for I had had trouble in crossing Whitechapel Road.

"'A big limousine had passed me a moment before, but as an electric tram was just going by on my off-side, between me and the limousine, I don't know where the limousine went. When I was clear of the tram I could not see it, and it may have gone down Cambridge Road and then down the same turning as the lady. I pulled up at the end of this turning, and could not see a sign of any one. It was quite deserted right to the end, and although I drove down, bore around to the right and finally came out near the top of Globe Road, I did not pass anyone. I waited about the district for over a quarter-of-an-hour and then drove straight to the police station, and they sent me on here to Scotland Yard to report what had occurred.'

"Have you anything to add to that?" said Dunbar, fixing his tawny eyes upon the cabman.

"Nothing at all," replied the man—a very spruce and intelligent specimen of his class and one who, although he had moved with the times, yet retained a slightly horsey appearance, which indicated that he had not always been a mechanical Jehu.

"It is quite satisfactory as far as it goes," muttered Dunbar. "I'll get you to sign it now and we need not detain you any longer."

"There is not the slightest doubt," said Dr. Cumberly, stepping forward and speaking in an unusually harsh voice, "that Helen endeavored to track this man Gianapolis, and was abducted by him or his associates. The limousine was the car of which we have heard so much . . ."

"If my cabman had not been such a . . . fool," broke in Denise Ryland, clasping her hands, "we should have had a different . . . tale to tell."

"I have no wish to reproach anybody," said Dunbar, sternly; "but I feel called upon to remark, madam, that you ought to have known better than to interfere in a case like this; a case in which we are dealing with a desperate and clever gang."

For once in her life Denise Ryland found herself unable to retort suitably. The mildly reproachful gaze of Leroux she could not meet; and although Dr. Cumberly had spoken no word of complaint against her, from his pale face she persistently turned away her eyes.

The cabman having departed, the door almost immediately reopened, and Sergeant Sowerby came in.

"Ah! there you are, Sowerby!" cried Dunbar, standing up and leaning eagerly across the table. "You have the particulars respecting the limousine?"

Sergeant Sowerby, removing his hat and carefully placing it upon the only vacant chair in the room, extracted a bulging notebook from a pocket concealed beneath his raincoat, cleared his throat, and reported as follows:

"There is only one car known to members of that division which answers to the description of the one wanted. This is a high-power, French car which seems to have been registered first in Paris, where it was made, then in Cairo, and lastly in London. It is the property of the gentleman whose telephone number is 18642 East—Mr. I. Gianapolis; and the reason of its frequent presence in the neighborhood of the West India Dock Road, is this: it is kept in a garage in Wharf-End Lane, off Limehouse Causeway. I have interviewed two constables at present on that beat, and they tell me that there is nothing mysterious about the car except that the chauffeur is a foreigner who speaks no English. He is often to be seen cleaning the car in the garage, and both the men are in the habit of exchanging good evening with him when passing the end of the lane. They rarely go that far, however, as it leads nowhere."

"But if you have the telephone number of this man, Gianapolis," cried Dr. Cumberly, "you must also have his address . . ."

"We obtained both from the Eastern Exchange," interrupted Inspector Dunbar. "The instrument, number 18642 East, is installed in an office in Globe Road. The office, which is situated in a converted private dwelling, bears a brass plate simply inscribed, 'I. Gianapolis, London and Smyrna.'"

"What is the man's reputed business?" jerked Cumberly.

"We have not quite got to the bottom of that, yet," replied Sowerby; "but he is an agent of some kind, and evidently in a large way of business, as he runs a very fine car, and seems to live principally in different hotels. I am told that he is an importer of Turkish cigarettes and . . ."

"He is an importer and exporter of hashish!" snapped Dunbar irritably. "If I could clap my eyes upon him I should know him at once! I tell you, Sowerby, he is the man who was convicted last year of exporting hashish to Egypt in faked packing cases which contained pottery ware, ostensibly, but had false bottoms filled with cakes of hashish . . ."

"But," began Dr. Cumberly.

"But because he came before a silly bench," snapped Dunbar, his eyes flashing angrily, "he got off with a fine—a heavy one, certainly, but he could well afford to pay it. It is that kind of judicial folly which ties the hands of Scotland Yard!"

"What makes you so confident that this is the man?" asked the physician.

"He was convicted under the name of G. Ionagis," replied the detective; "which I believe to be either his real name or his real name transposed. Do you follow me? I. Gianapolis is Ionagis Gianapolis, and G. Ionagis is Gianapolis Ionagis. I was not associated with the hashish case; he stored the stuff in a china warehouse within the city precincts, and at that time he did not come within my sphere. But I looked into it privately, and I could see that the prosecution was merely skimming the surface; we are only beginning to get down to the depths *now*."

Dr. Cumberly raised his hand to his head in a distracted manner.

"Surely," he said, and he was evidently exercising a great restraint upon himself—"surely we're wasting time. The office in Globe Road should be raided without delay. No stone should be left unturned to effect the immediate arrest of this man Gianapolis or Ionagis. Why, God almighty! while we are talking here, my daughter . . ."

"Morbleu! who talks of arresting Gianapolis?" inquired the voice of a man who silently had entered the room.

All turned their heads; and there in the doorway stood M. Gaston Max.

"Thank God you've come!" said Dunbar with sincerity. He dropped back into his chair, a strong man exhausted. "This case is getting beyond me!"

Denise Ryland was staring at the Frenchman as if fascinated. He, for his part, having glanced around the room, seemed called upon to give her some explanation of his presence.

"Madame," he said, bowing in his courtly way, "only because of very great interests did I dare to conceal my true identity. My name is Gaston, that is true, but only so far as it goes. My real name is Gaston Max, and you who live in Paris will perhaps have heard it."

"Gaston Max!" cried Denise Ryland, springing upright as though galvanized; "you are M. Gaston Max! But you are not the least bit in the world like . . ."

"Myself?" said the Frenchman, smiling. "Madame, it is only a man fortunate enough to possess no enemies who can dare to be like himself."

He bowed to her in an oddly conclusive manner, and turned again to Inspector Dunbar.

"I am summoned in haste," he said; "tell me quickly of this new development."

Sowerby snatched his hat from the vacant chair, and politely placed the chair for M. Max to sit upon. The Frenchman, always courteous, gently forced Sergeant Sowerby himself to occupy the chair, silencing his muttered protests with upraised hand. The matter settled, he lowered his hand, and, resting it fraternally upon the sergeant's shoulder, listened to Inspector Dunbar's account of what had occurred that night. No one interrupted the Inspector until he was come to the end of his narrative.

"Mille tonnerres!" then exclaimed M. Max; and, holding a finger of his glove between his teeth, he tugged so sharply that a long rent appeared in the suede.

His eyes were on fire; the whole man quivered with electric force.

In silence that group watched the celebrated Frenchman; instinctively they looked to him for aid. It is at such times that personality proclaims itself. Here was the last court of appeal, to which came Dr. Cumberly and Inspector Dunbar alike; whose pronouncement they awaited, not questioning that it would be final.

"To-morrow night," began Max, speaking in a very low voice, "we raid the headquarters of Ho-Pin. This disappearance of your daughter, Dr. Cumberly, is frightful; it could not have been foreseen or it should have been prevented. But the least mistake now, and"—he looked at

Dr. Cumberly as if apologizing for his barbed words—"she may never return!"

"My God!" groaned the physician, and momentarily dropped his face into his hands.

But almost immediately he recovered himself and with his mouth drawn into a grim straight line, looked again at M. Max, who continued:

"I do not think that this abduction was planned by the group; I think it was an accident and that they were forced, in self-protection, to detain your daughter, who unwisely—morbleu! how unwisely!—forced herself into their secrets. To arrest Gianapolis (even if that were possible) would be to close their doors to us permanently; and as we do not even know the situation of those doors, that would be to ruin everything. Whether Miss Cumberly is confined in the establishment of Ho-Pin or somewhere else, I cannot say; whether she is a captive of Gianapolis or of Mr. King, I do not know. But I know that the usual conduct of the establishment is not being interrupted at present; for only half-an-hour ago I telephoned to Mr. Gianapolis!"

"At Globe Road?" snapped Dunbar, with a flash of the tawny eyes.

"At Globe Road—yes (oh! they would not detain her there!). Mr. Gianapolis was present to speak to me. He met me very agreeably in the matter of occupying my old room in the delightful Chinese hotel of Mr. Ho-Pin. Therefore"—he swept his left hand around forensically, as if to include the whole of the company—"tomorrow night at eleven o'clock I shall be meeting Mr. Gianapolis at Piccadilly Circus, and later we shall join the limousine and be driven to the establishment of Ho-Pin." He turned to Inspector Dunbar. "Your arrangements for watching all the approaches to the suspected area are no doubt complete?"

"Not a stray cat," said Dunbar with emphasis, "can approach Limehouse Causeway or Pennyfields, or any of the environs of the place, tomorrow night after ten o'clock, without the fact being reported to me! You will know at the moment that you step from the limousine that a cyclist scout, carefully concealed, is close at your heels with a whole troup to follow; and if, as you suspect, the den adjoins the river bank, a police cutter will be lying at the nearest available point."

"Eh bien!" said M. Max; then, turning to Denise Ryland and Dr. Cumberly, and shrugging his shoulders: "you see, frightful as your suspense must be, to make any foolish arrests tonight, to move in this matter at all tonight—would be a case of more haste and less speed . . ."

"But," groaned Cumberly, "is Helen to lie in that foul, unspeakable den until the small hours of tomorrow morning? Good God! they may . . ."

"There is one little point," interrupted M. Max with upraised hand, "which makes it impossible that we should move tonight—quite apart from the advisability of such a movement. We do not know exactly where this place is situated. What can we do?"

He shrugged his shoulders, and, with raised eyebrows, stared at Dr. Cumberly.

"It is fairly evident," replied the other slowly, and with a repetition of the weary upraising of his hand to his head, "it is fairly evident that the garage used by the man Gianapolis must be very near to—most probably adjoining—the entrance to this place of which you speak."

"Quite true," agreed the Frenchman. "But these are clever, these people of Mr. King. They are Chinese, remember, and the Chinese—ah, I know it!—are the most mysterious and most cunning people in the world. The entrance to the cave of black and gold will not be as wide as a cathedral door. A thousand men might search this garage, which, as Detective Sowerby" (he clapped the latter on the shoulder) "informed me this afternoon, is situated in Wharf-End Lane—all day and all night, and become none the wiser. To-morrow evening"—he lowered his voice—"I myself, shall be not outside, but inside that secret place; I shall be the concierge for one night—Eh bien, that concierge will admit the policeman!"

A groan issued from Dr. Cumberly's lips; and M. Max, with ready sympathy, crossed the room and placed his hands upon the physician's shoulders, looking steadfastly into his eyes.

"I understand, Dr. Cumberly," he said, and his voice was caressing as a woman's. "Pardieu! I understand. To wait is agony; but you, who are a physician, know that to wait sometimes is necessary. Have courage, my friend, have courage!"

XXXVII

THE WHISTLE

Luke Soames, buttoning up his black coat, stood in the darkness, listening.

His constitutional distaste for leaping blindfolded had been over-ridden by circumstance. He felt himself to be a puppet of Fate, and he drifted with the tide because he lacked the strength to swim against it. That will-o'-the-wisp sense of security which had cheered him when first he had realized how much he owed to the protective wings of Mr. King had been rudely extinguished upon the very day of its birth; he had learnt that Mr. King was a sinister protector; and almost hourly he lived again through the events of that night when, all unwittingly, he had become a witness of strange happenings in the catacombs.

Soames had counted himself a lost man that night; the only point which he had considered debatable was whether he should be strangled or poisoned. That his employers were determined upon his death, he was assured; yet he had lived through the night, had learnt from his watch that the morning was arrived . . . and had seen the flecks at the roots of his dyed hair, blanched by the terrors of that vigil—of that watching, from moment to moment, for the second coming of Ho-Pin.

Yes, the morning had dawned, and with it a faint courage. He had shaved and prepared himself for his singular duties, and Said had brought him his breakfast as usual. The day had passed uneventfully, and once, meeting Ho-Pin, he had found himself greeted with the same mirthless smile but with no menace. Perhaps they had believed his story, or had disbelieved it but realized that he was too closely bound to them to be dangerous.

Then his mind had reverted to the conversation overheard in the music-hall. Should he seek to curry favor with his employers by acquainting them with the fact that, contrary to Gianapolis' assertion, an important clue had fallen into the hands of the police? Did they know this already? So profound was his belief in the omniscience of the invisible Mr. King that he could not believe that Power ignorant of anything appertaining to himself.

Yet it was possible that those in the catacombs were unaware how Scotland Yard, night and day, quested for Mr. King. The papers made no mention of it; but then the papers made no mention of another fact—the absence of Mrs. Leroux. Now that he was no longer panic-ridden, he could mentally reconstruct that scene of horror, could hear again, imaginatively, the shrieks of the maltreated woman. Perhaps this same active imagination of his was playing him tricks, but, her voice . . . Always he preferred to dismiss these ideas.

He feared Ho-Pin in the same way that an average man fears a tarantula, and he was only too happy to avoid the ever smiling Chinaman; so that the days passed on, and, finding himself unmolested and the affairs of the catacombs proceeding apparently as usual, he kept his information to himself, uncertain if he shared it with his employers or otherwise, but hesitating to put the matter to the test—always fearful to approach Ho-Pin, the beetlesque.

But this could not continue indefinitely; at least he must speak to Ho-Pin in order to obtain leave of absence. For, since that unforgettable night, he had lived the life of a cave-man indeed, and now began to pine for the wider vault of heaven. Meeting the impassive Chinaman in the corridor one morning, on his way to valet one of the living dead, Soames ventured to stop him.

"Excuse me, sir," he said, confusedly, "but would there be any objection to my going out on Friday evening for an hour?"

"Not at all, Soames," replied Ho-Pin, with his mirthless smile: "you may go at six, wreturn at ten."

Ho-Pin passed on.

Soames heaved a gentle sigh of relief. The painful incident was forgotten, then. He hurried into the room, the door of which Said was holding open, quite eager for his unsavory work.

In crossing its threshold, he crossed out of his new peace into a mental turmoil greater in its complexities than any he yet had known; he met M. Gaston Max, and his vague doubts respecting the omniscience of Mr. King were suddenly reinforced.

Soames' perturbation was so great on that occasion that he feared it must unfailingly be noticed. He realized that now he was definitely in communication with the enemies of Mr. King! Ah; but Mr. King did not know how formidable was the armament of those enemies! He (Soames) had overrated Mr. King; and because that invisible being could inspire Fear in an inconceivable degree, he had thought him all-powerful. Now, he realized that Mr. King was unaware of the existence of at least one clue held by the police; was unaware that his name was associated with the Palace Mansions murder.

The catacombs of Ho-Pin were a sinking ship, and Soames was first of the rats to leave.

He kept his appointment at the "Three Nuns" as has appeared; he accepted the blood-money that was offered him, and he returned to the garage adjoining Kan-Suh Concessions, that night, hugging in his bosom a leather case containing implements by means whereof his new accomplice designed to admit the police to the cave of the golden dragon.

Also, in the pocket of his overcoat, he had a neat Browning pistol;

and when the door at the back of the garage was opened for him by Said, he found that the touch of this little weapon sent a thrill of assurance through him, and he began to conceive a sentiment for the unknown investigator to whom he was bound, akin to that which formerly he had cherished for Mr. King!

Now the time was come.

The people of the catacombs acquired a super-sensitive power of hearing, and Soames was able at this time to detect, as he sat or lay in his own room, the movements of persons in the corridor outside and even in the cave of the golden dragon. That mysterious trap in the wall gave him many qualms, and tonight he had glanced at it a thousand times. He held the pistol in his hand, and buttoned up within his coat was the leather case. Only remained the opening of his door in order to learn if the lights were extinguished in the corridor.

He did not anticipate any serious difficulty, provided he could overcome his constitutional nervousness. In his waistcoat pocket was a brand new Yale key which, his latest employer had assured him, fitted the lock of the end door of Block A. The door between the cave of the dragon and Block A was never locked, so far as Soames was aware, nor was that opening from the corridor in which his own room was situated. Therefore, only a few moments—fearful moments, certainly—need intervene, ere he should have a companion; and within a few minutes of that time, the police—his friends!—would be there to protect him! He recognized that the law, after all, was omnipotent, and of all masters was the master to be served.

There was no light in the corridor. Leaving his door ajar, he tiptoed cautiously along toward the cave. Assuring himself once again that the pistol lay in his pocket, he fumbled for the lever which opened the door, found it, depressed it, and stepped quietly forward in his slippered feet.

The unmistakable odor of the place assailed his nostrils. All was in darkness, and absolute silence prevailed. He had a rough idea of the positions of the various little tables, and he stepped cautiously in order to skirt them; but evidently he had made a miscalculation. Something caught his foot, and with a muffled thud he sprawled upon the floor, barely missing one of the tables which he had been at such pains to avoid.

Trembling like a man with an ague, he lay there, breathing in short, staccato breaths, and clutching the pistol in his pocket. Certainly he had made no great noise, but . . .

Nothing stirred.

Soames summoned up courage to rise and to approach again the door of Block A. Without further mishap he reached it, opened it, and entered the blackness of the corridor. He could make no mistake in regard to the door, for it was the end one. He stole quietly along, his fingers touching the matting, until he came in contact with the corner angle; then, feeling along from the wall until he touched the strip of bamboo which marked the end of the door, he probed about gently with the key; for he knew to within an inch or so where the keyhole was situated.

Ah! he had it! His hand trembling slightly, he sought to insert the key in the lock. It defied his efforts. He felt it gently with the fingers of his left hand, thinking that he might have been endeavoring to insert the key with the irregular edge downward, and not uppermost; but no— such was not the case.

Again he tried, and with no better result. His nerves were threatening to overcome him, now; he had not counted upon any such hitch as this: but fear sharpened his wits. He recollected the fall which he had sustained, and how he had been precipitated upon the polished floor, outside.

Could he have mistaken his direction? Was it not possible that owing to his momentary panic, he had arisen, facing not the door at the foot of the steps, as he had supposed, but that by which a moment earlier he had entered the cave of the golden dragon?

Desperation was with him now; he was gone too far to draw back. Trailing his fingers along the matting covering of the wall, he retraced his steps, came to the open door, and reentered the apartment of the dragon. He complimented himself, fearfully, upon his own address, for he was inspired with an idea whereby he might determine his position. Picking his way among the little tables and the silken ottomans, he groped about with his hands in the impenetrable darkness for the pedestal supporting the dragon. At last his fingers touched the ivory. He slid them downward, feeling for the great vase of poppies which always stood before the golden image . . . .

The vase was on the *left* and not on the *right* of the pedestal. His theory was correct; he had been groping in the mysterious precincts of that Block B which he had never entered, which he had never seen any one else enter, and from whence he had never known any one to emerge! It was the fall that had confused him; now, he took his bearings anew, bent down to feel for any tables that might lie in his path, and crept across the apartment toward the door which he sought.

Ah! this time there could be no mistake! He depressed the lever handle, and, as the door swung open before him, crept furtively into the corridor.

Repeating the process whereby he had determined the position of the end door, he fumbled once again for the keyhole. He found it with even less difficulty than he had experienced in the wrong corridor, inserted the key in the lock, and with intense satisfaction felt it slip into place.

He inhaled a long breath of the lifeless air, turned the key, and threw the door open. One step forward he took . . .

A whistle (God! he knew it!) a low, minor whistle, wavered through the stillness. He was enveloped, mantled, choked, by the perfume of *roses!*

The door, which, although it had opened easily, had seemed to be a remarkably heavy one, swung to behind him; he heard the click of the lock. Like a trapped animal, he turned, leaped back, and found his quivering hands in contact with books—books—books . . .

A lamp lighted up in the center of the room.

Soames turned and stood pressed closely against the book-shelves, against the book-shelves which magically had grown up in front of the door by which he had entered. He was in the place of books and roses— in the haunt of *Mr. King!*

A great clarity of mind came to him, as it comes to a drowning man; he knew that those endless passages, through which once he had been led in darkness, did not exist, that he had been deceived, had been guided along the same corridor again and again; he knew that this room of roses did not lie at the heart of a labyrinth, but almost adjoined the cave of the golden dragon.

He knew that he was a poor, blind fool; that his plotting had been known to those whom he had thought to betray; that the new key which had opened a way into this place of dread was not the key which his accomplice had given him. He knew that that upon which he had tripped at the outset of his journey had been set in his path by cunning design, in order that the fall might confuse his sense of direction. He knew that the great vase of poppies had been moved, that night . . . .

God! his brain became a seething furnace.

There, before him, upstood the sandalwood screen, with one corner of the table projecting beyond it. Nothing of life was visible in the perfumed place, where deathly silence prevailed . . . .

No lion has greater courage than a cornered rat. Soames plucked the pistol from his pocket and fired at the screen—*once!—twice!*

He heard the muffled report, saw the flash of the little weapon, saw the two holes in the carven woodwork, and gained a greater, hysterical courage—the courage of a coward's desperation.

Immediately before him was a little ebony table, bearing a silver bowl, laden to the brim with sulphur-colored roses. He overturned the table with his foot, laughing wildly. In three strides he leapt across the room, grasped the sandalwood screen, and hurled it to the floor . . . .

In the instant of its fall, he became as Lot's wife. The pistol dropped from his nerveless grasp, thudding gently on the carpet, and, with his fingers crooked paralytically, he stood swaying . . . and looking into the face of *Mr. King!*

Soames' body already was as rigid as it would be in death; his mind was numbed—useless. But his outraged soul forced utterance from the lips of the man.

A scream, a scream to have made the angels shudder, to have inspired pity in the devils of Hell, burst from him. Two yellow hands leaped at his throat . . . .

XXXVIII

THE SECRET TRAPS

Gaston Max, from his silken bed in the catacombs of Ho-Pin, watched the hand of his watch which lay upon the little table beside him. Already it was past two o'clock, and no sign had come from Soames; a hundred times his imagination had almost tricked him into believing that the door was opening; but always the idea had been illusory and due to the purple shadow of the lamp-shade which overcast that side of the room and the door.

He had experienced no difficulty in arranging with Gianapolis to occupy the same room as formerly; and, close student of human nature though he was, he had been unable to detect in the Greek's manner, when they had met that night, the slightest restraint, the slightest evidence of uneasiness. His reception by Ho-Pin had varied scarce one iota from that accorded him on his first visit to the cave of the golden dragon. The immobile Egyptian had brought him the opium, and had departed silently as before. On this occasion, the trap above the bed had not been opened. But hour after hour had passed, uneventfully, silently, in that still, suffocating room . . . .

A key in the lock!—yes, a key was being inserted in the lock! He must take no unnecessary risks; it might be another than Soames. He waited—the faint sound of fumbling ceased. Still, he waited, listening intently.

Half-past-two. If it had been Soames, why had he withdrawn? M. Max arose noiselessly and looked about him. He was undecided what to do, when . . .

Two shots, followed by a most appalling shriek—the more frightful because it was muffled; the shriek of a man in extremis, of one who stands upon the brink of Eternity, brought him up rigid, tense, with fists clenched, with eyes glaring; wrought within this fearless investigator an emotion akin to terror.

Just that one gruesome cry there was and silence again.

What did it mean?

M. Max began hastily to dress. He discovered, in endeavoring to fasten his collar, that his skin was wet with cold perspiration.

"Pardieu!" he said, twisting his mouth into that wry smile, "I know, now, the meaning of fright!"

He was ever glancing toward the door, not hopefully as hitherto, but apprehensively, fearfully.

That shriek in the night might portend merely the delirium of some other occupant of the catacombs; but the shots . . .

"It was *Soames!*" he whispered aloud; "I have risked too much; I am fast in the rat-trap!"

He looked about him for a possible weapon. The time for inactivity was past. It would be horrible to die in that reeking place, whilst outside, it might be, immediately above his head, Dunbar and the others waited and watched.

The construction of the metal bunk attracted his attention. As in the case of steamer bunks one of the rails—that nearer to the door—was detachable in order to facilitate the making of the bed. Rapidly, nervously, he unscrewed it; but the hinges were riveted to the main structure, and after a brief examination he shrugged his shoulders despairingly. Then, he recollected that in the adjoining bathroom there was a metal towel rail, nickeled, and with a heavy knock at either end, attached by two brackets to the wall.

He ran into the inner room and eagerly examined these fastenings. They were attached by small steel screws. In an instant he was at work with the blade of his pocket-knife. Six screws in all there were to be dealt with, three at either end. The fifth snapped the blade and he uttered an exclamation of dismay. But the shortened implement proved to be an even better screw-driver than the original blade, and half a minute later he found himself in possession of a club such as would have delighted the soul of Hercules.

He managed to unscrew one of the knobs, and thus to slide off from the bar the bracket attachments; then, replacing the knob, he weighed the bar in his hand, appreciatively. His mind now was wholly composed, and his course determined. He crossed the little room and rapped loudly upon the door.

The rapping sounded muffled and dim in that sound-proof place. Nothing happened, and thrice he repeated the rapping with like negative results. But he had learnt something: the door was a very heavy one.

He made a note of the circumstance, although it did not interfere with the plan which he had in mind. Wheeling the armchair up beside the bed, he mounted upon its two arms and, *once—twice—thrice—* crashed the knob of the iron bar against that part of the wall which concealed the trap.

Here the result was immediate. At every blow of the bar the trap behind yielded. A fourth blow sent the knob crashing through the gauze material, and far out into some dark place beyond. There was a sound as of a number of books falling.

He had burst the trap.

Up on the back of the chair he mounted, resting his bar against the wall, and began in feverish haste to tear away the gauze concealing the rectangular opening.

An almost overpowering perfume of roses was wafted into his face. In front of him was blackness.

Having torn away all the gauze, he learned that the opening was some two feet long by one foot high. Resting the bar across the ledge he extended his head and shoulders forward through this opening into the rose-scented place beyond, and without any great effort drew himself up with his hands, so that, provided he could find some support upon the other side, it would be a simple matter to draw himself through entirely.

He felt about with his fingers, right and left, and in doing so disturbed another row of books, which fell upon the floor beneath him. He had apparently come out in the middle of a large book-shelf. To the left of him projected the paper-covered door of the trap, at right angles; above and below were book-laden shelves, and on the right there had been other books, until his questing fingers had disturbed them.

M. Max, despite his weight, was an agile man. Clutching the shelf beneath, he worked his way along to the right, gradually creeping further and further into the darkened room, until at last he could draw his feet through the opening and crouch sideways upon the shelf.

He lowered his left foot, sought for and found another shelf beneath, and descended as by a ladder to the thickly carpeted floor. Grasping the end of the bar, he pulled that weapon down; then he twisted the button which converted his timepiece into an electric lantern, and, holding the bar in one tensely quivering hand, looked rapidly about him.

This was a library; a small library, with bowls of roses set upon tables, shelves, in gaps between the books, and one lying overturned upon the floor. Although it was almost drowned by their overpowering perfume, he detected a faint smell of powder. In one corner stood a large writing-table with papers strewn carelessly upon it. Its appointments were markedly Chinese in character, from the singular, gold inkwell to the jade paperweight; markedly Chinese—and—*feminine*. A very handsome screen lay upon the floor in front of this table, and the rich carpet he noted to be disordered as if a struggle had taken place upon it. But, most singular circumstance of all, and most disturbing . . . there was no door to this room!

For a moment he failed to appreciate the entire significance of this. A secret room difficult to enter he could comprehend, but a secret room difficult to *quit* passed his comprehension completely. Moreover, he was no better off for his exploit.

Three minutes sufficed him in which to examine the shelves covering the four walls of the room from floor to ceiling. None of the books were dummies, and slowly the fact began to dawn upon his mind that what at first he had assumed to be a rather simple device, was, in truth, almost incomprehensible.

For how, in the name of Sanity, did the occupant of this room—and obviously it was occupied at times—enter and leave it?

"Ah!" he muttered, shining the light upon a row of yellow-bound volumes from which he had commenced his tour of inspection and to which that tour had now led him back, "it is uncanny—this!"

He glanced back at the rectangular patch of light which marked the trap whereby he had entered this supernormal room. It was situated close to one corner of the library, and, acting upon an idea which came to him (any idea was better than none) he proceeded to throw down the books occupying the corresponding position at the other end of the shelf.

A second trap was revealed, identical with that through which he had entered!

It was fastened with a neat brass bolt; and, standing upon one of the little Persian tables—from which he removed a silver bowl of roses—he opened this trap and looked into the lighted room beyond. He saw an apartment almost identical with that which he himself recently had quitted; but in one particular it differed. It was occupied . . . *and by a woman!*

Arrayed in a gossamer nightrobe she lay in the bed, beneath the trap, her sunken face matching the silken whiteness. Her thin arms drooped listlessly over the rails of the bunk, and upon her left hand M. Max perceived a wedding ring. Her hair, flaxen in the electric light, was spread about in wildest disorder upon the pillow, and a breath of fetid air assailed his nostrils as he pressed his face close to the gauze masking the opening in order to peer closely at this victim of the catacombs.

He watched the silken covering of her bosom, intently, but failed to detect the slightest movement.

"Morbleu!" he muttered, "is she dead?"

He rent the gauze with a sweep of his left hand, and standing upon the bottom shelf of the case, craned forward into the room, looking all about him. A purple shaded lamp burnt above the bed as in the adjoining apartment which he himself had occupied. There were dainty feminine trifles littered in the big armchair, and a motor-coat hung upon the hook of the bathroom door. A small cabin-trunk in one corner of the room bore the initials: "M. L."

Max dropped back into the incredible library with a stifled gasp.

"Pardieu!" he said. "It is Mrs. Leroux that I have found!"

A moment he stood looking from trap to trap; then turned and surveyed again the impassable walls, the rows of works, few of which were European, some of them bound in vellum, some in pigskin, and one row of huge volumes, ten in number, on the bottom shelf, in crocodile hide.

"It is weird, this!" he muttered, "nightmare!"—turning the light from row to row. "How is this lamp lighted that swings here?"

He began to search for the switch, and, even before he found it, had made up his mind that, once discovered, it would not only enable him more fully to illuminate the library, but would constitute a valuable clue.

At last he found it, situated at the back of one of the shelves, and set above a row of four small books, so that it could readily be reached by inserting the hand.

He flooded the place with light; and perceived at a glance that a length of white flex crossing the ceiling enabled anyone seated at the table to ignite the lamp from there also. Then, replacing his torch in his pocket, and assuring himself that the iron bar lay within easy reach, he began deliberately to remove all of the books from the shelves covering that side of the room upon which the switch was situated. His theory was a sound one; he argued that the natural and proper place for such a switch in such a room would be immediately inside the door, so that one entering could ignite the lamp without having to grope in the darkness. He was encouraged, furthermore, by the fact that at a point some four feet to the left of this switch there was a gap in the bookcases, running from floor to ceiling; a gap no more than four inches across.

Having removed every book from its position, save three, which occupied a shelf on a level with his shoulder and adjoining the gap, he desisted wearily, for many of the volumes were weighty, and the heat of the room was almost insufferable. He dropped with a sigh upon a silk ottoman close beside him . . . .

A short, staccato, muffled report split the heavy silence . . . and a little round hole appeared in the woodwork of the book-shelf before which, an instant earlier, M. Max had been standing—in the woodwork of that shelf, which had been upon a level with his head.

In one giant leap he hurled himself across the room— . . . as a second bullet pierced the yellow silk of the ottoman.

Close under the trap he crouched, staring up, fearful-eyed . . . .

A yellow hand and arm—a hand and arm of great nervous strength and of the hue of old ivory, directed a pistol through the opening above him. As he leaped, the hand was depressed with a lightning movement, but, lunging suddenly upward, Max seized the barrel of the pistol, and with a powerful wrench, twisted it from the grasp of the yellow hand. It was his own Browning!

At the time—in that moment of intense nervous excitement—he ascribed his sensations to his swift bout with Death—with Death who almost had conquered; but later, even now, as he wrenched the weapon into his grasp, he wondered if physical fear could wholly account for the sickening revulsion which held him back from that rectangular opening in the bookcase. He thought that he recognized in this a kindred horror—as distinct from terror—to that which had come to him with the odor of roses through this very trap, upon the night of his first visit to the catacombs of Ho-Pin.

It was not as the fear which one has of a dangerous wild beast, but as the loathing which is inspired by a thing diseased, leprous, contagious . . . .

A mighty effort of will was called for, but he managed to achieve it. He drew himself upright, breathing very rapidly, and looked through into the room—the room which he had occupied, and from which a moment ago the murderous yellow hand had protruded.

That room was empty . . . empty as he had left it!

"Mille tonneres! he has escaped me!" he cried aloud, and the words did not seem of his own choosing.

Who had escaped? Someone—man or woman; rather some *thing*, which, yellow handed, had sought to murder him!

Max ran across to the second trap and looked down at the woman whom he knew, beyond doubt, to be Mrs. Leroux. She lay in her death-like trance, unmoved.

Strung up to uttermost tension, he looked down at her and listened—listened, intently.

Above the fumes of the apartment in which the woman lay, a stifling odor of roses was clearly perceptible. The whole place was tropically hot. Not a sound, save the creaking of the shelf beneath him, broke the heavy stillness.

XXXIX

THE LABYRINTH

Feverishly, Max clutched at the last three books upon the shelf adjoining the gap. Of these, the center volume, a work bound in yellow calf and bearing no title, proved to be irremovable; right and left it could be inclined, but not moved outward. It masked the lever handle of the door!

But that door was locked.

Max, with upraised arms, swept the perspiration from his brows and eyes; he leant dizzily up against the door which defied him; his mind was working with febrile rapidity. He placed the pistol in his pocket, and, recrossing the room, mounted up again upon the shelves, and crept through into the apartment beyond, from which the yellow hand had protruded. He dropped, panting, upon the bed, then, eagerly leaping to the door, grasped the handle.

"Pardieu!" he muttered, "it is unlocked!"

Though the light was still burning in this room, the corridor outside was in darkness. He pressed the button of the ingenious lamp which was also a watch, and made for the door communicating with the cave of the dragon. It was readily to be detected by reason of its visible handle; the other doors being externally indistinguishable from the rest of the matting-covered wall.

The cave of the dragon proved to be empty, and in darkness. He ran across its polished floor and opened at random the door immediately facing him. A corridor similar to the one which he had just quitted was revealed. Another door was visible at one end, and to this he ran, pulled it open, stepped through the opening, and found himself back in the cave of the dragon!

"Morbleu!" he muttered, "it is bewildering—this!"

Yet another door, this time one of ebony, he opened; and yet another matting-lined corridor presented itself to his gaze. He swept it with the ray of the little lamp, detected a door, opened it, and entered a similar suite to those with which he already was familiar. It was empty, but, unlike the one which he himself had tenanted, this suite possessed two doors, the second opening out of the bathroom. To this he ran; it was unlocked; he opened it, stepped ahead . . . and was back again in the cave of the dragon.

"Mon dieu!" he cried, "this is Chinese—quite Chinese!"

He stood looking about him, flashing the ray of light upon doors which were opened and upon openings in the walls where properly there should have been no doors.

"I am too late!" he muttered; "they had information of this and they have 'unloaded.' That they intend to fly the country is proven by their leaving Mrs. Leroux behind. Ah, nom d'un nom, the good God grant that they have left also."

Coincident with his thoughts of her, the voice of Helen Cumberly reached his ears! He stood there quivering in every nerve, as: "Help! Help!" followed by a choking, inarticulate cry, came, muffled, from somewhere—he could not determine where.

But the voice was the voice of Helen Cumberly. He raised his left fist and beat his brow as if to urge his brain to super-activity. Then, leaping, he was off.

Door after door he threw open, crying, "Miss Cumberly! Miss Cumberly! Where are you? Have courage! Help is here!"

But the silence remained unbroken—and always his wild search brought him back to the accursed cave of the golden dragon. He began to grow dizzy; he felt that his brain was bursting. For somewhere—somewhere but a few yards removed from him—a woman was in extreme peril!

Clutching dizzily at the pedestal of the dragon, he cried at the top of his voice—

"Miss Cumberly! For the good God's sake answer me! Where are you?"

"Here, M. Max!" he was answered; "the door on your right . . . and then to your right again—quick! *Quick!* Saints! she has killed me!"

It was Gianapolis who spoke!

Max hurled himself through the doorway indicated, falling up against the matting wall by reason of the impetus of his leap. He turned, leaped on, and one of the panels was slightly ajar; it was a masked door. Within was darkness out of which came the sounds of a great turmoil, as of wild beasts in conflict.

Max kicked the door fully open and flashed the ray of the torch into the room. It poured its cold light upon a group which, like some masterpiece of classic statuary, was to remain etched indelibly upon his mind.

Helen Cumberly lay, her head and shoulders pressed back upon the silken pillows of the bed, with both hands clutching the wrist of the Eurasian and striving to wrench the latter's fingers from her throat, in the white skin of which they were bloodily embedded. With his left arm about the face and head of the devilish half-caste, and grasping with his right hand her slender right wrist—putting forth all his strength to hold it back—was Gianapolis!

His face was of a grayish pallor and clammy with sweat; his crooked eyes had the glare of madness. The lithe body of the Eurasian writing in his grasp seemed to possess the strength of two strong men; for palpably the Greek was weakening. His left sleeve was torn to shreds—to bloody shreds beneath the teeth of the wild thing with which he fought; and lower, lower, always nearer to the throat of the victim, the slender, yellow arm forced itself, forced the tiny hand clutching a poniard no larger than a hatpin but sharp as an adder's tooth.

"Hold her!" whispered Gianapolis in a voice barely audible, as Max burst into the room. "She came back for this and . . . I followed her. She has the strength of . . . a tigress!"

Max hurled himself into the melee, grasping the wrist of the Eurasian below where it was clutched by Gianapolis. Nodding to the Greek to release his hold, he twisted it smartly upward.

The dagger fell upon the floor, and with an animal shriek of rage, the Eurasian tottered back. Max caught her about the waist and tossed her unceremoniously into a corner of the room.

Helen Cumberly slipped from the bed, and lay very white and still upon the garish carpet, with four tiny red streams trickling from the nail punctures in her throat. Max stooped and raised her shoulders; he glanced at the Greek, who, quivering in all his limbs, and on the verge of collapse, only kept himself upright by dint of clutching at the side of the doorway. Max realized that Gianapolis was past aiding him; his own resources were nearly exhausted, but, stooping, he managed to lift the girl and to carry her out into the corridor.

"Follow me!" he gasped, glancing back at Gianapolis; "Morbleu, make an effort! The keys—the keys!"

Laying Helen Cumberly upon one of the raised divans, with her head resting upon a silken cushion, Max, teeth tightly clenched and dreadfully conscious that his strength was failing him, waited for Gianapolis. Out from the corridor the Greek came staggering, and Max now perceived that he was bleeding profusely from a wound in the breast.

"She came back," whispered Gianapolis, clutching at the Frenchman for support . . . "the hellcat! I did not know . . . that . . . Miss Cumberly was here. As God is my witness I did not know! But I followed . . . her—Mahara . . . thank God I did! She has finished me, I think, but"—he lowered the crooked eyes to the form of Helen Cumberly—"never mind . . . Saints!"

He reeled and sank upon his knees. He clutched at the edge of his coat and raised it to his lips, wherefrom blood was gushing forth. Max stooped eagerly, for as the Greek had collapsed upon the floor, he had heard the rattle of keys.

"She had . . . the keys," whispered Gianapolis. "They have . . . tabs . . . upon them . . . Mrs. Leroux . . . number 3 B. The door to the stair"— very, very slowly, he inclined his head toward the ebony door near which Max was standing—"is marked X. The door . . . at the top—into garage . . . B."

"Tell me," said Max, his arm about the dying man's shoulders—"try to tell me: who killed Mrs. Vernon and why?"

"Mr. King!" came in a rattling voice. "Because of the . . . carelessness of someone . . . Mrs. Vernon wandered into the room . . . of Mrs. Leroux. She seems to have had a fit of remorse . . . or something like it. She begged Mrs. Leroux to pull up . . . before . . . too late. Ho-Pin arrived just as she was crying to . . . Mrs. Leroux . . . and asking if she could ever forgive her . . . for bringing her here . . . . It was Mrs. Vernon who . . . introduced Mrs . . . . Leroux. Ho-Pin heard her . . . say that she . . . would tell . . . Leroux the truth . . . as the only means . . ."

"Yes, yes, morbleu! I understand! And then?"

"Ho-Pin knows . . . women . . . like a book. He thought Mrs. Vernon would . . . shirk the scandal. We used to send our women . . . to Nurse Proctor's, then . . . to steady up a bit . . . We let Mrs. Vernon go . . . as usual. The scene with . . . Mrs. Leroux had shaken . . . her and she fainted . . . in the car . . . Victoria Street . . . . I was with her. Nurse Proctor had . . . God! I am dying! . . . a time with her; . . . she got so hysterical that they had to . . . detain her . . . and three days later . . . her husband died; Proctor, the . . . fool . . . somehow left a paper containing the news in Mrs. Vernon's room . . . . They had had to administer an injection that afternoon . . . and they thought she was . . . sleeping."

"Morbleu! Yes, yes!—a supreme effort, my friend!"

"Directly Ho-Pin heard of Vernon's death, he knew that his hold . . . on Mrs. Vernon . . . was lost . . . . He . . . and Mahara . . . and . . . *Mr. King* . . . drove straight to . . . Gillingham . . . Street . . . to . . . arrange . . . . Ah! . . . She rushed like a mad woman into the street, a moment before . . . they arrived. A cab was passing, and . . ."

"I know this! I know this! What happened at Palace Mansions?"

The Greek's voice grew fainter.

"Mr. King followed . . . her . . . upstairs. Too late; . . . but whilst Leroux was in . . . Cumberly's flat . . . leaving door open . . . Mr. King went . . . in . . . Mahara . . . was watching . . . gave signal . . . whistle . . . of someone's approach. It was thought . . . Mr. King . . . had secured all the message . . . Mrs. Vernon . . . was . . . writing . . . . Mr. King opened the door of . . . the lift-shaft . . . lift not working . . . climbed down that way . . . and out by door on . . . ground floor . . . when Mr . . . . the Member of Parliament . . . went upstairs."

"Ah! pardieu! one last word! *Who is Mr. King?*"

Gianapolis lurched forward, his eyes glazing, half raised his arm—pointing back into the cave of the dragon—and dropped, face downward, on the floor, with a crimson pool forming slowly about his head.

An unfamiliar sound had begun to disturb the silence of the catacombs. Max glanced at the white face of Helen Cumberly, then directed the ray of the little lamp toward the further end of the apartment. A steady stream of dirty water was pouring into the cave of the dragon through the open door ahead of him.

Into the disc of light, leaped, fantastic, the witch figure of the Eurasian. She turned and faced him, threw up both her arms, and laughed shrilly, insanely. Then she turned and ran like a hare, her yellow silk dress gleaming in the moving ray. Inhaling sibilantly, Max leaped after her. In three strides he found his foot splashing in water. An instant he hesitated. Through the corridor ahead of him sped the yellow figure, and right to the end. The seemingly solid wall opened before her; it was another masked door.

Max crossed the threshold hard upon her heels. Three descending steps were ahead of him, and then a long brick tunnel in which swirled fully three feet of water, which, slowly rising, was gradually flooding the cave of the dragon.

On went the Eurasian, up to her waist in the flood, with Max gaining upon her, now, at every stride. There was a damp freshness in the air of the passage, and a sort of mist seemed to float above the water. This mist had a familiar smell . . . .

They were approaching the river, and there was a fog tonight!

Even as he realized the fact, the quarry vanished, and the ray of light from Max's lamp impinged upon the opening in an iron sluice gate. The Eurasian had passed it, but Max realized that he must lower his head if he would follow. He ducked rapidly, almost touching the muddy water with his face. A bank of yellow fog instantly enveloped him, and he pulled up short, for, instinctively, he knew that another step might precipitate him into the Thames.

He strove to peer about him, but the feeble ray of the lamp was incapable of penetrating the fog. He groped with his fingers, right and left, and presently found slimy wooden steps. He drew himself closely to these, and directed the light upon them. They led upward. He mounted cautiously, and was clear of the oily water, now, and upon a sort of gangway above which lowered a green and rotting wooden roof.

Obviously, the tide was rising; and, after seeking vainly to peer through the fog ahead, he turned and descended the steps again, finding himself now nearly up to his armpits in water. He just managed to get in under the sluice gate without actually submerging his head, and to regain the brick tunnel.

He paused for a moment, hoping to be able to lower the gate, but the apparatus was out of his reach, and he had nothing to stand upon to aid him in manipulating it.

Three or four inches of water now flooded the cave of the golden dragon. Max pulled the keys from his pocket, and unlocked the door at the foot of the steps. He turned, resting the electric lamp upon one of the little ebony tables, and lifting Helen Cumberly, carried her half-way up the steps, depositing her there with her back to the wall. He staggered down again; his remarkable physical resources were at an end; it must be another's work to rescue Mrs. Leroux. He stooped over Gianapolis, and turned his head. The crooked eyes glared up at him deathly.

"May the good God forgive you," he whispered. "You tried to make your peace with Him."

The sound of muffled blows began to be audible from the head of the steps. Max staggered out of the cave of the golden dragon. A slight freshness and dampness was visible in its atmosphere, and the gentle gurgling of water broke its heavy stillness. There was a new quality come into it, and, strangely, an old quality gone out from it. As he lifted the lamp from the table—now standing in slowly moving water—the place seemed no longer to be the cave of the golden dragon he had known . . . .

He mounted the steps again, with difficulty, resting his shaking hands upon the walls. Shattering blows were being delivered upon the door, above.

"Dunbar!" he cried feebly, stepping aside to avoid Helen Cumberly, where she lay. "Dunbar!"

XL

DAWN AT THE NORE

The river police seemed to be floating, suspended in the fog, which now was so dense that the water beneath was invisible. Inspector Rogers, who was in charge, fastened up his coat collar about his neck and turned to Stringer, the Scotland Yard man, who sat beside him in the stern of the cutter gloomily silent.

"Time's wearing on," said Rogers, and his voice was muffled by the fog as though he were speaking from inside a box. "There must be some hitch."

"Work it out for yourself," said the C. I. D. man gruffly. "We know that the office in Globe Road belongs to Gianapolis, and according to the Eastern Exchange he was constantly ringing up East 39951; that's the warehouse of Kan-Suh Concessions. He garages his car next door to the said warehouse, and tonight our scouts follow Gianapolis and Max from Piccadilly Circus to Waterloo Station, where they discharge the taxi and pick up Gianapolis' limousine. Still followed, they drive—where? Straight to the garage at the back of that wharf yonder! Neither Gianapolis, Max, nor the chauffeur come out of the garage. I said, and I still say, that we should have broken in at once, but Dunbar was always pigheaded, and he thinks Max is a tin god."

"Well, there's no sign from Max," said Rogers; "and as we aren't ten yards above the wharf, we cannot fail to hear the signal. For my part I never noticed anything suspicious, and never had anything reported, about this ginger firm, and where the swell dope-shop I've heard about can be situated, beats me. It can't very well be *under* the place, or it would be below the level of the blessed river!"

"This waiting makes me sick!" growled Stringer. "If I understand aright—and I'm not sure that I do—there are two women tucked away there somewhere in that place"—he jerked his thumb aimlessly into the fog; "and here we are hanging about with enough men in yards, in doorways, behind walls, and freezing on the river, to raid the Houses of Parliament!"

"It's a pity we didn't get the word from the hospitals before Max was actually inside," said Rogers. "For three wealthy ladies to be driven to three public hospitals in a sort of semi-conscious condition, with symptoms of opium, on the same evening isn't natural. It points to the fact that the boss of the den has *unloaded*! He's been thoughtful where his lady clients were concerned, but probably the men have simply been kicked out and left to shift for themselves. If we only knew one of them it might be confirmed."

"It's not worth worrying about, now," growled Stringer. "Let's have a look at the time."

He fumbled inside his overcoat and tugged out his watch.

"Here's a light," said Rogers, and shone the ray of an electric torch upon the watch-face.

"A quarter-to-three," grumbled Stringer. "There may be murder going on, and here we are."

A sudden clamor arose upon the shore, near by; a sound as of sledge-hammers at work. But above this pierced shrilly the call of a police whistle.

"What's that?" snapped Rogers, leaping up. "Stand by there!"

The sound of the whistle grew near and nearer; then came a voice—that of Sergeant Sowerby—hailing them through the fog.

"Dunbar's in! But the gang have escaped! They've got to a motor launch twenty yards down, on the end of the creek . . ."

But already the police boat was away.

"Let her go!" shouted Rogers—"close inshore! Keep a sharp lookout for a cutter, boys!"

Stringer, aroused now to excitement, went blundering forward through the fog, joining the men in the bows. Four pairs of eyes were peering through the mist, the damnable, yellow mist that veiled all things.

"Curse the fog!" said Stringer; "it's just our damn luck!"

"Cutter 'hoy!" bawled a man at his side suddenly, one of the river police more used to the mists of the Thames. "Cutter on the port bow, sir!"

"Keep her in sight," shouted Rogers from the stern; "don't lose her for your lives!"

Stringer, at imminent peril of precipitating himself into the water, was craning out over the bows and staring until his eyes smarted.

"Don't you see her?" said one of the men on the lookout. "She carries no lights, of course, but you can just make out the streak of her wake."

Harder, harder stared Stringer, and now a faint, lighter smudge in the blackness, ahead and below, proclaimed itself the wake of some rapidly traveling craft.

"I can hear her motor!" said another voice.

Stringer began, now, also to listen.

Muffled sirens were hooting dismally all about Limehouse Reach, and he knew that this random dash through the night was fraught with extreme danger, since this was a narrow and congested part of the great highway. But, listen as he might, he could not detect the sounds referred to.

The brazen roar of a big steamer's siren rose up before them. Rogers turned the head of the cutter sharply to starboard but did not slacken speed. The continuous roar grew deeper, grew louder.

"Sharp lookout there!" cried the inspector from the stern.

Suddenly over their bows uprose a black mass.

"My God!" cried Stringer, and fell back with upraised arms as if hoping to fend off that giant menace.

He lurched, as the cutter was again diverted sharply from its course, and must have fallen under the very bows of the oncoming liner, had not one of the lookouts caught him by the collar and jerked him sharply back into the boat.

A blaze of light burst out over them, and there were conflicting voices raised one in opposition to another. Above them all, even above the beating of the twin screws and the churning of the inky water, arose that of an officer from the bridge of the steamer.

"Where the flaming hell are *you* going?" inquired this stentorian voice; "haven't you got any blasted eyes and ears . . ."

High on the wash of the liner rode the police boat; down she plunged again, and began to roll perilously; up again—swimming it seemed upon frothing milk.

The clangor of bells, of voices, and of churning screws died, remote, astern.

"Damn close shave!" cried Rogers. "It must be clear ahead; they've just run into it."

One of the men on the lookout in the bows, who had never departed from his duty for an instant throughout this frightful commotion, now reported:

"Cutter crossing our bow, sir! Getting back to her course."

"Keep her in view," roared Rogers.

"Port, sir!"

"How's that?"

"Starboard, easy!"

"Keep her in view!"

"As she is, sir!"

Again they settled down to the pursuit, and it began to dawn upon Stringer's mind that the boat ahead must be engined identically with that of the police; for whilst they certainly gained nothing upon her, neither did they lose.

"Try a hail," cried Rogers from the stern. "We may be chasing the wrong boat!"

"Cutter 'hoy!" bellowed the man beside Stringer, using his hands in lieu of a megaphone—"heave to!"

"Give 'em 'in the King's name!'" directed Rogers again.

"Cutter 'hoy," roared the man through his trumpeted hands,—"heave to—in the King's name!"

Stringer glared through the fog, clutching at the shoulder of the shouter almost convulsively.

"Take no notice, sir," reported the man.

"Then it's the gang!" cried Rogers from the stern; "and we haven't made a mistake. Where the blazes are we?"

"Well on the way to Blackwall Reach, sir," answered someone. "Fog lifting ahead."

"It's the rain that's doing it," said the man beside Stringer.

Even as he spoke, a drop of rain fell upon the back of Stringer's hand. This was the prelude; then, with ever-increasing force, down came the rain in torrents, smearing out the fog from the atmosphere, as a painter, with a sponge, might wipe a color from his canvas. Long tails of yellow vapor, twining—twining—but always coiling downward, floated like snakes about them; and the oily waters of the Thames became pock-marked in the growing light.

Stringer now quite clearly discerned the quarry—a very rakish-looking motor cutter, painted black, and speeding seaward ahead of them. He quivered with excitement.

"Do you know the boat?" cried Rogers, addressing his crew in general.

"No, sir," reported his second-in-command; "she's a stranger to me. They must have kept her hidden somewhere." He turned and looked back into the group of faces, all directed toward the strange craft. "Do any of you know her?" he demanded.

A general shaking of heads proclaimed the negative.

"But she can shift," said one of the men. "They must have been going slow through the fog; she's creeping up to ten or twelve knots now, I should reckon."

"Your reckoning's a trifle out!" snapped Rogers, irritably, from the stern; "but she's certainly showing us her heels. Can't we put somebody ashore and have her cut off lower down?"

"While we're doing that," cried Stringer, excitedly, "she would land somewhere and we should lose the gang!"

"That's right," reluctantly agreed Rogers. "Can you see any of her people?"

Through the sheets of rain all peered eagerly.

"She seems to be pretty well loaded," reported the man beside Stringer, "but I can't make her out very well."

"Are we doing our damnedest?" inquired Rogers.

"We are, sir," reported the engineer; "she hasn't got another oat in her!"

Rogers muttered something beneath his breath, and sat there glaring ahead at the boat ever gaining upon her pursuer.

"So long as we keep her in sight," said Stringer, "our purpose is served. She can't land anybody."

"At her present rate," replied the man upon whose shoulders he was leaning, "she'll be out of sight by the time we get to Tilbury or she'll have hit a barge and gone to the bottom!"

"I'll eat my hat if I lose her!" declared Rogers angrily. "How the blazes they slipped away from the wharf beats me!"

"They didn't slip away from the wharf," cried Stringer over his shoulder. "You heard what Sowerby said; they lay in the creek below the wharf, and there was some passageway underneath."

"But damn it all, man!" cried Rogers, "it's high tide; they must be a gang of bally mermaids. Why, we were almost level with the wharf when we left, and if they came from *below* that, as you say, they must have been below water!"

"There they are, anyway," growled Stringer.

Mile after mile that singular chase continued through the night. With every revolution of the screw, the banks to right and left seemed to recede, as the Thames grew wider and wider. A faint saltiness was perceptible in the air; and Stringer, moistening his dry lips, noted the saline taste.

The shipping grew more scattered. Whereas, at first, when the fog had begun to lift, they had passed wondering faces peering at them from lighters and small steamers, tow boats and larger anchored craft, now they raced, pigmy and remote, upon open waters, and through the raindrift gray hulls showed, distant, and the banks were a faint blur. It seemed absurd that, with all those vessels about, they nevertheless could take no steps to seek assistance in cutting off the boat which they were pursuing, but must drive on through the rain, ever losing, ever dropping behind that black speck ahead.

A faint swell began to be perceptible. Stringer, who throughout the whole pursuit thus far had retained his hold upon the man in the bows, discovered that his fingers were cramped. He had much difficulty in releasing that convulsive grip.

"Thank you!" said the man, smiling, when at last the detective released his grip. "I'll admit I'd scarcely noticed it myself, but now I come to think of it, you've been fastened onto me like a vise for over two hours!"

"Two hours!" cried Stringer; and, crouching down to steady himself, for the cutter was beginning to roll heavily, he pulled out his watch, and in the gray light inspected the dial.

It was true! They had been racing seaward for some hours!

"Good God!" he muttered.

He stood up again, unsteadily, feet wide apart, and peered ahead through the grayness.

The banks he could not see. Far away on the port bow a long gray shape lay—a moored vessel. To starboard were faint blurs, indistinguishable, insignificant; ahead, a black dot with a faint comet-like tail—the pursued cutter—and ahead of that, again, a streak across the blackness, with another dot slightly to the left of the quarry . . .

He turned and looked along the police boat, noting that whereas, upon the former occasion of his looking, forms and faces had been but dimly visible, now he could distinguish them all quite clearly. The dawn was breaking.

"Where are we?" he inquired hoarsely.

"We're about one mile northeast of Sheerness and two miles southwest of the Nore Light!" announced Rogers—and he laughed, but not in a particularly mirthful manner.

Stringer temporarily found himself without words.

"Cutter heading for the open sea, sir," announced a man in the bows, unnecessarily.

"Quite so," snapped Rogers. "So are you!"

"We have got them beaten," said Stringer, a faint note of triumph in his voice. "We've given them no chance to land."

"If this breeze freshens much," replied Rogers, with sardonic humor, "they'll be giving *us* a fine chance to sink!"

Indeed, although Stringer's excitement had prevented him from heeding the circumstance, an ever-freshening breeze was blowing in his face, and he noted now that, quite mechanically, he had removed his bowler hat at some time earlier in the pursuit and had placed it in the bottom of the boat. His hair was blown in the wind, which sang merrily in his ears, and the cutter, as her course was slightly altered by Rogers, ceased to roll and began to pitch in a manner very disconcerting to the lands-man.

"It'll be rather fresh outside, sir," said one of the men, doubtfully. "We're miles and miles below our proper patrol . . ."

"Once we're clear of the bank it'll be more than fresh," replied Rogers; "but if they're bound for France, or Sweden, or Denmark, that's *our* destination, too!"

On—and on—and on they drove. The Nore Light lay astern; they were drenched with spray. Now green water began to spout over the nose of the laboring craft.

"I've only enough juice to run us back to Tilbury, sir, if we put about now!" came the shouted report.

"It's easy to *talk!*" roared Rogers. "If one of these big 'uns gets us broadside on, our number's up!"

"Cutter putting over for Sheppey coast, sir!" bellowed the man in the bows.

Stringer raised himself, weakly, and sought to peer through the driving spray and rain-mist.

"By God! They've turned—Turtle!"

"Stand by with belts!" bellowed Rogers.

Rapidly life belts were unlashed; and, ahead, to port, to starboard, brine-stung eyes glared out from the reeling craft. Gray in the nascent dawn stretched the tossing sea about them; and lonely they rode upon its billows.

"Port! Port! Hard a-port!" screamed the lookout.

But Rogers, grimly watching the oncoming billows, knew that to essay the maneuver at that moment meant swamping the cutter. Straight ahead they drove. A wave, higher than any they yet had had to ride, came boiling down upon them . . . and twisting, writhing, upcasting imploring arms to the elements—the implacable elements—a girl, a dark girl, entwined, imprisoned in silken garments, swept upon its crest!

Out shot a cork belt into the boiling sea . . . and fell beyond her reach. She was swept past the cutter. A second belt was hurled from the stern . . .

The Eurasian, uttering a wailing cry like that of a seabird, strove to grasp it . . .

Close beside her, out of the wave, uprose a yellow hand, grasping—seeking—clutching. It fastened itself into the meshes of her floating hair . . .

"Here goes!" roared Rogers.

They plunged down into an oily trough; they turned; a second wave grew up above them, threateningly, built its terrible wall higher and higher over their side. Round they swung, and round, and round . . .

Down swept the eager wave . . . down—down—down . . . It lapped over the stern of the cutter; the tiny craft staggered, and paused, tremulous—dragged back by that iron grip of old Neptune—then leaped on—away—headed back into the Thames estuary, triumphant.

"God's mercy!" whispered Stringer—"that was touch-and-go!"

No living thing moved upon the waters.

XLI

WESTMINSTER—MIDNIGHT

Detective-Sergeant Sowerby reported himself in Inspector Dunbar's room at New Scotland Yard.

"I have completed my inquiries in Wharf-end Lane," he said; and pulling out his bulging pocketbook, he consulted it gravely.

Inspector Dunbar looked up.

"Anything important?" he asked.

"We cannot trace the makers of the sanitary fittings, and so forth, but they are all of American pattern. There's nothing in the nature of a trademark to be found from end to end of the place; even the iron sluice-gate at the bottom of the brick tunnel has had the makers' name chipped off, apparently with a cold chisel. So you see they were prepared for all emergencies!"

"Evidently," said Dunbar, resting his chin on the palms of his hands and his elbows upon the table.

"The office and warehouse staff of the ginger importing concern are innocent enough, as you know already. Kan-Suh Concessions was conducted merely as a blind, of course, but it enabled the Chinaman, Ho-Pin, to appear in Wharf-end Lane at all times of the day and night without exciting suspicion. He was supposed to be the manager, of course. The presence of the wharf is sufficient to explain how they managed to build the place without exciting suspicion. They probably had all the material landed there labeled as preserved ginger, and they would take it down below at night, long after the office and warehouse Staff of Concessions had gone home. The workmen probably came and went by way of the river, also, commencing work after nightfall and going away before business commenced in the morning."

"It beats me," said Dunbar, reflectively, "how masons, plumbers, decorators, and all the other artisans necessary for a job of that description, could have been kept quiet."

"Foreigners!" said Sowerby triumphantly. "I'll undertake to say there wasn't an Englishman on the job. The whole of the gang was probably imported from abroad somewhere, boarded and lodged during the day-time in the neighborhood of Limehouse, and watched by Mr. Ho-Pin or somebody else until the job was finished; then shipped back home again. It's easily done if money is no object."

"That's right enough," agreed Dunbar; "I have no doubt you've hit upon the truth. But now that the place has been dismantled, what does it look like? I haven't had time to come down myself, but I intend to do so before it's closed up."

"Well," said Sowerby, turning over a page of his notebook, "it looks like a series of vaults, and the Rev. Mr. Firmingham, a local vicar whom I got to inspect it this morning, assures me, positively, that it's a crypt."

"A crypt! exclaimed Dunbar, fixing his eyes upon his subordinate.

"A crypt—exactly. A firm dealing in grease occupied the warehouse before Kan-Suh Concessions rented it, and they never seem to have suspected that the place possessed any cellars. The actual owner of the property, Sir James Crozel, an ex-Lord Mayor, who is also ground landlord of the big works on the other side of the lane, had no more idea than the man in the moon that there were any cellars beneath the place. You see the vaults are below the present level of the Thames at high tide; that's why nobody ever suspected their existence. Also, an examination of the bare walls—now stripped—shows that they were pretty well filled up to the top with ancient debris, to within a few years ago, at any rate."

"You mean that our Chinese friends excavated them?"

"No doubt about it. They were every bit of twenty feet below the present street level, and, being right on the bank of the Thames, nobody would have thought of looking for them unless he knew they were there."

"What do you mean exactly, Sowerby?" said Dunbar, taking out his fountain-pen and tapping his teeth with it.

"I mean," said Sowerby, "that someone connected with the gang must have located the site of these vaults from some very old map or book."

"I think you said that the Reverend Somebody-or-Other avers that they were a crypt?"

"He does; and when he pointed out to me the way the pillars were placed, as if to support the nave of a church, I felt disposed to agree with him. The place where the golden dragon used to stand (it isn't really gold, by the way!) would be under the central aisle, as it were; then there's a kind of side aisle on the right and left and a large space at top and bottom. The pillars are stone and of very early Norman pattern, and the last three or four steps leading down to the place appear to belong to the original structure. I tell you it's the crypt of some old forgotten Norman church or monastery chapel."

"Most extraordinary!" muttered Dunbar.

"But I suppose it is possible enough. Probably the church was burnt or destroyed in some other way; deposits of river mud would gradually cover up the remaining ruins; then in later times, when the banks of the Thames were properly attended to, the site of the place would be entirely forgotten, of course. Most extraordinary!"

"That's the reverend gentleman's view, at any rate," said Sowerby, "and he's written three books on the subject of early Norman churches!

He even goes so far as to say that he has heard—as a sort of legend—of the existence of a very large Carmelite monastery, accommodating over two hundred brothers, which stood somewhere adjoining the Thames within the area now covered by Limehouse Causeway and Pennyfields. There is a little turning not far from the wharf, known locally—it does not appear upon any map—as Prickler's Lane; and my friend, the vicar, tells me that he has held the theory for a long time"—Sowerby referred to his notebook with great solemnity—"that this is a corruption of Pre-aux-Clerce Lane."

"H'm!" said Dunbar; "very ingenious, at any rate. Anything else?"

"Nothing much," said Sowerby, scanning his notes, "that you don't know already. There was some very good stuff in the place—Oriental ware and so on, a library of books which I'm told is unique, and a tremendous stock of opium and hashish. It's a perfect maze of doors and observation-traps. There's a small kitchen at the end, near the head of the tunnel—which, by the way, could be used as a means of entrance and exit at low tide. All the electric power came through the meter of Kan-Suh Concessions."

"I see," said Dunbar, reflectively, glancing at his watch; "in a word, we know everything except . . ."

"What's that?" said Sowerby, looking up.

"The identity of Mr. King!" replied the inspector, reaching for his hat which lay upon the table.

Sowerby replaced his book in his pocket.

"I wonder if any of the bodies will ever come ashore?" he said.

"God knows!" rapped Dunbar; "we can't even guess how many were aboard. You might as well come along, Sowerby, I've just heard from Dr. Cumberly. Mrs. Leroux . . ."

"Dead?"

"Dying," replied the inspector; "expected to go at any moment. But the doctor tells me that she may—it's just possible—recover consciousness before the end; and there's a bare chance . . ."

"I see," said Sowerby eagerly; "of course she must know!"

The two hastened to Palace Mansions. Despite the lateness of the hour, Whitehall was thronged with vehicles, and all the glitter and noise of midnight London surrounded them.

"It only seems like yesterday evening," said Dunbar, as they mounted the stair of Palace Mansions, "that I came here to take charge of the case. Damme! it's been the most exciting I've ever handled, and it's certainly the most disappointing."

"It is indeed," said Sowerby, gloomily, pressing the bell-button at the side of Henry Leroux's door.

The door was opened by Garnham; and these two, fresh from the noise and bustle of London's streets, stepped into the hushed atmosphere of the flat where already a Visitant, unseen but potent, was arrived, and now was beckoning, shadowlike, to Mira Leroux.

"Will you please sit down and wait," said Garnham, placing chairs for the two Scotland Yard men in the dining-room.

"Who's inside?" whispered Dunbar, with that note of awe in his voice which such a scene always produces; and he nodded in the direction of the lobby.

"Mr. Leroux, sir," replied the man, "the nurse, Miss Cumberly, Dr. Cumberly and Miss Ryland . . ."

"No one else?" asked the detective sharply.

"And Mr. Gaston Max," added the man. "You'll find whisky and cigars upon the table there, sir."

He left the room. Dunbar glanced across at Sowerby, his tufted brows raised, and a wry smile upon his face.

"In at the death, Sowerby!" he said grimly, and lifted the stopper from the cut-glass decanter.

In the room where Mira Leroux lay, so near to the Borderland that her always ethereal appearance was now positively appalling, a hushed group stood about the bed.

"I think she is awake, doctor," whispered the nurse softly, peering into the emaciated face of the patient.

Mira Leroux opened her eyes and smiled at Dr. Cumberly, who was bending over her. The poor faded eyes turned from the face of the physician to that of Denise Ryland, then to M. Max, wonderingly; next to Helen, whereupon an indescribable expression crept into them; and finally to Henry Leroux, who, with bowed head, sat in the chair beside her. She feebly extended her thin hand and laid it upon his hair. He looked up, taking the hand in his own. The eyes of the dying woman filled with tears as she turned them from the face of Leroux to Helen Cumberly—who was weeping silently.

"Look after . . . him," whispered Mira Leroux.

Her hand dropped and she closed her eyes again. Cumberly bent forward suddenly, glancing back at M. Max who stood in a remote corner of the room watching this scene.

Big Ben commenced to chime the hour of midnight. That frightful coincidence so startled Leroux that he looked up and almost rose from his chair in his agitation. Indeed it startled Cumberly, also, but did not divert him from his purpose.

"It is now or never!" he whispered.

He took the seemingly lifeless hand in his own, and bending over Mira Leroux, spoke softly in her ear:

"Mrs. Leroux," he said, "there is something which we all would ask you to tell us; we ask it for a reason—believe me."

Throughout the latter part of this scene the big clock had been chiming the hour, and now was beating out the twelve strokes of midnight; had struck six of them and was about to strike the seventh.

Seven! boomed the clock.

Mira Leroux opened her eyes and looked up into the face of the physician.

Eight! . . .

"Who," whispered Dr. Cumberly, "is he?"

Nine!

In the silence following the clock-stroke, Mira Leroux spoke almost inaudibly.

"You mean . . . *Mr. King?*"

Ten!

"Yes, yes! Did you ever *see* him?"

Every head in the room was craned forward; every spectator tensed up to the highest ultimate point.

"Yes," said Mira Leroux quite clearly; "I saw him, Dr. Cumberly . . . He is . . ."

Eleven!

Mira Leroux moved her head and smiled at Helen Cumberly; then seemed to sink deeper into the downy billows of the bed. Dr. Cumberly stood up very slowly, and turned, looking from face to face.

"It is finished," he said—"we shall never know!"

But Henry Leroux and Helen Cumberly, their glances meeting across the bed of the dead Mira, knew that for them it was not finished, but that Mr. King, the invisible, invisibly had linked them.

Twelve!

THE END

Lightning Source UK Ltd.
Milton Keynes UK
UKOW051629210612

194838UK00002B/158/A